DARING TO DREAM

---- ❋ ----

WOMEN'S HISTORY IN SHORT STORIES

Two companion volumes:

OLD MAIDS
Short Stories by Nineteenth-Century US Women Writers
Compiled and with an Introduction by Susan Koppelman

DARING TO DREAM
Utopian Stories by United States Women: 1836-1919
Compiled, edited and introduced with annotated bibliography
by Carol Farley Kessler

Editorial consultant: Annette Kolodny

Daring to Dream

Carol Farley Kessler is assistant professor of English and
American Studies, The Pennsylvania State University, Delaware
County Campus, Media, Pennsylvania, USA. She has a PhD in
American Civilization from the University of Pennsylvania.

Cover illustration and design   Marion Dalley.

P A N D O R A   P R E S S

DARING TO DREAM

*

UTOPIAN STORIES BY
UNITED STATES WOMEN,
1836-1919

*Compiled, edited and introduced with
annotated bibliography, by*

CAROL FARLEY KESSLER

PANDORA PRESS
Boston, London, Melbourne and Henley

First published in 1984
by Pandora Press (Routledge & Kegan Paul plc)
9 Park Street, Boston, Mass. 02108, USA
14 Leicester Square, London WC2H 7PH, England
464 St Kilda Road, Melbourne,
Victoria 3004, Australia and
Broadway House, Newtown Road,
Henley-on-Thames, Oxon RG9 1EN, England

Set in Sabon by Columns of Reading
and printed in Great Britain
by Cox & Wyman Ltd, Reading

Library of Congress Cataloging in Publication Data

Daring to dream.
Bibliography: p.
Includes index.
1. American fiction – Women authors. 2. Utopias –
Fiction. 3. Feminism – Fiction. 4. American fiction –
19th century. 5. American fiction – 20th century.
I. Kessler, Carol Farley.
PS648.U85D37   1984   813'.009'372   84-5827

ISBN 0-86358-013-0 (pbk.)

CONTENTS

※

PREFACE

————————— ❋ —————————

This collection spans 1836-1919, beginning with the first Utopia known to have been written by a woman in the United States and ending with what can be seen as a feminist revision of Edward Bellamy's popular and influential *Looking Backward* (1888). The selection – limited to feminist fiction by United States women – includes six shorter selections, and significant excerpts from ten novels, each excerpt carefully selected to maintain the integrity of the original and to demonstrate themes common to this period and mode of writing by United States women. All selections have inherent dramatic interest. Their forms vary widely, including dream vision, satiric dialogue, alternative future, exotic journey, and communitarian romance. Authors currently available in reasonably priced editions do not appear. Work by the Utopist Charlotte Perkins Gilman (1860-1935) is thus omitted, though included in the bibliography.

All of the selections have literary and historical interest in their own right. The collection constitutes an overview of Utopian literary types and spans the nineteenth-century women's movement from the Jacksonian era to suffrage enactment. Thus the collection traces the imaginative roots of United States feminism. The selections delineate the social arrangements women wanted and demonstrate the feminist thread in United States Utopian fiction.

The fictional materials, plus accompanying introduction and bibliography, are relevant to a variety of contexts: cross-disciplinary courses in American Studies, Peace Studies, Utopian Studies, and Women's Studies; classes in American literature, popular culture, and United States history (reform, communitarianism); discussion of political theory, of ideal social structure, such as introductory courses in political science or philosophy could entail. Thus the anthology could be used at a variety of educational levels – from advanced high school pupils to graduate students.

The introduction discusses feminist Utopias only, there being some 53 from the Annotated Bibliography of 137 items. Nonfeminist Utopias seem to fit what has been a major trend in Western Utopian writing from Plato to the present, namely, the subordination of women to men – even in Utopia – and the treatment of sexuality as negatively disruptive. The countertrend in this tradition, which encompasses the feminist thread in United States Utopias, emerged in the nineteenth century. It values both women as full citizens of Utopia, and sexuality as a positively energizing social force. (See Kaplan, Selected Critical References, p. 00). This feminist Utopian thread receives an overview, its broad outlines sketched. The overview is not meant to be definitive or exhaustive, but rather suggestive. Its endnotes can be used as a guide to supplementary reading.

Headnotes to the selections include where available biographical information about the author, historical background or sources for themes she stresses, but not detailed literary analysis, which is the burden of the reader. If a selection is an excerpt, its relation to the rest of the work receives clarification. In addition, a list of references appears with each selection as well as a listing of pages excerpted.

The Annotated Bibliography covers 1836 to 1983. A headnote explains its parameters. A brief list of criticism on United States women and Utopia follows. A bar graph, showing the distribution of the works, precedes the annotations. You will of course find omissions: please tell me about them. No one bibliographer, no matter how diligent, can hope to cover all possibilities.

The research for a project such as this gathers numerous debts in the process of completion. The book and its compiler seem to me the mere apex of a supporting pyramid, an essential foundation permitting her work. Thus may I acknowlege most heartily and gratefully this human pyramid.

The research upon which this collection is based has been supported by funds from the Institute for Arts and Humanistic Studies, the Faculty Scholarship Support Fund, and the Liberal Arts College Fund for Research, all at the Pennsylvania State University, as well as by a Residential Fellowship for College

Teachers from the National Endowment for the Humanities, held at the University of Maryland, 1981-1982. I wish to thank all of the foregoing for this invaluable support.

The staffs at McKeldin Library of the University of Maryland and at the Library of Congress aided me with unfailing good humor. Charles Mann, Curator, and Sandy Stelts of the Rare Book Room, Pattee Library, The Pennsylvania State University, provided both advice and books. Janet Quinlan, Susan Ware, and Sara Whildin, Head, at Penn State's Delaware County Campus Library, ordered interlibrary loan and reference materials from what must have seemed an interminable stream of requests. May I thank them all for their boundless patience.

For their critique and camaraderie, I thank Maggie Cullen, Cheri Jennings, Laura Noell, and Phyllis Mael, members of the NEH Seminar at the University of Maryland.

In addition fellow researchers and bibliographers, both in published work and personal correspondence, have made a mountainous task more easily scalable. To each for helpful advice, I thank Janet Bardzik, Marleen S. Barr, Lucy Freibert, R. Gordon Kelly, Lee Cullen Khanna, Annette Kolodny, Susan Huddis Koppelman, Ann J. Lane, Arthur O. Lewis, Daphne Patai, Carol S. Pearson, Carolyn Rhodes, Jewell Parker Rhodes, Kenneth M. Roemer, Lyman Tower Sargent, and Lynn Williams.

I thank my typist Jean Patrick, who provided good cheer as well as interest and expertise.

And my family participated as well: I thank mother, daughter, son, and husband, for the many special contributions each can enumerate better than I.

For any remaining errors or oversights, I apologize and ask not your forbearance, but your information!

Carol Farley Kessler
The Pennsylvania State University
Delaware County Campus
Media, Pennsylvania 19063

INTRODUCTION
FEMINIST UTOPIAS BY
UNITED STATES WOMEN

'Pretty plain to see,' I went on. 'We men, having all human power in our hands, have used it to warp and check the growth of women. We, by choice and selection, by law and religion, by enforced ignorance, by heavy overcultivation of sex, have made the kind of woman we so made by nature, that that is what it was to be a woman. Then we heaped our scornful abuse upon her, ages and ages of it, the majority of men in all nations still looking down on women. And then, as if that was not enough – really, my dear, I'm not joking, I'm ashamed, as if I'd done it myself – we, in our superior freedom, in our monopoly of education, with the law in our hands, both to make and execute, with every conceivable advantage – we have blamed women for the sins of the world!'

'Put yourself in my place for a moment, Van. Suppose in Herland we had a lot of – subject men. Blame us all you want to for doing it, but look at the men. Little creatures, undersized and generally feeble. Cowardly and not ashamed of it. Kept for sex purposes only or as servants; or both, usually both. I confess I'm asking something difficult of your imagination, but try to think of Herland women, each with a soft man she kept to cook for her, to wait upon her and to – 'love' when she pleased. Ignorant men mostly. Poor men, almost all, having to ask their owners for money and tell what they wanted it for. Some of them utterly degraded creatures, kept in houses for common use – as women are kept here. Some of them quite gay and happy – pet men, with pet names and presents showered upon them. Most of them contented, piously accepting kitchen work as their duty, living by the religion and laws and customs the women made. Some of them left out and made fun of for being left – not owned at all – and envying

1

those who were! Allow for a surprising percentage of mutual love and happiness, even under these conditions; but also for ghastly depths of misery and a general low level of mere submission to the inevitable. Then in this state of degradation fancy these men for the most part quite content to make monkeys of themselves by wearing the most ridiculous clothes. Fancy them, men, with men's bodies, though enfeebled, wearing open-work lace underclothing, with little ribbons all strung through it; wearing dresses never twice alike and almost always foolish; wearing hats –' she fixed me with a steady eye in which a growing laughter twinkled – 'wearing such hats as your women wear!'

Charlotte Perkins Gilman
'With Her in Ourland' (1916)[1]

Many with an interest in Utopias have read Gilman's *Herland* (1915), one of the few recovered feminist classics. The foregoing segments of a conversation from its sequel, 'With Her in Ourland', suggest how both women and men can learn from reading Utopias by and about women. Let's look more closely.

'I' of the first passage is Vandyck Jennings, sociologist and husband of Herlander Ellador; the two are making a tour of Ourland (Earth) at the time of World War I. With satiric result, Gilman shows Ourland as seen through the eyes of a visitor from an all-female society, where crime, poverty, and war never existed. Ellador – whose innocent eye and rational mind inform Van, and incidentally us readers, too – has just exclaimed with regard to stereotypic gender differences, 'I call it "The Great Divergence." There is no other such catastrophic change in all nature – as far as I've been able to gather' (p. 291). Realizing that Ellador can hardly in good grace complain to him about men's role in women's degradation, Van gallantly begins as above to explain the 'worst result' of men's conduct – 'the petted women, the contented women, the "happy" women' (p. 292). His inventory of wrongs receive amplification in the selections that follow, as do those Ellador mischievously enumerates. But Gilman does not stop here. Ellador then points out to Van that a women's movement has achieved the availability of education and money for women, that although the "woman man made" is deplorable, she could have – but hasn't – objected or changed very greatly. Note then that in

2

Gilman's view, all of us share some responsibility, for being where we are. Elsewhere she observed satirically, 'The woman is narrowed by the home, and the man is narrowed by the woman,' her home – the quoted passage implies – having been narrowed by the man![2] A defeating circularity, to be sure. And only all of us together – each feeling his or her responsibility for doing so – can stop this cycle.

Historians contend that those who do not know the past are doomed to repeat it. Literary Utopias are not of course 'the past' in the sense intended. But if we understand that Utopias usually index – however obliquely – the wrongs, the lacks, the needs experienced or recognized by authors of the past, then by reading these Utopias we obtain a sense of history-as-experienced that statistics or political documents cannot provide.[3] From these Utopias we can learn what the wrongs have been. Knowing them, we can seek to change. No one of us is an island: if circumstances diminish any of us, we all stand deprived of enjoying the accomplishments any diminished person might have attained. Hence the recovery of woman's past is imperative, that we may no longer be deprived of her potential. Hence the reading of Utopias, those visions of better worlds to inspire us to greater efforts in our own. As Gilman notes, 'How to make the best kind of people and how to keep them at their best and growing better – surely that is what we are here for' (p. 297).

The word *Utopia* was coined by Sir Thomas More to name his 1516 fiction of a non-existent, ideal society (from the Greek *ou* no, *topos* place). A fictional society, of course, is not real, but an ideal nowhere. More's *Utopia*, however, contains a pun or deliberate ambiguity, deriving from the word's etymology: an ideal nowhere appears a good society compared to what writer or author has experienced (from the Greek *eu* good). More recently, by anaology to More's *Utopia*, a depiction of a bad society is called *dystopia* (from the Greek *dys* bad). Utopia, using the metaphor of the city or the society, can convey a state of mind (not a geographical territory), or a world view. Jung considers the city or society to be a metaphor of the female principle, of a woman sheltering inhabitants as if children. (Since today we would not wish to restrict the capacity to shelter to women only, we might call this a 'nurturing' principle, and thus render the term free of sex bias.) Utopia then becomes a refuge or shelter wherein we may

3

safely envision a changed society. And although mere metaphor located in no real place, Utopia nonetheless has power. Utopian ideals or ideas change minds: changed minds then change worlds. A critic of recent feminist Utopias, Lee Cullen Khanna, notes that we find 'Utopia in the process of experiencing a convincing fiction . . . not "out there" in another time and place – but within the self.'[4] In this power to change, convert, renew, Utopias can be spiritual or religious in their effect.

The view of literature expressed here is unashamedly didactic, a tradition encompassing such diversity as the classical Aesop's *Fables* and the medieval morality play *Everyman*, as well as much United States fiction written at the end of the nineteenth century, lately decried by twentieth-century critics as moralistic. But perhaps, given the outpouring of Utopian writing during the 1970s, we need to reconsider the label 'moralistic' as a pejorative. Recent didactic fiction – of which the Utopia and *Bildungs-roman* are two genres currently in evidence – again receives approval. In a recent discussion of Doris Lessing, Marge Piercy, and Joanna Russ, feminist critic Rachel Blau DuPlessis revived the label *apologue* (from the Greek *apologos* story) for the Utopias these authors have written. Such novels, DuPlessis explains, 'contain embedded elements from 'assertive discourse' – genres like sermon, manifesto, tract, fable or speech and marriage contract, as in selections here. Such genres usually 'guide or inform the action'. Though occurring in a variety of tones or moods, the speculation they provide is central to the action of the work. The source of interest in these works is not the typical plot or character, but 'speculative and didactic discourse'. Plot and character in apologues embody 'philosophical propositions or moral arguments,' in order to persuade readers to believe them.

'Second,' DuPlessis continues, 'these teaching fictions often contain an analysis of the past and a projection into the future – both within one work. . . . [W]hen a novel travels through the present into the future, as these can do, social or character development can no longer be felt as complete, nor [can] our "space" as reader (beyond the ending) [be] perceived as untrammeled. If the future is no longer a resolved place, then in the same way, the past – history itself – no longer has fixity or authority. These future visions are visions of the past as well. . . .'

'Third,' DuPlessis notes, 'characters in a teaching story are

4

not the classic "well-rounded" personages with whom one identifies and who seem to take on a life of their own.' Rather they may be flat because they represent a cluster of typical traits. Further, they embody 'Socratic questions: that is, ideas, not characters, are well-rounded. Socratic questions, it must be remembered, are questions to which Socrates already had an answer': in an apologue, the character exists to act out an author's answers to questions or to illustrate her ideals or speculations, but not to act out her life. Also the characters 'often fuse into multi-personed or cluster protagonists.' For example, Russ's characters in *The Female Man* – Janet, Jeannine, Joanna, and Jael – constitute such a cluster, as do the families in Piercy's Mattapoisett, the eutopia in *Woman on the Edge of Time* (see Annotated Bibliography, Russ, 1975; Piercy, 1976). 'The group protagonist presents a collective self, rather than individual selves, and therefore proposes the values which go with collectivity, especially unity of social purpose.' The 'cluster protagonist' appears to embody new values both concerning the person '(the individual and individual conflict are less stressed than communal growth),' and concerning 'the importance of interdependence and recognition of the need for collective survival.' Also the action of such books may include 'speculative, fantasy, or "science fiction" elements such as time travel or sex changes.' Such 'unreal elements . . . estrange the reader from the rules of the known world,' thereby loosening the mind and rendering it more receptive to the stories' revelations of needed changes in values and institutions. 'An ethical art moves the reader beyond acceptance of existing values and institutions.'[5]

To the foregoing condensation of DuPlessis's informative extended definition of the apologue, I would add a first warning footnote: no Utopia, a type of apologue, should be taken as a social blueprint, ready for implementation. Rather Utopias, as apologues, foment speculation, offer alternative *vicarious* experience, spur us as readers to reevaluate and act upon our own world – create new consensus, establish new community. Utopias are spiritual guides, demonstrations of values, experiences of societies that while not perfect are in some ways better than our own. And Elizabeth Janeway would add a second cautionary note – that we beware of the Utopist's occupational hazard of fastening too narrowly upon goals: even more significant is the choice of *means* to a goal. She prefers to focus upon process, upon techniques. At the conclusion of *Powers of the Weak* (1980), she writes, 'I believe that we may accomplish so much more than we can yet imagine that laying down goals is a bad idea: it limits us and it may misdirect our energies.'[6] So long as we keep in mind these two cautions, apologues as Utopias can inspire potential re-vision and subsequent revolution. If we recall sociologist Karl Mannheim's understanding of Utopianism as revolutionary social innovation 'that breaks the bonds of the existing order,' and if we recall that bonds enslave, then the study of Utopia must have a liberating effect.[7] And if we see in feminism the expression of holistic and communitarian values missing from the present order, then feminism itself is a type of Utopianism. Literary critic Annette Kolodny claims that feminists attempt 'a revolution in consciousness so thorough going as to truly dislodge, not simply alter or reform, reigning belief systems.'[8] Hence feminist Utopian visions help us frame a new consciousness permitting the exploration of a more complete range of human possibilities. Apologues are fables toward our future.

Such feminist eutopias constitute a persistent vision, the vision of a critical outsider wondering at the folly of the crowd. Their 'American Dream' is different – less ruggedly individualistic, more responsibly communitarian. And because theirs are dreams experienced by outsiders and thus always entail risk of censure by insiders, the dreams require that a dreamer be daring to express them.[9] The anthology title *Daring to Dream* varies a line from an 1880 poem by Elizabeth Stuart Phelps (1844-1911), one of the authors excerpted here. The line – 'Ideal of ourselves! We dream and dare.' – effectively expresses thought becoming act, Utopia realized in life.[10] The word *dare* has not varied from its Greek meaning, 'to be courageous,' but *dream* has lost earlier significance: in Old English 'joy' or 'music,' in Old Frisian, 'shout of joy.' This earlier meaning seems embedded still in the expression 'a dream come true!' Interestingly a Malay tribe, the Senoi, take dreams so much more seriously than those of us shaped by Western cultural systems that they have incorporated dreams into daily routine. They use dreams to stimulate creative life: they teach children to remember dreams, to direct those dreams (this *is* possible), and to retain from dreams a dance, poem, or other creative act or idea. The dreamer then shares the dream and its creative outcome with the rest of the tribe the following morning. The

Senoi are reportedly 'the most democratic group in anthropological literature' and experience 'no violent crime or intercommunal conflict,' an actual Utopia if these traits are among the indices of an ideal society. (A recent feminist Utopia is strikingly similar: see Bryant, 1971.)[11]

When studying or imagining a eutopia, we pursue a rite of passage to a better future. As we dare to dream of the not yet known, we change our mindset concerning the possible. As we try to imagine the unimagineable – namely, where we're going before we're there, we move ourselves toward new and as yet unrealized ends. In a 1971 poem 'for two voices, female and male' called 'Councils,' Marge Piercy notes,

> The women must learn to dare to speak. . . .
> The women must learn to say, I think this is so. . . .[12]

Much has been said and written about men's visions of eutopia; we know far less about women's.

Women's dreams of a 'good' society, a eutopia – not necessarily 'perfect,' but simply 'superior' to an author's experience – do have a different focus from men's. Women more than men imagine Utopias where the intangible features of human existence receive more prominent consideration. Consequently, where United States Utopias by men stress as *ends* in themselves matters of public policy – be they political, economic, or technological, women's Utopias are more likely to include these matters primarily as they provide a *means to the social end* of fully developed human capacity in all people.[13] Typically, women make issues of family, sexuality, and marriage more central than do men. During the period covered by the annotated bibliography concluding this volume, 1836-1983, a major thematic variation occurs in United States women's Utopian writing. Before 1970, women's autonomy is more often viewed negatively as freedom from domination, especially in marriage where women typically exchange services for economic support. The 1960s mark a transition period hinting at a changed version of the theme. Since the 1970s women's autonomy is more often viewed positively, as freedom for the development and expression of potential, especially within the context of a supportive community, occasionally composed of women only. Before 1970, marriage typically appears as the center of woman's experience: marriage reform, rather than suffrage, is the change more frequently called for in Utopias by women. For example, between 1836 and 1920 where 64 per cent of 59 examples treated marriage as a problem, only 24 per cent presented suffrage as part of a solution to women's place in society. Here is vindication for words of Elizabeth Cady Stanton, who in 1853 wrote Susan B. Anthony, 'I feel this whole question of women's rights turns on the point of the marriage relation, and sooner or later it will be the question for discussion.'[14] Since 1970, Utopian society-at-large becomes woman's arena at last: it, rather than marriage, is the new locus for change.

Over the century-and-a-half time-span, Utopias by United States women have shown the same range of contradictory or ambivalent positions as the women's movement, with the difference that the communitarian dimension may be larger in fiction than in history: 57 per cent of the 137 Utopias surveyed include some degree of co-operative practice. A probable source of the ambivalence in both the fiction and the social movement is feminism's divided intellectual roots. Olive Banks, in *Faces of Feminism: A Study of Feminism as a Social Movement* (1980), finds three intellectual sources informing feminist thought and accounting for the range and divergence among positions considered 'feminist.'[15] She cites three eighteenth-century sources, whose principles continue to the present. First is evangelical Christianity, which led to moral and social reform as well as to the ideology of women's moral guardianship of society. In the present, some radical feminists continue to believe in women's moral superiority. Second is Enlightenment philosophy with its stress upon reason, environmental influence, and natural rights. This philosophy is also the intellectual source of the feminist emphasis upon liberation, self-realization, and autonomy. Current expression of the former resides with equal rights advocates; of the latter, with liberationists. Third is communitarian socialism, with its economic, political and social innovations. Especially important for women are changes in the family such as communal child care, and changes in marriage, such as less-restrictive sexual relationships. This third set of principles has had the smallest following of the three, but gains adherents among current radical feminists and has always been more prominent in Utopian practice and fiction than in the women's movement in general.

The current expression of feminism seems to divide between equal rights advocates and liberationists, but lines are hardly clear. This general division can focus our backward look toward the imaginative roots of the women's movement as well as toward the literary tradition of which the current flood of feminist Utopias is simply the most recent example: educational, political, and economic rights are one branch of concern while social conditions in marriage and family as well as concern for co-operative or communitarian experiments constitute a second branch. The 1970s and 1980s seem to be moving toward a consensus that rights can only exist within a supportive community, that the existence of these rights will change society as we now know it, that autarchy or autonomy for women can exist only when society itself changes substantially.

The discussion that follows will concentrate upon feminist eutopias, about 40 per cent (or 54) or the 137 Utopias included in this study.[16] Since headnotes discuss each Selection in this collection, most illustrations will come from works not included, the more broadly to cover the feminist Utopian tradition.[17] Thus this introductory survey provides a context and reference point for the selections that follow. The 137 Utopias fall into three periods, divided according to events in women's history, and rate of output. The first period parallels this volume – over eighty years from the first Utopia written by a woman, through the 1848 Declaration of Sentiments, to the ratification of Constitutional Amendment XIX, granting suffrage to women in 1920 (29 feminist Utopias, or 49 per cent of the United States Utopias by women, 1836-1920). A second period, 1920-1960, includes the Depression and World War II (6 feminist works, or 22 per cent of the period's output: no feminist works appeared during the 1950s). A third period, 1960-1983, includes the transitional decade of the 1960s, 4 of 9 works published having feminist values. The five-year span 1975-79 astonishes: of the 24 works published, 11 or 46 per cent achieve consensus over a wide range of feminist concerns, a contrast to earlier diversity of vision. During these five years more Utopias were written by United States women than during any previous period. The average rate of output is one feminist Utopia every third year before 1920; one such work every fifth year, 1920-1970; and thereafter, one feminist Utopia every 10 months! The 1970s feminist Utopias appear to be one of many indicators suggesting that a cultural paradigm shift is in process and that feminist values are central to the emerging paradigm.[18]

I 1836-1920

Of the 12 feminist Utopias published during this period but not included in this collection, two short stories – 'The Rappite's Economy' (Davis, 1866) and 'Transcendental Fruitlands' (Alcott, 1873) – and one novel – *World War I Ourland* (Gilman, 1916) – are satiric Utopias; a fourth – the African eutopia *Liberia* (Hale, 1853) – is the only work before 1900 to consider race. All of these reveal the hegemony of patriarchal ideology, particularly in the control of women's labor. Rebecca Harding Davis in 'The Harmonists' decries one man's power to maintain in a 'communist village' a 'utopia of prophets and poets,' who appear to a visitor as 'gross men' and 'poor withered women' with 'faded and tired' faces showing a 'curious vacancy' (pp. 531, 533, 535, 537). Louisa May Alcott in 'Transcendental Wild Oats' wryly describes 'the most ideal of all these castles in Spain,' where to the question posed by Mrs Lamb – 'are there any beasts of burden on the place?' – another – seeing how overworked she was – responded, 'Only one woman!' Fruitlands fails: 'The world was not ready for Utopia yet' and Mrs Lamb wonders to her disappointed husband, 'Don't you think Apple Slump would be a better name for it, dear?' (pp. 1570, 1571). In each short story, women supply the labor to achieve a man's ideal and in both cases, the ideal fails to materialize as anticipated. (In two novels, Alcott shows women's co-operative ventures succeeding – four young women in *An Old-fashioned Girl* who share rooms, and the heterogeneous community of women concluding *Work*.)[19] Editor of *Godey's Lady's Book*, Sarah Josepha Hale in *Liberia; or Mr. Peyton's Experiments* provides yet another version of female labor in the service of male ideology. Black Keziah, indomitable manager of Mr Peyton's household, directs the labor of her husband Polydore in several of Mr Peyton's experiments to provide his 'servants' with an economic basis for living outside slavery. (Though racist by 1980s standards, for its time Hale's novel shows a measure of sympathy.) Hale, Davis, and Alcott all subscribe to the concept of women's moral guardianship of society. Gilman however, as noted above, saw women and men as both degenerate and remediable.

Several other works, while predominantly eutopian, use bad marriages to show how social regulation of woman's sexuality works to her disadvantage. First the marriage 'bargain' is shown corrupt: 'The man wants a housekeeper, the woman a home' (Shelhamer, 1885, p. 12); he married her to 'be stunning,' she him for money, called 'the god of civilization' (Pittock, 1890, ch. 22). Both exchange of services and exchange of objects – especially when one object is a person – do not work. Second, such corrupt marriages set eutopian sexual arrangements in relief: the freedom of exotic bronze-skinned women to select their sexual partners on a tropic island where mates 'strive to please each other' make a 'civilized' mate's demand to be pleased the more objectionable (Pittock, p. 60, ch. 12). Third, the children resulting from such corrupt marriages receive inadequate financial support: a deserted mother of three small children tries taking in boarders as a livelihood, but crying infants drive boarders away. Then her husband abducts her son (Fry, 1905, chs 12-15).

To correct men's control of women's labor and sexuality, feminist eutopias of this period suggest several possibilities: paid work, education, suffrage, and co-operation. 'A New Society' envisioned by a Lowell 'mill girl' paid equal wages regardless of sex, limited the work day to eight hours, and required three hours daily of mental or manual labor, whichever was not a person's means of livelihood (Chamberlain, 1841). In general both women and men work with access to the full range of jobs (Shelhamer, 1885; Richberg, 1900; Fry, 1905; Gilman, 1911, 1915). A short story called 'Friend Island' boasts a sea-captain heroine: 'a true sea-woman of that elder time when woman's superiority to man had not been so long recognized' (Bennett, 1918, p. 126). The story is her reminiscence of a sentient island, an early science-fiction tale that anticipates 1970s strategies for demonstrating interrelationships among human, animal, plant, and earth.

A second strategy for avoiding control is education – for daughters as well as sons (Chamberlain, 1841), especially to make 'an honorable living' instead of submitting to 'the best we can get' in a marriage (Shelhamer, 1885). And such self-sufficient women would of course keep their own names when they married (Fry, 1905, ch. 28; Gilman, 1915, pp. 118ff).

A third strategy, suffrage, is far more emphasized by subsequent histories of women than by Utopists: of the 59 Utopias appearing before 1920, only 14 or 24 per cent favor suffrage, though 10 more consider political issues, including general activity and office holding. Typical of a feminist viewpoint is a passage from Mary Theresa Shelhamer's *Life and Labor in the Spirit World* (1885):

> She should have a voice in the affairs of the country under whose laws she lives and educates her children. . . . Some people pretend to fear that when women vote they will have no time for domestic affairs, and the institution of the home itself will be destroyed. . . . From the fuss made . . . one would think it took a week to put a small slip of paper into a medium-sized box. Why, we have known of men who could put in half a dozen in less than half that time, and no one suspects women to be less clever than men (p. 13).

The passage is interesting for its acknowledgment of popular fears that women would no longer perform traditional domestic roles once they were admitted to the political sphere reserved for men. Many accepted the view that women, family, and home were the calm center in a raging storm of social flux, that to permit change there would ensure complete social chaos. (One anti-feminist Utopia *Pantaletta* showed women's political control to be a comedy of error: Wood, 1882.) Shelhamer ridicules this popular fear at the same time that she assumes the sexes to be equally clever, such equality of intelligence more readily assumed however in Utopian fiction than by the public at large. Women Utopists ignore woman's traditional restriction to the home and thereby imply that integrating the public and private spheres for women will be no more disastrous than for men.[20]

More important than suffrage in feminist eutopias are co-operative or communitarian solutions to social control: some 54 per cent (32) for this period include such solutions. They take two forms – co-operative services or self-sufficient experimental communities. The earlier of two communitarian examples is *A New Aristocracy*, of 'brain and heart,' to be established in Idlewild, New York, upon a Parisian suburban model (Bartlett, 1891). As in works by Howland and Graul

(Selections 5 and 12), independent wealth makes possible the establishment of a factory, with workers' cottages and cultural buildings (pp. 306-9). *Other Worlds* describes a society called 'The Colony,' to which members contribute an entry fee and work to support the Colony (compare Selection 9, Mason, 1889). Members own stock in their Colony, and enjoy its services. For example, a Nursery with a professionally trained staff cares for children, thus the single parent and a working couple are assured of responsible childrearing (Fry, 1905). Such child care service is the major focus of *Reinstern* ('pure star'), 'a planet as yet undiscovered by your astronomers, who waste lifetimes searching with telescopes for what inner vision will readily disclose when you allow the real self to predominate' (Richberg, 1900, p. 10). This eutopia presents an apprentice system to educate young adults for shared parenting, such training believed prerequisite to marriage (pp. 19-20). Parents of each sex receive 'equal honors, salaries, and privileges,' (pp. 23-4), but biological parents are not solely responsible for children and systematically receive support appropriate to their children's ages. *Moving the Mountain*, another eutopia having co-operative services, also includes detailed nursery and child garden arrangements (Gilman, 1911, ch. 4). In addition by the 1940s apartment residences for self-supporting women had become common in the United States with facilities to provide food hygienically and knowledgeably (ch. 4)! (Gilman was particularly outraged by 'the waste of private housekeeping' and devoted the novel *What Diantha Did* (1910) to demonstrating an alternative.)[21]

Two points emerging from this group of eutopias are especially salient for the concerns of Utopias during the 1970s. First, the observation that the 'nowhere' of Utopia can be the 'somewhere' of 'inner vision' marks the 1970s recognition of Utopia as a state of mind showing a spiritual or religious motive to underlie Utopia (Alexander, 1971; Bryant, 1971; Staton, 1975; Piercy, 1976). Some nineteenth-century Utopists called this visionary 'nowhere' by more theological names: 'heaven' (Selection 6, Phelps, 1883) or the 'spirit world' (Shelhamer, 1885). Several recent analysts of current Utopias by women consider these to be intrinsically spiritual.[22] In fact some would see women's liberation itself as a 'spiritual quest.'[23] Second, on a more mundane level, the domestic labor typically a concern of these communitarian eutopias before

1920 currently receives broadly based investigation in research, as well as visionary alternative solution in Utopia. Economists, historians, and anthropologists provide studies of women's triple labor loads: unpaid childcare and housekeeping work added to underpaid salaried work.[24] That 1970s eutopias completely restructure society to remove from women this triple burden should not surprise us. It is worth noting that the particular domestic solutions envisioned in Utopias before 1920 have not come to pass, but the domestic problems that we now seek to address were accurately forecast. Utopias, though not blueprints, can be harbingers.

II   1920-60

After 1920, the writing of Utopias declined until 1960. Apparently the passage of Amendment XIX lulled women into thinking that all needs could now be met, but history has shown suffrage to be a more limited achievement than predicted. Only 6 of 27 Utopias published can claim to have feminist content. Of these 6, half focus upon the relationship between women and men as the central feature of a woman's life (Pettersen, 1924; Dardenelle, 1943; McElhiney, 1945). This narrowing of focus after the wide-ranging visionary alternatives appearing before 1920 is troubling, especially since the non-feminist Utopias all enclose women in traditional marriages and families. Thus only 3 of 27 works do not see sex as woman's central concern (Cleghorn, 1924; Spotswood, 1935; Short, 1949) although two works include women space travellers from Venus (Pettersen, 1924; Short, 1949) and two women aviators (McElhiney, 1945; Short, 1949). The heterosexual love bond is seen to be benefited (1) by sex communication – taught to an Earth woman by two Venusian experts (Pettersen, 1924); (2) by a nudist existence – after technological disaster results in a warmer climate (Dardenelle, 1943); and (3) by astral means from the Island of Heaven somewhere in the Pacific – a stage of consciousness where death is absent (McElhiney, 1945). Although sexuality receives positive treatment, its excess centrality suggests Freudian influence. And the consistent appearance of marriage may be reflective not only of social possibilities, but also of a need for self-realization missing in the traditional institution. As current research has shown, women enjoying a marriage they claim is 'happy' can exhibit paradoxically disturbing symptoms – ill health, both mental and physical – the claim to 'happiness' perhaps more accurately labelled 'reconciliation.'[25]

The 3 broader Utopias suggest the diversity of both the earlier and the later periods. One Utopia contains four varied – partially narrative, partially discursive – explanations for social evolution by 1995 to a Family Order of society, practicing a Discipline of Happiness enhanced by a 1963 revival of Nomadry (Cleghorn, 1924). The non-hierarchical, non-racist, egalitarian values make this a harbinger of the 1970s fiction. Another, a satiric Utopia, depicts heroine Tellectina on her *Unpredictable Adventure* from Smug Harbor in the Land of Err to scale the heights of Nithking (Spotswood, 1935). Along her path is the Colony of the New Chimera, where free women worship the Goddess Frewo, but the *free love* they revere as the Priestess Frelo turns out to be a deception – a critique of the 1920s Flapper (ch. 5). Third, Gertrude Short's *A Visitor from Venus* (1949), except for allusions to World War II, resembles 1970s eutopias or Herlander's view of Ourland (Gilman, 1916). An Earthwoman aviator accidentally hears a radio report to a eutopia on Venus: she finds herself classed as a 'woe-man' and discovers a boss is a 'man-ag-her' (pp. 13-14). Sexism, racism and war are roundly condemned as 'immature destructiveness' (pp. 19-20, 28; compare Selection 11, Waisbrooker, 1894). Women must make their compassion felt in the world to erase war: love should be neither exclusive nor possessive (pp. 30, 32). Thus three twinkling candles glimmer between the slats of a bushel basket stretching across four decades.

The decade of the 1920s – when Freud and the Flapper reigned – also firmly established that 'wifehood and womanhood are the normal status of women,' the words in 1923 of Perkins Gilman, appalled at what she called 'sex mania.'[26] Where previously feminists had wanted to reconcile work, marriage, and family, suddenly only the last two needs remained, with a new need added – to avoid at all costs the unnatural status of not-married. A single woman as 'spinster' or 'old maid' was a social reject. Women's solidarity in a social movement was dispersed into numerous individual households by requiring that the indication of her normalcy and maturity be attractiveness to a male sexual partner – whose home she would keep and whose children she would bear and rear.[27] In addition to such social mythology, two post-World War decades added momentum to a return to traditional practices; a 1930s Depression decreased women's access to the labor market. Only the 1940s need to fill jobs vacated by enlisted men sent to fight World War II momentarily raised women's hope for pecuniary recognition. Some of the animus of Short's 1949 Utopia may derive from then-mounting ideological barriers to women's continued employment. But women were never again to stay home as before World War II: historians demonstrate the steady march toward paid labor outside the home.[28]

III 1960-83

These years since 1960 'are increasingly being viewed as a watershed in the history of Western civilization.' Although the words belong to an analyst of religion, feminists, sociologists, ecologists, physicists, futurists – to name a few – express the same view.[29] Feminist eutopias by United States women are one source for establishing the characteristics of an emerging cultural paradigm.

Although no feminist Utopias appeared during the 1950s, the publication of Utopias in general increased after the lull of the 1930s and 1940s. This increase continued during the 1960s. Hints of feminist values to become widespread during the 1970s do appear in four works of the 1960s. Zenna Henderson's stories about a People from the planet Home, who have landed in the United States Southwest, demonstrate the healing and empowering function storytelling can have, not to permit domination, but to enable expression and cohesion within a community (1961, 1967). For instance, a teacher replaces her pupils 'Home-sickness' with a dream-come-true of doing all that each is capable of doing, even to practicing super-psychic capacities unknown (hence deplored?) by the mainstream society (Henderson, 1961, pp. 63, 95). Power exists among the People not to control, but to release capacity in others. Ursula Le Guin's *Left Hand of Darkness* (1969) shows similar values in the relationship between two main characters, both men. In this science fiction Le Guin experiments with gender: a person is sexually neuter (though referred to as *he*) unless attraction to another triggers 'kemmer,' the male or female sex-phase, each person having the involuntary capacity for either phase (pp. 63-64, 177; ch. 8). Moving beyond gender-stereotyping will become a major feature of post-1970 feminist eutopias. Another feature will be moving beyond race-bias, a theme heralded by Alice M. Lightner [Hopf] in *The Day of the Drones* (1969), a race-reversal post-catastrophe dystopia set in Afria, where a young woman can grow up to lead her society. As in 1970s Utopias, Afrian women have considerable political power, including state headship. What these 1960s transition works lack is the centrality of women and women's concerns that characterize the 1970s feminist eutopias.

A surprising consensus exists among a third (14 of 42) of the works published since 1970 (with all but 4 appearing 1975-9).[30] Although many of the themes occurring since 1970 also appeared in Utopias from 1840 to 1920, the later Utopias each contain a cluster of themes, only several of which typically appeared in any one earlier work. This cluster includes three general areas: communitarian values, nature-awareness, and spiritual quest.[31]

The communitarian values, those least a part of the historical women's movement, seem most apparent in current eutopias. Several strands interweave. First, property is typically common, as the residence of the Wayward Women (Broner, 1978), with each individual having space of her own – a room (Young, 1979) or a mat (Charnas, 1978).[32] Second, the community is responsible to meet individual needs for food, clothing, education, medical care, travel, or recreation, as inoculations for a tribe (McIntyre, 1978) or singing of songs (Gearhart, 1979). Third, no one class or sex performs domestic work, which may be accomplished by the rotation of small groups, for preparing food (Piercy, 1976), or by the responsibility of the whole for childcare (Bryant, 1971). Fourth, children enjoy the concern of several parents – three (Piercy, 1976; Neeper, 1975) or five (Charnas, 1978) or seven (Gearhart, 1979), or a child may be assigned to a particular mentor who will oversee her development (Staton, 1975). Fifth, women work not only as parents but also in all the society's occupations, from carpenter (Singer, 1980) to scientist (LeGuin, 1974). Sixth, community responsibility for individual welfare also means safety from rape or assault (Russ, 1975). Thus individuals develop autarchy, or self-governance, in societies where their needs are met and they are expected responsibly to meet the needs of others: hurting another is forbidden (Bradley, 1976; Broner, 1978). Responsiveness to each other includes sexual permissiveness: diversity ranges from exclusive to open partnerships between people of the same or different sex, the individual herself determining the choice that suits her (Piercy, 1976). And because individuals develop autarchy, they also maintain egalitarian groups, where each has equal say and disagreements are talked through to consensus (Charnas, 1978; Gearhart, 1979).

One further characteristic of these eutopian communities needs mention – that half of the 14 contain all-female societies. At first glance it might seem that such fictions could polarize readers. But the 'wild zone' concept explicated by critic Elaine Showalter enables us to see an integrating outcome. This 'wild zone' is a peripheral area to mainstream (masculine-dominant) culture, a veritable 'no-man's-land' where women's culture and women's reality exist apart. Although subordinate groups must know about the range of dominant culture, a dominant group need not know what lies beyond the pale of their definition of society. This 'wild zone' provides the content of all-female Utopias, which then have the possible social function of moving the 'wild zone' within the realm of shared, rather than gender-specific, reality. Thus the insistence upon Utopia-from-a-female viewpoint effects not separation, but communication.[33]

The second general thematic area, nature-awareness, stresses a holistic or organic relationship between human and natural worlds. Typically this theme appears in these Utopias' use of scientific knowledge not to control nature, but to function in concert with her – for example, natural rather than artificial fertilizers to avoid upsetting chemical balance (Piercy, 1976). Characters also have a super-sentient capacity to commune with flora and fauna, a capacity leading to deep caring for all of life (Neeper, 1975; LeGuin, 1978; Gearhart, 1979). Cycles of community life parallel seasonal cycles (Bryant, 1971).[34]

And not only does the holism entail humankind and Earth, but humankind, Earth, and a universe beyond. This enlarged concept appears in the changed settings of the Utopias. No longer is present-day United States typical, as was true before 1970. Rather, action occurs in a seemingly limitless variety of otherworldly, interplanetary futures. Increasingly since 1920 features typical of science fiction appear, so that, by the 1970s, utopian writing frequently merges with the psychological, futuristic subtype called New Wave.[35] Utopists have thus launched characters beyond our known world and its learned stereotypes to enact alternative ways of being. These ways tie the human back to the natural, in a basically religious sense (from the Latin *re* back, *ligare* to bind or fasten).

Thus the third thematic area is a spiritual dimension encompassing both human community and natural earth. The storytelling that occurs within these Utopias (Bryant, 1971; Gearhart, 1979) as well as the story each book reveals becomes part of a process of healing and inspiriting. Characters move in quest of growth – a child on a dream-quest to achieve self-dependence and hence openness to others (Staton, 1975), an adolescent on a solo wilderness venture as passage to adulthood (Piercy, 1976) – journeys into the self that strengthen, the interior journey manifest as external events. The archetypal quest of the hero resulting in self-renewal lies at the basis of these Utopias. Crucial to the success of the quest is how it proceeds, what way or process guides a seeker's steps. A vicarious experience, Utopia is for the reader a journey to the frontier of a new state of mind, a *Gedänkenexperiment* revealing new possibilities.[36]

The new possibilities exist for both men and women – for men to learn to value what our culture has labelled as female, that unknown 'wild zone' whose practices may be crucial to the survival of humankind, and for women to reclaim the values of the 'wild zone' for the range of social activity from private living to the pinnacles of public power. The tradition of Utopian writing by United States feminists provides a record of dreams from this 'wild zone' of women's culture – where power enables and constructs, where experience not dogma informs behavior, where support comes from varied social groupings, where sensuality and bodily expression share communicative primacy with the word, where feeling as well as mind inform human knowledge, where holism and integration – rather than fragmentation and alienation – guide a group's way.[37]

We have returned to the starting point, Utopia as a call to action. As apologues, these novels teach. They persuade us to act. In her recent *The Anatomy of Freedom*, Robin Morgan quotes nineteenth-century poet Adelaide Proctor, 'Dreams grow holy when put in action.'[38] Can we together become 'ideals of ourselves' who dare to dream, and dreaming, dare to act?[39]

NOTES

1 *The Forerunner* VII (1916: 292-93) (ch. 11).
2 Charlotte Perkins Gilman, *The Home: Its Work and Influence* (1903; rpt Urbana, Illinois: University of Illinois Press, 1972), p. 277.
3 Frank E. Manuel and Fritzie P. Manuel, *Utopian Thought in the Western World* (Cambridge: Belknap/Harvard, 1982), pp. 23-4.
4 On Jung, see J.E. Cirlot, *A Dictionary of Symbols* (New York: Philosophical Library, 1962), pp. 46-7; Lee Cullen Khanna, 'Women's Worlds: New Directions in Utopian Fiction,' *Alternative Futures* 4(2-3) 1981: 58-9.
5 Rachel Blau DuPlessis, 'The Feminist Apologues of Lessing, Piercy, and Russ,' *Frontiers: A Journal of Women Studies* 4,(1) Spring 1979; my argument is strongly indebted to her definitional section (pp. 1-2). For the term 'apologue', DuPlessis credits Sheldon Sacks, *Fiction and the Shape of Belief* (Berkeley: University of California Press, 1964, p. 26); see pp. 7-8, n.2. In a revised form, DuPlessis's work will appear as *Writing Beyond the Ending: Narrative Strategies of Twentieth Century Women's Writing* (forthcoming, Indiana University Press).
6 Elizabeth Janeway, *Powers of the Weak* (New York: Knopf, 1980), p. 320.
7 Karl Mannheim, *Ideology and Utopia* (New York: Harcourt, Brace, Jovanovich, 1936), p. 192.
8 Annette Kolodny, 'Not-So-Gentle Persuasion: A Theoretical Imperative of Feminist Literary Criticism,' in *Feminist Literary Criticism* (Research Triangle Park, North Carolina: National Humanities Center, 1981), p. 7; see also Leah Fritz, *Dreamers and Dealers: An Intimate Appraisal of the Women's Movement* (Boston: Beacon Press, 1979), esp. ch. 10.
9 For a discussion of the woman as outsider, see Virginia Woolf, *Three Guineas* (1938; rpt New York: Harbinger, 1966); Vivian Gornick, 'Woman as Outsider' in *Woman in Sexist Society* (1971; rpt New York: New American Library, 1972), pp. 126-44.

10 Elizabeth Stuart Phelps, 'Victurae Salutamus' (Latin: 'we women, who are about to attain our goal, call upon you'; for the translation, I thank Emily J. Puder Farley, my mother and a Latin scholar), *Songs of the Silent World and Other Poems* (Boston: Houghton, Mifflin, 1885), p. 99.

11 Eric Partridge, *Origins: A Short Etymological Dictionary of Modern English* (New York: Macmillan, 1959), pp. 140, 166; Ann Faraday, *Dream Power* (1972; New York: Berkley Medallion, 1973), pp. 297-8. Citations by author and year refer to the Annotated Bibliography concluding this volume. Chapters and pages cited appear parenthetically within the text.

12 Marge Piercy, *Circles on the Water* (New York: Knopf, 1982), pp. 116-17.

13 For a discussion of predominantly male authors, see Kenneth M. Roemer, *The Obsolete Necessity: America in Utopian Writings, 1888-1900* (Kent, Ohio: Kent State University Press, 1976). Of the sample of 154 works, only 14 (less than 10 per cent) are by women, hence generalizations summarize men's far more than women's views.

14 *Elizabeth Cady Stanton/Susan B. Anthony: Correspondence, Writings, Speeches*, Ellen Carol DuBois, ed. (New York: Schocken, 1981), p. 56. And for a recent hypothesis stressing the impact of sex ratio in a society upon women's status in dyadic relationships, see Marcia Guttentag and Paul E. Secord, *Too Many Women? The Sex Ratio Question* (Beverly Hills, California: Sage, 1983), esp. chs 1, 6, 9.

15 Olive Banks, *Faces of Feminism: A Study of Feminism as a Social Movement* (New York: St Martin's Press, 1981), esp. chs 1 and 13.

16 Of course, the sample contains omissions. No one bibliographer can hope to cover all possibilities. So please join in the labor of recovery and completion by writing to me (c/o Routledge & Kegan Paul) whatever *you* find that this book omits. I thank you.

17 Those Utopias that I have called 'feminist' show several of the following characteristics: provide a critique of women's status, offer alternative ways of being female, recommend reforms benefiting women, place women centrally in the plot, show either sex atypically. See Annotated Bibliography for a bar graph of the Utopia distribution, 1836-1983.

18 Robert T. Francoeur, 'Religious Reactions to Alternative Lifestyles' in Eleanor D. Macklin and Roger H. Rubin, eds, *Contemporary Families and Alternative Lifestyles: Handbook on Research and Theory* (Beverly Hills, California: Sage, 1983), pp. 371-99; Daniel Yankelovich, *New Rules: Searching for Self-Fulfillment in a World Turned Upside Down* (New York: Random House, 1981).

19 Louisa May Alcott, *An Old-fashioned Girl* (Boston: Roberts, 1870), ch. 13: 'The Sunny Side'; *Work: A Story of Experience* (1873; rpt New York: Schocken, 1977), ch. 20.

20 For background see, Barbara Welter, 'Anti-Intellectualism and the American Woman, 1800-1860,' in *Dimity Convictions: The American Woman in the Nineteenth Century* (Athens, Ohio: Ohio University Press, 1976), pp. 71-82; Julia Ward Howe, ed., *Sex and Education* (1874; rpt New York: Arno, 1972), a collection of articles responding to Dr Edward H. Clarke, *Sex in Education* (1873).

21 Charlotte Perkins Gilman, 'The Waste of Private Housekeeping,' *Annals of the American Academy of Political and Social Science* (July 1913): 91-5; *What Diantha Did* (New York: Charlton, 1910).

22 See Khanna, note 4 above; Carol Pearson and Katherine Pope, *The Female Hero in American and British Literature* (New York: Bowker, 1981), pp. 260-5.

23 Carol P. Christ, *Diving Deep and Surfacing: Women Writers on Spiritual Quest* (Boston: Beacon Press, 1980), esp. pp. 1-12; Carol P. Christ and Judith Plaskow, eds, *Womanspirit Rising: A Feminist Reader in Religion* (San Francisco: Harper & Row, 1979), esp. pp. 1-17, 43-52, 217-19.

24 For examples, see John Kenneth Galbraith, 'The Economics of the American Housewife,' *Atlantic* 232 (Aug. 1973): 78-83; Delores Hayden, *The Grand Domestic Revolution: A History of Feminist Designs for American Homes, Neighborhoods, and Cities* (Cambridge, Mass: MIT Press, 1981); Eleanor Leacock, 'History, Development, and the Division of Labor by Sex: Implications for Organization,' *Signs: Journal of Women in Culture and Society* 7 (1981): 474-91; Bettina Berch, *The Endless Day: The Political Economy of Women and Work* (New York: Harcourt Brace Jovanovich, 1982); Susan Strasser, *Never Done: A History of American Housework* (New York: Pantheon, 1982).

25 Jessie Bernard, 'The Paradox of the Happy Marriage' in
    Vivian Gornick and Barbara K. Moran, eds, *Woman in
    Sexist Society; Studies in Power and Powerlessness* (1971;
    rpt New York: New American Library, 1972), pp. 145-62.

26 Quoted by June Sochen, *Movers and Shakers: American
    Women Thinkers and Activists, 1900-1970* (New York:
    Quadrangle/New York Times, 1973), p. 100.

27 See Sochen, above, esp. ch. 3 on 1920-1940; Elizabeth
    Janeway, *Man's World, Woman's Place: A Study in Social
    Mythology* (New York: William Morrow, 1971).

28 William Chafe, *The American Woman: Her Changing
    Social, Economic, and Political Role, 1920-1970* (New
    York: Oxford, 1972), esp. Pt II; Lois Banner, *Women in
    Modern America: A Brief History* (New York: Harcourt
    Brace Jovanovich, 1974), esp. ch. 4, and Tables, pp. 256-
    60.

29 Francoeur, note 18 above, p. 379; Yankelovich, note 18;
    many hold the view. For instances, see Fritjof Capra, *The
    Turning Point: Science, Society, and the Rising Culture*
    (New York: Simon & Schuster, 1982); Robin Morgan, *The
    Anatomy of Freedom: Feminism, Physics, and Global
    Politics* (New York: Anchor/Doubleday, 1982); Carolyn
    Merchant, *The Death of Nature: Women, Ecology, and the
    Scientific Revolution* (San Francisco: Harper & Row,
    1980); Janet Zollinger Giele, *Women and the Future:
    Changing Sex Roles in Modern America* (New York: Free
    Press/Macmillan, 1978). For a popular cross-disciplinary
    survey, see Marilyn Ferguson, *The Aquarian Conspiracy:
    Personal and Social Transformation in the 1980s* (Los
    Angeles: J.P. Tarcher, 1980).

30 Because of the consensus among these 14 works, I will
    discuss them as a group: Bryant, 1971; LeGuin, 1974,
    1978; Neeper, 1975; Russ, 1975; Staton, 1975; Piercy,
    1976; Bradley, 1976; Broner, 1978; Charnas, 1978;
    McIntyre, 1978; Gearhart, 1979; Young, 1979; Singer,
    1980.

31 The following articles have influenced my discussion: Lucy
    Freibert, 'World Views in Utopian Novels by Women,'
    Journal of Popular Culture, 17(1983): 49-60; Carol S.
    Pearson, 'Towards a New Language, Consciousness and
    Political Theory: The Utopian Novels of Dorothy Bryant,
    Mary Staton and Marge Piercy,' *Heresies: A Feminist*

Publication on Art and Politics 13 (1981): 84-7; Joanna Russ, 'Recent Feminist Utopias,' in Marleen S. Barr, ed., *Future Females: A Critical Anthology* (Bowling Green, Ohio: Bowling Green State University Popular Press, 1981), pp. 71-85.

32 I use a generic *she/her* throughout this discussion for two reasons: first, because authors and central characters make up a female majority; second, because we need to realize and practice the conceptualization of the 'female' as a norm equally available and valuable to each of us, man or woman.

33 Elaine Showalter, 'Feminist Criticism in the Wilderness,' in *Critical Inquiry* 8 (1981): esp. 200-1; see also Annette Kolodny, 'A Map for Rereading or, Gender and the Interpretation of Literary Texts,' *New Literary History* 11 (1979-80): 467, n.25. See also Nina Auerbach, *Communities of Women: An Idea in Fiction* (Cambridge, Mass.: Harvard University Press, 1978). On female culture, see Jessie Bernard, *The Female World* (New York: Free Press/Macmillan, 1981); Anne Wilson Schaef, *Women's Reality: An Emerging Female System in the White Male Society* (Minneapolis: Winston, 1981); Carol Gilligan, *In a Different Voice: Psychological Theories and Women's Development* (Cambridge, Mass.: Harvard University Press, 1982), esp. ch. 6.

34 For background, see Capra and Merchant, note 29 above; J.E. Lovelock, *Gaia: A New Look at Life on Earth* (London: Oxford University Press, 1979); Sandra Harding and Merill B. Hintikka, eds, *Discovering Reality: Feminist Perspectives on Epistemology, Metaphysics, Methodology, and Philosophy of Science* (Boston: D. Reidel, 1983).

35 William Sims Baimbridge, 'Women in Science Fiction,' *Sex Roles* 8 (1982): 1081-93.

36 For a discussion of archetypes, see Carol Pearson and Katherine Pope, *The Female Hero in American and British Literature* (New York: Bowker, 1981), esp. ch. 8; Annis Pratt, *Archetypal Patterns in Women's Fiction* (Bloomington: Indiana University Press, 1981), esp. ch. 6.

37 See Berit Ås, 'On Female Culture: an attempt to formulate a theory of women's solidarity and action,' *Acta Sociologica* 18 (1975): 142-61; Gayle Kimball, ed., *Women's Culture: The Women's Renaissance of the Seventies* (Metuchen, New

Jersey: Scarecrow, 1981); Maggie Tripp, ed., *Woman in the Year 2000* (New York: Arbor House, 1974). Also a reminder: although this study looks only at women, feminist writing by men has its own tradition, several examples being Charles Brockden Brown, *Alcuin* (1798); Alcanoan O. Grigsby, *Nequa* (1900); Ernest Callenbach, *Ecotopia* (1975).

38 Quoted by Morgan, p. 83; see note 29 above.

39 See Phelps, note 10 above.

SELECTIONS

1
'THREE HUNDRED YEARS HENCE'
(1836)

---- * ----

Mary Griffith (d. 1877)

We know little about Mary Griffith. In fact, Camperdown, *which contains this selection, appeared only as 'by the Author of* Our Neighborhood.' *A widowed mother, she made a living from agriculture and authorship — perhaps an historical antecedent for Susie Dykes in Howland's* Papa's Own Girl *(1874). She resided in Charlies Hope, New Jersey — a locale no longer appearing on maps. She received honorary membership in the Massachusetts Horticultural Society in 1830. She belonged also to the Horticultural Society of Pennsylvania.*

Beyond these few details, she left four books — a scientific work entitled Discoveries in Light and Vision *(1836); two novels,* Our Neighborhood *(1831) and* The Two Defaulters *(1842); and a volume of tales,* Camperdown; or News from Our Neighborhood *(1836), containing the following selection.* Our Neighborhood, *an epistolary novel of some 38 entries, incorporates a lecture on 'Women' (pp. 246-83), which presents in essay form many of the eutopian practices that 'Three Hundred Years Hence' shows women to enjoy. 'Women' emphasizes economic and educational rights, but omits concern for political rights. Griffith lists four evils which women 'suffer, for complaint they make none': lack of respect for her merit, lack of mental development in marriage with the result that her husband soon far outpaces her, lack of understanding for her husband's business affairs, and lack of occupational opportunity for supporting children, should he die (p. 260). 'Women' ends on the note that 'Three Hundred Years Hence' will develop: 'We are persuaded that all the misery in this world, which is dependent on vice, arises from the limited sphere of action in which woman is compelled to move' (p. 283, italics original).*

'Three Hundred Years Hence' is a dream vision of the United States, realistically projected three centuries into the future. The male narrator Edgar Hastings, whose dream follows, receives information from an alleged male descendant of the same name. Though women's rights receive central focus, women characters strangely do not. Except for the omission of political rights, a female version of Jacksonianism emerges – a spirit of expanded possibilities for the common woman. Deleted from the following is the contemporary literary frame introducing and concluding the selection.

REFERENCES:
Nelson F. Adkins, 'An Early American Story of Utopia,' The Colophon I (Summer 1935): 122-32; Arthur O. Lewis, Introduction to American Utopias: Selected Short Fiction (New York: Arno, 1971), pp. x-xi; Barbara Quissell, 'The New World That Eve Made' in America as Utopia, ed. Kenneth M. Roemer (New York: Franklin, 1981), pp. 159-61, 172-3; Beverly Seaton, 'Mary Griffith' in American Women Writers (New York: Ungar, 1980), vol. 2: 183-5.

SELECTION
Includes pp. 40-9, 67-76, 82-7 of the original pp. 9-92.

'THREE HUNDRED YEARS HENCE'

※

... 'In the year 1835 – alas, it seems to me that but a few days ago I existed at that period – was there not an Orphan Asylum here?'

'Yes, my dear sir, the old books speak of a small establishment of that kind, founded by several sensible and benevolent women; but it was attended with very great personal sacrifices – for there was in that century a very singular, and, we must say, disgusting practice among all classes, to obtain money for the establishment of any charitable, benevolent, or literary institution. Both men and women – women for the most part, because men used then to shove off from themselves all that was irksome or disagreeable – women, I say, used to go from door to door, and in the most humble manner beg a few dollars from each individual. Sometimes, the Recorder of Self-Inflicted Miseries says, that men and women of coarse minds and mean education were in the habit of insulting the committee who thus turned beggars. They did not make their refusal in decent terms even, but added insult to it. In the course of time the Recorder goes on to say, men felt ashamed of all this, and their first step was to relieve women from the drudgery and disgrace of begging. After that, but it was by degrees, the different corporate bodies of each state took the matter up, and finally every state had its own humane and charitable institutions, so that there are now no longer any private ones, excepting such as men volunteer to maintain with their own money.'

'Did the old Orphan Asylum of Philadelphia, begun by private individuals, merge into the one now established?'

'No,' replied Edgar; 'the original asylum only existed a certain number of years, for people got tired of keeping up a charity by funds gathered in this loose way. At length, another man of immense wealth died, and bequeathed all his property to the erection and support of a college for orphan girls – and this time the world was not in doubt as to the testator's meaning. From this moment a new era took place with regard to women, and we owe the improved condition of our people entirely to the improvement in the education of the female poor; blessed be the name of that man.'

'Well, from time to time you must tell me the rise and progress of all these things; at present I must try and find my way in this now truly beautiful city. This is Market street, but so altered that I should scarcely know it.'

'Yes, I presume that three hundred years would improve the markets likewise. But wherein is it altered?'

'In my day the market was of one story, or rather had a roof supported by brick pillars, with a neat stone pavement running the whole length of the building. Market women not only sat under each arch and outside of the pillars, but likewise in the open spaces where the streets intersected the market. Butchers and fish sellers had their appropriate stalls; and clerks of the market, as they were called, took care that no imposition was practised. Besides this, the women used to bawl through the streets, and carry their fish and vegetables on their heads.'

'All that sounds very well; but our old friend, the Recorder of Self-Inflicted Miseries, mentions this very market as a detestable nuisance, and the manner of selling things through the streets shameful. Come with me, and let us see wherein this is superior to the one you describe.'

The two friends entered the range above at the Schuylkill, for to that point had the famous Philadelphia market reached. The building was of two stories, built of hewn stone, and entirely fire-proof, as there was not a particle of wood-work or other ignitable matter in it. The upper story was appropriated to wooden, tin, basket, crockery, and other domestic wares, such as stockings, gloves, seeds, and garden utensils, all neatly arranged and kept perpetually clean. On the ground floor, in cool niches, under which ran a stream of cold, clear water, were all the variety of vegetables; and there, at this early season, were strawberries and green peas, all of which were raised in the neighbourhood. The finest of the strawberries were those that three centuries before went by the name, as it now did, of the *dark hautbois*, rich in flavour and delicate in perfume. Women, dressed in close caps and snow white aprons, stood or sat modestly by their baskets – not, as formerly, bawling out to the passers-by and entreating them to purchase of them, but waiting for their turn with patience and good humour. Their hair was all hidden, save a few plain braids or plaits in front, and their neck was entirely covered. Their dress was appropriate to their condition, and their bearing had both dignity and grace.

'Well, this surpasses belief,' said Hastings. 'Are these the descendants of that coarse, vulgar, noisy, ill dressed tribe, one half of whom appeared before their dirty baskets and crazy fixtures with tawdry finery, and the other half in sluttish, un-couth clothes, with their hair hanging about their face, or stuck up behind with a greasy horn comb? What has done all this?'

'Why, the improvement which took place in the education of women. While women were degraded as they were in your time' –

'In my time, my dear Edgar,' said Hastings, quickly – 'in my time! I can tell you that women were not in a degraded state then. Go back to the days of Elizabeth, if you please; but I assure you that in 1835 women enjoyed perfect equality of rights.'

'Did they! then our old friend, the Recorder of Self-Inflicted Miseries, has been imposing on us – but we will discuss this theme more at our leisure. Let us ask that neat pretty young woman for some strawberries and cream.'

They were ripe and delicious, and Hastings found, that however much all other things had changed, the fine perfume, the grateful flavour, the rich consistency of the fruit and cream were the same – nature never changes.

There were no unpleasant sights – no rotten vegetables or leaves, no mud, no spitting, no – in short, the whole looked like a painting, and the women all seemed as if they were dressed for the purpose of sitting for their portraits, to let other times have a peep at what was going on in a former world.

'If I am in my senses,' said Hastings, 'which I very much doubt, this is the most pleasing change which time has wrought; I cannot but believe that I shall wake up in the morning and find this all a dream. This is no market – it is a picture.'

'We shall see,' said Edgar. 'Come, let us proceed to the butchers' market.'

33

So they walked on, and still the rippling stream followed them; and here no sights of blood, or stained hands, or greasy knives, or slaughter-house smells, were present. The meats were not hung up to view in the open air, as in times of old; but you had only to ask for a particular joint, and lo! a small door, two feet square, opened in the wall, and there hung the identical part.

'This gentleman is a stranger,' said Edgar, to a neatly dressed man, having on a snow white apron; 'show him a hind quarter of veal; we do not want to buy any, but merely to look at what you have to sell.'

The little door opened, and there hung one of the fattest and finest quarters Hastings had ever seen.

'And the price,' asked he.

'It is four cents a pound,' replied the man.

A purchaser soon came; the meat was weighed within; the man received the money, and gave a ticket with the weight written on it; the servant departed, and the two friends moved on.

'Our regulations are excellent,' said Edgar; 'formerly, as the old Recorder of Self-Inflicted Miseries says, the butchers weighed their meats in the most careless manner, and many a man went home with a suspicion that he was cheated of half or three quarters of a pound. Now, nothing of this kind can take place, for the clerks of the market stand at every corner. See! those men use the graduated balance; the meat is laid, basket and all, on that little table; the pressure acts on a wheel – a clicking is heard – it strikes the number of pounds and quarters, and thus the weight is ascertained. The basket you saw, all those you now see in the meat market, are of equal weight, and they are marked 1,2,3,4 or more pounds, as the size may be. Do you not see how much of labour and confusion this saves? I suppose, in your day, you would have scorned to legislate on such trifling objects; but I assure you we find our account in it.'

'I must confess that this simplifies things wonderfully; but the cleanliness, order and cheerfulness that are seen throughout this market – these are things worthy of legislation. I suppose all this took place gradually?'

'Yes, I presume so; but it had arrived to this point before my time; the water which flows under and through the market was conveyed there upward of a century ago. But here is beef, mutton, all kinds of meat – and this is the poultry market – all sold by weight, as it should be; and here is the fish market – see what large marble basins; each fishmonger has one of his own, so that all kinds are separate; and see how dexterously they scoop up the very fish that a customer wants.'

'What is this?' said Hastings, look through one of the arches of the fish market; 'can this be the Delaware?'

'Yes,' replied Edgar; 'the market on which we are now, is over the Delaware. Look over this railing, we are on a wide bridge – but let us proceed to the extremity; this bridge extends to the Jersey shore, and thus connects the two large cities Philadelphia and Camden.'

'In my day, it was in contemplation to build a bridge over the Delaware; but there was great opposition to it, as in that case there would be a very great delay, if not hinderance, to the free passage of ships.'

New wonders sprung up at every step – vessels, light as gossamer, of curious construction, were passing and repassing under the arches of the bridge, some of three and four hundred tons burden, others for the convenience of market people, and many for the pleasure of the idle. While yet they looked, a beautiful vessel hove in sight, and in a moment she moved gracefully and swiftly under the arches, and by the time that Hastings had crossed to the other side of the bridge she was fastened to the pier.

'Is this a steamboat from Baltimore?' said Hastings. 'Yet it cannot be, for I see neither steam nor smoke.'

'Steamboat!' answered his companion – 'don't speak so loud, the people will think you crazy. Why, steamboats have been out of date for more than two hundred years. I forget the name of the one who introduced them into our waters, but they did not continue in use more than fifty years, perhaps not so long; but so many accidents occurred through the extreme carelessness, ignorance and avarice of many who were engaged in them, that a very great prejudice existed against their use. No laws were found sufficiently strong to prevent frequent occurrences of the bursting of the boilers, notwithstanding that sometimes as many as nine or ten lives were destroyed by the explosion. That those accidents were not the consequence of using steam power – I mean a *necessary* consequence – all sensible men knew; for on this river, the Delaware, the bursting of the boiler of a steam engine was never known, nor did such dreadful accidents ever occur in Europe. But, as I was saying, after one of the most awful catastrophes that ever took place, the bursting of a boiler which scalded to death forty-one members of Congress, (on their way home,) besides upwards of thirty women and children, and nine of the crew, the people of this country began to arouse themselves, and very severe laws were enacted. Before, however, any farther loss of lives occurred, a stop was put to the use of steamboats altogether. The dreadful accident of which I spoke occurred in the year 1850, and in that eventful year a new power was brought into use, by which steamboats were laid aside for ever.'

'What is the new principle, and who first brought it to light?'

'Why, a lady. The world owes this blessed invention to a female! I will take you into one of our small boats presently, where you can handle the machinery yourself. No steam, nor heat, nor animal power – but one of sufficient energy to move the largest ship.'

'Condensed air, is it? – that was tried in my time.'

'No, nor condensed air; that was almost as dangerous a power as steam; for the bursting of an air vessel was always destructive of life. The Recorder of Self-Inflicted Miseries mentions several instances of loss of life by the bursting of one of the air machines used by the manufacturers of mineral waters. If that lady had lived in *this* century, her memory would be honoured and cherished; but if no memorial was erected by the English to Lady Mary Wortley Montagu, a reproach could not rest upon us for not having paid suitable honours to the American lady.'

'Why, what did lady Mary Wortley Montagu do?' said Hastings; 'I recollect nothing but that she wrote several volumes of very agreeable letters – Oh, yes, how could I forget – the small-pox! Yes, indeed, she did deserve to have a monument; but surely the English erected one to her memory?'

'Did they? – yes – that old defamer of women, Horace Walpole, took good care to keep the public feeling from flowing in the right channel. He made people laugh at her dirty hands and painted cheeks, but he never urged them to heap honours on her head for introducing into England the practice of innoculation for the small-pox. If this American lady deserved the thanks and gratitude of her country for thus, for ever, preventing the loss of lives from steam, and I may say, too, from shipwreck – still farther was Lady Mary Wortley

Montagu entitled to distinction, for the very great benefit she bestowed on England. She saved thousands of lives, and prevented, what sometimes amounted to hideous deformity, deeply scarred faces, from being universal. – Yes, the benefit was incalculable and beyond price – quite equal, I think, to that which the world owes to Dr. Jenner, who introduced a new form of small-pox, or rather the small-pox pure and unadulterated by any affinitive virus. This modified the disease to such a degree, that the small-pox, in its mixed and complicated state, almost disappeared. The Recorder of Self-Inflicted Miseries states, that after a time a new variety of the small-pox made its appearance, which was called *varioloid*; but it was quite under the control of medical skill.'

'Well, you live in an age so much in advance of mine, and so many facts and curious phenomena came to light during the nineteenth century, that you can tell me what the settled opinion is now respecting small-pox, kine-pox, and varioloid.'

'The settled opinion now is, that they are one and the same disease. Thus – the original disease, transferable from an ulcer of the cow's udder to the broken skin of a human being, produced what is called the kine or cow-pox. This virus of the kine-pox, in its original state, was only capable of being communicated by contact, and only when the skin was broken or cut; but, when *combined* with the other poison, infected the system by means of breathing in the same atmosphere. The poison from the ulcer called cow-pox was never communicated to or by the lungs, neither was the poison which had so strong an affinity for it communicated in that way; but when the two poisons united, and met in the same system, a third poison was generated, and the *small-pox was the result*. But here we are discussing a deep subject in this busy place – what gave rise to it? – oh, steamboats, the new power now used, Lady Mary Wortley, and Dr. Jenner.'

'I presume,' said the attentive Hastings, 'that Dr. Jenner fared no better than your American lady and Lady Mary Wortley.'

'You are much mistaken,' said Edgar. 'Dr. Jenner was a *man*, which in your day was a very different circumstance. I verily believe if it had been a woman who brought that happy event about, although the whole world would have availed itself of the discovery, her name would scarcely be known at this day.' . . .

[S]mall offences were winked at as if defrauding the revenue of a dollar were not a crime *per se* as well as defrauding it of a thousand dollars – just as if murdering an infant were not as much murder as if the life had been taken from a man – just as if killing a man in private, because his enemy had paid you to do it, was not as much murder in the first degree as if the government had paid you for killing a dozen men in battle in open day – just as if' –

'Just as if what?' said the astonished Hastings, 'has the time come when killing men by wholesale, in war, is accounted a crime?'

'Yes, thank Heaven,' said Edgar, 'that blessed time has at length arrived; it is upwards of one hundred and twenty years since men were ordered to kill one another in that barbarous manner. Why the recital of such cruel and barbarous deeds fills our young children with horror. The ancient policy of referring the disputes of nations to single combat, was far more humanizing than the referring such disputes to ten thousand men on each side; for, after all, it was 'might that made right.' Because a strong party beats a weaker one, that is not a proof that the *right* was in the strong one; yet, still, if men had no other way of settling their disputes but by spilling blood, then that plan was the most humane which only sacrificed two or one man. As to national honour! why not let the few settle it? why drag the poor sailors and soldiers to be butchered like cattle to gratify the fine feelings of a few morbidly constructed minds?'

'Oh, that my good father, Valentine Harley, could have seen this day,' said Hastings. 'But this bloodthirsty, savage propensity – this murdering our fellow creatures in cold blood, as it were, was cured by degrees I presume. What gave the first impulse to such a blessed change?'

'The old Recorder states that it was brought about by the *influence of women*; it was they who gave the first impulse. As soon as they themselves were considered as of equal importance with their husbands – as soon as they were on an equality in *money matters*, for after all, people are respected in proportion to their wealth, that moment all the barbarisms of the age disappeared. Why, in your day, a strange perverted system had taken deep root; *then*, it was the *man that was struck* by another who was disgraced in public opinion, and not the one who struck him. It was that system which fermented and promoted bloodthirstiness, and it was encouraged and fostered by men and by women both.

'But as soon as women had more power in their hands, their energies were directed another way; they became more enlightened as they rose higher in the scale, and instead of encroaching on our privileges, of which we stood in such fear, women shrunk farther and farther from all approach to men's pursuits and occupations. Instead of congregating, as they did in your time, to beg for alms to establish and sustain a charity, that they might have some independent power of their own – for this craving after distinction was almost always blended with their desire to do good – they united for the purpose of exterminating that *war seed* above mentioned – that system which fastened the *disgrace* of a blow on the one who received it. This was their first effort; they then taught their children likewise, that to kill a man in battle, or men in battle, when mere national honour was the war cry, or when we had been robbed of our money on the high seas, was a crime of the blackest die, and contrary to the divine precepts of our Saviour. They taught them to abstain from shedding human blood, *excepting in self defence* – excepting in case of invasion.

'They next taught them to reverence religion; for until bloodthirstiness was cured, how could a child reverence our Saviour's precepts? How could we recommend a wholesome, simple diet to a man who had been accustomed to riot in rich sauces and condiments? They had first to wean them from the savage propensities that they had received through the maddening influence of unreflecting men, before a reverence for holy things could be excited. Then it was that clergymen became the exalted beings in our eyes that they now are – then it was that children began to love and respect them. As soon as their fathers did their mothers the poor justice of trusting them with all their property, the children began to respect her as they ought, and then her words were the words of wisdom. It was then, and not till then, that war and duelling ceased. We are amazed at what we read. What! take away a man's life because he has robbed us of money! Hang a man because he has forged our name for a few dollars! No: go to our prisons, there you will see the murderer's fate – solitary confinement, at hard labour, for life! that is his punishment; but murders are very rare now in this country. A man stands in greater dread of solitary confinement at hard labour than he does of hanging. In fact, according to our way of thinking, now, we have no right, by the Divine law, to take that away from a human being for which we can give no equivalent. It is right to prevent a murderer from committing still farther crime; and this we do by confining him for life at hard labour, *and alone*.'

'Women, you say, produced a reform in that miserable code called *the law of honour*.'

'Yes, thanks be to them for it. Why, as the old Recorder states, if a man did not challenge the fellow who struck him, he was obliged to quit the army or the navy, and be for ever banished as a coward, and it was considered as disgraceful in a private citizen to receive a blow without challenging the ruffian that struck him. But the moment that women took the office in hand, that moment the thing was reversed. They entered into a compact not to receive a man into their society who had struck another, unless he made such ample apology to the injured person as to be forgiven by him; and not only that, but his restoration to favour was to be sued for by the injured party himself. A man soon became cautious how he incurred the risk.'

'It often occurred to me,' said Hastings, 'that women had much of the means of moral reform in their power; but they always appeared to be pursuing objects tending rather to weaken than to strengthen morals. They acted with good intentions, but really wanted judgment to select the proper method of pursuing their benevolent schemes. Only look at their toiling as they did to collect funds towards educating poor young men for the ministry.'

'Oh, those young men,' replied Edgar, 'were, no doubt, their sons or brothers, and even then they must have been working at some trade to assist their parents or some poor relation, and thus had to neglect themselves.'

'No, indeed,' said Hastings, 'I assure you these young men were entire strangers, persons that they never saw in their lives, nor ever expected to see.'

'Then, all I can say is, that the women were to be pitied for their mistaken zeal, and the men ought to have scorned such aid – but the times are altered; no man, no poor man stands in need of women's help now, as they have trades or employments that enable them to educate themselves. Only propose such a thing *now*, and see how it would be received; why a young man would think you intended to insult him. We pursue the plan so

admirably begun in your day by the celebrated Fellenberg.*
When we return this way again, I will show you the work-
shops attached to the college – the one we saw in Princeton.'

'While we are thus far on the road, suppose that we go to
New York,' said Hastings, 'I was bound thither when that
calamity befell me. I wonder if I shall see a single house
remaining that I saw three hundred years ago.'

Edgar laughed – 'You will see but very few, I can tell you,'
said he, 'houses, in your day, were built too slightly to stand
the test of *one* century. At one time, the corporation of the city
had to inspect the mortar, lest it should not be strong enough
to cement the bricks! And it frequently happened that houses
tumbled down, not having been built strong enough to bear
their own weight. A few of the public buildings remain, but
they have undergone such changes that you will hardly
recognize them. The City Hall, indeed, stands in the same
place, but if you approach it, in the rear, you will find that it is
of marble, and not freestone as the old Recorder says it was in
your time. But since the two great fires at the close of the years
1835 and 1842 the city underwent great alterations.'

'Great fires; in what quarter of the city were they? They
must have been disasters, indeed, to be remembered for three
hundred years.'

'Yes, the first destroyed nearly seven hundred houses, and
about fifteen millions of property; and the second, upwards of
a thousand houses, and about three millions of property; but
excepting that it reduced a number of very respectable females
to absolute want, the merchants, and the city itself, were
greatly benefited by it. There were salutary laws enacted in
consequence of it, that is, after the second fire; for instance, the
streets in the burnt districts were made wider; the houses were
better and stronger built; the fire engines were drawn by horses,
and afterwards by a new power: firemen were not only exempt
from jury and militia duty, but they had a regular salary while
they served out their seven years' labour; and if any fireman
lost his life, or was disabled, his family received the salary for a
term of years. The old Recorder says that there was not a
merchant of any enterprise who did not recover from his losses
in three years.'

*Philip Emanuel von Fellenberg (1771-1884), a Swiss educator noted for
establishing in Bern a school to train poor boys to be self-supporting.

41

'But what became of the poor women who lost all their property? did they lose insurance stock? for I presume the insurance companies became insolvent.'

'The poor women? – oh, they remained poor – nothing in *your* day ever happened to better their condition when a calamity like that overtook *them*. Men had enough to do to pity and help themselves. Yes, their loss was in the insolvency of the insurance companies; but stock is safe enough now, for the last tremendous fire (they did not let the first make the impression it ought to have done,) roused the energies and *sense* of the people, and insurance is managed very different. Every house, now, whether of the rich or the poor man, is insured. It has to pay so much additional tax, and the corporation are the insurers. But the tax is so trifling that no one feels it a burden; our houses are almost all fire-proof since the discovery of a substance which renders wood almost proof against fire. But I have a file of the Recorder of Self-Inflicted Miseries, and you will see the regular gradation from the barbarisms of your day to the enlightened times it has been permitted you to see.'

'But the water, in my day,' – poor Hastings never repeated this without a sigh – 'in my day the city was supplied by water from a brackish stream, but there was a plan in contemplation to bring good water to the city from the distance of forty miles.'

'Where, when was that? I do not remember to have read any thing about it. – Oh, yes, there was such a scheme, and it appears to me they did attempt it, but whatever was the cause of failure I now forget; at present they have plentiful supply by means of boring. Some of these bored wells are upwards of a thousand feet deep.'

'Why the Manhattan Company made an attempt of this kind in my time, but they gave it up as hopeless after going down to the depth of six or seven hundred feet.'

'Yes, I recollect; but only look at the difficulties they had to encounter. In the first place, the chisel that they bored with was not more than three or four inches wide; of course, as the hole made by this instrument could be no larger, there was no possibility of getting the chisel up if it were broken off below, neither could they break or cut it into fragments. If such an accident were to occur at the depth of six hundred feet, this bored hole would have to be abandoned. We go differently to work now; with our great engines we cut down through the earth and rock, as if it were cheese, and the wells are of four feet diameter. As they are lined throughout with an impervious cement, the overflowing water does not escape. Every house is now supplied from this neverfailing source – the rich, and the poor likewise, use this water, and it is excellent. All the expense comes within the one yearly general tax: when a man builds he knows that pipes are to be conveyed through his house, and he knows also that his one tax comprehends the use of water. He pays so much per centum for water, for all the municipal arrangement, for defence of harbour, for the support of government, &c., and as there is such a wide door open, such a competition, his food and clothing do not cost half as much as they did in your day.'

'You spoke of wells a thousand feet deep and four feet wide; what became of all the earth taken from them – stones I should say.'

'Oh, they were used for the extension of the Battery. Do you remember, in your day, an ill constructed thing called Fort William, or Castle Garden? Well, the Battery was filled up on each side from that point, so that at present there are at least five acres of ground more attached to it than when you saw it, and as we are now levelling a part of Brooklyn heights, we intend to fill it out much farther. The Battery is a noble promenade now.'

They reached New York by the slow line at two o'clock, having travelled at the rate of thirty miles an hour; and after walking up Broadway to amuse themselves with looking at the improvements that had taken place since Hastings last saw it – three hundred years previous – they stopped at the Astor Hotel. This venerable building, the City Hall, the Public Mart, the St. Paul's Church, and a stone house at the lower end of the street, built by governor Jay, were all that had stood the test of ages. The St. Paul was a fine old church, but the steeple had been taken down and a dome substituted, as was the fashion of all the churches in the city – the burial yards of all were gone – houses were built on them: – vaults, tombs, graves, monuments – what had become of them?

The Astor Hotel, a noble building, of simple and chaste architecture, stood just as firm, and looked just as well, as it did when Hastings saw it. Why should it not? stone is stone, and three hundred years more would pass over it without impairing

43

it. This shows the advantage of stone over brick. Mr. Astor built for posterity, and he has thus perpetuated his name. He was very near living as long as this building; the planning and completing of it seemed to renovate him, for his life was extended to his ninety-ninth year. This building proves him to have been a man of fine taste and excellent judgment, for it still continues to be admired.

'But how is this?' said Hastings, 'I see no houses but this one built by Mr. Astor that are higher than three stories; it is the case throughout the city, stores and all.'

'Since the two great fires of 1835 and 1842, the corporation forbid the building of any house or store above a certain height. Those tremendous fires, as I observed, brought people to their senses, and they now see the folly of it.

'The ceilings are not so high as formerly; more regard is shown to comfort. Why the old Recorder of Self-Inflicted Miseries states, that men were so indifferent about the conveniences and comforts of life, that they would sometimes raise the ceilings to the great height of fourteen and fifteen feet! Nay, that they did so in despite of their wives' health, never considering how hard it bore on the lungs of those who were affected with asthma or other visceral complaints. Heavens and earth! how little the case and pleasure of women were consulted in your day.'

'Yes, that appears all very true,' said Hastings, 'but you must likewise recollect that these very women were quite as eager as their husbands to live in houses having such high flights of stairs.'

'Poor things,' exclaimed Edgar, 'to think of their being trained to like and desire a thing that bore so hard on them. Only consider what a loss of time and breath it must be to go up and down forty or fifty times a day, for your nurseries were, it seems generally in the third story. We love our wives too well now to pitch our houses so high up in the air. The Philadelphians had far more humanity, more consideration; they always built a range of rooms in the rear of the main building, and this was a great saving of time and health.' . . .

'Yes,' said Edgar, '. . . here is a neat building – you had nothing of this kind in your time. This is a house where the daughters of the poor are taught to sew and cut out wearing apparel. I suppose you know that there are no men tailors now.'

'What, do women take measure?'

'Oh, no, men are the measurers, but women cut out and sew. It is of great advantage to poor women that they can cut out and make their husbands' and children's clothes. The old Recorder states that women – poor women – in the year 1836, were scarcely able to cut out their own clothes. But just about that date, a lady of this city suggested the plan of establishing an institution of this kind, and it was adopted. Some benevolent men built the house and left ample funds for the maintenance of a certain number of poor girls, with a good salary for those who superintend it. And here is another house: this is for the education of those girls whose parents have seen better days. Here they are taught accounts and book-keeping – which, however, in our day is not so complicated as it was, for there is no credit given for any thing. In short these girls are instructed in all that relates to the disposal of money; our women now comprehend what is meant by stocks, and dividends, and loans, and tracts, and bonds, and mortgages.'

'Do women still get the third of their husband's estate after their husband's death?'

'Their thirds? I don't know what you mean – Oh, I recollect; yes, in your day it was the practice to curtail a woman's income after her husband's death. A man never then considered a woman as equal to himself; but, while he lived, he let her enjoy the whole of his income equally with himself, because he could not do otherwise and enjoy his money; but when he died, or rather, when about making his will, he found out that she was but a poor creature after all, and that a very little of what he had to leave would suffice for her. Nay, the old Recorder says that there have been rich men who ordered the very house in which they lived, and which had been built for their wives' comfort, during their life time, to be sold, and who thus compelled their wives to live in mean, pitiful houses or go to lodgings.'

'Yes,' said Hastings, – quite ashamed of his own times, – 'but then you know the husband was fearful that his wife would marry again, and all their property would go to strangers.'

'Well, why should not women have the same privileges as men? Do you not think that a woman had the same fears? A man married again and gave his money to strangers – did he not? The fact is, we consider that a woman has the same

45

feelings as we have ourselves – a thing you never once thought of – and now the property that is made during marriage is as much the woman's as the man's; they are partners in health and in sickness, in joy and in sorrow – they enjoy every thing in common while they live together, and why a woman, merely on account of her being more helpless, should be cut off from affluence because she survives her husband, is more than we of this century can tell. Why should not children wait for the property till after her death, as they would for their father's death? It was a relic of barbarism, but it has passed away with wars and bloodshed. We educate our women now, and they are as capable of taking care of property as we are ourselves. They are our trustees, far better than the trustees you had amongst you in your day – they seldom could find it in their hearts to allow a widow even her poor income. I suppose they thought that a creature so pitifully used by her husband was not worth bestowing their honesty upon.'

'But the women in my day,' said Hastings, 'seemed to approve of this treatment; in fact, I have known many very sensible women who thought it right that a man should not leave his wife the whole of his income after his death. But they were beginning to have their eyes opened, for I recollect that the subject was being discussed in 1835.'

'Yes, you can train a mind to acquiesce in any absurd doctrine, and the truth is, that as women were then educated, they were, for the most part, unfit to have the command of a large estate. But I cannot find that the children were eventually benefited by it; for young men and women, coming into possession of their father's estate at the early age of twenty-one, possessed no more business talent than their mother; nor had they even as much prudence and judgment in the management of money matters, as she had. Men seldom thought of this, but generally directed their executors to divide the property among the children as soon as they became of age – utterly regardless of the injustice they were doing their wives, and of the oath which they took when they married – that is, if they married according to the forms of the Episcopal church. In that service, a man binds himself by a solemn oath 'to endow his wife with *all* his worldly goods.' If he swears to endow her with all, how can he in safety to his soul, *will* these worldly goods away from her. We consider the practice of depriving a woman of the right to the whole of her husband's property after his death, as a monstrous act of injustice, and the laws are now peremptory on this subject.'

'I am certain you are right,' said Hastings, 'and you have improved more rapidly in this particular, during a period of three hundred years, than was done by my ancestors in two thousand years before. I can understand now, how it happens, that children have the same respect for their mother, that they only felt for their father in my time. The custom, or laws, being altogether in favour of equality of rights between the parents, the children do not repine when they find that they stand in the same relation of dependence to their mother, that they did to their father; and why this should not be, is incomprehensible to me now, but I never reflected on it before.'

'Yes, there are fewer estates squandered away in consequence of this, and society is all the better for it. Then to this is added the great improvement in the business education of women. All the retail and detail of mercantile operations are conducted by them. You had some notion of this in your time; for, in Philadelphia, although women were generally only employed to make sales behind the counter, yet some were now and then seen at the head of the establishment. Before our separation from Great Britain, the business of farming was also at a low ebb, and a farmer was but a mean person in public estimation. He ranks now amongst the highest of our business men; and in fact, he is equal to any man whether in business or not, and this is the case with female merchants. Even in 1836, a woman who undertook the business of a retail shop, managing the whole concern herself, although greatly respected, she never took her rank amongst the first classes of society. This arose, first, from want of education, and, secondly, from her having lived amongst an inferior set of people. But when women were trained to the comprehension of mercantile operations, and were taught how to dispose of money, their whole character underwent a change, and with this accession of business talent, came the respect from men for those who had a capacity for the conducting of business affairs. Only think what an advantage this is to our children; why our mothers and wives are the first teachers, they give us sound views from the very commencement, and our clerkship begins from the time we can comprehend the distinction of right and wrong.'

'Did not our infant schools give a great impulse to this improvement in the condition of women, and to the improvement in morals, and were not women mainly instrumental in fostering these schools?'

'Yes, that they were; it was chiefly through the influence of their pen and active benevolence, that the scheme arrived at perfection. In these infant schools a child was early taught the mystery of its relation to society; all its good dispositions and propensities were encouraged and developed, and its vicious ones were repressed. The world owes much to the blessed influence of infant schools, and the lower orders were the first to be humanized by them. But I need not dwell on this particular. I shall only point to the improvement in the morals of our people at this day, to convince you that it is owing altogether to the benign influence of women. As soon as they took their rank as an equal to man, equal as to property I mean, for they had no other right to *desire*; there was no longer any struggle, it became their ambition to show how long the world had been benighted by thus keeping them in a degraded state. I say degraded state, for surely it argued in them imbecility or incapacity of some kind, and to great extent, too, when a man appointed executors and trustees to his estate whilst his wife was living. It showed one of three things – that he never considered her as having equal rights with himself; or, that he thought her incompetent to take charge of his property – or, that the customs and laws of the land had so warped his judgment, that he only did as he saw others do, without considering whether these laws and customs were right or wrong. But if you only look back you will perceive, that in every benevolent scheme, in every plan for meliorating the condition of the poor, and improving their morals, it was women's influence that promoted and fostered it. It is to that healthy influence, that we owe our present prosperity and happiness – and it is an influence which I hope may forever continue.' . . .

2
'SEQUEL TO "THE VISION OF BANGOR IN THE TWENTIETH CENTURY"'
(1848)

---*---

Jane Sophia Appleton (d. 1884)

About Jane Sophia Appleton we know little more than her name as it appears in Voices from the Kenduskeag, *a collection she edited with Cornelia Crosby Barrett to benefit the Bangor [Maine] Female Orphan Asylum in 1848. According to an obituary in the* Bangor Daily Whig and Courier, *she wrote on temperance and 'women's progress.' One such essay was called 'End and Aim of the Present System of Female Education.'*

Appleton's 'Sequel' appeared in Voices from the Kenduskeag *as a response to 'Vision of Bangor' by then-governor Edward Kent, likewise a dream vision of Bangor, Maine, a century into the future. But Appleton labels Kent's narrator a misogynist. Her 'Sequel,' which follows, is a woman's dream of a society rewarding to women. Appleton's vision corrects Kent's errors in viewpoint: a male guide informs a female dreamer, who imagines herself to be Kent's original male visitor!*

REFERENCES
Arthur O. Lewis, Introduction to *American Utopias: Selected Short Fiction* (New York: Arno, 1971), pp. xi-xiii; Barbara Quissell, 'The New World That Eve Made' in *America as Utopia*, ed. Kenneth M. Roemer (New York: Franklin, 1981), pp. 150-2, 170-1.

SELECTION
Omission from pp. 246-50 of original pp. 243-65.

'SEQUEL TO "THE VISION OF BANGOR IN THE TWENTIETH CENTURY" '

'Your young men shall see visions, and your old men shall dream dreams.'

One day happening by chance to peep into a gentleman's escritoire, I discovered a 'Vision of Bangor in the twentieth century.' To my shame be it spoken, I did not resist the temptation thus spread before me, but allowed my curiosity the gratification of reading it from beginning to end. The same night having supped on oysters, *I*, too, had a dream, and what was very singular, it appeared to *join on* most remarkably to the one which had amused me so much in the morning. I seemed even to have entered into the person of the quondam dreamer, and to be actually the same individual. I shall plead therefore the extravagance of a dream, as my apology for merging my identity in his, as I relate the scenes which passed before me.

I stood by a building of very singular and imposing architecture, constructed of hewn stone, and adorned with magnificent paintings from the top to the bottom, which on nearer examination, I found to be emblematic and exquisitely beautiful representations of the triumph of the spirit of peace over that of strife and conquest, among the nations of the earth. I turned to ask the name of this building of the individual who had hitherto acted as my guide, but to my surpirse he had disappeared, and in his place stood a hale, hearty old gentleman, with a right honest countenance, and an eye wherein a spice of roguery was bewitchingly blended with a deep, manly earnestness. He seemed to be aware of my situation as a stranger, and as one who had long been absent from these sublunary scenes, and answered me with the utmost good nature.

'That,' said he, 'is a building wherein are kept the weapons of war, (so far as they could be obtained,) which have been used in all ages of the world.'

'They are preserved both as curiosities, and as affecting memorials of the atrocities which the indulgence of evil passions, and the imagined necessity of maintaining what was falsely called "national honor," once led the human race to commit.'

I had scarcely expressed my congratulations upon the great moral advance of society which the existence of such an edifice for such a purpose argued, when I espied in a neighboring street, in the midst of magnificent piles of stone and marble, a ruined structure, which looked as if it might have been a church, but was so fallen into decay and covered with the 'moss of ages,' that one could hardly distinguish its original form.

'And what ruin have we here?' I asked. 'That was once, I believe, an Episcopal church, although the Episcopalians hardly acknowledge it now. Their present structures are all so splendid, they are unwilling to believe that there was ever an Episcopal church built of wood in this great city. There is an old organ in this building, which report says sometimes sends forth strange sounds at the "witching hour of night." The rumor may perhaps be founded upon a tradition, representing it as a most wonderful organ in its day, – being determined to "go," with or without hands, unless it was constantly watched! What strange power the eyes of the "three watchers," who, the legend says, sat by it day and night, were endowed with, that they could "*hold*" the heavenly harmonies, I know not; but that they had some such power, the fact that whenever they were careless enough to fall asleep, the "troublesome thing *would* go," strongly intimates.'

'What is the present state of religious sects here?' I asked. 'Have they, as some prophesied in my day, been merged in one universal church?'

'No, they have not, but they have done what I think is quite as well, "agreed to disagree." Each still maintains some distinctive doctrines, but with so much Christian harmony, that a stranger might think them one united body, divided for convenience into distinct congregations. There has been a great change in the specific items of faith held by some sects since your time, and others have disappeared entirely. But the greatest change has been in the *spirit* which pervades the religious community. Where once all was rancor, misrepresentation, and hostility, now all is forbearance and love. The great

51

secret of this change has been, and is, that sects have ceased to *set themselves in antagonism with each other*. They go on quietly in their own course, teach, preach, and live the truths which they think the gospel inculcates, and *let each other alone*. The hateful voice of religious controversy is now scarcely heard in our land. Sects do not, even by implication, or by the application of exclusive titles to themselves, condemn each other. Calvinists no longer proclaim their '*evangelical*' distinctions, nor do Unitarians plume themselves on their '*liberal*' tendencies. The word 'Orthodox' is obsolete as applied to a sect, and a Unitarian would stare in astonishment if you should call him a 'liberal Christian.' Baptists have opened their arms wide to welcome the Christian world to the communion of their Lord, and, what is the greatest triumph of all, Episcopalians have done talking about '*the church*,' and Swedenborgians have conceded that somebody besides Swedenborg *can* have a new idea! Thank God, the times of religious *cant* are over!

'So soon as sects ceased to place themselves in a controversial attitude, so soon they began to see that really there was "some light" in their neighbors.'

'Trinitarians found it possible to believe that Unitarians "*might* be saved upon a pinch," and Unitarians that Trinitarians were "not such fools after all," (as, in spite of their "*liberality*," even the most intelligent of their body were apt to think a hundred years ago). The next step in reform, after they had come to *see* clearly the good and truth existing in their neighbors, was, in all Christian humility to adopt it, which they have done, and are daily doing. Thus renouncing their own errors, and receiving others' truths, they are becoming constantly more similar, although whether some great points will ever be harmonized so as to merge the various sects in one church, remains a matter of doubt.'

I mused awhile on the delightful state of things I had heard described, and then my thoughts turned to an institution which had always ranked in my estimation next to the church.

'Can you tell me, sir, how many lodges of Odd Fellows there are here?' He put his hand to his head with a bewildered expression – 'Odd Fellows,' said he, 'Odd Fellows – I am sure I have heard the name, and yet I cannot imagine where. Ah! I have it! I have read of them in a volume in the Antiquarian library. I had forgotten the *name* only, for the history of the decline of the institution I remember well. I think they disappeared about the year 1868. . . .'

Just as my companion paused in his discourse, I observed a lady approaching us, on whom my eyes were immediately riveted. Grace and dignity were blended in her mien with a noble simplicity; and the expression of command enthroned upon her brow, was chastened by the winning sweetness which distinguished the lower part of her expressive face.

'Do you know her?' I eagerly asked. 'Oh yes, very well; and if she enters the gallery of paintings, whither I think she is bending her steps, we will go in, and you shall know her also.'

Our hopes were realized, and in the space of a few moments, we all found ourselves together in the gallery. After an introduction, some cursory discussion of the pictures, and going through some of the commonplaces with which I was familiar in my day, I began, as my contemporaries were much in the habit of doing, to express the admiration I really felt for her, but in a style respectful and delicate. She appeared surprised and embarrassed, but spoke not. Presuming she did not understand me, I endeavored to make my language more unequivocal, and thinking it might seem in better taste than the more personal adulation I had commenced with, I included her whole sex in my expressions of admiration.

She turned her large earnest eyes full upon me, and remained lost in astonishment. Determined that I *would* make an impression upon her by my gallantry, I returned to the attack with increased vigor, and begged that she 'would not be offended or imagine that I was flattering her, for upon my honor I was truly sincere in every word I had uttered. That woman had been all I had described her, to *me*, during my pilgrimage on earth, and that even if I had had no experience in the matter until now, I should be equally sure of the truth of what I had said, for who could look upon the incomparable being before me, and doubt that woman was to man the "morning star" that shone through his youthful dreams, the "day-star" that gilded his manly prime, the "evening-star" that shed a halo over his declining years, and – and –'

'You might add the "dog-star," ' which plainly revealed the struggle that was going on in her mind, between politeness and mirth. The struggle was but for an instant. The beautiful lips parted, and out came a peal of uncontrollable laughter. Again it was checked, – the 'eloquent blood spoke' in her cheek, and pleading 'shopping,' while she gracefully apologized for her rudeness she left us. (So the women 'shop' yet, thought I.)

'Now in the name of wonder, tell me what is the meaning of all this,' I ejaculated, turning to my friend. To my great vexation, I found him laughing as heartily as she had done. As soon as he had recovered himself a little, he replied, '*I* was in as much of a maze as the lady, to hear your style of conversation, until I remembered having read in worm-eaten volumes of something similar. But talking to ladies after that fashion was obsolete many years ago.'

'What? Obsolete, do you say?' 'Yes, truly so. Woman is no longer considered as a mere object for caresses and pretty words. Men might as well attempt to cut away the Andes with a penknife, as to carve themselves a place in her esteem by flattery. She is not now petted and pacified with adulation, while her true dignity is forgotten, nor does she obtain "sugar-plums" when she only asks for *justice*. *Your* age *fondled* woman. *Ours* honors her. You gave her *compliments*. *We* give her *rights*.

'Your contemporaries, if I have read rightly, looked upon woman as a mere *adjunct* to man. As merely the 'companion to cheer *his* pathway,' the 'angel to soothe *his* sorrows,' the 'wife to adorn *his* fireside,' etc. etc. With you, all things in woman had a reference to *man*. We think not so, but regard her as *complete in herself*. (Not indeed independent of man, nor man of her, but both, in a high and noble sense, created for each other.) Not needing man to *eke her out into an individual*, but in *herself* the 'image of God.' Not 'God's last, best gift to *man*,' but *with* man, not *next* to him, or *before* him, 'God's last, best gift' to creation. Man is not thought of as the solid masonry in life, and woman as the *gingerbread-work*, but both together, as the solemn and beautiful architectural pile of humanity; which, without either, or with either subordinate to the other, would lose half its majesty and harmony.

'Admired, woman may be, and *is*, in these latter times, but not for the fair hair, or the azure eye, nor yet for the graceful manner, or elegant accomplishment alone, but for the *soul* that burns within her, and now only has freedom to show itself. Nor, much as we elevate and reverence her, do we aim to abolish the difference in the intellect and constitution of man and woman. On the contrary, we acknowledge and cherish it, only waiving the worn-out question of the intellectual *rank* of the sexes.

'The old-fashioned notions about woman that prevailed in your day, are now scarcely remembered as having existed, except by the antiquarian and the scholar. Some ancient books, with whose lore *they* alone are conversant, still preserve the recollection of them. 'Tis well that my memory has been recently refreshed by one of these very books, as well as by a "History of the manners, customs and opinions of the past," or I should be lost in astonishment at the light in which you contemplate the sex. There is one book, however, whose almost inspired pages are open not alone to the scholar, – I refer to Milton's "Paradise Lost," in which there is an allusion to some such ideas as your contemporaries had. It is in this remarkable address from Eve to Adam: "God thy law, thou, mine." There has been an immense amount of controversy upon this passage, but I believe commentators at length agree in considering it a false reading. Although of course aware of the condition of woman, at the time in which Milton lived, they believe him to have been incapable of putting a sentiment into the mouth of his ideal of womanly perfection, which makes God a God to *her*, only *through her husband*. They are the more confirmed in this, as in another immortal poem, "Comus" he makes his heroine a model of all that is free and noble, and as a still more ancient and world famed poet, Shakespeare, represents woman in quite a different way.'

'What is the standard of intellectual cultivation among women now?'

'Culture of the broadest kind is considered necessary to both men and women, to fit them for their entrance into the cares and toils of life.'

'But how do women find time for this? They could not do so in my day.'

'You know the old adage, "where there's a will, there's a way." Since woman has awoke to the importance of self-culture, the means are found quite practicable. And besides, there are the increased facilities for domestic labor, to be considered in this matter. The household arrangements of this age are somewhat different from those of yours, I imagine. At this moment, you may see an exemplification of it, in the gay groups of people which you notice yonder, just filling the streets, as they go to their eating houses.'

'Eating houses! Ah, it seems to me that looks a little like Fourierism, but the tall individual whom I met in the morning, told me that the community system "died out" long ago, and that people lived in families and women cooked and scrubbed, baked and patched, as of old.'

'And so people do live in families, and always will, I reckon; Ah! your tall friend! I know him like a book! A cross-grained, conservative old creature, who cannot endure the modern improvements which leave woman freedom to pursue her individual tastes. He spoke of things as he wished them to be, rather than as they are. Never believe a word he tells you on this subject. Poor fellow! he was once of goodly proportions, fully rounded out, sleek and fair; one of the most popular men in society. In early life he possessed a wife, a most exemplary woman, who devoted herself unusually to the promotion of his comfort; but having had the misfortune to lose her, he could find no other so docile and obedient, and he has really become the melancholy, attenuated being you saw, by venting his indignant ire against the progress of the sex in these days. "Woman's rights," as he sneeringly terms them, are the constant theme of his discourse, and the rich old fellow having been refused by at least a dozen ladies, revenges himself by slurs upon the whole woman part of creation.'

'Rich! is he? and will not his long purse procure him a wife?'

'Riches procure him a wife here! You forget, my dear sir, that women are not bought and sold now, as in your day.'

'Oh, they were not exactly that, in my day, but then, as now, I suppose, they found it necessary to be clothed and fed, and to move in genteel society, and what would you have them do, if they had no money of their own, the father bankrupt, perhaps, and a homeless old age before them? What better *could* they do, than marry a rich husband, and so provide for themselves, and destitute sisters perhaps? For my part, I always pitied, more than blamed, when I saw them doing so.'

' "Pitied!" "blamed!" Let me tell you, my good friend, that things have indeed changed with woman. As to "clothing and food," she provides them, (when necessity or inclination prompts) by her own hands or head, and what is more, can follow the impulses of her heart, in maintaining a feeble brother or sister, or an aged parent. She is therefore not obliged to enter the marriage state, as a harbor against poverty. And as for "genteel society," riches neither admit nor exclude from that, but man and woman both mingle in the circle for which talent or cultivation fit them, and take their places as easily as flowers turn to the light, or fold their leaves in the shade. And for this progress, we are mainly indebted to the genius of Charles Fourier, who, by his profound insight into the evils of society, induced such changes as gave due compensation to all industry, whether in man, woman or child. Cooperation substituted for competition, has in a great measure removed indigence from society, and division for labor in domestic art has increased the facilities of housekeeping as much as electricity has that of conveying news. Yet the labor of woman was lightened more reluctantly than other improvements, and the natural patience of that sex, and the selfishness of ours, might have made the eternal track of household labor go on as of old, but for the impossibility of getting female domestics for an occupation which brought so much social degradation and wear and tear of body and clothes! The factory, the shop, and the field even, came to be preferred before it, and men found that they must either starve, or contrive some better way of being fed.

'True, there are no "Associations" properly, and many things that the genius of Fourier dreamed of, have never been realized. The reformer's plans seldom *are* fulfilled, as he foresees them, but much that that great man taught has been heeded, and men now bless his labor, and respect his name.

'Taking the hint from him, the poor first combined to purchase their supplies at shops established expressly for them, that their small parcels might come to them at wholesale prices. Rich men built comfortable, cheap dwellings, with the privilege for each tenant of a certain right in a common bakery, school, etc. Other changes followed. Philanthropists guided legislation in the poor man's behalf, till he gradually lost sight of his poverty, while the *hoarder* became unable to heap up wealth from the sweat of his less prosperous brother.

'True, we do not live in the "phalanx," but you have noticed the various houses for eating which accommodate the city. Covered passages in some of the streets, the arcade style of building generally adopted in others, and carriages for the more isolated and wealthy residences, make this a perfectly convenient custom, even in our climate, and 'tis so generally adopted by our people, that only now and then a fidgetty man, or a *peremptory woman*, attempts anything like the system of housekeeping in your day. Nothing but extraordinary wages enables a man now to have a little tea, a little cake, a little meat, a little potato, cooked under his own roof, served all by itself, on a little table for him especially. But the recluse and monk will be found in all ages.

'You would hardly recognize the process of cooking in one of our large establishments. Quiet, order, prudence, certainty of success, govern the process of turning out a ton of bread, or roasting an ox! – as much as the weaving a yard of cloth in one of our factories. No fuming, no fretting over the cooking stove, as of old! No "roasted lady" at the head of the dinner table! Steam, machinery, division of labor, economy of material, make the whole as agreeable as any other toil, while the expense to pocket is as much less to man, as the wear of patience, time, bone and muscle, to woman.

'Look at that laundry establishment on the other side of the old Penobscot! See the busy boys and girls bearing to and fro the baskets of snowy linen, in exchange for the rolled and soiled bundle of clothes. There is a little fellow, now, just tumbling his load into this end of the building; – by the time he fairly walks round to the other side, it will be ready to place on his shoulders, clean, starched, and pressed with mirror-like polish! Ah, you did not *begin to live* in your benighted nineteenth century! Just think of the absurdity of one hundred housekeepers, every Saturday morning, striving to enlighten one hundred girls in the process of making pies for one hundred little ovens! (Some of these ovens remain to this day, to the great glee of antiquarians.) What fatigue! What vexation! Why, ten of our cooks, in the turning of a few cranks, and an hour or so of placing materials, produce pies enough to supply the whole of this city; – rather more than all your ladies together could do, I fancy. Window cleansing, carpet shaking, moving, sweeping, and dusting, too, are processes you would never know now, though, by the way, there is much less of this to do than there used to be, owing to a capital system of laying the dust by artifical showers which has long been used. Indeed, this was hinted at in your day I think, by a very acute observer of nature, laughed at then, as a dreamer. "Professor Espy" was his name.'

'I asked a while ago, how women could find *time* for the culture you were speaking of, but I am constrained to change my question now, and ask, what, for mercy's sake, is there left for them to do?' said I, indignantly, thinking of the unceasing turmoil of 'washing-day,' baking and ironing day, which my poor wife had always been obliged to submit to. 'How lazy your women must be!'

'Lazy! why they take part in all these very processes. Labor no longer makes them fear to lose caste, and they join in hand or head work as they please, and from having greater variety of employments, those which were deemed more exclusively theirs, such as sewing or teaching, not being crowded, command as high remuneration as any. No, woman is not made lazy by this social progress. She finds abundance of work and freedom to do it. In every station, pecuniary independence is her own. Her duties as mother and daughter are now more faithfully fulfilled than ever, as freedom is more favorable to the growth of the affections than coercion, while in the marriage relation the change is too great to describe. No longer induced to enter it as a refuge from the ennui of unoccupied faculties, free also from the injurious public opinion which makes it necessary to respectability to wed, woman as well as man may go to her grave single if she pleases, without being pitied for having failed of the great end of her existence. Marriage is therefore seldom entered, except from mutual choice and strong affection. True, mistakes are made now, as in your day, by the young with vivid imaginations, but the prevailing habit of useful occupation makes such mistakes far rarer now than then. The family and the home are indeed sacred, and the bond only broken by death. Children are reared under holy influences, and the generations grow and increase in the love and wisdom of God and man.'

'But your women do not take part in the affairs of state, do they? At least, so the "cross-grained, conservative old creature," as you called him, who answered my question this morning, told me.'

'Oh no, they have no wish to do so.'

'But that individual told me they had made the attempt;' and here I recapitulated the description he had given me of women in the halls of legislation.

'Oh, that was all a joke! And a capital one it was too.'

'A joke! How can that be?'

'Why, men were strangely sore and sensitive upon that subject, always imagining that women wanted to rule. If a word of fault was found with woman's condition, they would immediately take fire, and reply, "Oh, you want a share in government do you? Better stay at home and darn your stockings." If a sigh was breathed over woman's want of freedom, intellectual and social, "Ah! you'd like to go to the polls would you? Better learn to make a good pudding!" To which women answered in effect, that they hadn't any particular objection to "darning their hose," and that they liked of all things to *eat* "*good* puddings"; and in the then condition of "help" they couldn't reasonably expect to eat unless they made them, and as they were really quite indifferent to taking a share in government, they thought they should accept the advice offered them, and go on, for a while at least, "darning their stockings and making good puddings."

'But men were not so easily satisfied. Still, when the lovers of progress expressed a wish for a broader female culture, they shrugged their shoulders and ejaculated, "Oh! a share- in government!" and if some unlucky dog chanced to stumble on the word "woman," – "Humph! Good pudding." Still went on the deep, silent current of reform, and still men pricked up their ears and looked fearfully about them, scared lest woman was beginning to "rule." Still woman cried "onward," and still man groaned, "darn stockings!" They bore this patiently for some time. At last some mischievous ones declared "they would bear it no longer. It was too good a subject for fun to be longer treated seriously. It was quite too bad that men had for so many years cried 'wolf' in vain. Now the wolf should really come!" And so, indeed, he did; these female wags actually enacted the very scenes you have described to me, in their zeal to "quiz" their male tormentors. How well they succeeded in quizzing them, you can judge from the story you heard.

'But women were at one time obliged to take part in government, which was "*no* joke."'

'Ah! how happened it?'

'Men became completely eaten up with the love of money. This frightful disease had begun to show itself in your day, but it afterward made much more rapid and terrible advances. It became a raging pestilence, destroying everything within its reach. It prevailed over our whole country, but more fatally than anywhere else, in this our good city. All other things became subordinate to this burning fever. Social intercourse was abandoned. Amusement was ridiculed as absurd. The church was deserted. The Sabbath habitually desecrated. And even the master-passion, *love*, was forgotten. The effect of this money-leprosy (for I think of no more appropriate name) upon the body, was truly terrific; withering the skin, and changing it to a lurid copper color, with large livid spots upon it, seeming like the ghosts of dollars, (which, like the Lady Macbeth's spots of blood, "would not out"); giving the eyes the appearance of burning cents, sunk deep in the head; impregnating the breath with a fœtid metallic odor, and, as some declared, even imparting to the blood a dull coppery tinge; causing the hands to grope and fumble in vacancy, as if in search of bank bills, while the tongue muttered continually, "dollars," "interest," "stock," "dividends" and other words of pecuniary import.

'Of course, with this fearful disease upon them men neglected their duties in the Legislature, in Congress, in courts of law, etc., except those which related directly to their pecuniary interests.

'If their attention was called to any other matters than those which touched their pockets, they would look as bewildered as an owl in the day time, − blushing stammering, and finally ejaculating, "Well − I − don't know, but − I'll − I'll − go home and ask my wife!" And so "go home and ask their wives" they did, and their wives, poor things! having never turned their attention to these matters, and not feeling that they knew much about them, actually had to go to work and make themselves acquainted with all sorts of statistics, political economy, and even law, to help their money-crazed husbands out of their difficulties; so that for a long time women had as much, and even more, to do with the affairs of state than men.

'At last, things got to such a pass that the female part of the community concluded it would not do. That something must be done to stop the progress of the disease which was desolating their homes, and turning society topsy-turvy. And something *was* done. I will not stop to relate all the details of their mode of operations, but will be satisfied with saying, that a system was immediately commenced, which, after sundry discourage-ments and years of laborious effort, was at length crowned with success. (This much I will say, however, that with the exception of establishing hospitals for the treatment of the infected, their methods of restoration were altogether of the domestic kind.) Once more order and beauty were restored to society, and men became men again.'

The scene changed. I was in the midst of a large and brilliant assembly. Thousands of lights gleamed from the ceiling upon the festive throng. Music was heard in the alcoves. The merry laugh sounded from group to group, as the sparkling witticism flashed along the circle; and 'many-twinkling feet' were heard in the distance, 'wreathing the fantastic dance.'

My faithful friend was at my elbow. 'Where are we?' I asked in some surprise. 'At a levee at Mrs. —'s. You must open your eyes wide and see all there is to be seen, for you will not have a better opportunity of learning the social peculiarities of our age.' I took his hint, and wandered from circle to circle, to discover, if possible, the bent of the social tastes which I was to see exhibited. My first impression had been, that the assembly I found myself in the midst of was very similar to the festive gatherings of my own age; but I was soon convinced of my error. Externally, it is true, it was so. There were the same graceful exteriors, the same courtly manners; the same beaming faces. There was man in his pride and woman in her beauty. But under all these there was a *soul*.* The courtly manners, the graceful exteriors, and the beaming faces, veiled *a spirit*. Man was there in his manly sincerity, as well as pride, and woman in her majesty, as well as beauty. The assembly went not there to pass an idle hour in mere frivolity, or to obey the demands of ceremony or fashion. They went for the pure interchange of social joys. Friend greeted friend, and heart met heart. Man went not to flatter and cajole, and then boast of his victory over poor ensnared woman. Woman went not to be admired and caressed for a thoughtless hour, and then flung lightly away as a plaything to the winds. But both to meet each other as friends and companions, as spirits bound to the same haven, and created for the same objects.

I have spoken of the sparkling witticism, – and truly it was abundant. Fresh and clear it gushed from the well of thought, and gladdened all within its reach. But it was not, as in my day, *all* the evidence of mind allowed to appear in the festive circle. *Freedom* was there as well as wit, and the guests were not forbidden by the voice of imperious fashion to be serious or gay, as their humor moved them.

I found myself a listener to many circles where subjects which my contemporaries would have thought quite shocking in the social assembly, from their seriousness or profoundness,

---

*God forbid I should intimate that those who frequented social assemblies in my day had no souls. Only that they usually left them at home when they 'went into company.'

were chaining a delighted group in closer and closer interest. *Woman*, too, joined in them, and no fear of the world's smile cramped the vigorous intellect, and no visions of 'blue stockings' repressed the soul that *would* be free.

To other circles, where the grave and gay, the profound and brilliant, were elegantly blended, I lent a willing ear, and joined with a whole heart, and lungs most glad to do their office, in the 'laugh' which varied and vivified the entertainment. (They did laugh, those girls, as if they were afraid of no mortal. – And God bless them! why should they be?)

I observed that some of the assembly were quietly reading, as if they had been in their own parlors, others, in secluded corners or curtained alcoves, were reciting or reading aloud to a neighbor, others were engaged in playing chess and kindred games, and others still were seen tête-à-tête for a great length of time with one individual. I was much surprised at this, and asked an explanation of my companion, remarking that 'anything of the kind would not have been allowed in my day, and that indeed *I* could not consider it quite polite, as one would think the guest might find time at home for such purposes.' 'Oh, that,' said he, 'is a matter of opinion. *We* think it the truest politeness to allow our guests to find amusement for themselves, provided their way of doing so does not annoy others. Freedom is with us the highest enjoyment.'

At this moment my eye was caught by a strange looking object in a corner, examining a picture through a quizzing glass, with most grotesque contortions. His hair was brushed perfectly upright on the crown of his head, and trimmed very precisely in *points*, while from the crown to the neck it fell in elaborate ringlets, powdered and perfumed with all the art of the friseur. His whiskers were abundant, and finished in points like his hair. (Points were 'all the rage,' as I afterwards learned.) An immense moustache 'cultivated' into ringlets at the ends, adorned his upper lip, and a delicate goatee his under.

The rest of his toilet was in keeping. Loads of gold and silver lace decorated his green velvet coat, and the richest of thread lace his crimped shirt-bosom! Immense gold and pearl pendants hung from his ears, and his watch, set in pearl, dangled in full relief against his black velvet pantaloons. On his diminutive hands were squeezed gloves of the most dazzling whiteness, over which sparkled numerous rings of various value and beauty. Apertures in the fingers of these admitted to the light nails a full half inch in length, gracefully curled upward, and ending in the usual finishing of points! His pantaloons were short enough to display an exquisitely turned ancle; and shoes of white satin, embroidered with flosses of the richest hues, and ornamented with gold and pearl buckles, completed the toilet of this singular being.

My companion had been observing my minute scrutiny of the grotesque object before me, and at length asked me 'what I thought of him.' 'I cannot decide. Is he a man? and if not, to what title *can* he lay claim?'

'I suppose he must *pass* for a man,' he said, laughing. 'He is one of the *exquisites* of the day.'

'What! In the high state of social progress where I find you is it possible you have "exquisites?" Has woman made so great an advance as you have represented, and does man still remain so far behind her as to allow such a thing as a dandy to exist?'

'It is even so, although to do ourselves justice I must say that such creatures are very rare, and hardly tolerated in society. He was not invited here to-night I understand, but got in by some trick of his remarkable assurance.'

I looked again at the 'exquisite,' attracted by a strange sound, which seemed to come from his vicinity. He was laughing, as near as I could judge by the singular contortions of his phiz and the nervous agitation of his body, although the sound I never should have recognized as that of mirth, it being part squeal, part cackle, and part a suppression of both. It is said laughing is infectious. However this may be usually, *his* most assuredly was, and accordingly my friend and I began to *shake* in unison, then to laugh audibly, and finally to roar. Our unearthly noises seemed strangely to agitate our 'surroundings.' The walls began to totter. The flame of the lamps waved hither and thither. The furniture rocked. The floor rose and fell like the sea in a storm. A hapless Falstaff, overturned and set rolling by the 'swell,' came tumbling over my unlucky 'corns,' and bawling, I awoke.

3
'MY VISIT TO UTOPIA'
(1869)

---*---

Elizabeth T. Corbett (n.d.)

Elizabeth T. Corbett is literally a name on this page. No one has yet been able to discover more about her. Her Utopia appeared in Harper's New Monthly Magazine.

'My Visit to Utopia' continues the argument begun by Mary Griffith in her lecture on 'Women' (1831) that improved marital conditions would for women constitute eutopia. Marriage is made to woman's order, its oppressive potential for her now removed. This Utopia contrasts with the requirements of the nineteenth-century 'cult of true womanhood' – namely, purity, piety, domesticity, and submission (see Welter below), and with the twentieth-century 'paradox of the happy marriage' – a wife's claims of happiness beside the paradoxical evidence of both her mental and physical ill health (see Bernard below). According to science-fiction author and critic Joanna Russ, 'women's position in marriage' is still a 'dangerous' issue (13th Moon: A Feminist Literary Magazine, VI, 1982, p. 59). *Though Corbett may today be unknown, we can applaud this dream, daring for her time.*

REFERENCES
Jessie Bernard, see Introduction, endnote 25 on 'Paradox'; Jessie Bernard, *The Future of Marriage* (New York: World, 1972); Barbara Quissell, 'The New World That Eve Made' in *America as Utopia*, ed. Kenneth M. Roemer (New York: Franklin, 1981), pp. 152, 171; Barbara Welter, see Introduction, endnote 20 (on 'Cult,' pp. 21-41).

SELECTION
Omits pp. 203-4 or Part III of the original pp. 200-4.

'MY VISIT TO UTOPIA'

———————— ✳ ————————

I

It would occupy too much time, and perhaps trespass to largely on your patience, if I should tell you exactly why or how I went to Utopia, or even the precise geographical locality of that much-disputed place. Suffice it that I have been there, and that what I saw and heard during my brief sojourn was so remarkable that I recorded it at the time, and feel that it is quite worthy of your attention now.

It was late in the afternoon of a day last April when I reached my destination – so late that, after the customary delay in identifying my trunk, I looked down the fast-darkening street with a very slight decrease of my courage. I said 'slight' because I ·remembered even then that I was in Utopia, and that remembrance tended to reassure me; so I walked briskly out of the waiting-room at the station to the nearest corner.

By one of those fortunate chances which are common to dreams and novels, but so seldom occur in real life, I had in my porte-monnaie the card of an old school-mate and friend, long since married, like myself, but who, I was certain, had not forgotten me; so I determined to pay her a visit at once.

Feeling naturally doubtful as to the direction of my steps I asked the necessary information of a well-dressed man who presently overtook me, and I must say that I was agreeably disappointed at receiving, instead of a gruff answer thrown over his shoulder and scarcely audible at that, such a careful and courteous direction as once more reminded me that I was in Utopia.

As the distance was trifling, I soon reached my friend's house, and, ascertaining from the servant that Mrs. Jenkins was at home, I sent in my card and awaited her coming.

I had not long to wait; in an instant my friend was at my side, while her affectionate embrace spoke as plainly as her words of welcome of her pleasure at seeing me. There was no such thing as resisting her cordiality; and almost before I knew it I found myself comfortably seated in her cozy library, with my bonnet and cloak put out of sight, a tempting supper on a small table beside me, and a messenger dispatched for my trunk.

'For you must make your home with us, of course,' said Laura, decidedly; 'and we'll try to make your visit as pleasant as we can; won't we, William?'

'We will, indeed, dear,' said Mr. Jenkins; and added so many expressions of satisfaction at seeing his wife's particular and oft-mentioned friend at last that I yielded, well content, and began to make myself, as Laura urged, 'very much at home.'

After she had asked, and I had answered, countless questions as to the fortunes and whereabout of mutual acquaintants, and we had both exclaimed, a dozen times at least:

'Why, how natural it seems to see you again!' and, 'Who would have thought it?' I said, looking at an open volume on the table:

'Don't let me interrupt the employment of the evening, Laura. I am sure you were reading before I came in, for I fancied I heard you as I stood in the hall.'

'No,' said Laura; 'that was William reading the newspaper, and he had just finished it when you came.'

'And nearly finished you with it,' laughed her husband, 'for you were almost asleep when Jane announced your friend.'

Laura laughed too, as she replied: 'Well, I believe I was; for the paper was uncommonly stupid, and I was very tired. You don't know how fretful the baby has been all day, and he wouldn't let the nurse touch him.'

'Well, never mind,' said Mr. Jenkins, soothingly; 'I'll manage him to-night, so you will be rested and wide-awake for to-morrow evening.'

'Truly, Laura,' I said, softly, 'you have a model husband — reading the paper to you instead of enjoying it in silence, as is the manner of husbands in general, and, more wonderful still, proposing to take care of your baby at night merely to let you sleep. I'm afraid you are not half grateful enough for such a prize.'

Laura looked at me with an air of genuine astonishment, which speedily gave place to a smile, as she answered:

'Oh, I had really forgotten; you are not accustomed to the ways and manners of our country, and therefore even such a small matter as this surprises you, but –'

'*Small matter!*' I interrupted. 'Do you call it such a small matter to have a husband who cares not only for your amusement, but for your comfort as well?'

Laura smiled again as she replied: 'I suppose it is only in Utopia that one finds husbands quite perfect and wives quite satisfied; therefore I can easily imagine that you think William quite a paragon, when in fact he is only acting as any man ought to act under the same circumstances – that is, trying to lessen, by sharing, his wife's cares and duties; and to increase, by division, his own pleasures.'

'But,' I began, 'it is generally conceded that it is a woman's especial duty to –'

'To wear herself out! Yes, I know it is so believed in your part of the world,' said Laura, warmly; 'but I am happy to say that no such belief exists in Utopia, and even orthodox suicides are unheard-of in consequence. We decided long ago that the heaviest burdens should not be suffered to fall on the weaker partner in the matrimonial contract (of course, when I say "the weaker," I mean physically weak), and our children are educated accordingly. As a natural consequence our husbands are not ignorant of *their* duties; and the man who could sleep tranquilly while his wife walked the floor with the baby, or who could enjoy an unsociable cigar or paper in the evening, when his wife needed the cheer and comfort of his words as well as of his presence, would be voted a monster and punished as he deserved.'

'And how would that be?' I asked.

'Why, by depriving him of his home – a very appropriate discipline too for any man who doesn't know how to value a home. Such an offender would be sent to the "House of Correction for Bachelors," I suppose, and there he would be obliged to wait upon others in exact proportion to the degree in which he had allowed his wife to overtask herself for him. Imagine the misery of a married man suddenly deprived of all the comforts of his home and the kind attentions of his wife, with not even the poor satisfaction of fault-finding left to him, and tell me if you don't think the wife will be amply avenged!'

'Doubtless he will think so, but you made one remark just now, Laura, which I would like you to qualify; you spoke of "the cheer and comfort of a husband's *words* as well as his presence," and I was thinking that if he was a grumbler, or even an habitually fretful man, the "cheer and comfort of his words" might be questionable, to say the least.'

'Your hypothesis might be worth discussing, my dear, if it were not so impossible,' answered Laura, with a mischievous smile. 'You are continually forgetting that this is Utopia, and that husbands of the types you instance are only found in less happy localities. Grumblers indeed! Why, a woman could get a divorce here without a week's delay if she could prove that her husband was addicted to such a vice.'

Too much bewildered to say anything more, I was silent for a few moments. Mr. Jenkins, who had been an amused listener thus far, now took up the argument.

'I should suppose that you would fall in readily with Laura's views,' he began, 'since they tend so directly to the benefit of your sex. To be her husband's *companion* in truth, as well as in name, must conduce to a true woman's happiness, while at the same time it necessitates mental culture and constant development. She must be worthy of the position assigned her, and so we begin by teaching her aspiration through possession – not aspiration without the possibility of attainment, as is the common practice.'

'Oh! I see it all now,' said I; 'you have tutored your husband to defend the oft-vexed question of "Women's Rights" very creditably. Do you, then, approve of female suffrage and the rest?' I added, returning to Mr. J.

'Indeed you astonish me, my friend,' he said, earnestly, 'for I have but spoken a truth so simple that it is in danger of becoming a platitude, even from more eloquent lips than mine; and yet you treat it as if it were, to you at least, a novelty. But I won't discuss this subject with you to-night, for I trust that during your sojourn with us you will learn as much from facts as from theories; besides you are fatigued, as I see.'

'But one thing you said certainly did surprise me,' now said Laura, as she rose at my request to show me to my room; 'you spoke of female suffrage as if it did not exist in your country. Can it be possible that women vote nowhere but in Utopia?'

'Even so,' I answered, as I bade Mr. Jenkins good-night, and I retired to bed with a lively curiosity to know more of this strange country, and a vague wish that I too lived in Utopia. And so wishing I fell asleep.

II

The next morning as we sat chatting over the breakfast-table Laura said:

'How fortunate it is! we are invited to a wedding this evening, and you can go with us; it will give you an insight into our customs and ways of thinking that I know you will enjoy, besides the ever-new delight of seeing two people tied together "for better for worse." '

I was too anxious to see the workings of this new system; as I called it, to make any demur; so after a discussion as to what I should wear, a matter, by-the-way, which is never ignored in Utopia, where people are always expected to look their best, the thing was settled. Another good long talk with Laura and a drive filled up the day, and soon after dinner we made our toilets and sat down to wait the arrival of the carriage. We were joined presently by Mr. Jenkins, also in holiday costume; but Laura, after a critical survey of his *tout ensemble*, examined:

'Oh, William! your collar is too high, and it isn't at all becoming to you.'

'Think not?' asked the husband, surveying himself complacently in the mirror. 'Why, Laura, this is the newest style of collar, and all the rage just now.'

'I can't help that; they don't look well on you,' said Laura. 'Now do go and get on another before the carriage comes, to please me.'

Up stairs went Mr. J., while I sat speechless with surprise. At last Laura broke the silence.

'I see,' said she, 'you are amazed because William is changing his collar to please me, isn't it so?'

'It is; and I am more amazed than I can express. I never saw a man do such a thing before.'

'Well, of course, I don't know how it is with you, but with us a man is just as much bound to please his wife as the wife to please her husband. I wear this dress because William admires it, then why shouldn't he defer to my taste? The obligation is certainly mutual.'

'Ah yes! that's all very well in Utopia,' I sighed, as the carriage was announced, and our conversation ended.

We were somewhat later than we had intended to be, so we found the bridal party already in their places when we were ushered into the rooms, and very natural they looked too – not unlike the bridal parties I had seen often before. This was somewhat surprising at first, but afterward I reflected that love was more or less Utopian in its origin and character; and I began to wonder whether most newly married pairs did not aim at Utopia on their wedding-tours.

'And how did you like our marriage service?' questioned Laura, as she drew me to a sofa at one end of the room.

'To tell you the truth, I missed so much that I am accustomed to hear that I don't think I was particularly pleased. In the first place, the minister omitted entirely the promise to "love, honor, and obey," on the wife's part; and in the next, he said nothing at all of the husband's duty as protector and guardian of his wife, or of her duty as regards proper deference to his will – absolutely leaving out of his address all the things that are most indispensable, as well as touching on such occasions. Why, I was astonished.'

Laura looked amused as she replied: 'Ah, my friend! your prejudices will not let you understand or appreciate these things yet. Don't you know that in Utopia people always marry for love? and, therefore, we do not exact at the very altar a promise to love each other, since we know that the sentiment can not be compelled by any form of words. As for the honoring and obeying, why surely true love always honors and (better than obeying) always seeks to please its object; so we drop the obsolete and useless sentence out of our service. Did you not observe that the minister (taking for granted that these two people really loved each other as they should do) spoke much of mutual effort and forbearance, much of reciprocal tenderness and courtesy, addressing husband and wife equally? Did you not hear him say, too, that people when they marry ought to strive to make each other wiser and happier, and therefore better, all the time? and could any more be said? But come, I want to introduce you to some of our friends here, so we must not pursue this subject at present.'

'Tell me first,' I said, detaining her as she rose from her seat, 'who are these young people directly in front flirting so desperately?'

'Flirting!' said Laura, beginning to laugh as usual at my words, but she grew grave directly as she continued: 'That is another of your educational errors, my dear, and a very unfortunate one, let me tell you. There can be no candid and profitable intercourse between young men and young women if it is liable to such a construction as the one you have just alluded to; and therefore, as we regard this same companion-ship not only as a pleasure, but also as a means of culture for both parties, we encourage it in every possible way, and particularly by never commenting upon it. You will never hear any of our young people say that "Mr. So-and-so has been very devoted," or that "Miss This or That has given him the mitten;" and the very name of *flirt* is unknown to them. A young man may have, and should have, many female friends whom he admires and respects, without of necessity being in love with any of them; and, of course, a young girl has the same privilege. What more natural than that they should enjoy each other's society? and what more unfortunate than that they should grow up with a mutual distrust of each other?'

'I am reduced to my usual answer,' I exclaimed. 'This is all very well in Utopia, but it would not answer –'

'Well, then, let me answer for both of you, that supper is ready, and I would like some,' said Mr. Jenkins, as he offered an arm to each, and ended our conversation, which was not resumed during the rest of the evening. . . .

III

Early the next morning we parted, with many expressions of esteem and friendship, and a cordial invitation from Laura and Mr. Jenkins that I would visit them soon again.

But I have not complied with their wishes, nor do I think, much as I enjoyed my sojourn there, that I shall ever return to Utopia; for – I might as well confess it – the effect even of my brief stay in that favored land was to make me (at least so my husband said) 'very unreasonable and exacting.'

One word more. I have become very tolerant of all those reformers, as they are too often derisively called, who are fighting, with too much violence and too little grace, perhaps, in the cause of progress, on the side of liberality.

I am, as I said before, tolerant of all these, notwithstanding that I do not indorse them fully or approve their manner of warfare; because I see that they too have been in Utopia, and that they are striving to reproduce even a dim outline of that symmetry and beauty which have led their souls, as mine, captive.

4
MAN'S RIGHTS; OR, HOW WOULD YOU LIKE IT? (1870)

*

Annie Denton Cridge (n.d.)

Of Annie Denton Cridge we know that her brother William Denton (1823-83) of Boston published Man's Rights. *Apparently she herself resided in Pennsylvania. She was believed to be a psychometer, a person having the power 'to see all that has ever happened' to any piece of matter placed in contact with her. In 1868 she published a children's book called* The Crumb-Basket. *She had died by 1884 when her son Alfred Denton Cridge advertised himself as son of 'the late' Mrs Cridge and as author of* Utopia: or, The History of an Extinct Planet. *The son's* Utopia *shows his mother's feminist influence in that women's equality characterizes those societies evolving to a high level.*

Man's Rights *consists of five satiric dreams in which a female narrator-author imagines a gender-role reversal: in a society on Mars, men are confined to housekeeping and baby tending while women run the government and enjoy all privileges. Cridge ridicules the 'cult of true womanhood' by exposing its contradictions, made glaring when enacted by men. Marriage practices continue to receive criticism.*

REFERENCES
Allibone's Supplement (Philadelphia: Lippincott, 1892); *Encyclopedia of Occultism & Parapsychology*, ed. L. Shepard (Detroit: Gale, 1979); Barbara Quissell, 'The New World That Eve Made' in *America as Utopia*, ed. Kenneth M. Roemer (New York: Franklin, 1981), pp. 153-4, 171.

SELECTION
Dreams One-Three complete, or pp. 3-32 of the original pp. 3-48.

MAN'S RIGHTS; OR, HOW WOULD YOU LIKE IT?

— ✳ —

Last night I had a dream, which may have a meaning.

I stood on a high hill that overlooked a large city. The proud spires of many churches rose high, here and there; and round about the city were beautiful, sloping hills, stretching away, away into the distance: while a broad river wound here and there, extending a kindly arm toward the city.

As I stood there, wondering what manner of city it was, its name, and the character of its inhabitants, all at once I found myself in its very midst. From house to house I flitted; from kitchen to kitchen: and lo! everywhere the respective duties of man and woman were reversed; for in every household I found the men in aprons, superintending the affairs of the kitchen. Everywhere men, and only men, were the Bridgets and housekeepers. I thought that those gentleman-housekeepers looked very pale, and somewhat nervous; and, when I looked into their spirits (for it seemed in my dream that I had the power), I saw anxiety and unrest, a constant feeling of unpleasant expectancy, – the result of a long and weary battling with the cares of the household.

As I looked at those men-Bridgets and gentleman-house-keepers, I said to myself, 'This is very strange! Why, these men seem unsexed! How stoop-shouldered they are! how weak and complaining their voices.'

I found, too, that not only was the kitchen exclusively man's, but also the nursery: in fact, all the housework was directed and done by men. I felt a sad pity for these men, as I flitted from house to house, from kitchen to kitchen, from nursery to nursery.

I saw them in the houses of the door, where the 'man did his own work.' I saw him in the morning arise early, light the fire, and begin to prepare the breakfast, his face pale and haggard. 'No wonder!' I thought, when I saw how he hurried, hurried, while in his spirit was a constant fear that the baby would awake. Very soon I heard the sharp cry of the baby; and away ran the poor father, soon returning with baby in his arms, carrying it around with him, while he raked the fire, fried the meat, and set the table for breakfast. When all was ready, down came two or three unwashed, unkept children, who must be attended to: and, when all this was done, I observed that the poor gentleman's appetite was gone; and, pale and nervous, he sat down in the rocking-chair, with the baby in his arms. But what greatly astonished me was to see how quietly and composedly the lady of the house drank her coffee and read the morning paper; apparently oblivious of the trials of her poor husband, and of all he had to endure in connection with his household cares.

It was wash-day, and I watched him through that long and weary day. First at the wash-tub, while baby slept; then rocking the cradle and washing at the same time; then preparing dinner, running and hurrying here and there about the house: while in his poor, disturbed mind revolved the thought of the sewing that ought to be done, and only his own hands to do it.

Evening came, and the lady of the house returned to dinner. The children came to meet her; and as she lifted up one, and then another, and kissed them, I thought! 'Why, how beautiful is that woman!' Then in my dream I seemed to behold every woman of that strange city; and, ah! the marvellous beauty of those women! Eye hath not seen, neither hath it entered into the heart of man to conceive; for a beauty almost angelic was so charmingly combined with intellect, and health brooded so divinely over all, that, at the *tout ensemble*, I was profoundly astonished and intensely delighted.

Then I turned myself about, and was again in the home I had left. It was evening: the lamp on the table was lighted, and there sat the poor husband I have described, in his rocking-chair, darning stockings and mending the children's clothes after the hard day's washing. I saw that it had rained; that the clothes-line had broken, and dropped the clothes in the dirty yard; and the poor man had had a terrible time rinsing some and washing others over again; and that he had finally put them down in wash-tubs, and covered them with water he had brought from a square distant. But the day's work was over;

and there he moved to and fro, while his wife, in comfortable slippers, sat by the fire reading.

'Well,' I said to myself, 'such is the home of the lowly; but how is it where one or more servants can be kept?' Then, as by magic, I saw how it was, for I found myself in a kitchen where a male Bridget was at work, his hair uncombed, his face and hands unwashed, and his clothes torn and soiled. Bridget was cooking breakfast, a knife in his hand, while he was bending over the cooking-stove, moodily talking to himself. The gentleman-housekeeper, pale and unhappy, opened the door, looked at Bridget, but said nothing, and soon went into the dining-room. As soon as his back was turned, Bridget turned around, lifted the arm that held the knife, and, with a fiendish look, whispered to himself, 'I would like to strike you with this.'

Breakfast on the table, I looked, and beheld bad coffee, burned meat, and heavy biscuits; and I heard the lady of the house, who sat in a morning-robe and spangled slippers, say to the poor gentleman, —

'My dear, this breakfast is bad, very bad: you ought to attend to things better.'

I observed how sad he felt at these words; and I did pity the poor fellow. It seemed to me that I staid a whole day with this poor gentleman. His health was very feeble: he was suffering from dyspepsia. I saw him attending the children, saw him sewing, saw him go nervously into the kitchen, and sadly and wearily attend to things there, while the dark glances of the male Bridget followed him viciously everywhere. I saw the waste and thieving of that man-Bridget, and saw how completely that poor gentleman felt crushed and held by his help. My heart yearned toward that poor, feeble housekeeper, unable to do his own work, and so much at the mercy of that terrible Bridget; and I ceased to wonder at the pale faces of the men everywhere.

The homes of the wealthy I visited; and almost everywhere I found those gentleman-housekeepers anxious and worried, no matter how many servants were kept. There was trouble about washing, trouble about ironing, trouble about children: there was waste, there was thieving; and, oh! the number of poor, sickly gentlemen I found made me very sad.

And while, in my dream, my heart was going out in pity and commiseration toward those gentleman-housekeepers, I found

77

myself in the midst of a large assembly, composed exclusively of these men. Here almost every man in the city had congregated to hold an indignation-meeting, – a housekeeper's indignation-meeting. Every man wore a white kitchen-apron, and some I noticed whose sleeves were white with flour, while others had pieces of dough here and there stuck on their clothes: others, again, had hanging on their arms dish-clothes and towels. Very many, too, had babies in their arms, and one or more children at their side.

Then I listened to some of their speeches. One gentleman said, –

'I have kept house sixteen years; and I know what it is to be poor and do my own work; and I know what it is to have servants: and I tell you, gentlemen, the whole system of housekeeping, as now conducted, is a bad one. It is, in the first place, wasteful and extravagant; and, in the next place, it wears out our bodies and souls. See how pale and feeble we are! It is time there was a change.'

'We don't each of us make our own shoes,' said another speaker; 'we don't each of us spin our own yarn, or weave our own cloth: the hand-loom has departed, and it is now done by machinery, which has so far come to our rescue. It is not so bad for us as for our grandfathers, who had to weave on a hand-loom all the muslin and cloth for the family; but it is bad enough. Here we are kept every day of our lives over the cook-stove, wash-tub, or ironing-table, or thinking about them. Can nothing be done to remedy this? Can not all the domestic work be done by machinery? Can not it be done on wholesale principles? I say it can: there is no more need for a kitchen to any house than for a spindle or a loom.'

Then, followed many more speeches about the extravagance of the present system, whereby one or two persons, and often more, were employed in doing the work of a small family, when it might be done at much less expense for one-fourth the labor, were the wholesale principle applied to that as it is to other things.

One man remarked that the kitchen was a small retail shop to every house: another called it a dirt-producing establishment for every family, sending its fumes and filth to every room. Another gentleman said that the fine pictures painted about the domestic hearth, happy homes, &c., were all moonshine, and would continue so just as long as the present state of things continued.

'I protest against the present state of things,' said a tall, delicate man, with a large, active brain. 'We have this matter in our own hands; and let us here and now begin something practical. Instead of forty little extravagant cooking-stoves, with each a Bridget, and so many gentlemen employed as housekeeper's, let us have one large stove, and do our cooking, washing, and ironing on a large scale.'

Well, I thought in my dream that I listened to hundreds of speeches and protests and denunciations.

Then the scene changed; and forthwith there sprang up large cooking-establishments in different parts of the city, that could, as if by magic, supply hundreds of families with their regular meals. I looked, and lo! what machinery had done in the weaving of cloth, above and beyond what had been effected by the hand-loom, was accomplished here. The inventive genius of the age had been at work; and the result was a wondrous machine that could cook, wash, and iron for hundreds of people at once.

'I must see the workings of that establishment,' I said in my dream; and forthwith a polite gentleman, who said that he had been a housekeeper twenty-five years, and knew all the petty annoyances of the old system, kindly proposed to show me the various doings of the machinery.

'We are going to cook dinner now,' he said, as he walked toward a monster machine. He touched a handle, and then about fifty bushels of potatoes were quietly let down into a large cistern, where they were washed, and then moved forward into a machine for peeling; which operation was accomplished in a minute or two by its hundreds of knives, and the potatoes came out all ready to be cooked. Turnips went through the same process, and other vegetables were prepared and made ready for the huge cooking apparatus. All was done by machinery: there was no lifting, no hauling, no confusion; but the machines, like things of life, lifted, prepared, and transferred as desired.

I saw what was called a 'self-feeding pie-maker,' that reminded me of a steam printing-press, where the paper goes in blank at one end and comes out printed at the other. So the flour, shortening, and fruit were taken in all at once at three separate receptacles, and came out at the other end pies ready for the oven, to which they were at once, over a small tramway, transferred by machinery. Another machine made cakes and pies.

79

Meal-time came: the dinner was to be served. Two large wooden doors opened by means of a spring which the gentleman touched with his foot. Through them came filing past us, one after another, small, curiously constructed steam-wagons, the motion of which caused but little noise, as the wheels were tired with vulcanized India-rubber: those wagons were so arranged as to travel on common roads, and much resembled caravans. They moved past machines which were called 'servers,' where meals were dished and transferred to the steam caravans, which latter were termed 'waiters.' All this was done systematically, quietly, yet rapidly, by a few persons in charge of the machines by which meals were prepared for and distributed to hundreds of families. I saw that there were hundreds of these 'servers,' as well as hundreds of waiters; so that the dinner was dished and served almost simultaneously, in double-tin cases, containing all requisites for the table.

Then away went the steam 'waiters,' delivering the meals almost simultaneously at the houses, which, by the by, were rapidly being 'reconstructed' to meet the new state of things, with dining-rooms to accommodate hundreds at once, in blocks, or hollow squares, with cook-houses, laundries, &c., at the center, or in circles similarly arranged, combining, in a most inconceivable degree, economy with beauty.

To return to the steam waiters: At a time understood they called for the tin cases containing dishes and *débris*, and then wended their way back to head-quarters, where all the dishes were washed and transferred to their places by steam-power.

The washing and ironing, I discovered, was done in the same expeditious manner, by machinery; several hundred pieces going in at one part of the machine dirty, and coming out at the other end a few minutes afterward, rinsed and ready to dry. The ironing was as rapid as it was perfect, — smooth, glossy, uncreased unspecked; all done by machinery.

Then I looked once more into this strange city, and, behold! an emancipated class! The pale, sickly faces of the men were giving place to ruddy health. Anxiety, once so marked in their features, was departing. No Bridget to dread now; no washing-day any more; no sad faces nor neglected children: for now the poor gentleman-housekeepers had time to attend to the children, and to the cultivation of their own minds; and I saw that the dream of the poet and of the seer was realized: for husband and wife sat side by side, each sharing the joys of the other. Science and philosophy, home and children, were cemented together; for peace, sweet peace, had descended like a dove on every household.

I awoke: it was all a dream. My husband stood at my bedside. 'Annie, Annie!' he said: 'awake, Annie! that new girl of yours is good for nothing. You will have to rise and attend to her, else I shall have no breakfast. I have been late at the office for several days past, and I fear I shall be late again.'

I arose: and, as my husband ate his breakfast, I pondered over my strange dream. As soon as he was gone, I transferred it to paper, feeling that it really did mean something, and is intended as a prophecy of the 'good time coming,' when woman will be rid of the kitchen and cook-stove, and the possibilities of the age actualize for woman that which I have dreamed for man.

DREAM NUMBER TWO

Once again I have visited that strange city in dream-land, where men, and only men, were the housekeepers and Bridgets.

It is midnight: I have just awakened from my dream, and risen to pen it down, lest in the morning I should find my memory treacherous. My good husband has protested against writing by gas-light, and very gravely given his opinion on midnight writing; and – ah, well! he is sound asleep now, I see; and so at once to my dream.

I thought my husband and I were walking along some beautiful streets, when all at once I exclaimed, 'Why, husband! here we are together in that very city I told you about, where the men are the housekeepers and kitchen girls. Oh, I'm glad! Let us find out every thing about these inhabitants, both men and women.'

While we were talking together, several gentlemen, pale and delicate in appearance, passed us. Some were dressed in calico suits, trimmed with little ruffles – ruffles round the bottom of the pants, ruffles down the front and round the tails of the coats; and on both sides of the button-holes of their vests were rows of small ruffles. From some of their little flat hats flowed ribbon-streamers; while on others were placed, jauntily and conspiciously, feathers and flowers.

More and more gentlemen passed us. What a variety of

costume! I was almost bewildered; gentlemen in red, green, yellow, drab, and black suits, trimmed in such elaborate and fanciful styles! Some suits were parti-colored; that is to say, the pants perhaps yellow or red, the vest blue, the coat green, crimson, or drab. Some of these suits were trimmed with lace: lace down the sides of the pants and round the bottoms; lace round the edges of the coat, and beautifully curving hither and thither as a vine, over the backs and down the fronts of the coats; and also over the fronts of the vests. Some suits were almost covered with elaborate embroidery, or satin folds, or piping, or ribbon, while bows and streamers of the same or contrasting colors, according to taste, were placed on the backs of the coats, shoulders; and, here and there, on the vest and pants. It really makes me laugh at this moment to think of that comical sight. Their head-dresses, too, were most fantastic; flowers, bits of lace, tulle or blonde, feathers, and even birds, were mixed in endless profusion with ribbon, tinsel, glitter, and (*ad libitum*) grease. Many of these gentlemen carried little portemonnaies, which hung on their jewelled fingers by tiny chains. Others carried fans, some edged with feathers, or covered with pictures, or inlaid with pearl, &c., varying, I suppose, according to the purse.

Each of these gentlemen seemed particularly interested in every other gentleman's costume; for they turned and looked at each other, while several exclamations reached my ear; such as, 'What a superb suit!' 'What a splendid coat!' 'What a darling vest!' 'What a love of a hat!'

These gentlemen had a swinging gate, something like that of a sailor, that made their coat-tails move to and fro as they walked. I noticed, too, that they were very careful of their pants, which were decidedly wide; for on passing over a gutter or soiled part of the pavement, they carefully and daintily raised the legs of the pants with the finger and thumb. This impressed me favorably as to their love of cleanliness; for otherwise the laces, ribbons, embroidery, or ruffles which graced the bottoms of their pants, would have come in contact with the mud of the streets.

As we stood looking at those strange gentlemen, my husband suggested the idea of a masquerade. Then suddenly I found myself alone, and flitting from dwelling to dwelling, from home to home; and everywhere the gentlemen were dressed in flimsy materials, and all more or less decked with trimmings.

I found the majority of gentlemen busy with needlework, some doing the sewing of the family; but many, very many, with their sons, dressed in delicate morning suits, doing fancy-work. Some were working little cats and dogs on footstools; others were busy with embroidery, fancy knitting, and all the delicate nothings that interest only ladies in this waking world of ours.

As I listened to their conversation, which was generally composed of gossip, fashion, or love-matters, – for the male sex took the fashion-books, and not ladies, and these I found in the majority of homes, headed 'Gentlemen's Magazine of Fashions,' – as I listened to their conversation, I repeat, and observed all this, my soul was filled with unutterable sadness. 'Alas! alas!' I said: 'what means this degradation? Why have the lords of creation become mere puppets or dolls? Where is the loftiness and intellectuality of *man – noble man!*'

Just then I was aroused from my reverie by an aspiring young gentleman who was sewing some ruffles on the legs of his pants, saying to his father, 'I don't see, pap, why men can not earn money as well as women: I want to learn a business.'

'That is all nonsense,' replied his father: 'your business is to get married. There is no necessity for a *boy* to learn a *business*: what you have to do is to learn to be a good housekeeper; for you will be married some day, and will have to attend to your children and your wife; and that is enough business for any man.'

'But I may not marry,' said the boy; 'and I know I will not, unless I can get a woman with money, that can give me a good home.'

Then they talked about Mr. Some-one – I could not catch the name – that had married well: his wife was worth over fifty thousand dollars, and was very kind to him, taking him to theaters and concerts, and wherever he wanted to go: she let him, too, have all the dress he wanted. She had only one fault: she would not allow him to go anywhere unless she accompanied him.

Oh! my soul was sick with sympathy and pity for that race of poor degraded men! 'What does it mean?' I asked myself: 'why are they in this pitiable condition?'

Then, for the first time, I realized that this city was the capital of a great nation; that women, and only women, were the lawmakers, judges, executive officers, &c., of the nation;

that every office of honor and emolument was filled by women; that all colleges and literary institutions, with very few exceptions, were all built for women, and only open to women, and that men were all excluded. I went from school to school, from college to college; and, ah! the beauty, the dignity, of those women! Science and art had truly crowned them with their own best gifts: their faces seemed to me almost divine; and, ah! what a contrast to the vain, silly, half-educated men who staid at home, or paraded the streets, thinking principally of fashion and dress! for these women were everywhere dressed in plain, substantial clothing, which lent to them such a charm that I realized instinctively there was something about them far more beautiful than beauty.

As I looked upon these women in the colleges, as students and professors, as lawyers, judges, and jurors, as I looked upon them in the lecture-room and the pulpit, the house of representatives and the senate-chamber, – yea, everywhere, – I observed their quiet dignity, clothed in their plain flowing robes; and I was almost tempted to believe that Nature had intended – in this part of the world at least – that woman, and only woman, should legislate and govern; and that here, if nowhere else, woman should be superior to man.

In the galleries of the legislative bodies were hundreds of gentlemen, young and old, looking on, and listening to the speeches made by the lady members. How they fluttered and fanned and whispered and smiled!

'Alas, for fallen man!' I said. Then, in an instant, I had, as by one glance, looked into the pockets of every lady and gentleman present, and also into the acquisitive pockets of the brain of each; and the result proved to me, that, as man held the purse with us, so woman held the purse in that wonderful dream-land. To obtain money from their wives, those weak, silly men would often resort to cajolery and deceit. Only from their wives could they obtain money for dress or any thing else; and so, as by common consent, nearly all the husbands had seemingly decided that they had a right to get all they could out of their wives, with out any reference to the question whether the wife could afford it or not. Thus I found, that the woman being the purse-holder, she the giver and he the receiver, worked most disastrously; for it made the interests of wife and husband separate: the interest of the wife was not the interest of the husband, his greatest care being to get all he could, and spend all he could get.

I left those buildings, and took the street-cars. Here those noble-looking, stately women escorted the gentlemen to the cars, stood while the gentlemen walked in first, then demurely stepped on board, and paid the car-fare for both. What impressed me as much as any thing I saw was, with what matter-of-course style the gentlemen, in their dainty, flimsy, flying garments, occupied the seats of the cars, while the ladies stood; or, if a lady had a seat, with what noble demeanor she rose and gave it up if a gentleman stepped on board. I saw that those ladies took gentlemen to theaters and places of amusement; ladies took those gentlemen to church, and very kindly saw them safely home; ladies told those gentlemen how beautiful they looked, how prettily they were dressed, &c.; and I saw that it gave these poor, weak-minded men much pleasure.

In ice-cream saloons and other places of refreshment, these gentlemen were as kindly and as gallantly taken by the ladies, who, in all cases, paid for the refreshments.

I looked into the churches, which were principally filled with elegantly-dressed gentlemen. 'Ah!' I said to myself, 'in religion these down-trodden men find some consolation;' but, in an instant, I was shocked by realizing that more than half went from custom, or to show their dress and see the fashions.

I looked into the prayer-meetings, and (being, of course, all the time invisible) was also present at the confessionals; and in both, the excess of men who attended was a remarkable fact.

Men got up sewing-societies and mite-societies; and, in these, many sad, sorrowful men found a few moments, sometimes, of happy, useful existence.

Occasionally, in those public places I found a man who had risen above his fellows, who had become famous in literature. I met with some male poets, and several conversant with science in a degree equal to the best of women. And I said to myself, 'If these *few* men have proved themselves equal to the best of women, then is it not strong presumptive evidence that *all* these men would be equal to women, were they equally educated?'

Then I seemed in my dream to grasp the *cause* of all this difference between the sexes; and that these beautiful, noble women might have been in the same deplorable condition had they been trained and educated as these degraded men, — without a motive in life, limited in education and culture, shut out of every path to honor or emolument, and reduced to the condition of paupers on the bounty of the opposite sex. I saw that the disadvantages under which one sex thus labored constituted a curse that extended to both; and that, though the drudgery of the kitchen had been removed, it was not the millennium, by any means, as I had supposed in my last dream, but only the beginning of the millennium. Man was not the only sufferer, but the wrong done to man acted and re-acted on woman; for men, being defrauded in their education, and nearly all avenues to pecuniary independence closed to them, marriage, with those half-educated, dependent creatures called men, was necessarily their highest ambition. There was no other way for them to obtain wealth or a home; hence they devoted all their powers to the one grand object of catching a woman with money; hence woman became also the sufferer, being often trapped into marriage by one of these silly, worthless men, who had learned well the arts and schemes of wife-catching.

I looked into the thought-cells of these ladies' brains, and found stored therein, in almost every instance, a decided belief that men constituted the inferior, and woman the superior sex.

There is a bright side, however, to every picture; and even my dream had its bright side. For instance: I had dreamed that I looked in on the gentleman with pale face and haggard countenance, of whom I spoke in my first dream as a man that 'did his own work;' and now, instead of toil and anxiety about meals, washing, ironing, &c., he was in the garden with his children, planting vegetable-seeds and flower-seeds; and as I with pleasure noted his returning health and strength, I listened to his talk with the children, whom he was interesting with a story.

How I lingered with that gentleman! I accompanied him to the house, and saw him reading; I looked over his book, and was delighted to find that he was studying physiology. By and by he began to talk with the children about the nerves, which he called electric wires carrying messages to the brain; which delighted the children: and I said in deep reverence, 'Thank God, that man has been emancipated from the kitchen! he will work out his own salvation: the golden key of the universe has he grasped with his own right hand, and it will open to him every door in the arcana of Nature. Not for ever will man be considered woman's inferior.'

Then, like a flash, came to me the mental and moral status of every man in that great country: and I realized that with emancipation from the kitchen had come a hungering and thirsting for education, for mental aliment.

Then I turned; and, lo! I stood in the street, where great posters caught my eye:—

'MAN'S RIGHTS!
A LECTURE ON MAN'S RIGHTS,'

I read.

Fain would I have attended a lecture on man's rights; but, in my eagerness to do so, I awoke.

P.S. – It is morning; and, to my great joy, I have had another dream. As I retired to my bed after writing the above, instantly Dreamland was present, and the thread taken up where it was dropped. I have attended lectures on *Man's Rights*, and Man's Rights Conventions; all of which I must write down at once, even if my husband has to go without his breakfast; for dreams so often take to themselves wings and fly away!

DREAM NUMBER THREE

Who can divine the philosophy of dreams? Who can account for the fact that persons visit again and again places they have never beheld by physical eyes, and talk with people they have only known in Dreamland? How real become to us the places and the people we have repeatedly visited in our dreams! Who have not experienced something of this reality in their own dreaming?

But it does seem especially remarkable to me, that, after having penned down at midnight one dream, I should, on returning to my pillow, have found myself in the very spot where my late dream ended; again in that strange city, again looking at the large posters headed, –

'MAN'S RIGHTS!!
MR. SAMMIE SMILEY, MR. JOHNNIE SMITH, AND OTHERS,
Will address the meeting on the
RIGHTS OF MAN!'

I was pleased on coming to these words: 'Discussion is invited.' 'I will go,' I said, and turned to follow the crowd; but, as by magic, was transferred to one of the large cooking-establishments which I saw in my first dream, and soon recognized it to be the same.

There were the huge machines at work cooking dinner, while in a comfortable rocking-chair sat the same gentleman who had in that same dream showed me over the establishment. He was reading a newspaper. 'Ah!' he said, as he looked up from his paper, 'glad to see you, madam. You see I have time to read while the dinner is cooking. All goes on well. We supply one-eighth of the city with meals, and everybody is satisfied, nay, more than satisfied: they are delighted with the arrangement; for every poor man is relieved of washing, ironing, and cooking. And yet all this is done at less cost than when every house had its little selfish, dirty kitchen.'

'And what is this about "man's rights"?' I asked. 'I see posters all over your city, headed, "Man's Rights!"'

He smiled as he replied, 'Well, madam, emancipating man from the drudgery of the kitchen has given him leisure for thought; and, in his thinking, he has discovered that he labors under many wrongs, and is deprived of quite as many rights. The idea of men lecturing, men voting, men holding office, &c., excites considerable ridicule; but ridicule proves nothing.'

'Are you going to the lecture?' I asked.

'I will go if I have company,' he replied; 'but it would not look well for me to go alone: besides, I would be afraid to go home so late.'

I made no answer; but I thought musingly, 'Afraid! afraid of what? of what can these men be afraid? I wonder if there are any wild beasts prowling around this strange city at night. Perhaps there are wolves or mad dogs; but then he is a man, and could carry a revolver and protect himself.' But, as by a flash, the truth came to me, and I wondered I had not thought of it before. In this land, *woman*, is the natural protector; and so, of course, he was afraid to go without a lady to take care of him.

I had scarcely arrived at this conclusion, when I found myself *en rapport* with every husband in that city. 'I would like to go to the lecture on "men's rights,"' I heard one man say to his wife very timidly.

'I shall go to no such place,' replied his wife loftily; 'neither will you. "Man's rights," indeed!'

'Let us go to the lecture,' said another husband to his wife, with a pleasant smile on his face.

'No, no, my dear,' replied the lady: 'I like you just as you are; and I don't admire womanish men. Nothing is more disgusting than feminine men. We don't want men running to the polls, and electioneering: what would become of the babies at such times?'

Then I looked in on a bevy of young boys ranging in age from sixteen to twenty. How they did laugh at the very mention of 'man's rights,' as they put on their pretty coats and hats, looking in the mirror, and turning half round to see how their coat-tails looked!

'Man's rights!' said one. 'I have all the rights I want.'

'So have I,' said a young boy of nineteen. 'I don't want any more rights.'

'We'll have rights enough, I presume, when we get married,' said a tall boy of seventeen, as he touched up the flowers in his pretty hat, and perched it carefully on his head.

'Are you all ready?' said a lady, looking into the room. 'Come, I want you all to learn your rights tonight. I warrant that after to-night you will want to carry the purse, don the long robes, and send us ladies into the nursery to take care of the babies!'

Hundreds of ladies and gentlemen were on their way to the meeting; and it rejoiced me greatly to find in the hearts of many of the ladies a profound respect for the rights of man, and a sincere desire that man should enjoy every right equally with themselves.

Then I found myself in the lecture-room, which was well filled with ladies and gentlemen, many of whom seemed greatly amused as they whispered and smiled to each other. Very soon three little gentlemen and one rather tall, thin, pale-faced gentleman walked to the platform, and were received with great demonstrations of applause and suppressed laughter. The audience were evidently not accustomed to hear *gentlemen* lecture.

'How ridiculous those men look!' I heard one elderly lady say. 'What does it look like to see a parcel of men pretending to make speeches, in their tawdry pants and fly-away coat-tails, covered with finery and furbelows?'

'They sadly lack the dignity,' said another female, 'that

belongs to ladies and long robes.'

'They are decidedly out of their sphere,' I heard another remark.

The meeting was opened by the tall gentleman being nominated as president, who at once introduced Mr. Sammie Smiley to the audience, remarking that Mr. Sammie Smiley, with whom they were probably all acquainted by reputation, would address the audience on the all-important subject of *Man's Rights*.

'*Sammie Smiley!*' said a young lady contemptuously. 'Suppose we should call ourselves *Lizzie* instead of Elizabeth, or *Maggie* instead of Margaret. Their very names lack dignity.'

Mr. Sammie Smiley stepped to the front of the platform with remarkable self-possession for one of the gentleman of that Dreamland. He wore a suit of black silk, – coat, vest, and pants all alike, bordered with broad black lace. He wore no ornaments, except ear-rings, a plain breastpin, and one or two rings on the fingers. Very good taste, I thought.

'Ladies and gentlemen,' he said, 'our subject this evening is the *Rights of Man*; but to properly understand this question, it would be well, before considering man's *rights*, to define his *wrongs*.'

'Hear, hear!' applauded the audience.

'Education,' he continued, 'commences with childhood; and men's wrongs also commence with childhood, inasmuch as they are restricted from healthful physical exercise. The merry, active boy, that would romp and play like his sister, is told that it would be improper for a boy. How often your little son has to be reminded that a *boy* must not do so and so: he must be a dear little gentleman, and not rough and boisterous like a girl.

'He is kept in over-heated rooms; seldom breathes the pure air of heaven; and when he is taken out, how different his dress from that of the girl! Look at his flimsy pants of white muslin; look at his flimsy jacket and paper shoes: and contrast them with the warm cloth dress, the substantial over-garments, and thick shoes of the girl! Think how seldom the boy is permitted to inhale the life-giving, open atmosphere! The girl may romp and play in the snow, climb fences and trees, and thus strengthen every muscle; while the little pale-faced boy presses his nose against the window-pane, and wishes – alas! vainly – that he, too, had been a girl.

'The course of training for our boys causes weakness and

disease in after-life, and more than a natural degree of muscular inferiority. The pale faces of boys are a sad contrast to the rosy-cheeked girls in the same family. In our boys is laid, not by Nature, but by ignorance and custom, the foundation for bodily weakness, consequently dependence and mental imbecility: in our girls, muscular strength and their accompaniments, independence and vivacity, both of body and mind. Were boys subject to the same physical training as girls (and no valid reason can be given why they should not be), the result would prove that no natural inferiority exists.

'True education I conceive to be the harmonious development of the whole being, both physical and mental. The natural or physical is before the intellectual. First the stalk, then the ear, and then the full corn in the ear. Through ignorance of these primary truths, many well-intentioned fathers hurry their children to premature graves.

'Why is it that, of all the children born, one-fifth die annually? Can not this large mortality be traced to the present ignorance of *males?* Can it not be traced to their flimsy and imperfect educational training? If men had their rights, were all literary institutions as free to one sex as to the other, our young men would be taught what is of the utmost importance for them to know, but what is kept sedulously from them; viz., a knowledge of mental and physical science.

'Let man be educated as liberally as woman; let him be made to feel the value of a sound mind, and that the brightest ornament to man, as well as woman, is intellect: then, and not until then, will he stand forth in all his beauty.

'We frequently hear that woman's mind is superior to man's; and therefore he ought not to have equal educational facilities. If, as is stated by the opponents of man's rights, men are naturally and necessarily inferior to women, it must follow that they should have superior opportunities for mental culture. If, on the other hand, men are by nature mentally equal to women, no reason can be given why they should not have equal educational facilities.'

In the midst of the audience, a beautiful, stately woman rose, and said, that, if it was not out of order, she would like to ask a question: Did not the literature written expressly for men — gentlemen's magazines, gentlemen's fashion-books, &c., — prove their inferiority? This question caused a laugh, and round after round of applause; but the little gentleman-speaker smilingly replied, that many gentlemen never read the trash prepared for them just as simple reading is prepared for children: but the works written for *women* to read, they study and digest, feeling that they were as much for them as for women. The lecturer then continued by stating the appreciative estimates of the truths of science and philosophy evinced by men as well as women, which would be the case to a still greater extent as the *opportunities* for culture were increased, when gentlemen's books and their flimsy trash would disappear; that even were man weaker in judgment than woman, it did not follow that he should never use it; and, if women did all the reasoning for man, it would not be surprising if he had lost the power to reason.

'Pretty good, Mr. Sammie Smiley,' said a lady near me.

'Smiley can reason pretty well: that is pretty good logic,' remarked another. Then applause after applause arose, accompanied by stamping and clapping of hands, while some young folks in the back of the hall crowed like roosters.

It was really very funny; but Mr. Sammie Smiley took no notice of the proceeding. He referred to the exclusion of men from nearly all occupations, from governing States to measuring tape; also that men were paid only one-third of the wages of women, even for the same work, their occupations being mainly restricted to sewing and teaching; while women could do both these, and whatever else they chose. He urged the gentlemen to push their way into the employment and professions of women, and be equal sharers in the rights of humanity.

Mr. Johnnie Smith then made an excellent speech on man's civil and political rights; but the discussion that followed so interested me that I can not at this moment recall it. When he sat down, a lady arose, and said, that, as discussions were allowed, she desired to make a few remarks.

'Take the platform! take the platform!' said several voices, which she accordingly did.

'What ease! what dignity!' said I mentally, as she stood there in her long, flowing robes. 'Ah, woman! thou art verily transfigured.'

Then I looked around on that audience, and am compelled to say that the comparison between the sexes was any thing but flattery to the gentlemen. Woman as I am, I love above all things to behold the beautiful face of a woman; but here was womanly beauty exceeding our highest conceptions; and in profound reverence I said, 'Our Father in heaven, I thank thee for human beauty. Teach us the laws of beauty, that we, thy children, may people this earth with beautiful beings. Homeliness is akin to ignorance and sin; while beauty of form and beauty of intellect constitute God's best gifts to mortals.'

'Those two gentlemen,' said the lady, 'have given us many good things to-night. There are very few persons who do not know that our sons and husbands ought to be better educated and better paid for their labor; but shall we, for this reason, make them presidents and senators? How would they look in the senate-chamber in their style of dress, so lacking in dignity? Why, we should have them quarreling and pulling hair very soon!'

'Ha, ha!' laughed the audience.

'No, no, gentlemen! you can discuss fashion and money-spending far better than national affairs. Besides, what would become of the babies? Do you propose that we, the women, shall take these your duties upon us? Depend upon it you are wrong, gentlemen: the sphere of man is *home*; and I am decidely opposed to taking man out of his sphere. Let us for a moment see what Nature teaches on this subject; let us look at man divested of his embroidery and trimming; look at his angular, long form; look at his hairy face. Is he not in his outward structure and appearance more allied to the lower animals? Look at him, and do you not at once think of the monkey? [Hear, hear!] Now turn to woman. Look at her! Does not Nature delight in curves as in lines of beauty?

'See how the planets as they revolve in their orbits delight in curves? It is Nature's perfect method of form and motion. Now look at woman's beautifully curved face and bust, and compare her form in its curved outlines with the angular outlines of man's form, and tell me if Nature herself has not put the stamp of inferiority on man! Ah, woman's face is enough! No mask of hair does she wear; but clear as the sun and fair as the moon shines clearly every feature, thus conclusively attesting her superiority. Again: how well Nature knows the superiority of woman and the inferiority of man, inasmuch as she has chosen woman for maternity. Ah! Nature knew where to find the perfect mould for her handiwork; Nature knew which is the superior sex:-

> ' "Very near to the infinite nature,
>   Very near to the hand of God,
> More rich than the hills of Beulah,
>   Which the white feet of angels trod,
> Is the sacred heart of woman;
>   The nature by which alone
> The divine can become embodied,
>   And the spirit reach its home." '

'Let us look at this matter from another stand-point. Nature is harmonious in all her parts. If, as I have proved, woman is physically superior, then she is mentally superior; and as man is physically inferior, so, as he must be harmonious in all his parts, he is necessarily and unmistakably inferior in all other respects.'

I thought in my dream that I was greatly dissatisfied with the lady's speech, and I did pity the little gentlemen on the platform who were forced to hear so much about their inferiority.

'One more argument,' said the lady, 'and I am done; and this argument is also drawn from Nature. Woman has phrenologically a larger organ of language than man. Now, what does this teach us? It teaches us this (and it ought to teach every man the same truth): *that woman is the natural orator*; that it is she who should be the lecturer, the speech-maker, the orator, and not man. It teaches us that women as senators and representatives, as lecturers and orators, are where they belong, where Nature intended they should be. It teaches us more than this: that, as man has smaller language than woman, his sphere is the domestic; is the quiet, the silent, the unobtrusive; is one of *silent* influences, not public and demonstrative like that of woman.'

She sat down, and I was really glad. 'Woman superior to man!' I exclaimed to myself. 'Well, some people can prove any thing. I do hope that little gentleman will demolish their sophistry.' But, just as Mr. Sammie Smiley arose to reply, I awoke; and, behold! it was all a dream; and I gladly realized, that, in this waking world of ours, man is not considered the inferior of woman, neither is he deprived of his just rights; and I wish sincerely that I could transfer our men to their Dreamland, and that there, at least, in God's universe, there might be one spot where men and women could stand side by side as equals.

5
PAPA'S OWN GIRL
(1874)

---*---

Marie Stevens Case Howland
(1836-1921)

Born in Lebanon, New Hampshire, Marie Stevens moved in her teens to Lowell, Massachusetts, where she became a millworker to support younger twin sisters after her father's death, and where from boarding house living, she learned both independence and co-operation. Becoming a New York City school principal in 1857, she in the same year married radical lawyer Lyman W. Case. They had met at The Club, a meeting place for feminists, anarchists, free-love advocates, and other social reformers. In the early 1860s with Lyman's approval, Marie Case and Edward Howland traveled to Guise, France, to experience the Familistère being constructed by Jean Godin (1817-1888). Begun in 1859, this was a Fourierist experiment in establishing a co-operative community, to be financed by an ironworks that manufactured stoves. Both Marie and Edward reported their impressions to the United States press. They returned to the USA a married couple. During the late 1870s, the Howlands were part of the group responsible for Woodhull & Claflin's Weekly, a periodical that kept censors in business! This free love group became Section 12 of the International Workingmen's Association (IWA). But in July 1872 Section 12 was expelled from IWA for overt support of women's emancipation. By the mid-1870s the Howlands were involved in Pacific City, a co-operative community in Topolobampo, Mexico, where Marie lived from 1888 to 1893. (Edward died there in 1890.) She designed living quarters permitting domestic co-operation — a practice advocated as well by Charlotte Perkins Gilman (1860-1935), whom Marie influenced. Before this colony failed, Marie moved to Alabama where she worked as a librarian at the Fairhope Single Tax Colony until her death.

Howland's visit to Godin's Familistère inspired her novel Papa's Own Girl *(Jewett, 1874; John Lovell, 1885, 1890), which appeared in France as* La Fille de Son Père *(1880). A third US edition appeared as* The Familistere *(Christopher, 1918). She also translated Godin's writings as* Social Solutions *(John Lovell, 1886). She likely wrote a substantial portion of* Integral Co-operation *by Albert K. Owen (John Lovell, 1885), an explanation of the principles guiding the Topolobampo Colony. Her living and her writing made a continuous whole.* Papa's Own Girl *accurately reflects the range of her concerns − from individual autonomy to community responsibility for the general welfare. Her communitarian romance reveals her admiration for Godin's Familistère, her concern for the whole of workers' lives, her advocacy of one standard to govern relations between the sexes, and her dedication to women's rights.*

The novel takes its title Papa's Own Girl *from the signature Clara Forest uses on letters written from Stonybrook College to her father Dr Forest, a physician in L −, Massachusetts. He is one of the two male characters advocating women's rights. He educates his daughter, takes into his household young Susie Dykes − pregnant from his son's heartless folly, finances Susie's florist business (recall Mary Griffith), and welcomes home a daughter who divorces her philandering husband, Dr Albert Delano. The second spokesperson for Howland's views is Count von Frauenstein ('Ladies' Rock' in German), a wealthy advocate of social experimentation. He also invests in the florist business, adopts in order to educate Susie's daughter Minnie (called 'Min'), and in his person provides a spouse worthy of Clara − although in so doing he removes her need to be economically independent, a condition he has claimed essential to women's happiness (p. 358). Nonetheless, 'Papa's Own Girl' has matured from the schoolgirl who read about social wrongs in George Sand's* Jacques *(ch. 6) to a social reformer who rights such wrongs by working in the Social Palace. Excerpts illustrate Howland's dual stress upon women's rights and social reform.*

REFERENCES

Robert S. Fogarty, Introduction to *The Familistere* (Philadelphia: Porcupine Press, 1975); Dolores Hayden, *The Grand Domestic Revolution* (Cambridge, Mass.: MIT Press, 1981), ch. 5; 'Marie Howland,' Vicki Lynn Hill in *American Women Writers* (New York: Ungar, 1980), vol. 2: 345-7; Barbara Quissell, 'The New World That Eve Made' in *America as Utopia*, ed. Kenneth M. Roemer (New York: Franklin, 1981), pp. 161-3, 173.

SELECTION
Includes pp. 343-5, 306-9, 371-4, 534-7.

PAPA'S OWN GIRL

❋

Another year has passed – a busy and prosperous year for the firm of 'Dykes & Delano, Florists.' Miss Galway, the modiste, still continued to dispose of the small bouquets, and for two years, finding the supply constant and the demand certain, she had devoted one of her windows exclusively to them, furnished it with a little fountain, and given it into the hands of the little girl, her sister, who sold a part of Susie's first installment on the Common. On the promise of Miss Galway to devote the whole proceeds of this window to the education of the little girl, our florists had agreed to continue the supply two years more, though they now had their own showroom and order department in the city, conducted by Annie, now Mrs. Storrs, assisted by another woman as book-keeper; for the firm of Dykes & Delano were 'sworn,' as the doctor declared, to never employ a man when a woman could be found to do the work required. . . .

Orders came in constantly, after the first six months; and although the firm had opened business relations with a great English nursery establishment in another part of the State, which supplied them with young shade-trees, shrubs, and evergreens from rare foreign invoices, they could hardly supply the demand. Ten acres of Minnie's legacy from Mrs. Buzzell had been put in order as a nursery, and the propagation of shrubs and trees was progressing finely. Clara and Susie became more and more enterprising and ambitious. The taste in Oakdale and neighboring towns for lawn and park cultivation, was rapidly increasing, and the young firm looked forward to getting their supplies directly from England, instead of receiving them at second hand. One man was now constantly employed in the nursery, and other help indoors and out, when the busier part of the season demanded more hands.

One morning, as Clara was busy in the conservatory, Susie brought her the card of a gentleman who was waiting in the sitting-room.

'Frauenstein?' said Clara, looking at the card, on which was written, in pencil underneath the name, 'sends his compliments to Mrs. Delano and her partner, and would esteem it a favor to be admitted into her conservatories.'

'Bring him in, Susie. I cannot present myself in the drawing-room in this rig. Don't you think I shall make an impression on his countship?' she asked, glancing at her looped-up dress and bibbed apron.

'Why not? You are beautiful in any dress.'

'You wicked little flatterer! Well, send in his Exalted Highness, the Count Von Frauenstein.'

Before Clara had scarcely glanced at the face of the count, she was strongly impressed with the distinguished air of the man. He wore a dark-blue circular, reaching nearly to the knee, and as he stepped through the folding-doors into the broad, central passage in the conservatory, he removed a very elegant shaped hat of soft felt, and seeing Clara, bowed silently, with a simply, courtly air, seldom attained except by men of the Continent. Clara returned the salute, but remembering the European custom, did not offer him her hand.

'Madam,' he said, 'I have had several glimpses of your flowers from the outside, and I greatly desire to have a better view, if you will pardon my presumption.'

'I am very glad to see you, sir,' Clara replied. 'My father has often spoken of you, for he is one of your ardent admirers.'

'He flatters me greatly. I am proud of his good opinion, for it is worth more than that of other men.'. . .

[The Count von Frauenstein] had just returned from Guise, in France, where he had visited the grand social palace founded by a great French capitalist for his workmen. 'I tell you, Dr. Forest,' he said, with enthusiasm, 'the age is ripe for a grand spring toward social organization, and the sight of that palace of workers inspires me with new hope. There are over a thousand people, honest wealth-producers, surrounded by a sum of conveniences and luxuries to be found nowhere else on the planet, even among the rich. . . . There are nurseries and schools on a magnificent scale, for the children. There are swimming and hot and cold baths for all, medical service of the best, a restaurant, a billiard saloon, a café, a charming theatre, a library and reading-room, societies for various objects, such as music and the drama, beside the board, composed of men and women, who manage the internal affairs of the palace. All the courts of the palace are covered with glass, and the various suites of apartments open on corridors in these courts. . . . [E]very one of the advantages I have named, and many more, are included in the rents, and Monsieur Godin, the founder, makes six per cent on the capital invested. It has been in successful operation some twelve years. . . . [T]here is no congenial society for me anywhere, as life is ordered at present. I must help to build up a society of men and women who can be honest and free, because sure of the present and of the future for themselves and their children. I found more intelligence, more faith in humanity, and more freedom of expression among those workingmen at Guise, than I ever met among any set of people in my life; and the children, madam: O, the children! I can give you no idea of their rosy health, their frank expression of advanced opinions, and their courteous manners.'

It was a clear, balmy day in the first week of April that the count sought this interview with the doctor. So far in his life, he had never found a man who was so much 'after his own heart.' He believed in him fully from the first hour he conversed with him, since when they had corresponded, expressing their views fearlessly; and thus far had found them in perfect accord. To say they loved each other like brothers would by no means express the sentiment existing between these two men, so unlike in many respects, yet so closely in sympathy that thought answered to thought like the voice of one's own soul. During the drive, for they went past the fifty acres away into the country, neither asking for what reason, the count gave in detail his plans. 'If I build this palace,' he said, 'I shall do it with this clear granite sand of the river. I know the secret of making stones of it – bricks, we call them – which, moulded in any shape, and tinted any hue, will last for centuries. I can have a man here in three days to conduct the work. He will guarantee that they shall be finished this summer. If I do it, it shall be a magnificent structure, beside which the palace of Versailles will seem the work of a "prentice hand." I can profit by the original palace at Guise, and make it much handsómer, though that is truly splendid. The apartments must be larger, and the whole should accommodate about two thousand people. Now, I have already one industry for its occupants. What is your idea for a second?'

'Making these very bricks,' said the doctor, 'if only you have got at the secret of their perfect durability, as you have, I know, or you would not speak so positively. But this industry would not suit all. You want one more.'

'Of course. One that will employ women. What shall it be? I have thought of silk-weaving, for a certain reason of my own. It is proverbial, you know, that those who make the silks, laces, and velvets – pure luxuries, and the most costly – are the worst paid of any laborers in the world. Look at Spitalfields, England, and Lyons, the great velvet manufacturing centre of France. In India, those who make the fabulous-priced Cashmere shawls are the most pitiably paid of all. I am willing, if necessary, to lose a considerable fortune to prove that good wages can be paid to silk-makers, and yet have a fair profit on the product. I should go into that manufacture with some advantages. I have a first-class steamer already plying between San Francisco and China. I can get silk as cheap as anybody.'

'Good!' said the doctor. 'Let the third industry be silk-weaving.' The count had not mentioned the first, but the doctor knew well he meant floriculture.

'There's only one thing lacking, doctor, and that is – the motive: the motive for the first step. That depends –' And suddenly checking himself and turning his horse in the road, he asked, abruptly, 'Doctor, have you ever been in love?'

'With a woman – no; with a man, yes.'

'I understand. You have met a man who responded to all the needs a man could respond to, but never a woman to respond to what you need there. That is my own case exactly, though I have loved, of course – few men more, I think.'

'If men only knew,' said the doctor, 'how they cramp their own growth by making idols of women!'

'By idols, you mean slaves. Only free women are worthy of free men; and the time is not come, though it is near, when they will be emancipated. Then we shall see the dawn of the Golden Age. Men think they are free; but they are bound by many shackles, only they have thrown off some which they still compel women to wear.'

'And some they cannot throw off,' said the doctor, 'until women are recognized as their political equals. I have great

101

patience with the women; they are coming up slowly, through much tribulation.'

Here the count gave a detailed description of the organization and working of the Social Palace system, and then he continued: . . .

'The primal object of society should be to make perfect men and women – perfect citizens. This cannot be accomplished without scientific training for the mind, and the free and harmonious development of the muscles through labor, with gymnastic exercises and games for the development of those muscles not brought into play by the ordinary industrial occupations. When a man continues many hours a day using only one set of muscles, as the blacksmith his arm, he must do it at the expense of grace, and strength, and beauty, which we should be taught to seek as a duty to ourselves and to our fellow-beings, since we have no moral right to transmit disease and ugliness to posterity. [Cheers.] No one should dream of finishing his education until he dies. Besides the exercise of the muscles by industry, every human being should have time during the twenty-four hours, for amusing games, for bathing, for dressing elegantly and becomingly, for social converse, for music or the drama, for regular study and drill in classes, and finally for sleep. All this may not be accomplished for the wronged and cheated adult generation of the present; all this and more will be the proud heritage of the children growing up under the blessings of a nobly organized social and industrial life. [Great applause.] Children growing up under such conditions, will be strong and beautiful, tender and wise. They will be strong through constant exercise, a varied and plentiful diet, and the natural stimulation of happiness. They will be beautiful, because to develop their bodies harmoniously will be the object of scientific study; and their faces will be beautiful because they will be moulded, not by anger, and cunning, and selfishness, but by generosity, candor, and love. They will be tender, because they will be taught to be proud of exemplifying the devotion of love, the grandest of all our passions, for it is the only one that exalts us to the dignity of the creative mood. Finally, they will be wise, for they will have acquired the sentiment of the brotherhood of man. . . . This spirit is based on the sentiment of equality, the recognition of human rights everywhere, and is most significant, for it is full of promise for the future success of our great effort. And here I will mention one thing, not out of malice, but simply as a lesson. I am accused of advocating the "leveling" principle. "Frauenstein, you are a leveler," said a friend to me to-day. Well, there is some truth in that: I would bring all the races and individuals on the globe up to the highest level; but I should be very sorry to do anything toward bringing my artisan friends down to the physical, intellectual, or moral level of certain aristocrats whom I know. [Laughter and applause.] It is undeniably the fact, that to-day the soundest views on education, on politics, on finance, on social organization, are supported, not by those who hold themselves above their kind — the drones of the community, who feed on the mechanic's labor — but by those who have an honest right to everything they own, and much more. The more I associate with laborers, even those who have had little advantage from schools, the more I am stuck with the saving virtue that is in them.'. . .

6
SELECTIONS BY ELIZABETH STUART PHELPS (1844-1911)

———————————— ✳ ————————————

(a) 'A DREAM WITHIN A DREAM' (1874)
(b) *BEYOND THE GATES* (1883)

Author of some 56 books, Elizabeth Stuart Phelps grew up and lived in the Greater Boston region. She was educated in Andover, the daughter of popular author, Elizabeth Stuart Phelps, and Andover Theological Seminary President, Austin Phelps. Her mother died only three years into a writing career when daughter Elizabeth was eight. Christened 'Mary Gray' after a maternal friend, the daughter assumed her mother's name, and apparently her career, too. An early regional writer, the mother Phelps had depicted women's domestic constraints in The Sunny Side *(1851) and* A Peep at 'Number Five' *(1853). From these and from her mother's overburdened life, the daughter early gained an awareness of women's wrongs and rights. She commented upon them more outspokenly than had her mother. Her pen was her pulpit. She established herself as both a popular and a serious writer in 1868.* The Gates Ajar *gained her widespread popular acclaim for its message – consolatory to post Civil War bereaved women – that they could believe in a eutopian heaven. An* Atlantic Monthly *story* 'The Tenth of January,' *– inspired by Rebecca Harding Davis's* Life in the Iron Mills *(1861), an exposé of industrialists' unconcern for labor needs – received critical approval from Thomas Wentworth Higginson and John Greenleaf Whittier.*

Thus established, Phelps continued to write 'for truth's sake.' Hedged In *(1870) criticized a double sexual standard while* A Silent Partner *(1871) faulted a double occupational standard. Also in 1871 a series of essays on a range of women's issues appeared first in* The Independent *and then in* The Woman's Journal: *one of these is an exposé of 'that dummy "the true woman."' After a period of ill health, from which Phelps was never free, she published her best work* The Story of Avis *(1877), a revelation of a woman's artistic talent being drained by the necessities of daily living.* Old Maids and Burglars in Paradise *(1879, 1886) in comic vein shows women vacationing in a summer cottage 'Paradise' without much use for 'male protection.'* Friends: A Duet *(1881) shows the impossibility of friendship between the sexes.* Doctor Zay *(1882) demonstrates a woman capably pursuing a typical male vocation.* Beyond the Gates *(1883) depicts a heavenly eutopia where women receive compensation for earth's deficits, whether in education, health, or affection, and where a father keeps house awaiting his family.* The Gates Between *(1887) develops a different facet of heaven: a father must learn to care for his son. This book was offered as a subscription premium by* The Woman's Journal. *In 1888 she married Herbert Dickinson Ward, a man seventeen years younger. She continued to write, but the only substantial work to emerge was* A Singular Life *(1895), a novel showing a man killed for his attempt to live according to a Social Gospel.*

Phelp's Utopian writing thus occurred within a lifetime of writing to raise awareness of women's needs. Although she lived most of her adulthood outside of marriage, she never gave up hope that woman and man could live equitably together. In the meanwhile she found friendships among women. Her 'Gates' books, read in isolation, might appear mere consolation for lost lives, but rather they depict as heaven a eutopian world in which women no longer exist in want. So popular were these books that as late as 1916 Edith Wharton in 'The Bunner Sisters' includes a 'Gates Ajar' funeral wreath, which her characters admire. The popularity of the 'Gates' books makes a provocative statement concerning the malaise in women's lives. Both the 1883 and 1887 books suggest death as escape from desolation:

> *To be dead was to be dead to danger, dead to fear. To be dead was to be alive to a sense of assured good chance that nothing in the universe could shake. (1883, p. 72) '. . . They call this death. Why, I never knew what it was to be alive before!' (1887, p. 152)*

105

The following selections stress Phelps's hope, couched in nineteenth-century language, for a future better relation between the sexes and, in 1883, for mutually beneficial relations between women of different social classes: Marie Sauvée now helps her former benefactress. For her audience, heavenly eutopias served much as science fiction eutopias do for us today – as imaginative transcendence of contemporary dystopia.

REFERENCES
Ann Douglas, *The Feminization of American Culture* (New York: Alfred A. Knopf, 1977), 'Heaven Our Home: Consolation Literature in the Northern United States, 1830-1880,' *American Quarterly* 26 (1974): 496-515; James D. Hart, *The Popular Book* (New York: Oxford, 1950), ch. 7; Carol Farley Kessler, *Elizabeth Stuart Phelps* (Boston: G.K. Hall, 1982) and 'The Heavenly Utopia of Elizabeth Stuart Phelps' in *Women and Utopia*, ed. Marleen Barr and Nick Smith (Lanham, Maryland: University Press of America, 1983); Helen Sootin Smith, Introduction to *The Gates Ajar* (Cambridge, Mass.: Harvard University Press, 1964); Elmer F. Suderman, 'Elizabeth Stuart Phelps and The Gates Ajar Novels,' *The Journal of Popular Culture* 3(1969): 91-105; Barbara Welter, 'Defenders of the Faith' in *Dimity Convictions* (Athens, Ohio: Ohio University Press, 1976), pp. 111-20.

SELECTION
'A Dream Within a Dream' omits about 250 words; *Beyond the Gates* includes pp. 118-29.

SELECTIONS BY ELIZABETH STUART PHELPS

---*---

(a) 'A DREAM WITHIN A DREAM' (1874)

. . . The Episcopal service — that most hallowed by churchly associations and most full of excellences — has yet egregious faults. Bad taste, bad grammar, and perjury may have their places; but a marriage service would not seem to be the place for them.

'I take thee *to* my wedded wife [or husband] . . . to have and to hold' is an awkwardness for which only long-inculcated reverence could feel so much rhetorical respect as not to mar a matrimonial ecstasy. 'Till Death us do part' is a dislocation in which the most devout Church woman must feel a pang. The inquiry 'Who *giveth* this woman to be married to this man?' is, to say the least of it, an anachronism. 'I pronounce you *man* and *wife*' flavors somewhat of the tenement-house patois, as of a couple henceforth to say, 'My man is abroad today,' or 'My woman is getting dinner.'

'With all my worldly goods I thee endow' is a fiction so stupendous as to be more amusing than impressive.

'Do you promise to obey him and serve him? The woman shall say, I will.' Herein we have the spectacle of a priest at the altar offering the most solemn and binding of vows to a woman who has not the lest intention of keeping it; who will not keep it, if she has; and who ought not to keep it, whether she has or not.

The Church service was written in a bygone age, for a bygone type of society. Its real beauties cannot save it intact to the future. The Marriage To-be will demand a pledge for which this is neither speech nor language.

Outside of the apostolic succession we fare scarcely better.

Most of the forms of marriage ceremony current among our pastors are mere abridgments and modifications of the old Church service. One of great beauty has, indeed, been written and circulated in private ministerial circles, with much acceptance. But even this, inimitable as a literary master-piece, must something fail of reaching the temper in which many men and women nowadays find themselves moved to exchange the marriage vows. Nor does the short, slippery formula of the civil justice help the matter much.

Musing thus, the other evening, Mr. Editor, I fell into a dream. . . .

For I dreamed that behold! I was invited to succeed the Rev. Mr. Murray as pastor of Park-street church; and that, having accepted the call, upon conditions not to the purpose to specify; and that, having been duly (I doubled the 1 in that word; but discovered the superfluity just in time) — duly ordained, settled, discussed, made in every respect as self-conscious and wretched as it is quite proper to make a somewhat bashful new pastor in a perfectly self-possessed old church; having delivered my inaugural, and received my first pair of worked slippers, and declined my first donation party, and denied my first ten or fifteen engagements, and quite become used to selecting housekeepers and conducting funerals, it fell to my lot, on a New Year's Eve, to marry my first couple.

Now, fifteen engagements is a small matter, and it is pure enjoyment to murder a donation party, and funerals and house-keepers have no effect upon my peace of mind, and it has been the one ungratified wish of my life that a young lady should work me a pair of slippers; but when it came to the wedding, I saw in my dream that my heart within me was troubled, for I doubted of the manner of the language in which I should perform this most difficult and delicate of duties satisfactorily to the young people and honorably to myself and my profession.

But I saw in my dream, and behold! when the youth and the maiden came before me, there were given unto me the words which I should speak, and that I married them according to the meaning of the words.

When I awoke, all particulars of that wedding had vanished from me. Whether there were cake and cards I know not; what the bride wore I cannot say; if there were bridesmaids or favors ask me not; but the words which I spoke remained unto me. . . .

MARRIAGE SERVICE

Which beginneth with the words 'Let us pray.'

(At the close of a brief prayer the minister shall say):

'In the presence of God and of those witnesses, we are now come to solemnize the covenant of this man and woman in marriage. Are you, Charles True, prepared, of your own free will's inclining and whole heart's desire, to take upon yourself the vows which shall make and keep you the husband of this woman as long as Death shall spare you one to the other?'

(He shall say): 'I am.'

'Are you, Charlotte Tender, prepared, of your own free will's inclining and whole heart's desire, to take upon yourself the vows which shall make and keep you the wife of this man as long as Death shall spare you one to the other?'

(She shall say): 'I am.'

'Is there to your inmost consciousness any hidden reason why you should not charge your lips with the utterance of these vows? Does the voice of your secret soul cry to you – by any reproach of memory, by any uncertainty of hope – to forbid these banns? If there be such a reason, if there be such a voice, in the presence of God and of these witnesses, regard it, before it be too late.'

(Both): 'There is none such.'

(Unto the man he shall say): 'If you feel within your honest heart that any other woman ought to hold – or in the sweet mood of your affection, that any other could hold – the place which this woman occupies to-day, for your soul's sake and for her soul's sake, acknowledge it before it be too late.'

(Unto the woman he shall say): 'If you feel within your honest heart that any other man ought to hold – or in the sweet mood of your affections, that any other could hold – the place which this man occupies to-day, for your soul's sake and for his soul's sake, acknowledge it before it be too late.'

(Receiving no responses, the minister shall proceed):

'Then reverently do I offer you and loyally may you take upon yourselves the covenant of true marriage.

'Do you, Charles True take this woman whose hand you hold to be your lawfully wedded wife?'

(He shall say): 'I do.'

'Do you, Charlotte Tender, take this man whose hand you hold to be your lawfully wedded husband?'

(She shall say): 'I do.'

'You promise to cleave unto each other in sickness and in health, in prosperity and in adversity, through trial and triumph, in temptation, peril, joy, sorrow, through life, unto death. You promise to be faithful each to the other in deed, word and truth. You promise to be considerate each of the other's happiness, above all other earthly claims. You promise to assist each other in your mutual and individual life's work, rendering each to each such tender thoughtfulness and such large estimate of the other's nature that neither shall absorb in petty exactions or in selfish blindness the other's subject life. You recognize it to be the duty of every man and of every woman to live a life of individual service to an individual God, and you hold it to be the especial aim of marriage to assist men and women in the pursuance of such a service, by a union which brings mutual responsibility, mutual forbearance, and mutual comfort, to replace solitary labors and lonely failures and unshared successes. You, therefore, promise to regard each the other's preference in all your plans of life, and to consider any claim of one to legislate for the other, as foreign to the spirit of a righteous marriage and to the letter of your-vows. You believe that the sweet restraints and large liberty of mutual love shall serve you in the settlement of all difference of opinion, and that your happiness will be increased by your recognition each of the other's freedom of personal judgment, and action. You promise to reverence in each other all that is essentially different in your natures, and to meet generously upon all that is common, and to elevate, each for the other and each in the other, your ideals of manhood, of womanhood, and of marriage. Do you thus believe and promise?'

(Both shall say): 'I do.'

'Then do I pronounce you to be husband and wife. The great necessity of love is laid upon you. Love is no longer its own, but another's. You are not any more your own, but each other's. You have set yourselves to learn the longest lessons of human experience. You have entered upon a condition of the highest duties, as well as of the deepest joys. As earnestly as you have come to it may it come to you. As solemnly as you have chosen each other may God's blessing choose out you. Even as tenderly as you are drawn to each other may his heart be drawn unto you. As sacredly as you cherish each other may his protection cherish you.

'"Love," we read, "is stronger than Death." Of whatever there shall be in human love which outlives human life, may the love of this man and woman be found worthy to partake!'

'For all that the love of man and woman may mean, in a world where they neither marry nor are given in marriage, God grant that this earthly marriage may fit these two Heaven-born souls!

'Amen.'

(b) *BEYOND THE GATES* (1883)

IX

The shore upon which we had landed was thickly populated, as I have said. Through a sweep of surpassingly beautiful suburbs, we approached the streets of a town. It is hard to say why I should have been surprised at finding in this place the signs of human traffic, philanthropy, art, and study – what otherwise I expected, who can say? My impressions, as Marie Sauvée led me through the city, had the confusion of sudden pleasure. The width and shining cleanliness of the streets, the beauty and glittering material of the houses, the frequent presence of libraries, museums, public gardens, signs of attention to the wants of animals, and places of shelter for travelers such as I had never seen in the most advanced and benevolent of cities below, – these were the points which struck me most forcibly.

The next thing, which in a different mood might have been the first that impressed me was the remarkable expression of the faces that I met or passed. No thoughtful person can have failed to observe, in any throng, the preponderant look of unrest and dissatisfaction in the human eye. Nothing, to a fine vision, so emphasizes the isolation of being, as the faces of people in a crowd. In this new community to which I had been brought, that old effect was replaced by a delightful change. I perceived, indeed, great intentness of purpose here, as in all thickly-settled regions; the countenances that passed me indicated close conservation of social force and economy of intellectual energy; these were people trained by attrition with many influences, and balanced with the conflict of various interests. But these were men and women, busy without hurry, efficacious without waste; they had ambition without unscrupulousness, power without tyranny, success without vanity, care without anxiety, effort without exhaustion, – hope, fear, toil, uncertainty it seemed, elation it was sure – but a repose that it was impossible to call by any other name than divine, controlled their movements, which were like the pendulum of a golden clock whose works are out of sight. I watched these people with delight. Great numbers of them seemed to be students, thronging what we should call below colleges, seminaries, or schools of art, or music, or science. The proportion of persons pursuing some form of intellectual acquisition struck me as large. My little guide, to whom I mentioned this, assented to the fact, pointing out to me a certain institution we had passed, at which she herself was, she said, something like a primary scholar, and from which she had been given a holiday to meet me as she did, and conduct me through the journey which had been appointed for me on that day. I inquired of her what her studies might be like; but she told me that she was hardly wise enough as yet to explain to me what I could learn for myself when I had been longer in this place, and when my leisure came for investigating its attractions at my own will.

'I am uncommonly ignorant, you know,' said Marie Sauvée humbly, 'I have everything to learn. There is book knowledge and thought knowledge and soul knowledge, and I have not any of these. I was as much of what you used to call a heathen, as any Fiji-Islander you gave your missionaries to. I have so much to learn, that I am not sent yet upon other business such as I should like.'

Upon my asking Marie Sauvée what business this might be, she hesitated. 'I have become ambitious in Heaven,' she answered slowly. 'I shall never be content till I am fit to be sent to the worst woman that can be found – no matter which side of death – I don't care in what world – I want to be sent to one that nobody else will touch; I think I might know how to save her. It is a tremendous ambition!' she repeated. 'Preposterous for the greatest angel there is here! And yet I – *I* mean to do it.'

I was led on in this way by Marie Sauvée, through and out of the city into the western suburbs; we had approached from the east, and had walked a long distance. There did not occur to me, I think, till we had made the circuit of the beautiful town, one thing, which, when I did observe it, struck me as, on the whole, the most impressive that I had noticed. 'I have not seen,' I said, stopping suddenly, 'I have not seen a poor person in all this city.'

'Nor an aged one, have you?' asked Marie Sauvée, smiling.

'Now that I think of it, – no. Nor a sick one. Not a beggar. Not a cripple. Not a mourner. Not – and yet what have we here? This building, by which you are leading me, bears a device above the door, the last I should ever have expected to find *here*.'

It was an imposing building, of a certain translucent material that had the massiveness of marble, with the delicacy of thin agate illuminated from within. The rear of this building gave upon the open country, with a background of hills, and the vision of the sea which I had crossed. People strolled about the grounds which had more than the magnificence of Oriental gardens. Music came from the building, and the saunterers, whom I saw, seemed nevertheless not to be idlers, but persons busily employed in various ways – I should have said, under the close direction of others who guided them. The inscription above the door of this building was a word, in a tongue unknown to me, meaning 'Hospital,' as I was told.

'They are the sick at heart,' said Marie Sauvée, in answer to my look of perplexity, 'who are healed there. And they are the sick of soul; those who were most unready for the new life; they whose spiritual being was diseased through inaction, *they* are the invalids of Heaven. There they are put under treatment, and slowly cured. With some, it takes long. I was there myself when I first came, for a little; it will be a most interesting place for you to visit, by-and-by.'

I inquired who were the physicians of this celestial sanitarium.

'They who unite the natural love of healing to the highest spiritual development.'

'By no means, then, necessarily they who were skilled in the treatment of diseases on earth?' I asked, laughing.

'Such are oftener among the patients,' said Marie Sauvée sadly. To me, so lately from the earth, and our low earthly way of finding amusement in facts of this nature, this girl's gravity was a rebuke. I thanked her for it, and we passed by the hospital – which I secretly made up my mind to investigate at another time – and so out into the wider country, more sparsely settled, but it seemed to me more beautiful than that we had left behind.

'There,' I said, at length, 'is to my taste the loveliest spot we have seen yet. That is the most homelike of all these homes.'

We stopped before a small and quiet house built of curiously inlaid woods, that reminded me of Sorrento work as a great achievement may remind one of a first and faint suggestion. So exquisite was the carving and coloring, that on a larger scale the effect might have interferred with the solidity of the building, but so modest were the proportions of this charming house, that its dignity was only enhanced by its delicacy. It was shielded by trees, some familiar to me, others strange. There were flowers – not too many; birds; and I noticed a fine dog sunning himself upon the steps. The sweep of landscape from all the windows of this house must have been grand. The wind drove up from the sea. The light, which had a peculiar depth and color, reminding me of that which on earth flows from under the edge of a breaking storm-cloud at the hour preceding sunset, formed an aureola about the house. When my companion suggested my examining this place, since it so attracted me, I hesitated, but yielding to her wiser judgment, strolled across the little lawn, and stood, uncertain, at the threshold. The dog arose as I came up, and met me cordially, but no person seemed to be in sight.

'Enter,' said Marie Sauvée in a tone of decision, 'You are expected. Go where you will.'

I turned to remonstrate with her, but the girl had disappeared. Finding myself thus thrown on my own resources, and having learned already the value of obedience to mysterious influences in this new life, I gathered courage, and went into the house. The dog followed me affectionately, rather than suspiciously.

For a few moments I stood in the hall or ante-room, alone and perplexed. Doors opened at right and left, and vistas of exquisitely-ordered rooms stretched out. I saw much of the familiar furniture of a modest home, and much that was unfamiliar mingled therewith. I desired to ask the names or purposes of certain useful articles, and the characters and creators of certain works of art. I was bewildered and delighted. I had something of the feeling of a rustic visitor taken for the first time to a palace or imposing town-house.

Was Heaven an aggregate of homes like his? Did everlasting life move on in the same dear ordered channel – the dearest that human experiment had ever found – the channel of family

114

love? Had one, after death, the old blessedness without the old burden? The old sweetness without the old mistake? The familiar rest, and never the familiar fret? Was there always in the eternal world 'somebody to come home to'? And was there always the knowledge that it could not be the wrong person? Was all *that* eliminated from celestial domestic life? Did Heaven solve the problem on which earth had done no more than speculate?

While I stood, gone well astray on thoughts like these, feeling still too great a delicacy about my uninvited presence in this house, I heard the steps of the host, or so I took them to be; they had the indefinable ring of the master's foot. I remained where I was, not without embarrassment, ready to apologize for my intrusion as soon as he should come within sight. He crossed the long room at the left, leisurely; I counted his quiet footsteps; he advanced, turned, saw me – I too, turned – and so, in this way, it came about that I stood face to face with my own father.

. . . I had found the eternal life full of the unexpected, but this was almost the sweetest thing that had happened to me yet.

Presently my father took me over the house and the grounds; with a boyish delight, explaining to me how many years he had been building and constructing and waiting with patience in his heavenly home for the first one of his own to join him. Now, he too, should have 'somebody to come home to.' As we dwelt upon the past and glanced at the future, our full hearts overflowed. He explained to me that my new life had but now, in the practical sense of the word, begun; since a human home was the center of all growth and blessedness. When he had shown me to my own portion of the house, and bidden me welcome to it, he pointed out to me a certain room whose door stood always open, but whose threshold was never crossed. I hardly feel that I have the right, in this public way, to describe, in detail, the construction or adornment of this room. I need only say that Heaven itself seemed to have been ransacked to bring together the daintiest, the most delicate, the purest, thoughts and fancies that celestial skill or art could create. Years had gone to the creation of this spot; it was a growth of time, the occupation of that loneliness which must be even in the happy life, when death has temporarily separated two who had been one. I was quite prepared for his whispered words, when he said, –

'Your mother's room, my dear. It will be all ready for her at any time.'

This union had been a *marriage* – not one of the imperfect ties which pass under the name, on earth. Afterwards, when I learned more of the social economy of the new life, I perceived more clearly the rarity and peculiar value of an experience which had in it the elements of which might be called (if I should be allowed the phrase) eternal permanency, and which involved, therefore, none of the disintegration and redistribution of relations consequent upon passing from temporary or mistaken choices to a fixed and perfect state of society. . . .

7
MIZORA: A PROPHECY
(1880-1)

*

Mary E. Bradley Lane (n.d)

*Another unknown and unknowable Utopist, Mary E. Bradley
Lane serialized* Mizora *in the* Cinncinati Commercial *from 6
November 1880 to 5 February 1881. She subtitled it 'A Mss.
found among the private papers of the Princess Vera Zarovitch;
Being a true and faithful account of her Journey to the Interior
of the Earth, with a careful description of the Country and its
Inhabitants, their Customs, Manners and Government. Written
by Herself.' Thus she concealed her authorship, even from her
husband, according to Murat Halstead. Apparently he was
associated with the* Commercial. *In a Preface to the 1889 book
edition, he notes that the narrative 'attracted a great deal of
attention . . . , and there was much more said about it than is
usual when works of fiction run through a newspaper in weekly
installments.' But no evidence survives today.*

What differentiates Mizora *from all other eutopias by
women until Charlotte Perkins Gilman's* Herland *(1915) is the
absence of men. This feature anticipates several 1970s eutopias
(see Bibliography 1973, 1975, 1978, 1979, 1980). The
narrator-visitor to Mizora searches constantly for some indication of men, but in the passage following she learns the history.
In contrast to* Herland *where the mother is the ideal role, in*
Mizora *the teacher ranks above all others. And in contrast to
Phelps's 'Gates' books, religion here is no more than superstition.*

*The narrator Princess Vera is a Russian adventurer-explorer,
who has escaped to the North Pole from her exile to Siberia,
lived with Eskimoes, then one day found her rowboat drawn
into a whirlpool that pulled her inside the Earth to Mizora, a
land of blonde women. (Unfortunately such race bias, as well
as hierarchical social structure, sets this apart from recent*

MARY E. BRADLEY LANE

feminist eutopias.) Wauna, daughter of the Preceptress of the National College, guides Vera about Mizora.

REFERENCES
Kristine Anderson, 'Introduction: A Woman's View,' pp. xi-xiii, and Stuart A. Teitler, 'Introduction,' pp. v-x, to *Mizora: A Prophecy* (Boston: G.K. Hall, 1975); Barbara Quissell, 'The New World That Eve Made' in *America as Utopia*, ed. Kenneth M. Roemer (New York: Franklin, 1981), pp. 167-9, 173-4.

SELECTION
Includes pp. 23-30, 94-105.

MIZORA: A PROPHECY

— * —

PART I CHAPTER IV

To facilitate my progress in the language of Mizora I was sent to their National College. It was the greatest favor they could have conferred upon me, as it opened to me a wide field of knowledge. Their educational system was a peculiar one, and, as it was the chief interest of the country, I shall describe it before proceeding farther with this narrative.

All institutions for instruction were public, as were, also, the books and other accessories. The state was the beneficent mother who furnished everything, and required of her children only their time and application. Each pupil was compelled to attain a certain degree of excellence that I thought unreasonably high, after which she selected the science or vocation she felt most competent to master, and to that she then devoted herself.

The salaries of teachers were larger than those of any other public position. The Principal of the National College had an income that exceeded any royal one I had ever heard of; but, as education was the paramount interest of Mizora, I was not surprised at it. Their desire was to secure the finest talent for educational purposes, and as the highest honors and emoluments belonged to such a position, it could not be otherwise. To be a teacher in Mizora was to be a person of consequence. They were its aristocracy.

Every State had a free college provided for out of the State funds. In these colleges every department of Science, Art, or Mechanics was furnished with all the facilities for thorough instruction. All the expenses of a pupil, including board, clothing and the necessary traveling fares, were defrayed by the state. I may here remark that all railroads are owned and controlled by the General Government. The rates of transportation were fixed by law, and were uniform throughout the country.

The National College which I entered belonged to the General Government. Here was taught the highest attainments in the arts and sciences, and all industries practised in Mizora. It contained the very cream of learning. There the scientist, the philosopher and inventor found the means and appliances for study and investigation. There the artist and sculptor had their finest work, and often their studios. The principals and subordinate teachers and assistants were elected by popular vote. The State Colleges were free to those of another State who might desire to enter them, for Mizora was like one vast family. It was regarded as the duty of every citizen to lend all the aid and encouragement in her power to further the enlightenment of others, wisely knowing the benefits of such would accrue to her own and the general good. The National College was open to all applicants, irrespective of age, the only requirements being a previous training to enter upon so high a plane of mental culture. Every allurement was held out to the people to come and drink at the public fountain where the cup was inviting and the waters sweet. 'For,' said one of the leading instructors to me, 'education is the foundation of our moral elevation, our government, our happiness. Let us relax our efforts, or curtail the means and inducements to become educated, and we relax into ignorance, and end in demoralization. We know the value of free education. It is frequently the case that the greatest minds are of slow development, and manifest in the primary schools no marked ability. They often leave the schools unnoticed; and when time has awakened them to their mental needs, all they have to do is to apply to the college, pass an examination, and be admitted. If not prepared to enter the college, they could again attend the common schools. We realize in its broadest sense the ennobling influence of universal education. The higher the culture of a people, the more secure is their government and happiness. A prosperous people is always an educated one; and the freer the education, the wealthier they become.'

The Preceptress of the National College was the leading scientist of the country. Her position was more exalted than any that wealth could have given her. In fact, while wealth had acknowledged advantages, it held a subordinate place in the estimation of the people. I never heard the expression 'very wealthy,' used as a recommendation of a person. It was always: '*She* is a fine scholar, or mechanic, or artist, or musician.' *She* excels in landscape gardening, or domestic work. *She* is a first-class chemist? But never '*She* is rich.'

The idea of a Government assuming the responsibility of education, like a parent securing the interest of its children, was all so new to me; and yet, I confessed to myself, the system might prove beneficial to other countries than Mizora. In that world, from whence I had so mysteriously emigrated, education was the privilege only of the rich. And in no country, however enlightened, was there a system of education that would reach all. Charitable institutions were restricted, and benefited only a few. My heart beat with enthusiasm when I thought of the mission before me. And then I reflected that the philosophers of my world were but as children in progress compared to these. Still traveling in grooves that had been worn and fixed for posterity by bygone ages of ignorance and narrow-mindedness, it would require courage and resolution, and more eloquence than I possessed, to persuade them out of these trodden paths. To be considered the privileged class was an active characteristic of human nature. Wealth, and the powerful grip upon the people which the organizations of society and governments gave, made it hereditary. Yet in this country, nothing was hereditary but the prosperity and happiness of the whole people. . . .

At the National College, where it is taught as a regular science, I witnessed the chemical production of bread and a preparation resembling meat. Agriculture in this wonderful land, was a lost art. No one that I questioned had any knowledge of it. It had vanished in the dim past of their barbarism. With the exception of vegetables and fruit, which were raised in luscious perfection, their food came from the elements. A famine among such enlightened people was impossible, and scarcity was unknown. Food for the body and food for the mind were without price. It was owing to this that poverty was unknown to them, as well as disease. The absolute purity of all that they ate preserved an activity of vital power long exceeding our span of life. The length of their year, measured by the two seasons, was the same as ours; but the women who had marked a hundred of them in their lifetime,

MARY E. BRADLEY LANE

looked younger and fresher, and were more supple of limb than myself, yet I had barely passed my twenty-second year.

I wrote out a careful description of the processes by which they converted food out of the valueless elements — valueless because of their abundance — and put it carefully away for use in my own country. There drouth, or excessive rainfalls, produced scarcity, and sometimes famine. The struggle of the poor was for food, to the exclusion of all other interests. Many of them knew not what proper and health-giving nourishment was. But here in Mizora, the daintiest morsels came from the chemists' laboratory, cheap as the earth under her feet.

I now began to enjoy the advantages of conversation, which added greatly to my happiness and acquirements. I formed an intimate companionship with the daughter of the Preceptress of the National College, and to her were addressed the questions I asked about things that impressed me. She was one of the most beautiful beings that it had been my lot to behold. Here eyes were dark, almost the purplish blue of a pansy, and her hair had a darker tinge than is common in Mizora, as if it had stolen the golden edge of a ripe chestnut. Her beauty was a constant charm to me.

The National College contained a large and well filled gallery. Its pictures and statuary were varied, not confined to historical portraits and busts as was the one at the College of Experimental Science. Yet it possessed a number of portraits of women exclusively of the blonde type. Many of them were ideal in loveliness. This gallery also contained the masterpieces of their most celebrated sculptors. They were all studies of the female form. I am a connoisseur in art, and nothing that I had ever seen before could compare with these matchless marbles, bewitching in every delicate contour, alluring in softness, but grand and majestic in pose and expression.

But I haunted this gallery for other reasons than its artistic attractions. I was searching for the portrait of a man, or something suggesting his presence. I searched in vain. Many of the paintings were on a peculiar transparent substance that gave to the subject a startlingly vivid effect. I afterward learned that they were imperishable, the material being a translucent adamant of their own manufacture. After a picture was painted upon it, another piece of adamant was cemented over it.

Each day, as my acquaintance with the peculiar institutions and character of the inhabitants of Mizora increased, my perplexity and a certain air of mystery about them increased with it. It was impossible for me not to feel for them a high degree of respect, admiration, and affection. They were ever gentle, tender, and kind to solicitude. To accuse them of mystery were a paradox; and yet they *were* a mystery. In conversation, manners and habits, they were frank to singularity. It was just as common an occurrence for a poem to be read and commented on by its author, as to hear it done by another. I have heard a poetess call attention to the beauties of her own production, and receive praise or adverse criticism with the same charming urbanity.

Ambition of the most intense earnestness was a natural characteristic, but was guided by a stern and inflexible justice. Envy and malice were unknown to them. It was, doubtless, owing to their elevated moral character that courts and legal proceedings had become unnecessary. If a discussion arose between parties involving a question of law, they repaired to the Public Library, where the statute books were kept, and looked up the matter themselves, and settled it as the law directed. Should they fail to interpret the law alike, a third party was selected as referee, but accepted no pay.

Indolence was as much a disgrace to them as is the lack of virtue to the women of my country; hence every citizen, no matter how wealthy, had some regular trade, business or profession. I found those occupations we are accustomed to see accepted by the people of inferior birth and breeding, were there filled by women of the highest social rank, refined in manner and frequently of notable intellectual acquirements. It grew, or was the result of the custom of selecting whatever vocation they felt themselves competent to most worthily fill, and as no social favor or ignominy rested on any kind of labor, the whole community of Mizora was one immense family of sisters who knew no distinction of birth or position among themselves.

There were no paupers and no charities, either public or private, to be found in the country. The absence of poverty such as I knew existed in all civilized nations upon the face of the earth, was largely owing to the cheapness of food. But there was one other consideration that bore vitally upon it. The dignity and necessity of labor was early and diligently impressed upon the mind. The Preceptress said to me:

'Mizora is a land of industry. Nature has taught us the duty of work. Had some of us been born with minds fully matured, or did knowledge come to some as old age comes to all, we might think that a portion was intended to live without effort. But we are all born equal, and labor is assigned to all; and the one who seeks labor is wiser than the one who lets labor seek her.'

Citizens, I learned, were not restrained from accumulating vast wealth had they the desire and ability to do so, but custom imposed upon them the most honorable processes. If a citizen should be found guilty of questionable business transactions, she suffered banishment to a lonely island and the confiscation of her entire estate, both hereditary and acquired. The property confiscated went to the public schools in the town or city where she resided; but never was permitted to augment salaries. I discovered this in the statute books, but not in the memory of any one living had it been found necessary to inflict such a punishment.

'Our laws,' said Wauna, 'are simply established legal advice. No law can be so constructed as to fit every case so exactly that a criminal mind could not warp it into a dishonest use. But in a country like ours, where civilization has reached that state of enlightenment that needs no laws, we are simply guided by custom.'

The love of splendor and ornament was a pronounced characteristic of these strange people. But where gorgeous colors were used, they were always of rich quality. The humblest homes were exquisitely ornamented, and often displayed a luxury that, with us, would have been considered an evidence of wealth.

They took the greatest delight in their beauty, and were exceedingly careful of it. A lovely face and delicate complexion, they averred, added to one's refinement. The art of applying an artificial bloom and fairness to the skin, which I had often seen practiced in my own country, appeared to be unknown to them. But everything savoring of deception was universally condemned. They made no concealment of the practice they resorted to for preserving their complexions, and so universal and effectual were they, that women who, I was informed, had passed the age allotted to the grandmothers in my country, had the smooth brow and pink bloom of cheek that belongs to a more youthful period of life. There was, however, a distinction between youth and old age. The hair was permitted to whiten, but the delicate complexion of old age, with its exquisite coloring, excited in my mind as much admiration as astonishment.

I cannot explain why I hesitated to press my first inquiry as to where the men were. I had put the question to Wauna one day, but she professed never to have heard of such beings. It silenced me – for a time.

'Perhaps it is some extinct animal,' she added, naively. 'We have so many new things to study and investigate, that we pay but little attention to ancient history.'

I bided my time and put the query in another form.

'Where is your other parent?'

She regarded me with innocent surprise. 'You talk strangely. I have but one parent. How could I have any more?'

'You ought to have two.'

She laughed merrily. 'You have a queer way of jesting. I have but one mother, one adorable mother. How could I have two?' and she laughed again.

I saw that there was some mystery I could not unravel at present, and fearing to involve myself in some trouble, refrained from further questioning on the subject. I nevertheless kept a close observance of all that passed, and seized every opportunity to investigate a mystery that began to harass me with its strangeness.

Soon after my conversation with Wauna, I attended an entertainment at which a great number of guests were present. It was a literary festival and, after the intellectual delicacies were disposed of, a banquet followed of more than royal munificence. Toasts were drunk, succeeded by music and dancing and all the gayeties of a festive occasion, yet none but the fairest of fair women graced the scene. It is strange, therefore, that I should have regarded with increasing astonishment and uneasiness a country in all respects alluring to the desires of man – yet found him not there in lordly possession?

Beauty and intellect, wealth and industry, splendor and careful economy, natures lofty and generous, gentle and loving – why has not Man claimed this for himself?

PART II CHAPTER II

I trembled at the suggestion of my own thoughts. Was this an enchanted country? Were the lovely blonde women fairies — or some weird beings of different specie, human only in form? Or was I dreaming?

'I do not believe I understand you,' I said. 'I never heard of a country where there were no men. In my land they are so very, very important.'

'Possibly,' was the placid answer.

'And you are really a nation of women?'

'Yes,' she said. 'And have been for the last three thousand years.'

'Will you tell me how this wonderful change came about?'

'Certainly. But in order to do it, I must go back to our very remote ancestry. The civilization that I shall begin with must have resembled the present condition of your own country as you describe it. Prisons and punishments were prevalent throughout the land.'

I inquired how long prisons and places of punishment had been abolished in Mizora.

'For more than two thousand years,' she replied. 'I have no personal knowledge of crime. When I speak of it, it is wholly from an historical standpoint. A theft has not been committed in this country for many many centuries. And those minor crimes, such as envy, jealousy, malice and falsehood, disappeared a long time ago. You will not find a citizen in Mizora who possesses the slightest trace of any of them.'

'Did they exist in earlier times?'

'Yes. Our oldest histories are but records of a succession of dramas in which the actors were continually striving for power and exercising all of those ancient qualities of mind to obtain it. Plots, intrigues, murders and wars, were the active employments of the very ancient rulers of our land. As soon as death laid its inactivity upon one actor, another took his place. It might have continued so; and we might still be repeating the old tragedy but for one singular event. In the history of your own people you have no doubt observed that the very thing plotted, intrigued and labored for, has in accomplishment proved the ruin of its projectors. You will remark this in the history I am about to relate.

'Many ages ago this country was peopled by two races — male and female. The male race were rulers in public and domestic life. Their supremacy had come down from prehistoric time, when strength of muscle was the only master.

126

Woman was a beast of burden. She was regarded as inferior to man, mentally as well as physically. This idea prevailed through centuries of the earlier civilization, even after enlightenment had brought to her a chivalrous regard from men. But this regard was bestowed only upon the women of their own household, by the rich and powerful. Those women who had not been fortunate enough to have been born in such a sphere of life toiled early and late, in sorrow and privation, for a mere pittance that was barely sufficient to keep the flame of life from going out. Their labor was more arduous than men's, and their wages lighter.

'The government consisted of an aristocracy, a fortunate few, who were continually at strife with one another to gain supremacy of power, or an acquisition of territory. Wars, famine and pestilence were of frequent occurrence. Of the subjects, male and female, some had everything to render life a pleasure, while others had nothing. Poverty, oppression and wretchedness was the lot of the many. Power, wealth and luxury the dower of the few.

'Children came into the world undesired even by those who were able to rear them, and often after an attempt had been made to prevent their coming alive. Consequently numbers of them were deformed, not only physically, but mentally. Under these conditions life was a misery to the larger part of the human race, and to end it by self-destruction was taught by their religion to be a crime punishable with eternal torment by quenchless fire.

'But a revolution was at hand. Stinted toil rose up, armed and wrathful, against opulent oppression. The struggle was long and tragical, and was waged with such rancor and desperate persistence by the insurrectionists, that their women and children began to supply the places vacated by fallen fathers, husbands and brothers. It ended in victory for them. They demanded a form of government that should be the property of all. It was granted, limiting its privileges to adult male citizens.

'The first representative government lasted a century. In that time civilization had taken an advance far excelling the progress made in three centuries previous. So surely does the mind crave freedom for its perfect development. the consciousness of liberty is an ennobling element in human nature. No nation can become universally moral until it is absolutely FREE.

'But this first Republic had been diseased from its birth. Slavery had existed in certain districts of the nation. It was really the remains of a former and more degraded state of society which the new government, in the exultation of its own triumphant inauguration, neglected or lacked the wisdom to remedy. A portion of the country refused to admit slavery within its territory, but pledged itself not to interfere with that which had. Enmities, however, arose between the two sections, which, after years of repression and useless conciliation, culminated in another civil war. Slavery had resolved to absorb more territory, and the free territory had resolved that it should not. The war that followed in consequence severed forever the fetters of the slave and was the primary cause of the extinction of the male race.

'The inevitable effect of slavery is enervating and demoralizing. It is a canker that eats into the vitals of any nation that harbors it, no matter what form it assumes. The free territory had all the vigor, wealth and capacity for long endurance that self-dependence gives. It was in every respect prepared for a long and severe struggle. Its forces were collected in the name of the united government.

'Considering the marked inequality of the combatants the war would necessarily have been of short duration. But political corruption had crept into the trust places of the government, and unscrupulous politicians and office-seekers saw too many opportunities to harvest wealth from a continuation of the war. It was to their interest to prolong it, and they did. They placed in the most responsible positions of the army, military men whose incapacity was well known to them, and sustained them there while the country wept its maimed and dying sons.

'The slave territory brought to the front its most capable talent. It would have conquered had not the resources against which it contended been almost unlimited. Utterly worn out, every available means of supply being exhausted, it collapsed from internal weakness.

'The general government, in order to satisfy the clamors of the distressed and impatient people whose sons were being sacrificed, and whose taxes were increasing, to prolong the war had kept removing and reinstating military commanders, but always of reliable incapacity.

'A man of mediocre intellect and boundless self-conceit

happened to be the commander-in-chief of the government army when the insurrection collapsed. The politicians, whose nefarious scheming had prolonged the war, saw their opportunity for furthering their own interests by securing his popularity. They assumed him to be the greatest military genius that the world had ever produced; as evidenced by his success where so many others had failed. It was known that he had never risked a battle until he was assured that his own soldiers were better equipped and outnumbered the enemy. But the politicians asserted that such a precaution alone should mark him as an extraordinary military genius. The deluded people accepted him as a hero.

The politicians exhausted their ingenuity in inventing honors for him. A new office of special military eminence, with a large salary attached was created for him. He was burdened with distinctions and emoluments, always worked by the politicians, for their benefit. The nation, following the lead of the political leaders, joined in their adulation. It failed to perceive the dangerous path that leads to anarchy and despotism – the worship of one man. It had unfortunately selected one who was cautious and undemonstrative, and who had become convinced that he really was the greatest prodigy that the world had ever produced.

'He was made President, and then the egotism and narrow selfishness of the man began to exhibit itself. He assumed all the prerogatives of royalty that his position would permit. He elevated his obscure and numerous relatives to responsible offices. Large salaries were paid them and intelligent clerks hired by the Government to perform their official duties.

'Corruption spread into every department, but the nation was blind to its danger. The few who did perceive the weakness and presumption of the hero were silenced by popular opinion.

'A second term of office was given him, and then the real character of the man began to display itself before the people. The whole nature of the man was selfish and stubborn. The strongest mental trait possessed by him was cunning.

'His long lease of power and the adulation of his political beneficiaries, acting upon a superlative self-conceit, imbued him with the belief that he had really rendered his country a service so inestimable that it would be impossible for it to entirely liquidate it. He exalted to unsuitable public offices his most intimate friends. They grew suddenly exclusive and aristocratic,

129

forming marriages with eminent families.

'He traveled about the country with his entire family, at the expense of the Government, to gradually prepare the people for the ostentation of royalty. The cities and towns that he visited furnished fetes, illuminations, parades and every variety of entertainment that could be thought of or invented for his amusement or glorification. Lest the parade might not be sufficiently gorgeous or demonstrative he secretly sent agents to prepare the programme and size of his reception, always at the expense of the city he intended to honor with his presence.

'He manifested a strong desire to subvert the will of the people to his will. When informed that a measure he had proposed was unconstitutional, he requested that the constitution be changed. His intimate friends he placed in the most important and trustworthy positions under the Government, and protected them with the power of his own office.

'Many things that were distasteful and unlawful in a free government were flagrantly flaunted in the face of the people, and were followed by other slow, but sure, approaches to the usurpation of the liberties of the Nation. He urged the Government to double his salary as President, and it complied.

'There had long existed a class of politicians who secretly desired to convert the Republic into an Empire, that they might secure greater power and opulence. They had seen in the deluded enthusiasm of the people for one man, the opportunity for which they had long waited and schemed. He was unscrupulous and ambitious, and power had become a necessity to feed the cravings of his vanity.

'The Constitution of the country forbade the office of President to be occupied by one man for more than two terms. The Empire party proposed to amend it, permitting the people to elect a President for any number of terms, or for life if they chose. They tried to persuade the people that the country owed the greatest General of all time so distinctive an honor. They even claimed that it was necessary to the preservation of the Government; that his popularity could command an army to sustain him if he called for it.

'But the people had begun to penetrate the designs of the hero, and bitterly denounced his resolution to seek a third term of power. The terrible corruptions that had been openly protected by him, had advertised him as criminally unfit for so responsible an office. But, alas! the people had delayed too long. They had taken a young elephant into the palace. They had petted and fed him and admired his bulky growth, and now they could not remove him without destroying the building.

'The politicians who had managed the Government so long, proved that they had more power than the people. They succeeded, by practices that were common with politicians in those days, in getting him nominated for a third term. The people, now thoroughly alarmed, began to see their past folly and delusion. They made energetic efforts to defeat his election. But they were unavailing. The politicians had arranged the ballot, and when the counts were published, the hero was declared President for life. When too late the deluded people discovered that they had helped dig the grave for the corpse of their civil liberty, and those who were loyal and had been misled saw it buried with unavailing regret. The undeserved popularity bestowed upon a narrow and selfish nature had been its ruin. In his inaugural address he declared that nothing but the will of the people governed him. He had not desired the office; public life was distasteful to him, yet he was willing to sacrifice himself for the good of his country.

'Had the people been less enlightened, they might have yielded without a murmur; but they had enjoyed too long the privileges of a free Government to see it usurped without a struggle. Tumult and disorder prevailed over the country. Soldiers were called out to protect the new Government, but numbers of them refused to obey. The consequence was they fought among themselves. A dissolution of the Government was the result. The General they had lauded so greatly failed to bring order out of chaos; and the schemers who had foisted him into power, now turned upon him with the fury of treacherous natures when foiled of their prey. Innumerable factions sprung up all over the land, each with a leader ambitious and hopeful to subduing the whole to his rule. They fought until the extermination of the race became imminent, when a new and unsuspected power arose and mastered.

The female portion of the nation had never had a share in the Government. Their privileges were only what the chivalry or kindness of the man permitted. In law, their rights were greatly inferior. The evils of anarchy fell with direct effect upon them. At first, they organized for mutual protection from the lawlessness that prevailed. The organizations grew, united and

131

MARY E. BRADLEY LANE

developed into military power. They used their power wisely, discreetly, and effectively. With consummate skill and energy they gathered the reins of Government in their own hands.

'Their first aim had been only to force the country into peace. The anarchy that reigned had demoralized society, and they had suffered most. They had long pleaded for an equality of citizenship with men, but had pleaded in vain. They now remembered it, and resolved to keep the Government that their wisdom and power had restored. They had been hampered in educational progress. Colleges and all avenues to higher intellectual development had been rigorously closed against them. The professional pursuits of life were denied them. But a few, with sublime courage and energy, had forced their way into them amid the revilings of some of their own sex and opposition of the men. It was these brave spirits who had earned their liberal cultivation with so much difficulty, that had organized and directed the new power. They generously offered to form a Government that should be the property of all intelligent adult citizens, not criminal.

'But these wise women were a small minority. The majority were ruled by the remembrance of past injustice. *They* were now the power, and declared their intention to hold the Government for a century.

'They formed a Republic, in which they remedied many of the defects that had marred the Republic of men. They constituted the Nation an integer which could never be disintegrated by States' Rights ideas or the assumption of State sovereignty.

'They proposed a code of laws for the home government of the States, which every State in the Union ratified as their State Constitution; thus making a uniformity and strength that the Republic of men had never known or suspected attainable.

'They made it a law of every State that criminals could be arrested in any State they might flee to, without legal authority, other than that obtained in the vicinity of the crime. They made a law that criminals, tried and convicted of crime, could not be pardoned without the sanction of seventy-five out of one hundred educated and disinterested people, who should weigh the testimony and render their decision under oath. It is scarcely necessary to add that few criminals ever were pardoned. It removed from the office of Governor the responsibility of pardoning, or rejecting pardons as a purely personal privilege. It abolished the power of rich criminals to bribe their escape from justice; a practice that had secretly existed in the former Republic.

'In forming their Government, the women, who were its founders, profited largely by the mistakes or wisdom displayed in the Government of men. Neither the General Government, nor the State Government, could be independent of the other. A law of the Union could not become such until ratified by every State Legislature. A State law could not become constitutional until ratified by Congress.

'In forming the State Constitutions, laws were selected from the different State Constitutions that had proven wise for state Government during the former Republic. In the Republic of men, each State had made and ratified its own laws, independent of the General Government. The consequence was, no two States possessed similar laws.

'To secure strength and avoid confusion was the aim of the founders of the new Government. The Constitution of the National Government provided for the exclusion of the male sex from all affairs and privileges for a period of one hundred years.

'*At the end of that time not a representative of the sex was in existence.*'

CHAPTER III

I expressed my astonishment at her revelation. Their social life existed under conditions that were incredible to me. Would it be an impertinence to ask for an explanation that I might comprehend? Or was it really the one secret they possessed and guarded from discovery, a mystery that must forever surround them with a halo of doubt, the suggestion of uncanny power? I spoke as deprecatingly as I could. The Preceptress turned upon me a calm but penetrating gaze.

'Have we impressed you as a mysterious people?' she asked.

'Very, very much!' I exclaimed. 'I have at times been oppressed by it.'

'You never mentioned it,' she said, kindly.

'I could not find an opportunity to,' I said.

'It is the custom in Mizora, as you have no doubt observed, never to make domestic affairs a topic of conversation outside of the family, the only ones who would be interested in them; and this refinement has kept you from the solution of our social system. I have no hesitancy in gratifying your wish to comprehend it. The best way to do it is to let history lead up to it, if you have the patience to listen.'

I assured her that I was anxious to hear all she chose to tell. She then resumed:

'The prosperity of the country rapidly increased under the rule of the female Presidents. The majority of them were in favor of a high state of morality, and they enforced it by law and practice. The arts and sciences were liberally encouraged and made rapid advancement. Colleges and schools flourished vigorously, and every branch of education was now open to women.

'During the Republic of men, the government had founded and sustained a military and naval academy, where a limited number of the youth of the country were educated at government expense. The female government re-organized the institutions, substituting the youth of their own sex. They also founded an academy of science, which was supplied with every facility for investigation and progress. None but those having a marked predilection for scientific research could obtain admission, and then it was accorded to demonstrated ability only. This drew to the college the best female talent in the country. The number of applicants was not limited.

'Science had hitherto been, save by a *very* few, an untrodden field to women; but the encouragement and rare facilities offered soon revealed latent talent that developed rapidly. Scarcely half a century had elapsed before the pupils of the college had effected by their discoveries some remarkable changes in living, especially in the prevention and cure of diseases.

'However prosperous they might become, they could not dwell in political security with a portion of the citizens disfranchised. The men were resolved to secure their former power. Intrigues and plots against the government were constantly in force among them. In order to avert another civil war, it was finally decided to amend the constitution, and give them an equal share in the ballot. They had no sooner obtained that than the old practices of the former Republic were resorted to to secure their supremacy in government affairs. The women looked forward to their former subjugation as only a matter of time, and bitterly regretted their inability to prevent it. But at the crisis, a prominent scientist proposed to let the race die out. Science had revealed the Secret of Life.'

She ceased speaking, as though I fully understood her.

'I am more bewildered than ever,' I exclaimed. 'I cannot comprehend you.'

'Come with me,' she said.

I followed her into the Chemist's Laboratory. She bade me look into a microscope that she designated, and tell her what I saw.

'An exquisitely minute cell in violent motion,' I answered.

'Daughter,' she said, solemnly, 'you are now looking upon the germ of *all* Life; be it animal or vegetable, a flower or a human being, it has that one common beginning. We have advanced far enough in Science to control its development. Know that the MOTHER is the only important part of all life. In the lowest organisms no other sex is apparent.'

I sat down and looked at my companion in a frame of mind not easily described. There was an intellectual grandeur in her look and mien that was impressive. Truth sat, like a coronet, upon her brow. The revelation I had so longed for, I now almost regretted. It separated me so far from these beautiful, companionable beings.

'Science has instructed you how to supercede Nature,' I said, finally.

'By no means. It has only taught us how to make her obey us. We cannot *create* Life. We cannot develop it. But we can control Nature's processes of development as we will. Can you deprecate such a power? Would not your own land be happier without idiots, without lunatics, without deformity and disease?'

'You will give me little hope of any radical change in my own lifetime when I inform you that deformity, if extraordinary, becomes a source of revenue to its possessor.'

'All reforms are of slow growth,' she said. 'The moral life is the highest development of Nature. It is evolved by the same slow processes, and like the lower life, its succeeding forms are always higher ones. Its ultimate perfection will be mind, where all happiness shall dwell, where pleasure shall find fruition, and desire its ecstasy.

'It is the duty of every generation to prepare the way for a higher development of the next, as we see demonstrated by

135

Nature in the fossilized remains of long extinct animal life, a preparatory condition for a higher form in the next evolution. If you do not enjoy the fruit of your labor in your own lifetime, the generation that follows you will be the happier for it. Be not so selfish as to think only of your own narrow span of life.'

'By what means have you reached so grand a development?' I asked.

'By the careful study of, and adherence to, Nature's laws. It was long years – I should say centuries – before the influence of the coarser nature of men was eliminated from the present race.

'We devote the most careful attention to the Mothers of our race. No retarding mental or moral influences are ever permitted to reach her. On the contrary, the most agreeable contacts with nature, all that can cheer and ennoble in art or music surround her. She is an object of interest and tenderness to all who meet her. Guarded from unwholesome agitation, furnished with nourishing and proper diet – both mental and physical – the child of a Mizora mother is always an improvement upon herself. With us, childhood has no sorrows. We believe, and the present condition of our race proves, that a being environed from its birth with none but elevating influences, will grow up amiable and intelligent though inheriting unfavorable tendencies.

'On this principle we have ennobled our race and discovered the means of prolonging life and youthful loveliness far beyond the limits known by our ancestors.

'Temptation and necessity will often degrade a nature naturally inclined and desirous to be noble. We early recognized this fact, and that a nature once debased by crime would transmit it to posterity. For this reason we never permitted a convict to have posterity.'

'But how have you become so beautiful?' I asked. 'For, in all my journeys, I have not met an uncomely face or form. On the contrary, all the Mizora women have perfect bodies and lovely features.'

'We follow the gentle guidance of our mother, Nature. Good air and judicious exercise for generations and generations before us have helped. Our ancestors knew the influence of art, sculpture, education, painting and music, which they were trained to appreciate.'

'But has not nature been a little generous to you?' I inquired.

'Not more so than she will be to any people who follow her

136

laws. When you first came here you had an idea that you could improve nature by crowding your lungs and digestive organs into a smaller space than she, the maker of them, intended them to occupy.

'If you construct an engine, and then cram it into a box so narrow and tight that it cannot move, and then crowd on the motive power, what would you expect?

'Beautiful as you think my people, and as they really are, yet, by disregarding nature's laws, or trying to thwart her intentions, in a few generations to come, perhaps even in the next, we could have coarse features and complexions, stoop shoulders and deformity.

'It has required patience, observation and care on the part of our ancestors to secure to us the priceless heritage of health and perfect bodies. Your people can acquire them by the same means.'

8
HIERO-SALEM: THE VISION OF PEACE
(1889)

———————————*———————————

Eveleen Laura Knaggs Mason (1838-1914)

Born in Boston, Eveleen Laura Knaggs 'in her early life' married the Rev. A. Frank Mason, D.D., a Baptist minister residing in Brookline. They had no children. The author was active in initiating a prototype of the Traveler's Aid, to meet young girls and women at railroad stations and steamboat landings. In addition she cared for orphaned or neglected children in her home. Eventually her husband's invalidism and her own health 'prevented her from continuing her activity in uplifting work.'

Between 1883 and 1909 she published six books, all developing themes appearing in Hiero-Salem. *Subtitled 'The Vision of Peace. A Fiction Founded on Ideals which Are Grounded in the Real that Is Greater than the Greatest of All Human Ideals' and dedicated 'to the upbuilding of Futurity by the Power of Freedom's purity,' Mason used as epigraph Coleridge's observation, 'The truth is, a great* mind *must be androgynous.' Mason used the label 'dualized' for those able to call upon their full human capacities beyond stereotypic gender limits. Set between 1849 and 1889, her story depicts one Midwestern couple's efforts to live their vision of a better future by raising their son and daughter according to ideals revealed in the United States Bill of Rights, Judaeo-Christian religious principles, and feminist values. Althea Eloi and Daniel Heem establish the Eloiheem (female and male aspects of the divine), household into which Robert then Ethel are born. The household expands into a community including members of diverse race, class, and religion. Peace and co-operation are communal goals, which reverence for a female principle will permit to evolve.*

REFERENCES
'Devoted Her Life to Good Work,' *Boston Evening Transcript*,
Sept. 8, 1914, p. 2, col. 6; Barbara Quissell, 'The New World
That Eve Made,' in *America as Utopia*, ed. Kenneth M.
Roemer (New York: Franklin, 1981), pp. 154-5, 171-2; 'Book
Reviews: *The Doings of the Dualized*,' *The Woman's Tribune*
(Washington, D.C.), 17 (10 March, 1900), and Mason's reply
'Preface and Purpose of "Hiero-Salem." By its Author,'
appearing 17 (7 April, 1900): 27.

SELECTION
Includes pp. 89-92, 300-4, 351-2, 505-6.

HIERO-SALEM: THE VISION OF PEACE

——————————————*——————————————

The West in those days was not the place in which to cultivate easy manners, but it was the place in which each person could find vent for his or her determination to make the most and best of self. So, even if this self were a bit boisterous and egotistical, it was yet a brilliantly adventurous and healthful self. There was so much work of every good kind to be done, and every one was so actively engaged with large plans, that each freely hastened along his and her chosen path, sure of results and fearless of criticism.

Althea was by no means slow to perceive and to avail herself of these advantages. She was only too glad that her environments were so well adapted to her tastes and her purposes. To her, this Western vivacity and joyous young energy was like exhilarating wine, and to her the Western man and woman seemed quite the typical American citizen. For were they not making a civilization for the coming generation? Meanwhile, she silently surmised that it was Daniel's opinion of what should go to the making up of the on-coming civilization, which had fixed him in his practical decision that the Eloiheem* home should bring to the community, not more of boisterous energy, but instead, should bring to it a new element of care-free repose.

As a result of this diversity of methods and manners, it came about that, when the Eloiheems had been for six years in their new home, Mrs. Eloiheem had three times gathered up land to hold on speculation, and had made other and lucky transactions satisfactory to herself. Meanwhile, Daniel's private

*'Eloiheem' comes from the Hebrew meaning 'male and female attributes of the Divine.'

opinion regarding the righteousness of speculating in land as greatly differed from Althea's and from the popular idea of the matter, as did his opinion on almost every other subject. Indeed, in those days, whatever he had to write or say on any topic seemed almost a burlesque on the bustling, self-seeking life of the people of that new and hurrying country. Whatever other change had come to Daniel, there had come to him no change in his satisfaction with his growing vision of the unity of life, nor in his recognition of the futility of an attempt on his part to live midst the strifes which were so satisfactory to Althea. So it had easily come about that each had fallen into the life most congenial.

The result — as it looked to the outer world — was, that Daniel Heem dwelt at home, with the boy and the garden, while Althea, consciously handsome, well dressed, and popular, led an out-door life, busy about, no one particularly inquired what, seeing every one else was equally busy and self-concerned. . . .

Robert was eight years old when one day Althea came home, looking and feeling as though she had the world under her feet. 'Why don't all married people take up life, each following his and her bent as we have done?' she asked. 'But of course, as Mr. Chelmitch says, few men would be willing to do as you do, Daniel. I told him, the money-fight was odious to you; that you better liked the solitude and silence of home-making. I told him I could not well do that part; but that I could see through the chances of a business plan a week ahead of his time. He said that men did not like to have women round in business, because in the money-fight it was not always easy to be chivalrous; and that women ought to be at home waiting to make things pleasant to the tired brains of the family. I told him we hadn't any tired brains in our family. Presently he said he would call up this evening. Then I asked him if Mrs. Chelmitch thought woman's place was at home waiting to rest tired brains? And when he said "certainly," I told him he would probably find her there, then, waiting to rest his. But as we had nothing of that kind in our family I would not for the world introduce such a thing into the cheerful Eloiheem evenings! So then he swore a whirling, Western oath, from which I escaped unscathed.'

Althea had told all this rapidly with a breezy tone and a laugh, neither constrained nor crude, adding, as she observed the flush that mounted Daniel's cheek, –

'O, it is a life worth living to live as we live! Why don't others unite their individualities?' thinking meanwhile that she was glad she had told of that disagreeable occurrence. For one effect and accompaniment of her free intercourse with men in business was to make her cordial to all and intimate with none, fearless in manner and guarded in personal reserves outside the house, and sufficiently frank at home.

Robert had looked quickly from Althea to Daniel, then steadily onto the floor, not even raising his eyes when Daniel had answered, –

'There is a whimsical receipt "how to make hare-pie," which begins with the words, "first catch the hare." And a receipt of how to unite the individuality of two persons in marriage should likewise commence with the words, "first catch your *individuals*." '

'We are becoming a conglomerate household, Robert. You see, we have now Tama and 'Dolph, the colored people, who are warm-hearted Methodists; and we have now, with us, Mrs. Mancredo's old coachman and his family, Sullivan, who is a Fenian, and a drinker of intoxicants; a Chinese laundry-man and a Japanese gardener, one a Confucian and the other a Hindoo; and we have Mrs. Mancredo, Baptist and Yankee, late from Boston; and Mrs. Aubrey, Romanist and Southerner, half French and wholly un-reconstructed. Besides these, there are the Othniels, brother and two married sisters, young, proud-spirited Hebrews, relatives of the Eloi family. Besides, of the family, but not dwelling permanently here, is Bertha Gemacht, of whom you have heard; a goddess-like-natured girl, but who, born under the difficulties of illegitimacy, has passed on to a child she was duped into bearing the same difficulties mid which she herself was born.

'But she has learned her lesson, – and it is a big one as unfolded by Ethel, – and is making use of all that she is, for the benefit of other such mothers as herself. Mothers, by the way, Robert, of the one sort who legally own the children to whom they give birth.

'Oh, had you never thought of that? I believe it is a fact, that in many states and countries, while mothers whose children are born out of wedlock own *those* children, married women are not everywhere the legal owners of their children.'

Robert had paled. Daniel continued. . . .

'It is a *Kinde*-garten, a Nature-garden, in which Ethel, the Nature-gardener, is working with nature, as women naturally do, instead of working against nature, as man-made society has heretofore done. Ethel serenely secures that nothing which has been begun shall be left to go to waste for want of timely encouragement and added suggestion in the way of carrying on the good beginnings.

'The delight here in doing well is contagious.

'True, the Chinaman did a little object to giving up his peculiar style of sprinkling the clothes; but he is satisfied now with using a rubber-bulb sprinkler instead of his mouth. He laundries all the clothes for the household; the Japanese gardener supplies us all with flowers, and the cook and her helpers supply us all with good food.

'John Sullivan at first felt it would spoil Nora for a poor man's wife if she had the washing and ironing and the cooking and dish-washing all done for her, and the clothes for herself and family all made by the "clothes artists;" and there's a long story about all that which will make a book in itself, when your mother gets at it; for the Othniels – two married sisters and their husbands – are the clothes artists. There are *four* children there. And Nora has six; and Nora, who is a great mother-heart, washes and dresses the ten of them. She was educated in a nunnery, and knows how to do some ordinary things extraordinarily well; especially to wash, dress, and comfort babies. And, besides, for every one here has a right to his and her pet way of making money, she knows how to mend and restore to their first beauty all textures coarse and fine. So *that* is her pet play at work. The Othniels are really clothes *artists* and fine judges of reliable material for clothes. They have time given them to do honest and beautiful work, and no anxiety to harass them while they are doing it. Oh, your mother's books will tell the story a few years hence.

'Of course, we Eloiheems make a point here, and wherever we reach people we make a point of protecting against itself the too self-neglectful woman-*heart*. For it is the woman-*heart* which the fearers of the woman-*brain* have so disproportion-ately cultivated in woman. The law of this house, you know, interposes, like a flaming sword, at the gate where liberty is met by incoming license. A husband's liberty tends to the *tres-pas*; that is, to go a step too far; because false teachers for centuries have taught woman to subject herself to her *husband's* demands, instead of leaving her to her inherent knowledge that not her husband's demands, but her self-recognized needs as priestess of the mother-mystery, is her great concern! Of course, we arrange things so that women under this law do not *have* to sin against themselves or their children in order to try to keep the peace with their husbands. *We sustain woman in that perfect freedom in which character-growths are best put forth; love of purity, self-poise, and love of the development of the higher hidden germs of new delights in life.*

'Understand, Robert? – Now, mark you, seeing that woman transmits her character-growths to her *sons*, this cultivation of free intellectual power, and of the love of purity, self-poise, and of the *love of the development* of the hidden germs of a life of new delights, – all this cultivation of a new order of faculties, I say, will be in the future the dower that free, natural women will give to their sons. Then these sons, in turn, will transmit their gains to their daughters, and so on and on. It takes time, but so it does to grow an oak or a cedar, and yet more time to make the diamond. But the eternal years are ours. The Roman church would have done all this long ago if they had had the wisdom to give perfect freedom to woman, and if they had *not* so foolishly feared her supremacy.

'I am unable to tell you what we are doing. But, of course, in true kindergarten-way, we are emphasizing the methods by which the ability of a crude workman is trained to that of the skilled artisan; and the skill of the artisan is then developed into that of the artist. We are a large, old company of associates, gods and goddesses, young and old, whom Ethel and I began picking up, and setting to work, and initiating into our plans slowly, on the day when she, at twelve years old, "went about the Father's business" of gathering up the fragments, that nothing should be lost. And now the House that Jack built is not only a center of influences rather far outreaching, but I myself, with Ethel, give three hours a day to the kindergarten work and play, at which the six little Catholics and the six little Hebrews are taught as you and Ethel were taught; and their parents, and all of the household who choose, come in and "play with the children," as we, Robert, used all to play together. That is the way we are going on.'

. . . . Ethel said, as simply as a child, –

'That is what I should have thought, too, if I were that slug living down there in the under-world among the beginnings of things. For probably I should have been so busy crawling about in the darkness that slugs enjoy, that I should never have noticed when, one day, a ray of light, striking down into the mud, won away that little wormlike-looking thing, and strengthened it to climb up and up, out of reach of my eyes, such as they were. So that, if any one had said to me, "Look, slug, that is a lily bud which is warming into life at your side. Look up, now, look up above you! She is out of the mud. She is standing, head up, in the midst of water, through which she is making her way! There are liquid heights above this mud. And through those heights the lily bud is climbing, drawn up, and up, by a thing called Light and heat! Away and away she will go, till some day she will find herself on the top of dancing waves; and there she will blossom, a circumference of purity with a heart of gold. A heart like, somewhat like, the rolling orb of furious fire, whose ray struck at and won her out of the mud at your side!" – I say, if some one had told me, the poor slug, these great things in ever so loud a tone, I, knowing nothing of "dancing waves," "heart of gold," nothing of heights, or light, or heat, and caring nothing, would never have heeded anything but my own life in the mud-world below! I would neither have believed nor disbelieved, I simply should have known nothing of things quite out of my world.

'So, when, some day, long afterwards, I might have seen at my side that which this slug here in the mud may be able to see – that is, the wormlike-looking thing which Nora pointed out, see it! – well, if I, as a slug, saw it, I, who had had no understanding of what I had been told of the uprising of the lily bud to its lily life upon the dancing wave, would now neither know nor care anything about who or what was this wormlike-looking thing, which is pressing head downward into the mud. For as I could have had no idea of all that had come and gone since a bud had climbed up to float in freedom on the dancing wave, under the heat of the ball of fire which rolled through the blue of the expanse above, still less could I understand, though one should tell me, that this Climber, having done all that which it befits a climbing lily bud blossomed into maturity to do, had, at last, *holily turned on its stem, and had come back down into the mud, to plant its life there, that from it new lilies might grow.*'

'O Madame!' cried the Japanese, '*down* into the mud, did you say? O Madame, down is up, in a world that turns. In my land, too, we tell it with awe, that "the Lotus springs from the mud!" And there, as here, we know that when the lily turns on her stem, and goes back to plant her life in the mud, she but seems to begin again with the beginnings of things; for that at the climax of her glory she had exhaled into the upper air an order of life, which could not be used in a world of *beginnings of things!* But, as that which was planted downward was lily-life, so was that which was exhaled upward. For the Tree of Life has roots both ways, so our sages tell us.' . . .

[Robert said to Ethel,] '. . . . You remind me that I, like thousands and thousands of real *gentle*-men, have had from birth a most majestic womanliness of being within, but that this womanliness is popularly covered over and trodden under foot by the Evil of all the old evils of other incarnations: — by the madman in us which ravages and rends the Ego from its own beloved comrade and compeer. Yes, I see. I was insane when I fought, feared, and yet desired to have, own, and dominate all womanhood, while yet among them all I found nowhere my real other self. I found no one to whom I honestly wished to be tied for this life, let alone Eternity. No, no more than either you, Alice, Daniel, or Althea sees in any man or woman the *real* other self!

'Oh, Ethel, it is like a new sight of things. For I have seen, I have re-cognized that other half of me, which makes of my divorced, fragmentary self a better being, a full-orbed duality, with *just such a work before its two halves* as was before Miss Eloi and Daniel Heem, when they (two entities) set about demonstrating the nuptial diagram of the Eloiheems. See? Mine is the business to, in a like way, work out the full development and the final Self-unification of *my OWN duality!*

'Oh, Ethel, I see now. This glorious work is so nearly done in your soul's palace, that, self-poised, self-continent, the dual power of the opposite currents within you generates a resistless force like that of the electric dynamo, and which, like that, is competent to utter itself in deeds of dire or of divine significance.

'And as for future marriages of the coming race, I see well that in the future it will not be an attempt to make of "two halves a whole one," with a result that that "one" shall be a miserably shackled and dominated man or woman. It will be rather that two times One Whole One is forever two Whole Ones, each of whom is a self-poised Continent of purpose, powers, and achievements. Oh, my sister, I am ready to become an Eloiheem.'

9
'A FEMININE ICONOCLAST'
(1889)

❋

Mary H. Ford (n.d.)

Of Mary H. Ford we know that she published Which Wins
(1891) and the following critique of Edward Bellamy's Looking
Backward *(1888) in* The Nationalist, *a magazine promulgating
his views. Ford calls Bellamy especially to task for his patronizing and paternalistic view of women. For instance, recall the
character Doctor Leete assuring the narrator that 'under no
circumstances is a woman permitted to follow any employment
not perfectly adapted both as to kind and degree of labor, to
her sex.' In the industrial army, she is 'under an entirely
different discipline.' Leete concludes, women are 'wardens of
the world to come,' a duty they respect with 'a sense of
religious consecration. It is a cult in which they educate their
daughters from childhood' (pp. 173, 180). Though as late as
1960 this sex-bias passed unrecognized, it is clear today.*

*Ford's critique takes the form of a conversation between two
women riding a street car, one of whom thrusts sharply satiric
jibes at Bellamy. An eavesdropper reports.*

REFERENCES
Edward Bellamy, *Looking Backward, 2000-1887* (1888; rpt.
New York: New American Library, 1960): Forward by Erich
Fromm; Vicki L. Hill, ' "A Distinctly Curious Collection of
Human Beings": American Women Writers in the Age of
Reform,' *PMLA* 98 (1983): 1094.

SELECTION
Complete.

'A FEMININE ICONOCLAST'

———————*———————

As I was sitting in the street-car the other day, the conductor rang the bell, and two ladies sat down beside me who were sufficiently beyond the ordinary in appearance to attract attention, and as the car was not full and they were animated, I became an involuntary listener. The younger one, of robust and beautifully developed figure, appeared rather fatigued, and, her companion alluding to the fact, she responded with considerable vivacity: 'Yes, I should think I might look tired, considering the number of shocks I've received, and the extent to which my opinions have been altered since I left home this morning!'

'Why, what is the matter?' replied her friend, looking decidedly amused, 'I should think you were sufficiently accustomed to have your opinions assailed and could resist all attack!'

'Assailed!' responded the other, 'certainly, but assailed and shaken are two very different things. I went down town this morning an enthusiastic Nationalist, and now I don't know what I am!'

'Dear me! that is rather serious,' answered the first speaker, for evidently Nationalism had been a strong enthusiasm with her young friend, 'but what is the matter with Mr. Bellamy now?'

'Oh! Mr. Bellamy is not exactly accountable for my idiosyncrasies, of course,' said the young lady with an amused little laugh, 'but I'll tell you how it is. You know,' she began playing with the tassel of her rather elegant umbrella, 'I have been connected with a newspaper for the last two years, and my salary has been a very acceptable addition to the family income since father's death. My brothers have not been

149

especially successful bread-winners,' (there was a little sadness in her voice as she said this) 'and my youngest brother would not be able to complete his college course without my assistance. Well, this morning at breakfast the young man commenced in that sophomoric tone which I never can endure, "Frances, I have finished Looking Backward," (his profound studies kept him from reading it before, you know,) "and I must say I have been much struck with it, especially with its treatment of the woman question. You see it fixes that up very nicely. It's all right for you women to settle your own affairs, but it might be a trifle irritating, I'll confess, to have you interfering with ours. And then, of course, in Mr. Bellamy's adjustment of the case, the question of capacity is not touched upon. There's no doubt that women can arrange their own matters properly without the intervention of men," – he had risen now, and stood before the fire-place curling the ends of his moustache – "and it's perfectly proper that they should do so." "How kind you are, Arthur," (I replied), "you don't happen to remember the name of that young woman, do you, who took a prize in the Harvard Annex some time ago? The prize was for the best essay descriptive of Rome in the time of the Caesars, I believe." No, Arthur didn't remember, – he has a very convenient forgetfulness about such things. "Well," I went on, "the prize was open to the whole college for competition. The successful young lady from the Annex signed her name to the winning essay just with initials – E. T. Dawson, or something like that, – and they thought the winner was a man, but when the judges found that they had unintentionally bestowed the prize upon a woman, they refused to give her the full amount of the prize money, which was one hundred dollars, but offered her half, which she very properly declined. I think in that case women would, as you say, have settled their own affairs properly, and they would have given E. T. Dawson all of the prize money." Arthur stopped curling his moustache at that, and I went out in a great hurry, fearful I might be ungenerously tempted to remind him to how great an extent I am managing his affairs just at present. Soon after, as I was walking down town I met Mr. Eaton; you know what a delicate little creature he is; well, he walked beside me while he was waiting for his car and talked Nationalism, he can't talk anything else nowadays, and presently he said: "Oh! we are going to provide for you ladies, Miss Frances, and we will be very careful of you, too; we shan't let you do anything beyond your strength, or exhaust yourselves with grinding arduous labors," and he skipped beside me with his cane making circles in the air, for all the world like a benignant musquito. "Mr. Eaton," I said, "are you going to take a car? Yes? well, your office is not so far down town as mine, but I walk every morning because I enjoy it, and I should think any woman who dressed sensibly and was not an invalid would do the same. I rather enjoy labor," I added, – for I certainly do, – "and if I had to choose between being a blacksmith and doing nothing, I certainly should be a blacksmith!" He grew so pale over that remark, I was glad his car came along, and I left him and walked on. When I reached the office, there lay The Dawn for this month. I opened it with a great deal of pleasure, for I had liked the preceding numbers exceedingly, and turning to the editorial page, the first thing I saw was an allusion to Nationalism and the woman question. Speaking of the same pet adjustment of woman's judicial functions which Arthur had alluded to, the editor says: "This would be justice to all, without doing violence to the true distinctions between man and woman which some fear would be violated in the ordinary development of woman's suffrage." Now that might have looked very innocent had I not already been exasperated by Arthur's much more frank statement of the same thing, but that had opened my eyes and I began to feel as if cords were tied around my ankles. Are the Nationalists afraid, I thought, that women will expect too much, that they already begin to draw the line so carefully beyond which we cannot go? I wonder if there are women angels,' she added, fixing her eyes dreamily on the distant sky, 'for if there is any sex in the other world, I don't want to go there, unless I can be a snail or a lizard or something so amorphous that my higher nature will never bother me.'

'But surely,' said her friend with a little sigh, 'it is better to have some privileges and liberties than to have none at all, isn't it?'

'No!' replied Miss Frances decidedly, 'I don't want to have any privileges doled out to me like slices of gingerbread cut thin! I want to feel that I can stand up under any star and shine just as independently and vigorously as I choose. The proper distinction between man and woman!' she added vindictively, 'what would I not give to be a plain human being, instead of having been born an ornament to society!'

'I heard of a woman today who would suit you,' replied her friend, 'I think you might call her a plain human being almost, in spite of her sex.'

'Who is that?' exclaimed Miss Frances eagerly.

'She is a delicate little woman not so stalwart as you are,' continued her friend, 'and was professor in a state university where the admirable law is in force that a married woman cannot hold the office of teacher. She fell in love with one of her pupils, and when he was fitted to take her place married him and let him be professor. After awhile as the proprieties were satisfied by the fact that the office was held by a male, the little wife let her husband go to Europe to complete his education, while she acted as substitute for him at home, did his work and supported him and their little girl during his absence. How she made the two ends meet out of her meagre salary I don't know, but she did all of that and smiles about it.'

'That was noble indeed!' cried Miss Frances heartily. 'And her husband, what does he think of woman's sphere and the proper distinction between the sexes?'

'What he?' asked the lady with a hearty laugh, 'I think if his wife wanted to enter the lists against John Sullivan he would consider it a perfectly legitimate activity for her, and he would have no hope whatever for Mr. Sullivan in the contest.'

Miss Frances sighed a trifle enviously. 'Ah! that is what I call love,' she remarked admiringly, 'Do you know,' she asked on a sudden, 'whether she darns his socks?'

'Very likely she does, if occasion demands it,' replied her friend, laughing still more heartily, 'but I happen to know likewise that he frequently mends his own socks and her stockings, while she reads Goethe to him.'

'I wish I could meet that man,' cried Miss Frances, 'and introduce him to Mr. Bellamy. I didn't tell you my last experience,' she added, seeing her friend's mystification. 'There is a young man on our journal who' (Miss Frances blushed a little, while she looked indignant) 'sometimes makes love to me – or at least says things which are very disagreeable.'

'Surely,' interpolated her friend mischievously, 'the two terms are not synonymous!'

'At any rate,' continued Miss Frances, 'he was talking to me this morning about Nationalism and he took occasion to quote a remark Mr. Bellamy makes descriptive of the marital happiness that will accrue from his system in those pleasant days when it is established. He says that husbands will have more time for love. I never thought any thing about it until that young man spoke of it, but I wish now that Mr. Bellamy had dilated upon the subject more fully, for certainly,' concluded Miss Frances with great decision, 'if his idea of love is the same as this young man's, I should wish that my husband had very little time for it.'

'Now, Frances!' exclaimed her friend smiling, 'you know that you are extremely romantic.'

'I know I am romantic,' cried Miss Frances, 'but you remember what Balzac says, there is nothing more ennobling than *l'Amour*, nothing so degrading as *la Passion*, and think of it!' she continued, 'the French language makes *l'Amour* masculine, and *la Passion* feminine; could ever anything show more plainly what men have made of women? When our Elysium comes,' she added, 'there will be no such thing as *la Passion*; *l'Amour* will bind the hearts of men and women so that they will go through life hand in hand without bothering their heads about the "proper distinction between the sexes." Then husband and friend will be synonymous terms, and a wife will not have to be continually adding a new patch to her opinions to make them fit those of her husband.'

'Do you think you will ever marry, Frances?' asked her friend, smiling as she paused for breath.

'Yes,' replied the young lady quickly; 'whenever I can find a Nationalist who I am sure will never want to go to the Club to talk over things!'

'But I thought you were not a Nationalist any longer, though I cannot see exactly why,' said Miss Frances's friend, after a momentary pause.

'Well,' replied Miss Frances slowly and thoughtfully, 'you see women have never yet had a fair chance at any thing. They have always been put in the position of mendicants, and if they received anything, the world said, in effect, "you are objects of charity and we will assist you." Even in the days of the Troubadours when poets were singing the names of fair ladies all over the land, and when those ladies' hearts must have been full of poetry, they could not sing. Oh, no! convention required them simply to be well-schooled and well-dressed and manage their adorers adroitly!'

'But I don't see what that has to do with Nationalism,'

interjected her friend gently.

'You don't?' responded Miss Frances sharply, 'then I suppose you fail to realize how selfish I am. I thought Nationalism was going to offer an equal chance to all mankind irrespective of sex, but it does nothing of the kind so far, it simply leaves us in the position of mendicants, saying, – very sweetly to be sure – "I'm going to take care of you, I'll let you do certain things which I am sure you are fitted for, and I'll see that you are fairly treated in doing them and that you have equal wages." That is very good,' admitted Miss Frances, 'but it is not what I want, and I am considering whether it is worth while to pin my faith to something which for me will only be a make-shift – whether in fact I can be magnanimous,' she added smiling.

'What would you have?' asked her friend thoughtfully.

'That is soon told,' replied Miss Frances. 'I prefer that the Nationalists should say to me, "my dear young lady, we don't know what you are fitted for, but we want you to do whatever you are capable of doing best, and if you cannot tell what this is, we will give you an education which will enable you to find it out for yourself." That is what I should call fair, and as long as they do not say this, they don't know what freedom is.'

'You see,' responded her friend, 'they have no conception of what a woman's life is, and how convention hedges her about even in this nineteenth century.'

'Yes, and do you know how I would teach them?' exclaimed Miss Frances warmly, 'I should like to take every Nationalist, and bind him hand and foot for a day to one of those straight-backed gilded chairs one sees so often in old palaces. I should bind him with golden chains, fan him with perfumed fans, and feed him meanwhile with ice cream and French candy. Then he would realize what it is to be a *fortunate* woman, and why I want freedom and fresh air in such large, unlimited doses!'

The two ladies left the car at this point in the conversation, and as I observed the swinging graceful gait of Miss Frances, I could not avoid thinking to myself, 'what dreadful things they said, and how true most of them are!' But surely, my thoughts ran on, Miss Frances will not give up her allegiance to the Nationalist cause. It can not afford to lose such staunch confederates.

10
UNVEILING A PARALLEL:
A ROMANCE
(1893)

---------------------------------*---------------------------------

Alice Ilgenfritz Jones (d. 1906) and Ella Merchant (n.d.)

Originally published over the authorship of 'Two Women of the West,' this Utopia again baffles efforts to learn about the writers. Of Ella Merchant, we know only her name. Alice Ilgenfritz Jones wrote three other books. Using the pseudonym 'Ferris Jerome,' she published Highwater Mark *(1879). Subsequently, she wrote about a quadroon in* Beatrice of Bayou Teche *(1895) and an historical romance in* The Chevalier of St. Denis *(1900).* Beatrice *is interesting in that the heroine resolves the dilemma of her love relationship with a white man not by self-sacrifice, but by establishing sisterly companionship with an Italian exile, a Boston marriage on a Batavian isle.*

The parallel unveiled in this novel emerges through several contrasts: between women and men, between two Martian societies – Thursia and Caskia, and between Mars and Earth. The central parallel unveiled is that between the sexes: capacities are revealed to be more parallel than different, varying according to social context. Both societies appear almost gender-role reversals compared to Earth; in Thursia, women enjoy the range of negative and positive freedoms men enjoy on Earth while in Caskia, traits ideal for nineteenth-century women typify both sexes. Given the constraints of 'true womanhood' Caskia is far less lively than Thursia, the first society visited by the Earth-man narrator. His conversations follow, first with Severnius – brother to Elodia, a model Thursian woman – and then with Elodia herself. Education, work, and marriage are the topics discussed.

REFERENCES
Barbara Quissell, 'The New World That Eve Made' in *America*

as Utopia, ed. Kenneth M. Roemer (New York: Franklin, 1981), pp. 155-9, 172.

SELECTION
Includes pp. 40-58, 158-78, 182-7.

UNVEILING A PARALLEL:
A ROMANCE

————————————— ✳ —————————————

'My father was a banker,' he said, 'and very rich. My sister inherited his gift and taste for finance. I took after my mother's family, who were scientists. We were trained, of course, in our early years according to our respective talents. At our parents' death we inherited their fortune in equal shares. Elodia was prepared to take up my father's business where he left it. In fact he had associated her with himself in the business for some time previous to his departure, and she has carried it on very successfully ever since.'

'She is a banker!' said I.

'Yes. I, myself, have always had a liking for astronomy, and I have been employed, ever since I finished my education, in the State Observatory.'

'And how do you employ your capital?' I asked.

'Elodia manages it for me. It is all in the bank, or in investments which she makes. I use my dividends largely in the interest of science. The State does a great deal in that direction, but not enough.'

'And what, may I ask, does she do with her surplus, – your sister, I mean, – she must make a great deal of money?'

'She re-invests it. She has a speculative tendency, and is rather daring; though they tell me she is very safe – far-sighted, or large-sighted, I should call it. I do not know how many great enterprises she is connected with, – railroads, lines of steamers, mining and manufacturing operations. And besides, she is public-spirited. She is much interested in the cause of education, – practical education for the poor especially. She is president of the school board here in the city, and she is also a member of the city council. A great many of our modern improvements are due to her efforts.'

My look of amazement arrested his attention.

'Why are you so surprised?' he asked. 'Do not your women engage in business?'

'Well, not to such an extraordinary degree,' I replied. 'We have women who work in various ways, but there are very few of them who have large business interests, and they are not entrusted with important public affairs, such as municipal government and the management of schools!'

'Oh!' returned Severnius with the note of one who does not quite understand. 'Would you mind telling me why? Is it because they are incapable, or – unreliable?'

Neither of the words he chose struck me pleasantly as applied to my countrywomen. I remembered that I was the sole representative of the Earth on Mars, and that it stood me in hand to be careful about the sort of impressions I gave out. It was as if I were on the witness' stand, under oath. Facts must tell the story, not opinions, – though personally I have great confidence in my opinions. I thought of our government departments where women are the experts, and of their almost spotless record for faithfulness and honesty, and replied:

'They are both capable and reliable, in as far as they have had experience. But their chances have been circumscribed, and I believe they lack the inclination to assume grave public duties. I fear I cannot make you understand, – our women are so different, so unlike your sister.'

Elodia was always my standard of comparison.

'Perhaps you men take care of them all,' suggested Severnius, 'and they have grown dependent. We have some such women here.'

'O, I do not think it is that entirely,' said I. 'For in my city alone, more than a hundred and seventy thousand women support not only themselves, but others who are dependent upon them.'

'Ah, indeed! but how?'

'By work.'

'You mean servants?'

'Not so-called. I mean intelligent, self-respecting women; teachers, clerks, stenographers, type-writers.'

'I should think it would be more agreeable, and easier, for them to engage in business as our women do.'

'No doubt it would,' I replied, feeling myself driven to a close scrutiny of the Woman Question, as we call it, for the first time in my life. For I saw that my friend was deeply interested and wanted to get at the literal truth. 'But the women of my country,' I went on, 'the self-supporting ones, do not have control of money. They have a horror of speculation, and shrink from taking risks and making ventures, the failure of which would mean loss or ruin to others. A women's right to make her living is restricted to the power within herself, powers of brain and hand. She is a beginner, you know. She has not yet learned to make money by the labor of others; she does not know how to manipulate those who are less intelligent and less capable than herself, and to turn their ignorance and helplessness to her own account. Perhaps I had better add that she is more religious than man, and is sustained in this seeming injustice by something she calls conscience.'

Severnius was silent for a moment; he had a habit of setting his reason to work and searching out explanations in his own mind, of things not easily understood.

As a rule, the Marsians have not only very highly developed physical faculties, such as sight and hearing, but remarkably acute intellects. They let no statement pass without examination, and they scrutinize facts closely and seek for causes.

'If so many women', said he, 'are obliged to support themselves and others beside, as you say, by their work simply, they must receive princely wages, – and of course they have no responsibilities, which is a great saving of energy.'

I remembered having heard it stated that in New York City, the United States Bureau gives the average of women's wages – leaving out domestic service and unskilled labor – as five dollars and eighty-five cents per week. I mentioned the fact, and Severnius looked aghast.

'What, a mere pittance!' said he. 'Only about a third as much as I give my stableman. But then the conditions are different, no doubt. Here in Thursia that would no more than fight off the wolf, as we say, – the hunger and cold. It would afford no taste of the better things, freedom, leisure, recreation, but would reduce life to its lowest terms, – mere existence.'

'I fear the conditions are much the same with us,' I replied.

'And do your women submit to such conditions, – do they not try to alter them, throw them off?'

'They submit, of course,' I said; 'I never heard of a revolt or an insurrection among them! Though there seems to be growing up among them, lately, a determination strong as death, to work out of those conditions as fast as may be. They realize – just as men have been forced to realize in this century – that work of the hands cannot compete with work of machines, and that trained brains are better capital than trained fingers. So, slowly but surely, they are reaching up to the higher callings and working into places of honor and trust. The odds are against them, because the 'ins' always have a tremendous advantage over the 'outs.' The women, having never been in, must submit to a rigid examination and extraordinary tests. They know that, and they are rising to it. Whenever, it is said, they come into competition with men, in our colleges and training schools, they hold their own and more.'

'What are they fitting for?' asked Severnius.

'Largely for the professions. They are becoming doctors, lawyers, editors, artists, writers. The enormous systems of public schools in my own and other countries is entirely in their hands, – except of course in the management and directorship.'

'Except in the management and directorship?' echoed Severnius.

'Of course they do not provide and disburse the funds, see to the building of school-houses, and dictate the policy of the schools!' I retorted. 'But they teach them; you can hardly find a male teacher except at the head of a school, – to keep the faculty in order.'

Severnius refrained from comment upon this, seeing, I suppose, that I was getting a little impatient. He walked along with his head down. I think I neglected to say that we were taking a long tramp into the country, as we often did. In order to change the conversation, I asked him what sort of a government they had in Paleveria, and was delighted when he replied that it was a free republic.

'My country is a republic also,' I said, proudly.

'We both have much to be thankful for,' he answered. 'A republic is the only natural government in the world, and man cannot get above nature.'

I thought this remark rather singular, – at variance with progress and high civilization. But I let it pass, thinking to take it up at some future time.

'How do you vote here?' I asked. 'What are your qualifications and restrictions?'

'Briefly told,' he replied. 'Every citizen may vote on all public questions, and in all elections.'

'But what constitutes citizenship?'

'A native-born is a citizen when he or she reaches maturity. Foreigners are treated as minors until they have lived as long under the government as it takes for a child to come of age. It is thus,' he added, facetiously, 'that we punish people for presuming to be born outside our happy country.'

'Excuse me,' I said, 'but do I understand you to say that your women have the right of suffrage?'

'Assuredly. Do not yours?'

'Indeed no!' I replied, the masculine instinct of superiority swelling within me.

Severnius wears spectacles. He adjusted them carefully on his nose and looked at me.

'But did you not tell me just now that your country is a republic?'

'It is, but we do not hold that women are our political equals,' I answered.

His face was an exclamation and interrogation point fused into one.

'Indeed! and how do you manage it, – how, for instance, can you prevent them from voting?'

'O, they don't often try it,' I said, laughing. 'When they do, we simply throw their ballots out of the count.'

'Is it possible! That seems to me a great unfairness. However, it can be accounted for, I suppose, from the fact that things are so different on the Earth to what they are here. Our government, you see, rests upon a system of taxation. We tax all property to defray governmental expenses, and for many other purposes tending toward the general good; which makes it necessary that all our citizens shall have a voice in our political economy. But you say your women have no property, and so–'

'I beg your pardon!' I interposed; 'I did not say that. We have a great many very rich women, – women whose husbands or fathers have left them fortunes.'

'Then they of course have a vote?'

'They do not. You can't make a distinction like that.'

'No? But you exempt their property, perhaps?'

'Of course not.'

'Do you tell me that you tax property, to whatever amount, and for whatever purpose, you choose, without allowing the owner her fractional right to decide about either the one or the other?'

'Their interests are identical with ours,' I replied, 'so what is the difference? We men manage the government business, and I fancy we do it sufficiently well.'

I expanded my chest after this remark, and Severnius simply looked at me. I think that at that moment I suffered vicariously in his scornful regard for all my countrymen.

I did not like the Socratic method he had adopted in this conversation, and I turned the tables on him.

'Do your women hold office, other than in the school board and the council?' I asked.

'O, yes, fully half our offices are filled by women.'

'And you make no discrimination in the kind of office?'

'The law makes none; those things adjust themselves. Fitness, equipment, are the only things considered. A woman, the same as a man, is governed by her taste and inclination in the matter of office-holding. Do women never take a hand in state affairs on the Earth?'

'Yes, in some countries they do, – monarchies. There have been a good many women sovereigns. There are a few now.'

'And are they successful rulers?'

'Some are, some are not.'

'The same as men. That proves that your women are not really inferior.'

'Well, I should say not!' I retorted. 'Our women are very superior; we treat them more as princesses than as inferiors, – they are angels.'

I was carried away in the heat of resentment, and knew that what I had said was half cant.

'I beg your pardon!' said Severnius quickly; 'I got a wrong impression from your statements. I fear I am very stupid. Are they all angels?'

I gave him a furtive glance and saw that he was in earnest. His brows were drawn together with a puzzled look.

I had a sudden vision of a scene in Five Points; several groups of frowsled, petticoated beings, laughing, joking, swearing, quarreling, fighting, and drinking beer from dirty mugs.

'No, not all of them,' I replied, smiling. 'That was a figure of speech. There are so many classes.'

'Let us confine our discussion to one, then,' he returned. 'To the women who might be of your own family; that will simplify matters. And now tell me, please, how this state of things came about, this subjection of a part of your people. I cannot understand it, – these subjects being of your own flesh and blood, I should think it would breed domestic discontent, where some of the members of a family wield a power and enjoy a privilege denied to the others. Fancy my shaking a ballot over Elodia's head!'

'O, Elodia!' I said, and was immediately conscious that my accent was traitorous to my countrywomen. I made haste to add,

'Your sister is – incomparable. She is unusual even here. I have seen none others like her.'

'How do you mean?'

'I mean that she is as responsible as a man; she is not inconsequent.'

'Are your women inconsequent?'

'They have been called so, and we think it rather adds to their attractiveness. You see they have always been relieved of responsibility, and I assure you the large majority of them have no desire to assume it, – I mean in the matter of government and politics.'

'Yes?'

I dislike an interrogative 'yes,' and I made no reply. Severnius added,

'I suppose they have lost the faculty which you say they lack, – the faculty that makes people responsible, – through disuse. I have seen the same thing in countries on the other side of our globe, where races have been held as slaves for several centuries. They seem to have no ideas about personal rights, or liberties, as pertaining to themselves, and no inclination in that direction. It always struck me as being the most pathetic feature of their condition that they and everybody else accepted it as a matter of course, as they would a law of nature. In the place of strength and self-assertion there has come to them a dumb patience, or an unquestioning acquiescence like that of people born blind. Are your women happy?'

'You should see them!' I exclaimed, with certain ball-room memories rushing upon me, and visions of fair faces radiant with the joy of living. But these were quickly followed by other pictures, and I felt bound to add, 'of late, a restless spirit has developed in certain circles, –'

'The working circles, I suppose,' interrupted Severnius. 'You spoke of the working women getting into the professions.'

'Not those exclusively. Even the women of leisure are not so satisfied as they used to be. There has been, for a great many years, more or less chaffing about women's rights, but now they are beginning to take the matter seriously.'

'Ah, they are waking up, perhaps?'

'Yes, some of them are waking up, – a good many of them. It is a little ridiculous, when one thinks of it, seeing they have no power to enforce their "rights," and can never attain them except through the condescension of men. Tell me, Severnius, when did your women wake up?'

Severnius smiled. 'My dear sir, I think they have never been asleep!'

We stalked along silently for a time; the subject passed out of my mind, or was driven out by the beauties of the landscape about us. I was especially impressed with the magnificence of the trees that hedged every little patch of farm land, and threw their protecting arms around houses and cottages, big and little; and with the many pellucid streams flowing naturally, or divided like strands of silk and guided in new courses, to lave the roots of trees or run through pasture lands where herds were feeding.

A tree is something to be proud of in Paleveria, more than a fine residence; more even than ancient furniture and cracked china. Perhaps because the people sit out under their trees a great deal, and the shade of them has protected the heads of many generations, and they have become hallowed through sacred memories and traditions. In Paleveria they have tree doctors, whose business it is to ward off disease, heal wounded or broken boughs, and exterminate destructive insects.

Severnius startled me suddenly with another question:

'What, may I ask, is your theory of Man's creation?'

'God made Man, and from one of his ribs fashioned woman,' I replied catechetically.

'Ours is different,' he said. 'It is this: A pair of creatures, male and female, sprang simultaneously from an enchanted lake in the mountain region of a country called Caskia, in the northern part of this continent. They were only animals, but they were beautiful and innocent. God breathed a Soul into them and they were Man and Woman, equals in all things.'

'A charming legend!' said I.

Later on I learned the full breadth of the meaning of the equality he spoke of. At that time it was impossible for me to comprehend it, and I can only convey it to you in a complete account of my further experiences on that wonderful planet. . . .

The social conditions in Thursia do not demand that women shall pose in a conciliatory attitude toward me – upon whose favor their dearest privileges hang. Marriage not being an economic necessity with them, they are released from certain sordid motives which often actuate women in our world in their frantic efforts to avert the appalling catastrophe of missing a husband; and they are at liberty to operate their matrimonial campaigns upon other grounds. I do not say higher grounds, because that I do not know. I only know that one base factor in the marriage problem, – the ignoble scheming to secure the means of living, as represented in a husband, – is eliminated, and the spirit of woman is that much more free.

We men have a feeling that we are liable at any time to be entrapped into matrimony by a mask of cunning and deceit, which heredity and long practice enable women to use with such amazing skill that few can escape it. We expect to be caught with chaff, like fractious colts coquetting with the halter and secretly not unwilling to be caught.

Another thing: women's freedom to propose – which struck me as monstrous – takes away the reproach of her remaining single; the supposition being, as in the case of a bachelor, that it is a matter of choice with her. It saves her the dread of having it said that she has never had an opportunity to marry.

Courtship in Thursia may lack some of the tantalizing uncertainties which give it zest with us, but marriage also is robbed of many doubts and misgivings. Still I could not accustom myself with any feeling of comfort to the situation there, – the idea of masculine pre-eminence and womanly dependence being too thoroughly ingrained in my nature.

Elodia, of course, did many things and held many opinions of which I did not approve. But I believed in her innate nobility, and attributed her defects to a pernicious civilization and a government which did not exercise its paternal right to cherish, and restrain, and protect, the weaker sex, as they should be cherished, and restrained, and protected. And how charming and how reliable she was, in spite of her defects! She had an atomic weight upon which you could depend as upon any other known quantity. Her presence was a stimulus that quickened the faculties and intensified the emotions. At least I may speak for myself; she awoke new feelings and aroused new powers within me.

Her life had made her practical but not prosaic. She had imagination and poetic feeling; there were times when her beautiful countenance was touched with the grandeur of lofty thought, and again with the shifting lights of a playful humor, or the flashings of a keen but kindly wit. She had a laugh that mellowed the heart, as if she took you into her confidence. It is a mark of extreme favor when your superior, or a beautiful woman, admits you to the intimacy of a cordial laugh! Even her smiles, which I used to lie in wait for and often tried to provoke, were not the mere froth of a light and careless temperament; they had a significance like speech. Though she was so busy, and though she knew so well how to make the moments count, she could be idle when she chose, deliciously, luxuriously idle, – like one who will not fritter away his pence, but upon occasion spends his guineas handsomely. At the dinner hour she always gave us of her best. Her varied life supplied her with much material for conversation, – nothing worth noticing ever escaped her, in the life and conduct of people about her. She was fond of anecdote, and could garnish the simplest story with an exquisite grace.

Upon one of her idle days, – a day when Severnius happened not to be at home, – she took up her parasol in the hall after we had had luncheon, and gave me a glance which said, 'Come with me if you like,' and we went out and strolled through the grounds together. Her manner had not a touch of coquetry; I might have been simply another woman, she might have been simply another man. But I was so stupid as to essay little gallantries, such as had been, in fact, a part of my youthful education; she either did not observe them or ignored them, I could not tell which. Once I put out my hand to assist her over a ridiculously narrow streamlet, and she paid no heed to the gesture, but reefed her skirts, or draperies, with her own un-occupied hand and stepped lightly across. Again, when we were about to ascend an abrupt hill, I courteously offered her my arm.

'O, no, I thank you!' she said; 'I have two, which balance me very well when I climb.'

'You are a strange woman,' I exclaimed with a blush.

'Am I?' she said, lifting her brows. 'Well, I suppose – or rather you suppose – that I am the product of my ancestry and my training.'

'You are, in some respects,' I assented; and then I added, 'I have often tried to fancy what effect our civilization would have had upon you.'

'What effect do you think it would have had?' she asked, with quite an unusual – I might say earthly – curiosity.

'I dare not tell you,' I replied, thrilling with the felicity of a talk so personal, – the first I had ever had with her.

'Why not?' she demanded, with a side glance at me from under her gold-fringed shade.

'It would be taking too great a liberty.'

'But if I pardon that?' There was an archness in her smile which was altogether womanly. What a grand opportunity, I thought, for saying some of the things I had so often wanted to say to her! but I hesitated, turning hot and then cold.

'Really,' I said, 'I cannot. I should flatter you, and you would not like that.'

For the first time, I saw her face crimson to the temples.

'That would be very bad taste,' she replied; 'flattery being the last resort – when it is found that there is nothing in one to compliment. Silence is better; you have commendable tact.'

'Pardon my stupid blunder!' I cried; 'you cannot think I meant that! Flattery is exaggerated, absurd, unmeaning praise, and no praise, the highest, the best, could do you justice, could –'

She broke in with a disdainful laugh:

'A woman can always compel a pretty speech from a man, you see, – even in Mars!'

'You did not compel it,' I rejoined earnestly, 'if I but dared, – if you would allow me to tell you what I think of you, how highly I regard –'

She made a gesture which cut short my eloquence, and we walked on in silence.

Whenever there has been a disturbance in the moral atmosphere, there is nothing like silence to restore the equilibrium. I, watching furtively, saw the slight cloud pass from her face, leaving the intelligent serenity it usually wore. But still she did not speak. However, there was nothing ominous in that, she was never troubled with an uneasy desire to keep conversation going.

On top of the hill there were benches, and we sat down. It was one of those still afternoons in summer when nature seems to be taking a siesta. Overhead it was like the heart of a rose.

167

The soft, white, cottony clouds we often see suspended in our azure ether, floated – as soft, as white, as fleecy – in the pink skies of Mars.

Elodia closed her parasol and laid it across her lap and leaned her head back against the tree in whose shade we were. It was an acute pleasure, a rapture indeed, to sit so near to her and alone with her, out of hearing of all the world. But she was calmly unconscious, her gaze wandering dreamily through half-shut lids over the wide landscape, which included forests and fields and meadows, and many windings of the river, for we had a high point of observation.

I presently broke the silence with a bold, perhaps an excusable question,

'Elodia, do you intend ever to marry?'

It was a kind of challenge, and I held myself rigid, waiting for her answer, which did not come immediately. She turned her eyes toward me slowly without moving her head, and our glances met and gradually retreated, as two opposing forces might meet and retreat, neither conquering, neither vanquished. Hers went back into space, and she replied at last as if to space, – as if the question had come, not from me alone, but from all the voices that urge to matrimony.

'Why should I marry?'

'Because you are a woman,' I answered promptly.

'Ah!' her lip curled with a faint smile, 'your reason is very general, but why limit it at all, why not say because I am one of a pair which should be joined together?'

The question was not cynical, but serious; I scrutinized her face closely to make sure of that before answering.

'I know,' I replied, 'that here in Mars there is held to be no difference in the nature and requirements of the sexes, but it is a false hypothesis, there is a difference, – a vast difference! all of my knowledge of humanity, my experience and observation, prove it.'

'Prove it to you, no doubt,' she returned, 'but not to me, because my experience and observation have been the reverse of yours. Will you kindly tell me,' she added, 'why you think I should wish to marry any more than a man, – or what reasons can be urged upon a woman more than upon a man?'

An overpowering sense of helplessness fell upon me, – as when one has reached the limits of another's understanding and is unable to clear the ground for further argument.

'O, Elodia! I cannot talk to you,' I replied. 'It is true, as you say, that our conclusions are based upon diverse premises; we are so wide apart in our views on this subject that what I would say must seem to you the merest cant and sentiment.'

'I think not; you are an honest man,' she rejoined with an encouraging smile, 'and I am greatly interested in your philosophy of marriage.'

I acknowledged her compliment.

'Well,' I began desperately, letting the words tumble out as they would, 'It is woman's nature, as I understand it, to care a great deal about being loved — loved wholly and entirely by one man who is worthy of her love, and to be united to him in the sacred bonds of marriage. To have a husband, children; to assume the sweet obligations of family ties, and to gather to herself the tenderest and purest affections humanity can know, is surely, indisputably, the best, the highest, noblest, province of woman.'

'And not of man?'

'These things mean the same to men, of course,' I replied, 'though in lesser degree. It is man's office — with us — to buffet with the world, to wrest the means of livelihood, of comfort, luxury, from the grudging hand of fortune. It is the highest grace of woman that she accepts these things at his hands, she honors him accepting, as he honors her in bestowing.'

I was aware that I was indulging in platitudes, but the platitudes of Earth are novelties in Mars.

Her eyes took a long leap from mine to the vague horizon line. 'It is very strange,' she said, 'this distinction you make, I cannot understand it at all. It seems to me that this love we are talking about is simply one of the strong instincts implanted in our common nature. It is an essential of our being. Marriage is not, it is a social institution; and just why it is incumbent upon one sex more than upon the other, or why it is more desirable for one sex than the other, is inconceivable to me. If either a man, or a woman, desires the ties you speak of, or if one has the vanity to wish to found a respectable family, then, of course, marriage is a necessity, — made so by our social and political laws. It is a luxury we may have if we pay the price.'

I was shocked at this cold-blooded reasoning, and cried, 'O, how can a woman say that! have you no tenderness, Elodia? no heart-need of these ties and affections, — which I have always been taught are so precious to woman?'

169

She shrugged her shoulders, and, leaning forward a little, clasped her hands about her knees.

'Let us not make it personal,' she said; 'I admitted that these things belong to our common nature, and I do not of course except myself. But I repeat that marriage is a convention, and — I am not conventional.'

'As to that,' I retorted, 'all the things that pertain to civilization, all the steps which have ever been taken in the direction of progress, are conventions: our clothing, our houses, our religions, arts, our good manners. And we are bound to accept every "convention" that makes for the betterment of society, as though it were a revelation from God.'

I confess that this thought was the fruit of my brief intercourse with the Caskians, who hold that there is a divine power continually operating upon human consciousness, — not disclosing miracles, but enlarging and perfecting human perceptions. I was thinking of this when Elodia suddenly put the question to me:

'Are you married?'

'No, I am not,' I replied. The inquiry was not agreeable to me; it implied that she had been hitherto altogether too indifferent as to my 'eligibility,' — never having concerned herself to ascertain the fact before.

'Well, you are perhaps older than I am,' she said, 'and you have doubtless had amours?'

I was as much astounded by the frankness of this inquiry as you can be, and blushed like a girl. She withdrew her eyes from my face with a faint smile and covered the question by another:

'You intend to marry, I suppose?'

'I do, certainly,' I replied, the resolution crystallizing on the instant.

She drew a long sigh. 'Well, I do not, I am so comfortable as I am.' She patted the ground with her slipper toe. 'I do not wish to impose new conditions upon myself. I simply accept my life as it comes to me. Why should I voluntarily burden myself with a family, and all the possible cares and sorrows which attend the marriage state! If I cast a prophetic eye into the future, what am I likely to see? — Let us say, a lovely daughter dying of some frightful malady; an idolized son squandering my wealth and going to ruin; a husband in whom I no longer delight, but to whom I am bound by a hundred intricate ties impossible to sever. I think I am not prepared to take the future on trust to so great an extent! Why should the free wish for fetters? Affection and sympathy are good things, indispensable things in fact, – but I find them in my friends. And for this other matter: this need of love, passion, sentiment, – which is peculiarly ephemeral in its impulses, not-with-standing that it has such an insistent vitality in the human heart, – may be satisfied without entailing such tremendous responsibilities.'

I looked at her aghast; did she know what she was saying; did she mean what her words implied?

'You wrong yourself, Elodia,' said I; 'those are the sentiments, the arguments, of a selfish person, of a mean and cowardly spirit. And you have none of those attributes; you are strong, courageous, generous –'

'You mistake me,' she interrupted, 'I am entirely selfish; I do not wish to disturb my present agreeable pose. Tell me, what is it that usually prompts people to marry?'

'Why, love, of course,' I answered.

'Well, you are liable to fall in love with my maid –'

'Not after having seen her mistress!' I ejaculated.

'If she happens to possess a face or figure that draws your masculine eye,' she went on, the rising color in her cheek responding to my audacious compliment; 'though there may be nothing in common between you, socially, intellectually, or spiritually. What would be the result of such a marriage, based upon simple sex-love?'

I had known many such marriages, and was familiar with the results, but I did not answer. We tacitly dropped the subject, and our two minds wandered away as they would, on separate currents.

She was the first to break this second silence.

'I can conceive of a marriage,' she said, 'which would not become burdensome, any more than our best friendships become burdensome. Beside the attraction on the physical plane – which I believe is very necessary – there should exist all the higher affinities. I should want my husband to be my most delightful companion, able to keep my liking and to command my respect and confidence as I hope to his. But I fear that is ideal.'

'The ideal is only the highest real,' I answered, 'the ideal is always possible.'

'Remotely!' she said with a laugh. 'The chances are many against it.'

'But even if one were to fall short a little in respect to husband or wife, I have often observed that there are compensations springing out of the relation, in other ways,' I returned.

'You mean children? O, yes, that is true, when all goes well. I will tell you,' she added, her voice dropping to the tone one instantly recognizes as confidential, 'that I am educating several children in some of our best schools, and that I mean to provide for them with sufficient liberality when they come of age. So, you see, I have thrown hostages to fortune and shall probably reap a harvest of gratitude, – in place of filial affection.'

She laughed with a touch of mockery.

I suppose every one is familiar with the experience of having things – facts, bits of knowledge, – 'come' to him, as we say. Something came to me, and froze the marrow in my bones.

'Elodia,' I ventured, 'you asked me a very plain question a moment ago, will you forgive me if I ask you the same, – have you had amours?'

The expression of her face changed slightly, which might have been due to the expression of mine.

'We have perhaps grown too frank with each other,' she said, 'but you are a being from another world, and that must excuse us, – shall it?'

I bowed, unable to speak.

'One of the children I spoke of, a little girl of six, is my own natural child.'

She made this extraordinary confession with her glance fixed steadily upon mine.

I am a man of considerable nerve, but for a moment the world was dark to me and I had the sensation of one falling from a great height. And then suddenly relief came to me in the thought, She is not to be judged by the standards that measure morality in my country! When I could command my voice again I asked:

'Does this little one know that she is your child, – does any one else know?'

'Certainly not,' she answered in a tone of surprise, and then with an ironical smile, 'I have treated you to an exceptional confidence. It is a matter of etiquette with us to keep these things hidden.'

As I made no response she added:

'Is it a new thing to you for a parent not to acknowledge illegitimate children?'

'Even the lowest class of mothers we have on Earth do not often abandon their offspring,' I replied.

'Neither do they here,' she said. 'The lowest class have nothing to gain and nothing to lose, and consequently there is no necessity that they should sacrifice their natural affections. In this respect, the lower classes are better off than we aristocrats.'

'You beg the question,' I returned, 'you know what I mean! I should not have thought that you, Elodia, could ever be moved by such unworthy considerations – that you would ever fear the world's opinions! you who profess manly qualities, the noblest of which is courage!'

'Am I to understand by that,' she said, 'that men on your planet acknowledge their illegitimate progeny, and allow them the privileges of honored sons and daughters?'

Pushed to this extremity, I could recall but a single instance, – but one man whose courage and generosity, in a case of the kind under discussion, had risen to the level of his crime. I related to her the story of his splendid and prolonged life, with its one blot of early sin, and its grace of practical repentance. And upon the other hand, I told her of the one distinguished modern woman, who has had the hardihood to face the world with her offenses in her hands, as one might say.

'Are you not rather unjust to the woman?' she asked. 'You speak of the man's acknowledgment of his sin as something fine, and you seem to regard hers as simply impudent.'

'Because of the vast difference between the moral attitude of the two,' I rejoined. 'He confessed his error and took his punishment with humility; she slaps society in the face, and tries to make her genius glorify her misdeeds.'

'Possibly society is to blame for that, by setting her at bay. If I have got the right idea about your society, it is as unrelenting to the one sex as it is indulgent to the other. Doubtless it was ready with open arms to receive back the offending, repentant man, but would it not have set its foot upon the woman's neck, if she had given it the chance, if she had knelt in humility as he did? A tree bears fruit after its kind; as does a code of morals. Gentleness and forgiveness breed repentance and reformation, and harshness begets defiance.' She added with a laugh, 'What a spectacle your civilization would present if all the women who have sinned had the genius and the spirit of a Bernhardt!'

'Or all the men had the magnanimity of a Franklin,' I retorted.

'True!' she said. . . .

'Elodia,' I said presently, 'You can hardly understand what a shock this – this conversation has been to me. I started out with saying that I had often tried to fancy what our civilization might have done for you. I see more clearly now. You are the victim of the harshest and cruelest assumption that has ever been upheld concerning woman, – that her nature is no finer, holier than man's. I have reverenced womanhood all my life as the highest and purest thing under heaven, and I will, I must, hold fast to that faith, to that rock on which the best traditions of our Earth are founded.'

'Do your women realize what they have got to live up to?' she asked ironically.

'There are things in men which offset their virtues,' I returned, in justice to my own sex. 'Where men are strong, women are gentle, where women are faithful, men are brave, and so on.'

'How charming to have the one nature dovetail into the other so neatly!' she exclaimed. 'I seem to see a vision, shall I tell it to you, – a vision of your Earth? In the Beginning, you know that is the way in which all our traditions start out, there was a great heap of Qualities stacked in a pyramid upon the Earth. And the human creatures were requested to step up and help themselves to such as suited their tastes. There was a great scramble, and your sex, having some advantages in the way of muscle and limb, – and not having yet acquired the arts of courtesy and gallantry for which you are now so distinguished, – pressed forward and took first choice. Naturally you selected the things which were agreeable to possess in themselves, and the exercise of which would most redound to your glory; such virtues as chastity, temperance, patience, modesty, piety, and some minor graces, were thrust aside and eventually forced upon the weaker sex, – since it was necessary that all the Qualities should be used in order to make a complete Human Nature. Is not that a pretty fable?'

She arose and shook out her draperies and spread her parasol. . . .

Severnius had returned. After dinner he invited me out onto the veranda to smoke a cigar, – he was very particular not to fill the house with tobacco smoke. . . .

My mind was so full of the subject Elodia and I had discussed that I could not forbear repeating my old question to him:

'Tell me, my friend,' I entreated, 'do you in your inmost soul believe that men and women have one common nature, — that women are no better at all than men, and that men may, if they will, be as pure as — well, as women ought to be?'

Severnius smiled. 'If you cannot find an answer to your first question here in Paleveria, I think you may in any of the savage countries, where I am quite positive the women exhibit no finer qualities than their lords. And for a very conclusive reply to your second question, — go to Caskia!'

'Does the same idea of equality, or likeness rather, exist in Caskia that prevails here?' I asked.

'O, yes,' said he, 'but their plane of life is so much higher. I cannot but believe in the equality,' he added, 'bad as things are with us'. . . .

Severnius added, apropos of what had gone before, 'It does not seem fair to me that one half of humanity should hang upon the skirts of the other half; it is better that we should go hand in hand, even though our progress is slow.'

'But that cannot be,' I returned; 'there are always some that must bear the burden while others drag behind.'

'O, certainly; that is quite natural and right,' he assented. 'The strong should help the weak. What I mean is that we should not throw the burden upon any particular class, or allow to any particular class special indulgences. That — pardon me! — is the fault I find with your civilization; you make your women the chancellors of virtue, and claim for your sex the privilege of being virtuous or not, as you choose.' He smiled as he added, 'Do you know, your loyalty and tender devotion to individual women, and your antagonistic attitude toward women in general — on the moral plane — presents the most singular contrast to my mind!'

11
A SEX REVOLUTION
(1894)

———————————————*———————————————

Lois Nichols Waisbrooker
(1826-1909)

Born Adeline Eliza Nichols to parents who worked hard but had little education, Lois Nichols Waisbrooker at 26 decided to cease 'working for others as a maid or cook' and spent two years in preparation for teaching. She then taught in Black schools. During the 1870s she was in Boston helping to organize the Boston Social Reform Convention with other sex radicals. She also wrote numerous tracts and novels at this time. She became an editor of Lucifer, the Light Bearer *(1883-1907), a free love journal. During the 1880s and 1890s she edited her own journal* Foundation Principles, *published in Kansas, Iowa, and California. She lectured widely. In 1900-2, she lived in the anarchist colony of Home (near Tacoma), Washington. Details of her personal life are unclear.*

Her didactic fiction of the 1870s stressed woman's rights — especially the ownership of her own body and of children she bore, the giving or withholding of love as she saw fit, the freedom of self-governance. In both Suffrage for Woman: The Reasons Why *(1868) and* Nothing Like It; or, Steps to the Kingdom *(1875), Waisbrooker argues that 'Woman everywhere is in bondage, is not accorded equal rights with men; has not the right even to the use of her maternal functions unless bound to some man' (1875, p. 128). All bonds enslave, including the marriage bond; therefore the only law appropriate to marriage is not the traditional bonds of matrimony but rather love alone, freely given and freely received, according to Waisbrooker and other sex radicals.*

Like Charlotte Perkins Gilman's Herland *(1915), Waisbrooker's* A Sex Revolution *idealizes the Mother. Here she is a nurturer and purveyor of Love throughout society. This dream vision reported by a female narrator reveals how women revolted against men to establish "a new heaven and a new earth," one at last free of war. Not alone a pleader for pacifism, also Mary Elizabeth McGrath Blake (1840-1907), published "The Coming Reform" (Boston: American Peace Society, 1889) and Elizabeth Stuart Phelps wrote "There Should Be No War"* (Boston Herald; *see her letter 18 Jan. 1892, Alderman Library, University of Virginia).*

REFERENCES
Delores Hayden, *The Grand Domestic Revolution* (Cambridge, Mass.: MIT Press, 1981), pp. 139, 144; Hal D. Sears, *The Sex Radicals* (Lawrence, Kansas: Regents Press of Kansas, 1977), pp. 219-36.

SELECTION
Includes chapters 3-4, or pp. 26-44 of the original pp. 5-61.

A SEX REVOLUTION

―――――――――――――― ✳ ――――――――――――――

PREFACE

DEAR READER: – The history of the past shows us that
nations rise, go through a longer or shorter period of prosperity
and then decay. The ruling motive in the life of nations, so far,
has always been the same, the aggressive or masculine. Self-
aggrandizement, *our* nation right or wrong, all to be laid upon
the national altar in the name of patriotism, a centralizing of
wealth and power in the hands of the few at the expense of the
many, and the result has always been what? Go, gather
together the human wrecks of any one nation and you have
your answer.

Now will not this latest and brightest of nations perish also
unless methods are changed, unless the social lever is reversed?
Already the seeds of decay are taking root; is there not some
law through which we may take a new lease of life, and what is
that law, if there be such, if it be not that

'WOMAN, TAKE THE LEAD?'

True, woman is already quite prominent, is becoming more
so, but she does not seem as yet to realize that with man's
methods she will succeed no better than man has done. She
must formulate her own methods before her true work can
appear. Woman must be free, must refuse to be led, must
believe in herself, before the evils attendant upon imperfect
motherhood can be eliminated, and as I see things, the only
hope of our nation lies in this direction.

Let us once rise above the necessity of armies, navies,
prisons, almshouses, asylums, etc., then the future will stretch

out before us with ever increasing brightness. The first step toward this desirable consummation is to believe that it *can* be done; the next that it *will* be done, and lastly to determine to do it *ourselves*.

L.W.

CHAPTER III.

'But *we* wont let you go.' I saw then as never before the assumption of the position that man takes; taking it for granted as he does, that he is woman's rightful ruler. If 'and he shall rule over thee,' was pronounced upon woman as a curse, the sooner she repudiates such rule the sooner will that curse be lifted. However there was not much assurance in the faces of the men there present when wives, mothers, sisters and daughters made that declaration. I never saw such an expression. They were speechless with astonishment.

'What does this mean?' said Selferedo, looking at Lovella as if he would like to annihilate her.

'It means, sir, that we are in earnest; it means that we do not intend that the men shall be killed off till large numbers of our women must live alone or violate the law.'

'Or violate the law,' he repeated inquiringly.

'Yes; you men make the laws, and you say that a man can have but one wife, which is right in itself, is Nature's law where you do not violate her conditions, and then you declare war and the men many of them, are killed: is that not practically decreeing an equal number of women to celibacy or a violation of natural law and legal statute?'

Selferedo looked as if a new, but unacceptable light was dawning on his mind. He evidently felt the force of what she said and could not readily reply to her argument, and she continued:

'In view of all this we have decided that if you go to war we will go with you, that we will share danger and death by your sides, that what God hath joined together, we will not permit you to put asunder.'

'And leave your children, such of you as have children, motherless!'

'Why not,' she asked. 'If you go to war to kill other

179

children's fathers or be killed yourselves, we will go too, and will kill other children's mothers or be killed ourselves.'

Selferedo and those with him looked horrified. He opened his lips as if to speak, then closed them again; at length he gasped in the same words he had used before, 'What does this all mean!'

'It means that the crucified God is rising from his tomb.'

'Not much God in woman's going to war,' he retorted.

'You do not understand; men cannot,' said Lovella gently. 'Woman represents the love element of the God-forces in Nature. Hitherto it has been a negative, a yielding, and consequently a crucified love. The love in woman's heart has suffered till its latent power is aroused, so aroused that it demands redemption or extinction; we repudiate eternal torture.'

'Eternal torture,' I repeated to myself, 'surely, woman's life has been little else.'

Selferedo did not seem to know what to say to this, but as Lovella made no further remark, he at length asked: 'And how much more are you going to demand? As I said awhile ago, when we conceded what you demanded in what you call a "Strike of a Sex," we supposed you would leave us alone so far as our way of doing things is concerned.'

'I believe you graciously conceded us the right to our own bodies,' she said in reply.

'We resigned all rights as husbands and put ourselves in the place of dependents upon your favor.'

'What right have you then to demand that we shall bear sons who must go to war, must kill or be killed. If we have the right to our own bodies how dare you ask us to use them as gestating rooms for sons who must be reared as marks for bullets or for cannon balls?'

'So you intend to separate from us again unless we grant what you demand?'

'Have not these said they will go with you, and die with you, if need be?'

'But that is what we do not want.'

'Why not say then in so many words that you want us to rear sons as an offering to the war demon, and daughters whose husbands are likely to be torn to pieces to satisfy that governmental pride which is ready to immolate its citizens on the altar of national ambition. If you persist in declaring war, this is what you mean and why not say it?'

'You are Anarchists, you do not believe in government.'

'Wait till you have given us a just government before you accuse us of being opposed to government as such. A just government will be a permanent one, you can rest assured of that.'

Again Selferedo was silent, while the vast concourse of both men and women stood waiting the result. At length he said: 'But you have not told us how much more you intend to demand.'

'How much do you think we ought to demand to make things as they should be?' she smilingly asked. To this there was no reply.

Lovella now turned to the men, who, enthused by Selferedo's eloquence, had volunteered for the war and asked: 'What will you do?'

'What can we do? we cannot see these dear ones die.'

'You have enlisted and you cannot go back; desertion is death,' thundered Selferedo in his most commanding tones.

'Then we must die for fight we will not,' was the equally positive response.

'And we will die with you,' said mothers, wives, sisters and daughters.

'No,' said Selferedo, 'we do not war on women.'

'When you take away fathers, sons, husbands and brothers, you do war on us, and you cannot prevent our dying if they die.'

Then there arose a great cry from the men who had not enlisted, and from the women who were with them. They said: 'These shall not die for we will not permit it.'

Selferedo trembled for he saw that his power was gone, while Lovella said: 'War does not tend to the elevation of humanity; on the contrary it brutalizes, drags us down. Its results are evil and only evil, therefore we demand that war shall cease; shall our demand be accorded?' and from the vast concourse of men came the response clear and strong: "Your demand shall be accorded." But Selferedo stood silent and rebellious. Lovella read his thought and said:

'You mistake in believing that the glory of our nation has departed because we ignore an insult rather than fight. National duelists are no more honorable than are individual duelists and the creed of honor once held by them has long since been discarded by gentlemen, by all honorable men. The real glory of our nation has but just commenced; from henceforth the nations of the earth will look to us as taking the lead in beating swords into ploughshares and spears into pruning hooks.' . . .

Selferedo replied to Lovella's gentle words with: 'Time will tell if a nation ruled by women can maintain its position. Judging by her yielding nature, such a nation will become the prey of surrounding nations, will be picked to pieces and divided amongst them; what does woman know of government?'

'Judging from the past, you mean; you forget that she is becoming a positive power.'

'If she becomes a positive power, in what will her methods differ from man's? How can she maintain her positive position without the sword?'

'You forget, sir, that positiveness and aggressiveness are not one and the same thing, even as force and power are not the same. We pay the nations the compliment of believing them capable of being swayed by moral weapons, if skillfully handled. Beside, as to woman's knowledge of government, has man evolved one that is satisfactory?'

To this Selferedo, as before, made no reply, and she continued:

'Man has had the control of affairs in all of the ages of the past; is it more than fair that there should be a sex revolution?'

'A sex revolution, what do you mean by that?' he asked.

'Let the subservient sex become the dominant one for a time. Man's forte is force, woman's love; suppose that force yields the reins of love?'

'Love is a syren; her dalliance leads to death if followed too far,' he said contemptuously.

'Alas,' she replied, 'how little you men understand love! With woman in the lead, love's true law will be learned, and man will cease to grovel in the dust of passion, unsanctified either by moral purpose or spiritual life. Then the central, the creative love, out of which all other loves spring, will become a refining instead of a consuming fire. It will then be like the bush that Moses saw, which burned and was not consumed, a glorifying fire, an uplifting power, a quickener in our search after truth.'

The man's reply was a sneer with the words: 'Oh, you are

very beautiful, but you cannot move me, if you can these others,' indicating with his hand the men assembled, 'and though defeated now I bide my time.'

'And so can I, to be understood' said Lovella with a sigh, 'but I will now try to tell what we demand. I do not like the word, demand, but as you have not heeded our requests, our pleading tears, the force of self assertion must be overcome by the force of love's assertion. We will conquer or die, not for ourselves, but for humanity, so I say we demand. You have conceded to us on the war question, for that it was evil did not need to be proven, and the how to remove it was already plain.

'But there are other evils that the way to cure them is not yet plain. We demand, no ask, for if they will not do so we must study them alone — we ask that our brothers study these questions with us, and when the cause of any evil is found, its working clearly understood, we then demand that said cause be removed at no matter what cost, for in the end, its removal will always cost less than its continuance.'

'That is, we men must be put in leading strings,' said Selferedo, scornfully.

'Why not;' she replied. "With what mete ye measure it shall be measured to you again" is a law of nature. One extreme must bring the other before the balance comes.

> For ages past the men have led
>   In church, and state, and home,
> And battlefields have strown with dead
>   To gild ambition's dome,
> But now the great transition comes,
>   Earth's slaves are being freed,
> Love's light is kindling in our homes,
>   With woman in the lead,

is the language of one of your own sex, is the declaration of a sex revolution and we propose to make it good, to practicalize it.'

'So you propose to run this world for the ages to come, do you?'

Lovella gave him a look such as a mother might give to a wayward child: 'No Selferedo, only till a balance is restored, then we can go on together,' she said.

'And how long, suppose you, will it take to bring the balance you talk of,' he asked in the same sneering tone in which he had so often spoken.

'Live for us as we have lived for you; give us the aid of your earnest thought, knowing the while, that the decision rests with us, say fifty years, and if the changes that we bring are not for the better, we will then concede you your old place.'

'Fifty years,' he repeated to himself, 'fifty years, just like a woman's calculation; what can they accomplish in that length of time,' then aloud: 'Well, it shall be so; if you think you can do so much in half a century, you shall have the chance to test your power.'

'And the credit of what we do will be yours as much as ours, for you have prepared the materials for our work; we shall only arrange it. We could not do what we wish to do but for what you have done.'

'If it is creditable,' added Selferedo, 'we will share the credit with you.'

'Would you prefer that it be otherwise than creditable?' asked Lovella, looking him calmly in the face.

'We shall see,' he said again, 'but remember, it is but fifty years, and at the end of that time I think you will have discovered your folly, if not long before.'

There came a sort of mist before my eyes just then, a hazy appearance which I involuntarily tried to brush away. The effort seemed to intensify the difficulty and I wondered what was the matter. Presently things cleared but the scene had changed. Instead of a plain filled with women, or even half filled, I was looking into a very large room in which there was a number of both sexes.

Lovella and Selferedo were there, and I seemed to have the power to look into the very soul of the latter. Externally he was as pleasant and agreeable as a man can make himelf when he has a purpose to accomplish, which he does not wish to have known. To all outward appearance he was as anxious to have Lovella's plans succeed as though they were his own. His manner said: 'Fair queen, I am your servant for the next fifty years, and well may you prosper,' but the internal thought was, 'yes, your plans shall be carried out and proven so foolish that we men will never have any more trouble from that source. Woman's rights will be a thing of the past, will have been thrown into the waste basket of rejected schemes, and from thence forth woman will fall back into her proper place, glad to yield the lead to us.'

I looked to see if any of the others felt as Selferedo did. Of

184

the some two or three dozen men present there were five who held positions of wealth and honor, were chosen rulers of the people. Of these, four shared Selferedo's feelings, while the other one really hoped that with 'woman in the lead,' something better would come to humanity. 'Four of the five only care for themselves,' was my silent comment, when, as if in answer to the thought, I heard the words:

'How hardly shall they who have riches enter into the kingdom of heaven.'

I turned to see who had spoken, and if ever there was a divine man in human form, here was one. I looked at him inquiringly, but was too much awed to speak.

'Yes,' he repeated, 'the kingdom of heaven, the kingdom of love with wisdom as a devoted counterpart. The prophecy of a new heaven and a new earth is no idle dream, but the conditions which will make things new here must be the work of woman, must be born of woman.'

Emboldened by his kindly manner I asked: 'Would you accept woman as leader?'

'Most certainly; woman alone can lead man to the divinest heights. Man was first, but the fact that he was incomplete without her showed that he needed a leader. He will finally accord her her true place.'

'It would indeed be a grand woman who could lead you,' was my thought.

'Yes, grand, and more than that, is she to whom I owe so much,' he said in response, 'but listen and learn.' Saying this he vanished.

CHAPTER IV

When I had in a measure recovered from my surprise, I heard Selferedo saying:

'Fifty years will soon be gone; if you would accomplish anything worth the while you, or I should say, we, must work fast.'

'The best way to facilitate a work is first to understand it,' replied Lovella.

'And what do you propose, my fair commander?'

'First of all a thorough investigation of the machinery of society, both as to its separate parts, and as to its relations, the effect of one part upon another; and here is where we want the aid of the best, the broadest, the wisest minds of both sexes.'

I could see that Selferedo was not well pleased, but he smilingly asked: 'And how much of your precious time must we devote to this work of investigation?'

'Enough to master the subject, five, perhaps ten years.'

'But there are some evils, dear lady, the causes of which are so plain there is no need that time be spent to investigate. The fifty years, as I have already said, will soon pass, and I should like to see something done that will tell upon the future. If we can do enough in that time, with "woman in the lead" to demonstrate her fitness to lead, then there is no more to be said. She will have proved her place. Yet it appears to me like assuming a great deal for her to make the attempt when the best men of the ages have failed to remedy the evils that seem to be inseparable from human nature.'

'You forget,' she said, 'what you men have already done. But for that, we could do no more than the squaw of the wigwam could do if such a work were proposed to her. You have been so intent, however, in evolving wonders from nature's store-house that you have overlooked their proper adjustment. It takes months to prepare the land, particularly if it be timbered land, and months more for the wheat, corn, potatoes, and whatever else is needed for a good meal, to grow and ripen, but when all is ready the housewife will prepare the meal in an hour.

'Fifty years, it is true, is but an hour compared with the time you have worked, but with your aid we expect in that time to be able to satisfy some of the hunger that now prevails.'

'I do not think that hunger prevails, or that it ever has to any great extent,' said Selferedo. 'Now and then some one may fail in getting enough to eat but compared with the whole people the cases are very rare, and if they were known a supply would be forth coming. Generally, when such cases do occur, it is the party's own fault, and there is the county house to go to, if no where else.'

Lovella sighed, when she found that Selferedo only thought of physical hunger. 'The county house is but a sorry refuge at its best,' she said, 'but there are other kinds of hunger than that demanding physical food. Heart hunger, soul hunger, spiritual starvation prevail everywhere, and these result from a lack of balance in societary relations, and from our ignorance of the finer forces of nature in their adaptation to soul needs.'

Selferedo seemed very much surprised at the idea of spiritual starvation. 'Why, really,' he said, 'I cannot understand you. Spiritual starvation, and church spires pointing heavenward from every village in the country. Surely, we are a very religious people.'

As he said this something wonderful occurred – something that made me think of the magicians of Egypt. Lovella waved her hand and there appeared before us a most loathsome and disgusting scene, brutal men, degraded women, ragged children contending for the garbage that had been gathered from the streets. It was a scene from one of the slums of the metropolis of our country, as I afterwards learned.

'Look,' she said. He did look and shuddered at the sight.

'How much spirituality is there in the churches when such places as that can exist almost beneath their very shadows?' she asked.

'And do you expect to purify such places as that?' he asked in reply.

'We expect to try and that you will help us. In your haste to evolve great things you have knocked down and trampled upon my weaker children. The churches have no healing for such as these; not that their intent is not good enough, but they don't know how; they do not understand causes. These are among the things to be investigated, and these poor wrecks are the ones that the spirit of motherhood must heal as far as is possible, and at the same time must find out and remove the causes that have produced such results.'

The conversation had so far been carried on between Lovella and Selferedo, but Lovella now turned to the others and said: 'We will now look upon some of the grand things that man has done,' and as she spoke there unrolled before their gaze immense forests that slowly changed into fertile fields, wigwams that gave place to comfortable dwellings, and still the change went on, till large cities, magnificent residences, storehouses filled with the choicest products of all lands, wonderful architecture, elevated railroads, hanging bridges, magnificent steamers, marvelous machinery, railroads upon which palace cars were gliding, telegraph and telephone lines, these were among the many things shown.

The glorious works of the artist, panoramas of scenes that were past, or in some other part of the globe, all these and more, to please the eye and charm the heart, while the rich melody of music and song, ravished the ear and enthused the soul – all these, and more than words can express, were shown with wonderful distinctness, while in and out were moving with stately tread, or flitting, dancing along, noble looking men, beautiful women and lovely children, all robed in rich garments, and all fair to look upon.

And in contrast with each of these achievements of man's skill, there came along beside them pictures of what had originally been of the savage condition from which all this had been evolved. It was grand, and Selferedo's eye kindled as he looked, and then turning to the others, he said.

'With all these achievements of man so illustrated before us, in view of all this we are now asked, have pledged ourselves to give to woman the lead. What has woman done to deserve such a concession?'

At this the men present began to murmur. 'Wait,' said Lovella, 'there is another side to this question. The men who have done all this – all and much more than has been shown us, have all been borne beneath woman's heart, have been fed from her bosom and dandled upon her knees, while these, her sons, have assumed to rule over her, refusing to give her a voice in their counsels; is this just, my brothers?'

'It is not just,' responded the women, but the men were silent. They ceased to murmur, however, because woman was given a trial leadership, while first one woman then another made some such remarks as these:

'I wonder how much of all this the men would have done if they had had the children to take care of.' 'Haven't we always stood by them, cared for them when sick and encouraged them when well, we surely deserve a share of the credit.' 'Credit, or no credit they couldn't do without us, could you?' said the last speaker, turning toward them a smiling face.

'We shouldn't like to try it,' was the general response, and then one of them remarked: 'We are waiting to have our work mapped out for us.'

'That in good time,' said Lovella; 'there is enough to be done, but we must go to work advisedly. The work of the past that has succeeded was man's to do, and he has done it in his own way, not under woman's direction; on the other hand, the work that woman can do, has tried to do and has succeeded so poorly in the trying, has had to be done in man's way, and

while contending with the adverse conditions which he has
furnished. Civilization as it exists to-day, reflects man not
woman. I have shown you some of the grand things that man
has done; I will now show you some other things – things that
have resulted from the lack of the mother element in his
work.' . . .

Lovella looked very sad when she proposed to show the
other side of the picture, but after a little hesitation as if
debating where to begin, there filed before me, before those
assembled in that room, thousands of the most wretched
looking women I ever saw, and upon whose foreheads was
written the word, 'prostitute,' but above that and traced by
some friendly hand, was written 'victim.'

'Prostitutes,' I exclaimed, looking at Lovella, 'I thought that
woman abolished prostitution at the time of what was called
the "Strike of a Sex".'

'Look again, and carefully,' was the reply; then, as I turned
to watch the long procession I saw what I had not noticed
before, a tablet upon the breast of each giving the causes that
had brought them into this condition.

I found that about one out of ten of the whole number,
being born with strongly passional natures, and not finding
satisfaction by marrying, had chosen this life in preference to
the tortures of celibacy, or the unsatisfactory relief of solitary
vice. These looked healthier and happier than the others, but
far from being satisfied with their lot.

Of the others about four tenths had been driven to
deperation by man's perfidy, and, cast out by society, had
rushed into prostitution as the only thing left them. The
remaining half had been driven to it by want, and sold
themselves to keep from starvation, to feed their hungry
children, or perhaps an aged parent; in some cases all three
were combined.

There were cases in which a loved but helpless companion
was thus furnished with some comfort while the means by
which it was obtained was carefully hidden from the sufferer,
the woman thus becoming a veritable sacrifice to love, and
beyond what man is capable of, Christ souls in woman bodies,
martyred with the supremest martyrdom possible to human
beings; nailed alive to that of which the cross is but a symbol,
the masculine organ of generation.

As Lovella noted my thought she said: 'Man may be nailed

to a wooden cross with spikes of iron, but woman groans from the torture inflicted by a cross of flesh and blood.'

Her earnestness awed me, and my heart went out in a great wave of pity toward this unfortunate class of my sisters, for in all that I saw, in the lowest degradations I witnessed, I realized the truth of what the apostle Paul said. I accepted the spirit thereof though I should word it differently. He said, 'but for the grace of God,' I say, 'but for different conditions, surroundings and motive powers brought to bear, I might have sunk to the level of the lowest.'

When I had fully noted the causes that crowd women into prostitution Lovella asked. 'Can you see now why woman cannot abolish this curse?'

I looked at her in a sort of dazed way, for though partially sensing the reason I could not put it into words.

'It is the economic problem,' she said. 'Man controls the bread and butter question; that must be rightly adjusted first.'

'But,' said I, 'woman's right to herself puts it in her power to demand such adjustment; she can refuse herself to man till he makes it.'

'True, but they have conceded to us half a century of leadership, together with their sympathy and aid and that is much better than an attempt to force matters in the way you suggest. Many children, more than the entire population of to day, will be born in that time and some of the first born will have children, and even grandchildren.

'All these gestated under the influence of, and with the idea of "women in the lead," this together with the influence of mutual searching for the causes which produce the evils which so mar our grand civilization – searching for with the full determination of removing them – such children will be a radical improvement upon those gestated and born under the influence of the old ideas, and surely, that is a much better way of doing than to stand aloof and demand what man himself does not yet know how to grant.'

Selferedo listened intently to what Lovella was saying and I saw from the change in his countenance that this power of heredity had not entered into his calculations, and his thought was: 'Here is a new factor, one that we must neutralize in some way or she will beat us yet,' and he centered his hopes on hurrying up, overdoing the matter. 'Come,' said he, 'this philosophizing is all very fine, but when are we to get to work?'

'We have already begun our work,' she smilingly replied. 'Men of sense build their homes ideally first – build them in their brains before putting them into visible shape, and women must act with equal discretion. We have a great work to do, and it must be idealized in detail before it can be actualized. Don't hurry us; we have waited your motion for ages now please give us our own time.' . . .

12
'HILDA'S HOME'
(1897)

---*---

Rosa Graul (n.d.)

Of Rosa Graul, we again know only her name. 'Hilda's Home' was serialized in Lucifer, the Light Bearer (1883-1907), a journal of sex radicalism. Sex radicalism must be construed not as licentiousness, but as a means to attain a fuller humanity. As here, its believers often intended to conserve family and gender ideals through a freer expression of sexual love. As early as 1853, Elizabeth Cady Stanton (1815-1902) wrote Susan B. Anthony (1820-1906) that

> A child conceived in the midst of hate, sin, and discord, nurtured in abuse and injustice cannot do much to bless the world or himself. If we properly understood the science of life – it would be far easier to give to the world, harmonious, beautiful, noble, virtuous children, than it is to bring grown-up discord into harmony with the great divine soul of all. (Stanton/Anthony, p. 55)

'Hilda's Home' depicts this 'science of life' guiding the community's residents. This sentimental novel reveals women and men falling out of and into love – a love which when freely expressed was believed to extend beyond the beloved individual and to infuse a whole community with well-being. The novel concludes with the establishment of a community dedicated to free love and free labor relations. Contrary to Howland's fiction of a Social Palace just ready to operate at the novel's conclusion, this community exists for several years. Both experiments, however, are founded upon individual wealth. Excerpts show family, community, and labor ideals.

REFERENCES
Hal D. Sears, *The Sex Radicals* (Lawrence, Kansas: Regents Press of Kansas, 1977), esp. pp. 273, 319; *Elizabeth Cady Stanton/Susan B. Anthony: Correspondence, Writings, Speeches*, Ellen Carol DuBois, ed. (New York: Schocken, 1981); Taylor Stoehr, *Free Love in America: A Documentary History* (New York: AMS, 1979).

SELECTION
Chapters 22-66 only seem to have survived, from which pp. 303-4, 311, 358, 365-6, 374, 381-2 follow.

'HILDA'S HOME'

---- ✳ ----

CHAPTER LVI

[Hilda] was explaining and trying to make plain that vague
sweet dream of her future co-operative home, and none so
attentive, or none more so than Owen. She spoke of the
spacious halls where the ardent searchers after knowledge of
any kind might find their teacher. Of the library stocked with
volumes from the ceiling to the floor; of the lecture hall and the
theater; of the opportunities where every talent could be
cultivated; of the liberty – the free life – where every fetter
should be broken. Of the dining hall where they would partake
of their evening meal midst flowers and music; of the common
parlor where every evening should be an entertainment for all
wherein love and genuine sociability should always preside; of
the sacred privacy of the rooms where each man or woman
should reign a king or queen – the sanctum of each, closed to
all intruders, consecrated to the holiest and divinest of
emotions and self-unfoldment. She spoke of the grand conservatories filled with choicest flowers – the sweet-scented
blossoms, the trailing vines, the exotic plants; of the spacious
gardens, the sparkling, everplaying fountains; of the delicious,
health-giving baths; of the life of unconventionality, – of the
abandon; of the nursery rooms where baby lips were lisping
their first words and little toddling feet taking their first
uncertain steps; of the things of beauty surrounding the
prospective mother; of the unutterably sweet welcome that
awaited each coming child; of the full understanding that
would be taught to woman of the responsibility of calling into
life a new being; of how man would revere her, how he would
wait and abide her invitation; of the sweet co-operation and

planning how all should be worked to keep up the financial part.

'O', said she, 'it should, it would be paradise! – this my dream. But ah me! it is only a dream.'

CHAPTER LVII

As a being transfigured Hilda stood among them, her eyes shining, her cheeks glowing, her bosom heaving, looking far beyond them into space. A feeling came over Lawrence Westcot as with bated breath his eyes rested on her, of how utterly unworthy he was of the love of a creature so grand, so superior. A still, small voice whispered, 'Make yourself worthy!' – and then and there a high resolve was formed in his mind that he would surely do so. A solemn vow rose as a silent prayer from the depths of his heart that some day he would realize that sweet invitation. With him every man in the room became conscious of a feeling of inferiority, but not an impulse to bow in humility. Rather each head was crested higher with a feeling of lofty aspiration. Owen Hunter answered the closing remarks of Hilda's dream picture:

'Why, my dreaming maiden, should your dream be but a dream?'

A sad smile played about her lips,

'You forget that it is such an expensive one. It would take a fortune, an almost limitless fortune, to build us such a home. Of course we could be very, very happy in our little circle, as it is, in a much smaller and less expensive home, but I would have it large, so that we might welcome all who possess the same lofty thought to our circle, so that we should be able to give to the world an object lesson in the art of making life worth living, so grand and so glorious that the whole world would want to imitate our example.'

Owen smiled.

'What an enthusiast! Take my advice, little one, and until this grand, this glorious home can be ours, help us with your lofty aspirations, and help us not to despise our more limited advantages and privileges. In the meantime we will try to become more worthy of so perfect a home – as some years must of necessity elapse ere it can be completed.'

'Have I not said it is only a *dream*? How can I dare to hope it could ever be realized; and when I come to this home, day after day, and realize what privileges are ours the feeling sometimes comes to me, how wrong-headed I am to be constantly sighing for still more.'

Owen shook his head.

'You are mistaken Miss Hilda. Your sentiments and aspirations are not wrong. Harmonious and beautiful as is the life that has been granted you through the mutual understanding and sympathy of our kind host and hostess it is by no means complete. So dream on, plan on, and if there is an architect in our midst he shall transfer these plans to paper, and as soon as practicable, we will look about us for a suitable site, and when the spring sunshine calls all nature again to life, work shall begin, and what has so long been only a vague dream shall, all in good time, bloom into a living reality.'

All eyes hung upon the lips of the speaker. All ears drank in his words. Could such a thing be possible? Only Cora seemed to understand. Pressing close to his side, she drew his hand with a caressing motion to her smiling lips. With a hasty movement he withdrew the hand to lay it on the head covered with the soft fluffy hair; he pressed it close to him. Hilda drew a step nearer and extending both hands,

'You mean – O, Mr. Hunter! do you really mean that it can be done? that the home can and shall be ours? But how? how?'

Cora slipped down upon her knees at Hilda's side and caught both those hands in hers,

'Did I not tell you long ago, when I told you that story of my heartaches and my noble lover, that he possessed almost limitless wealth? He could not be one of us did he not consecrate some of his millions to the happiness of others. It is in his power to lay the foundation stone for the future ideal society, by showing to the world an example of how people should live. Don't you see my Hilda? Owen is wealthy, and he is going to build us our home.'

CHAPTER LXIII

Five years have passed since the dedication of that beautiful home; years that have brought their changes, as time invariably does. The mystic rooms – the sanctum of the expectant mother – have been occupied, again and yet again. . . .

196

[T]he young mothers ... did not devote all their time to their darling babies. O, no! Dearly as they loved them they found that they had other work to do while the little ones were left in the care of those who were perfectly trustworthy. Not to be petted, not to be pampered and spoiled, but left to those who understood how to get to the depths of each baby nature.

When it is remembered what preparation had been made for their advent it is not surprising that they were wonderfully good babies. When it is remembered with what joy they were welcomed – welcomed while still in the first stages of foetal growth; how carefully the prospective mothers had been kept under calm, sweet and pure influences; how their minds had been kept active without taxing their strength; how constantly their souls had been bathed in the luxury of sympathy and love; how every part of their natures had been kept teeming with life – overflowing life; how carefully undue excitement had been warded off; how they were given every opportunity for cultivating the higher human instincts, – the spiritual nature; – when all this is remembered we cannot help seeing that, on the principle of natural causation, the children of such mothers and of such influences could not be other than exceptionally well endowed and exceptionally well behaved.

But when the months had passed, during which the mother should give her personal care and attention to her cherished babe, it was transferred to the sole care of the experienced nurse, and she herself returned to her usual work, whatever that work might happen to be. There were so many fields open, and each made her choice. The head gardener was glad to get help in the tending and nursing of his plants and flowers. Nimble, dextrous fingers were needed to fashion the garments to be worn by the occupants of the home, and this large and beautiful home needed many willing hands to keep it beautiful. All this however was work which could be entrusted to and performed by stronger hands, if other work should prove more attractive, work in which more than ordinary intelligence and skill were required. Among our band were teachers of music and song, as might be expected of the artist soul seeking expression. Margaret had kissed her lover and baby good-bye and had given another season to her loved profession and had returned again with, O, such longing and love for the home and the circle of loved ones it contained.

But there was other work. . . .

CHAPTER LXIV

After two years of life in their co-operative home its inmates were convinced of its success and felt almost like thieves that they should enjoy so many privileges which were beyond the reach of those to whom they gave employment, and then the plans were made for a new home, and again Owen's millions did service and now a beautiful, grand structure had been erected. But not so far away from the place of work as their own. That would have been cruelty to the morning 'turn' who were expected to be at their post at the hour of seven, and equally unpleasant for the afternoon 'turn' as it would cause them to be late for their evening meal.

Right on the outskirts of the city, where fifteen minutes would be all that would be required to bring them back and forth, a site was brought upon the brink of the beautiful river, elevated just enough to be beyond the reach of any possible flood. A park had been laid out which in time would be one of the handsomest the city could boast of, with its miniature lakes, its splashing fountains, its dense shrubbery, its gleaming statuary and flowery banks. And right in the midst of these beautiful surroundings this monster home was built. For three long years the workmen toiled, until when finished it was the finest of its kind that fancy could depict. A place where home pleasures would be given the workers, such as they had never known; where every arrangement had been made to amuse, to instruct, to educate, to develop the inmates. It boasted of its school rooms, its college, its sculpture hall and artist's studio, its lecture hall and theater, where the best of traveling troupes were to be engaged, with perfect arrangements for the accommodation of those troupes. Here the players would not have to undergo the extra fatigue, after their tiresome work, to again dress for the street, catch the last cold an[d d]reary car that was to take them to their place of lodging. No indeed! The theater of the workers' home was a marvel of its kind. Large, airy, comfortable and well furnished rooms were attached to it, a room to every player, so near and convenient to the stage that it was not required to dress in little boxes or holes for their work. Here they could dress in quiet and comfort and then rest until the signal to begin was given.

When through with their work, in the pleasant, comfortable dining room connected with the theater for the convenience of this hard-working class of people – how hard-working few, not of the profession, ever realize – a simple but refreshing repast was served, which repast was so restful and had so much real comfort in it that the traveling bands invariably forgot that wines and liquors were absent from it.

Then there was a library with its thousands of volumes containing reading matter of every kind, but always choice, always select, always instructive. A large billiard room was also there. Then came the gymnasium for the development of physical strength and where both sexes were expected to participate. There was to be a singing class and dancing school.

The baths were not forgotten. Larger, more complete than at the first home, so many more were to make use of them here.

All arrangements were complete. A large, airy hall where breakfast and the mid-day meal were to be served. But here, as in that other home, the evening meal, which would be the chief meal of the day, was to be taken amidst nature's beauties in a large and beautiful conservatory. Owen had spent a fortune in furnishing it with the required plants which were of the rarest kinds. A miniature lake was formed in its center, wherein the little golden speckled beauties were dashing and splashing about in their merry chase. A fountain was reared in its center composed of a half dozen nude mermaids holding their hands aloft, their finger tips forming a circle from which the water was flung aloft in showering spray. Sweet voiced songsters filled the air with their thrilling music. Flowers bloomed in wild profusion; huge vases were filled with their brilliant treasures wherever they could be suitably placed. . . .

CONCLUSION

The evening meal is over. All have gathered on the broad veranda to watch the golden sunset as it dips its slanting rays in the river beyond. They are unusually quiet, even for this serious band. Last night's merry making has made them just a little tired, besides which their hearts are full of unuttered prayers for the future success of that new home.

Mrs. Leland is sitting in the comfortable depths of an easy chair. A sturdy little man of four summers perches upon her knee, patting grandma's cheek, tossing her hair in his efforts to smooth it, taking her face between both chubby hands and drawing her head forward so that he can kiss her happy, smiling lips and altogether making love in the most approved fashion.

Margaret is sitting at her feet, her arm thrown across her mother's knee, while her eyes with a happy, tender light follow the movements of her boy, and her heart swells with fond tenderness and pride at the knowledge that he is her very own.

At grandma's back stands Wilbur whose eyes also follow the antics of the boy when they for a few moments lose sight of the glorious sunset.

Mr. Roland is a visitor at the home tonight, and sits a little to the right of this group, quietly drinking in the scene before him in the pauses of the animated conversation he is carrying on with the brilliant little lecturer, Althea Wood, who also is a guest at the home tonight.

Farther to the left are various groups. The two pairs of sisters – Imelda and Cora, Edith and Hilda – have formed a circle, their babies forming the center of their attention. Three little prattlers and one sweet little cooing innocent, lying close to Imelda's breast.

O, the joys of young motherhood! And the group of men that were standing a little apart felt the influence of the spell and each thought his lady love had never looked more fair.

Alice in delicate health was reclining in an easy chair while Milton with adoring eyes stood over her chair ready to do her slightest bidding. O, if she were only safely tided over the coming hour of trial! And as the sigh escapes him his hand caressingly toys with the bright mass of shining hair.

Lawrence has his Norma perched upon his knee answering her many questions. She has grown to be quite a big girl now, but has never outgrown her early love for her papa, and ever with the old delight greets his coming. The two are so near to Alice that she can comfortably watch them, and while a smile of proud tenderness wreathes her lips, it is Milton's hand to which they are laid.

'My baby!' She whispers the tender words.

'A little longer patience,' is Milton's whispered reply, 'and your baby will be your own!'

Her hand went up to his face with a caressing touch.

'I know,' she smiling said, 'but it was Norma I meant this time.'

He drew the hand to his lips as with a knowing smile he answered:

'Ah, I see!'

Lawrence now and then let his eyes wander to the mother of his child, then they would turn to the group of fair young women where a pair of sweet gray eyes met his in a tender glance, then to rest on the little one reclining against his bosom. Which did he love most? His eyes lit up with a glad tenderness as they rested on the little one and then he drew the fair curly head so near him, close to his heart and hid his face in the fluffy masses; could he himself answer the question?

Many other faces we see which are all new to us, but they are all men and women worthy to be called by these names.

A group of the younger people have strayed down to the sweet-scented gardens gathering flowers as they go. Osmond and Homer are fast friends. Both are young men untouched by the rough hand of fate. Their young manhood, so perfect in its strength and beauty giving them the appearance of young kings, so proud, so lofty, was their bearing. Elmer, too, could scarcely be termed a boy any longer. His twenty years sat well on his broad shoulders and the eyes of the fifteen year old Aleta shone bright as stars, her cheeks flushed as he chased her through the winding mazes of the park, and when he had caught her and kissed the rosy lips she submitted as a matter of course with the most natural grace.

Osmond had thrown himself at the feet of Hattie Wallace whose nineteen summers sat lightly on her shoulders. She was such a fairy and with rosy hued cheeks she listened to the soft, love-freighted words that fell in whispers from Osmond's lips.

Homer's companion was a dark, soft-eyed young girl, timid and shy who had been an inmate of the home for one year, where she had come with her mother who had fled in the dead of night from her husband and sought refuge in this haven of rest and Homer was teaching the sweet Katie her first experience in the mysteries of love.

Aleda, the youngest of the Wallace girls was also there, and seventeen years had developed a truly pretty and healthy girl from the delicate querulous child. Another new comer had engaged her attention. Reading from a volume of Tennyson, a boy scarcely older than herself was reclining at her feet. He too had been brought there by a mother, not one who had fled the cruelties of an unappreciative husband, as she had never applied the title to any man. He had been a child of love.

His mother, in the wild sweet delirium of a first love, had

abandoned herself to her artist lover without a thought of right or wrong. And he, pure and noble had no thought of wronging her. But disease had early marked him for its own, and ere the child of his Wilma had seen the light of day his own life had closed in that sleep that knows no waking, and she was left alone to buffet the storms of life as best she could, an orphan and without friends. With a babe in her arms of 'illegal' origin the path of her life had not been strewn with roses. But amidst all her privations and trials she had kept her love pure for her child and had fostered only instincts pure and holy in the young mind, and when she heard of the home she applied at its gates, telling her story in pure, unvarnished words, never dreaming of an effort to hide any of her past. Only by the light of truth could the delicate fair woman thread her path through the world.

As might be expected, she had been received with open arms. Wilma, the mother of Horace, our young poet, and Honor, Katie's mother, could now be seen as they stand arm in arm watching the golden sunset and the children whose future promises to bring with it less of the pain that has so early drawn silver threads through their own brown locks.

The world at large knew not the full meaning of this home as yet. The world is yet too completely steeped in superstition and ignorance to have permitted its existence had the full meaning been known. The 'Hunter Co-operative Home' it had been called, and thus it was known to the world. It was known that babes had made their advent therein, but none but the initiated knew that marriage as an institution was banished from its encircling walls.

Would you ask us if happiness was so unalloyed within those walls that no pangs of regret or of pain could enter there? Well, no! We are not so foolish as to make such claim. There are hours of temptation; there are moments of forgetfulness; there are sometimes swift, keen, torturing pangs that nothing earthly can completely shut out. Our heroes and heroines are not angels. They are — when the very best of them has been said — only intelligent, sensible and sensitive men and women — but men and women who are possessed of high ideals and who are striving hard to reach and practicalize them. They live in a world of thought. They do nothing blindly, inconsiderately; their every action is done with eyes wide open. In trying to gain the goal they have set themselves to reach, they strive not to think of self alone. The future of those who have been entrusted to their care, the young lives their love has called into existence, exacts from them much of self-denial. They are individualists, yet not so absolutely such that they do not realize that sometimes the ego must be held in check so as not to rob another of his, or her, birth right.

You ask again, 'Does this home life, as you have pictured insure against the possibility of the affections changing?'

And again we answer, No! Certainly not. Such changes will and must come. Yet is it not to be expected that where there is *liberty*, in the fullest sense of the word, *life will be a constant wooing*? Is it not the lack of liberty that deals the death blow to many a happy, many a once happy home? to many a home that was founded in the sweetest of hopes, the brightest of prospects, only to be shattered and wrecked in a few short years? aye, even a few short months or weeks? And when such a change does come, in spite of all efforts to prevent, how great a thing it must be to know yourself FREE? free to embrace the new love without the horrible stigma of 'shame!' as our modern society now brands it, and which stigma causes such unspeakable misery, such endless suffering.

And if a woman desires to repeat the experience of motherhood, why should it be wrong when she selects another to be the father of her child, instead of the one who has once performed this office for her? Why should the act be less pure when she bestows a second love, when the object of this second love is just as true, just as noble, just as pure-minded as was the first one? Why should an act be considered a crime with one partner which had been fully justified with another?

Reader, judge me not hastily. Judge not my ideas, my ideals, without having first made a careful study of life as you find it around you. My words are backed by personal experience and observation, experience as bitter as any that has been herein recorded. Indeed I doubt if I should, or could, ever have given birth to the thoughts expressed in these pages had it not been for that experience – which is one of a thousand – and when you have carefully weighed my words, think of the good that must result to future generations when unions are purely spontaneous, saying nothing of the increase of happiness of those who are permitted thus to choose, and to live.

When, O, when will the great mass of humanity learn and realize that in ENFORCED MOTHERHOOD, unwelcome motherhood, is to be found the chief cause of the degradation that gives birth to human woe. When will they see that enforced motherhood is the curse resting upon and crushing out the life energies of woman; while on the other hand, the consciousness of being the mother of a DESIRED babe, a child conceived in a happy, a loving embrace, needs no other blessing, no other sanction, than such act itself bestows.

13
'A DREAM OF THE TWENTY-FIRST CENTURY' (1902)

*

Winnifred Harper Cooley
(c. 1875-after 1955)

Although the only daughter of a famous woman, social activist Ida Husted Harper (1851-1931), facts about the life of Winnifred Harper Cooley resist recovery. Her parents married in 1871; she must have been born in Indiana about 1875 if she were about 21 upon receiving in 1896 an A.B. in Ethics from Stanford University. Her parents had divorced in 1890 and her mother moved to Indianapolis where Winnifred was then attending Girls' Classical School, established in 1882 by May Wright Sewell (1844-1920). Her mother apparently moved with her to California for the college years. In 1899 Winnifred married the Rev. George Elliot Cooley, a Unitarian minister. She was a widow by 1926, however. A journalist, lecturer, and teacher, she considered a diversity of subjects, among them women's issues, pure food, travel, literature, and current drama.

In 1904 Winnifred published The New Womanhood *in which she surveys the historical roots of women's personal liberty, formerly confined to the occasional genius, now more generally possible to women as a class, she thinks. In addition the book covers such issues as single women, divorce, co-operative housekeeping, population control, and occupational access. Later she wrote articles defending suffragists, first against upstart 'suffragettes' (Hearst's Mag. 15 (October 1908):1066-71) and second against conservative, outdated suffragists (Harper's Weekly 58 (27 September 1913):7-8). The dream vision that follows incorporates several of these concerns.*

REFERENCES
Notable American Women, vols II and III (Cambridge, Mass.:

Harvard University Press, 1971); Barbara Quissell, 'The New World that Eve Made' in *America as Utopia*, ed. Kenneth M. Roemer (New York: Franklin, 1981), pp. 166, 174; *Stanford* (University) *Class of '96* (Stanford, California: Stanford Alumni Assn, 1926), pp. 127-9.

SELECTION
Complete.

'A DREAM OF THE TWENTY-FIRST CENTURY'

————————— * —————————

It was New Year's night of the twentieth century. The new cycle of a hundred years had been ushered in by chimes and bugles, by jollity and revel, and I was wearied by all the excitement, and, sleeping, dreamed a dream. I dreamed that it was the first day of the *twenty-first* century, and that I, an old woman, somehow sojourning still upon the earth, was seeking knowledge as to the new conditions. My instructress was a radiant creature, in flowing, graceful robes – a healthful, glorious girl of the period: the product of a century of freedom.

'Tell me,' I said, 'what evolution has done for you, my fair Feminine Type.' The maiden answered: 'We have made such advances that I fear to seem egotistic if I tell you, for I have heard that at the beginning of the twentieth century the world actually considered itself civilized! I have tried to read the history of those days, but ignorance, cruel injustices, and utter irrationality existing in a supposed free land affect me as unpleasantly in retrospect as the Spanish Inquisition affected you.'

I felt somewhat insulted at this reflection upon my own times, and replied: 'But we of the nineteenth and twentieth centuries made marvelous additions to the wealth and knowledge of nations. We invented the automobile, wireless telegraphy, and the Roentgen ray; we gave you a fine system of education, a democracy –'

'Not so,' she interrupted. 'You gave a republic; a corrupt, subsidized government, manipulated by greed, controlled by one set of selfish mercenaries after another, under partizan leaders; a one-sided affair at best, where only one sex voted, and an absurd electoral college registered the votes of States instead of counting the majority of the people. Now, we have unqualified equal suffrage – for all of the citizens are educated,

207

and women are among the best voters; also the initiative and referendum, complete civil service, government control of public utilities –'

'Stop!' I cried; 'I never could straighten out those technical names.'

'You see,' she explained, 'in your day millionaires were made by getting control of that which the people were obliged to have, and charging what they wished, as if they were imitation gods, having a monopoly of Nature. They almost charged for the air you breathed! We have abolished oil trusts, private ownership of mines, railways, electric-light plants, and express and telegraph companies; and you would be amazed to see how the frightful discrepancies in individual wealth are done away with, without any artificial schemes of "dividing up" personal property and giving the belongings of the industrious man to the shiftless. Ambition and individuality are still allowed; also private incomes. All these businesses are run as smoothly in the cooperative spirit as the Post Office ever was; and they pay for themselves, besides allowing the poorer people to use the necessities and comforts for a nominal sum. I wish I might tell you of the marvelous changes wrought along industrial lines, but the instances are too numerous to explain.'

'You mean that sweat-shops are abolished?'

'All such, and a thousand other evils once considered almost a requisite of trade. The hours of labor in every department of work are greatly reduced. By using all the adults, permitting no dependent classes, either tramps, paupers, or idle rich, we have found that the world's work can be done by each healthy individual working five hours a day. You will readily understand how this benefits the indolent by compelling exercise, and the industrious by affording leisure,, not to speak of the good that accrues to society by having all its members in a normal state, with time at their command for inventions, art, and letters.'

'This accounts, also, doubtless, for the good health that seems to prevail?'

'There are many reasons – increased happiness, development of science, perfect sanitation everywhere existing. The abolition of slums was brought about chiefly by women.'

'In my time, excepting the college settlement workers and the Salvation Army, there were few who seriously labored along such dirty lines.'

'Some time ago women began to comprehend that, not alone for the safety of their own loved children but for that of all little ones, in the alleys as well as on the boulevards, there must be an eradication of disease, that the rising generation should not begin life hampered by unclean bodies and tainted morals. Hindered at first, by not having official power, the women did thier best with the insidious, left-handed influence that always was recommended to them by men; but when given political freedom they went to work with enthusiasm, using the 'influence' *necessary* to effect transformations – the ballot. And so we have a fine sanitary condition and a healthful race.'

'Marriage is as of old?' I timidly ventured.

'That depends upon what you consider was in vogue in your time. Monogamy was officially recognized but not universally practised, we have been told.'

'I thought perhaps it is now abolished,' I retorted.

'Oh, no; it is almost universal with us. The improvement in the average income has done away with the barrier of poverty, and a higher moral standard has abolished that nineteenth-century horror – the city bachelor. Every one marries, and the number of ideal unions is really very large. The age of marrying is a trifle higher, following the tendency of your time; but this is as it should be, for every one stays in college until at least twenty-two.'

'Every one?'

'Yes, our compulsory education extends through college, and all, including universities, are free. As in your day, the happiest marriages were those formed by the products of co-educational colleges; so now, you see, all the unions are happy ones.'

'I do not see many children?'

'No; they do not swarm the back streets like rats. But you will find, by our statistics, that the increase is sufficient to keep the race extant.'

'Goodness! Are families regulated by law?'

'Hardly that; but the advance of civilization seems to go hand in hand with a decrease in population. The tendency toward having fewer children has been encouraged instead of censured by public opinion, which now, as ever, is the greatest ruler of mankind. Instead of bewailing the "good old families of fifteen" or acting hypocritically, we frown upon people who bring more than two children into the world, unless they, by virtue of excessive wealth, health, morals, or talents, seem

209

unusually well qualified to educate and nurture a family. Social Control suggests that men and women devote much thought to the minds and hearts of their youth; consequently, the character of children has increased marvelously as the number has decreased. Even their longevity is now prolonged, and the death-rate of infants is remarkably small.'

'All this is strange and fascinating, though it would have shocked my contemporaries,' I ventured.

'It is not unnatural. It is but the logical working out of civilization. Another cause for the finer type of childhood today is the tender love and congeniality existing between parents. The abolition of multi-millionaires prevents mercenary marriages, and a few simple laws discourage discrepancies in age between men and women; but unless physically and morally unfit, two persons strongly attracted to each other are expected to wed.'

'All this is most remarkable; and, I doubt not, the inventions and all material matters have kept pace with these social and moral innovations. But how could such radical transformations be wrought – improvements, I grant, and desired by the prophets of my day – while human nature remained sordid, selfish, grasping, and sensual? Surely your last hundred years have not revolutionized the *heart of man?*'

'I think it is mainly due to our rational religion. It was a mighty struggle to overcome dogmatism, superstition, ritualism, emotionalism, and conservatism, especially as the leaders of our great Religion of Humanity had nothing exciting, dramatic, pompous, or mystical to offer in place of the old. But simplicity and sense at last conquered. The only weapon of the new church was Education; and at length all the old creeds crumbled away, and now are preserved in libraries, with the Icelandic myths and Vedic hymns, to record the development of the mind of man in its groping toward God.'

'Is the new religion Christian?'

'Yes; its essentials are based upon the moral teachings of Jesus, but it does not fear to inculcate the best that has been worked out by every people that has struggled and suffered and aspired beneath the sun. It does not scorn the simplest death-song of an Indian if this expresses some noble conception of immortality more clearly than do the sages.'

'And it is this world-religion that has wrought so many reforms in politics, economics, and morals?'

'Yes, and it has done more. By destroying the spite and fight over hair-splitting theological problems it has enabled men and women to turn their zeal and energy into practical ethics and philanthropy, and to believe that if all men are indeed children of God, and brothers, they must act as such; and so we have attained Universal Peace!'

'Indeed? This must be something like heaven. The Bible proclaimed "peace on earth," but for two thousand years Christians seemed content with bloody war.'

'We are not yet perfect, but we are no longer pessimists. The low rumble of insurrection heard in your day has died away, and all of us are bending every force toward the serious business of making life worth living and this world habitable, in a moral as well as in a material sense. Criminals, paupers, and tramps are practically unknown, and the strong public feeling toward one standard of purity – and that the highest – for men and women has elevated the social life of the whole world.'

'I should think you would want never to die!' I cried.

'The rate of mortality is much lower than formerly; we know little of old age, in the sense of decrepitude, as of yore. We live better as well as longer lives, too,' said the beautiful woman. 'We do not profess any didactic knowledge of a future existence, but we hope and long for personal immortality, as people always have hoped and longed, and our scientists and psychologists believe they are about to prove it. We all try to live so that if our activities continue after death we may have somewhat approximated perfection upon this earth.'

I awoke – to hear the ragged little newsboys (products of an imperfect social system) bellowing forth the financial crashes, murders, suicides, and scandals so glowingly regaled by the 'yellow journals.' I turned my face to the pillow, and prayed: 'O God, may I live to do my small part of the world's work, and help to hasten the conditions that I dare dream will prevail in the twenty-first century!'

14
SETH WAY: A ROMANCE OF THE NEW HARMONY COMMUNITY (1917)

———————————*———————————

Caroline Dale Parke Snedeker
(1871-1956)

Born in New Harmony, Indiana, a great-granddaughter of the
communitarian experimenter Robert Owen (1771-1858),
Caroline Dale Parke heard stories of early Harmony from her
grandmother Caro Neef Owen, wife of Owen's son David Dale
Owen. There she studied piano at the College of Music. In
1903 she married Charles H. Snedeker, Dean of the Cathedral
of Cincinnati. The couple moved to Hempstead, New York.
Until his death in 1927, her husband encouraged her career as
an author of children's books – several set in ancient Greece or
Rome, several depicting New Harmony. For example,
Downright Dencey (1927) and The Beckoning Road (1929)
concern a Quaker family of Nantucket, Massachusetts, who
decide to move to New Harmony. For adults, she wrote The
Town of the Fearless (1931), a fictionalized version of her own
family history as connected to New Harmony. She also edited
The Diaries of Donald MacDonald (1942), an Irish resident of
the New Harmony experiment. Seth Way (1917), from which
this excerpt comes, is a fictionalized biography of zoologist
Thomas Say, another community resident. For this book the
author used the pseudonym 'Caroline Dale Owen.' As in earlier
writing by Corbett, Howland, and Phelps, the position of
women in marriage receives prominent concern.

REFERENCES
Alethea K. Helbig, 'Caroline Dale Parke Snedeker' in American
Women Writers (New York: Ungar, 1982), vol. 4:122-4;
Junior Book of Authors, 2nd Ed. Rev., ed. Stanley J. Kunitz
and Howard Haycraft (New York: Wilson, 1951).

SELECTION
Includes pp. 398-401.

SETH WAY: A ROMANCE OF THE NEW HARMONY COMMUNITY

—— ❋ ——

'But what is this?' she exclaimed, — 'this legal paper addressed to me?'

'Suppose you open it,' I suggested.

Like a Christmas child she unfolded it.

'But I don't understand,' she said, glancing at the paper and stopping to question my face; 'is this a letter you have written me?'

'No,' I said; 'it is my marriage promise. I don't know how I had the courage to write it — for I wrote it months ago.'

She still seemed to question, so I went on:

'One day Robert-Dale and I talked together about you and how you had a right to your own perilous daring. And then I got him to show me those laws which even out here in this new Indiana give a woman no rights to her own property or her own sacred person. As I came home picturing you with your character subject to such laws, I grew very indignant. I tried to meditate what I ought to do to make you free of them if' — I smiled into her face — 'if I should ever have the chance. That night, very late, I came up here, lighted my candle, and wrote out this.'

'You good, generous man,' she called me with tears; for she had seen what the paper contained. 'Read it for me, Seth. You see I cannot.'

So I read it to her in a low voice, not disturbing Mr. Maclure at his work:

MARRIAGE LINES

This day I enter into a matrimonial engagement with Jessonda Lucrezia Maria Giovanni Battista Macleod, a

213

young woman whose opinions in all important subjects, and whose mode of thinking and feeling, coincide more intimately with my own than do those of any other individual with whom I am acquainted.

We contract a legal marriage, for we desire a tranquil life, in so far as it can be obtained without a sacrifice of principle.

We have selected the simplest ceremony which custom and the laws of the State recognize and which in consequence of the liberality of these laws involves not the necessity of calling in the aid of a member of the clerical profession –

'But we *are* calling a preacher,' she interrupted.

'I thought that, perhaps you would wish one, though when I wrote I had in mind the Quaker way.'

'Yes,' she answered, 'that is better, we will have it the Quaker way. Your father was a Quaker, Seth. Your own father and mother must have been married in that way.'

'Yes, they were,' I said. And taking her hand in mine I pursued my reading:

– a profession, the authority of which we do not recognize, and the influence of which we are led to consider often injurious to society. The Quaker ceremony, too, involves not the repeating of those forms which we deem offensive, inasmuch as they outrage the principles of human Liberty and Equality, by conferring rights and imposing duties unequally on the sexes.

The ceremony which we have chosen consists simply in the signature by each of us of a written contract in which we agree to take each other as husband and wife according to the laws of the State of Indiana, our signatures being attested by those of all our friends who may be present.

Of the *unjust rights* which, in virtue of this ceremony, a[n] iniquitous law tacitly gives me over the person and property of another, I cannot legally, but I *can morally*, divest myself. And I hereby earnestly desire to be considered by others as utterly divested, now and during the rest of my life, of any such rights – the barbarous relics of a feudal and despotic system, soon destined in the onward course of improvement to be wholly swept away, and the existence of which is a tacit insult to the good sense and good feeling of the present comparatively civilized age.

I now set down these sentiments on paper as a simple record of the views and feelings with which I enter into an engagement, important in whatever light we consider it – views and feelings which I believe to be shared by her who is to become my wife.

SETH WAY.

'Jessonda,' I said, as I folded the paper with unsteady hands, 'whatever you may receive from priest or magistrate, these will be your true marriage lines.'[1]

'Yes, oh, yes,' she whispered. Then suddenly she took the paper from my hand and ran with it to Mr. Maclure.

'Look!' she cried, her eyes yet bright with their tears. 'See what your dear, good son wrote for me long ago when I did not deserve it.'

Maclure adjusted his glasses and read it smiling – puzzled, of course. He stopped midway.

'But this date,' he declared, 'is six months back. Seth Way, this is the most audacious piece of presumption I ever heard of!'

'It is not, it is not!' cried Jessonda. 'They are the most honest, beautiful words a lover ever penned!'

Then she stopped in confusion.

Maclure ceased smiling; and I saw his face soften as he looked at my darling's flushed cheeks and glad eyes.

'Jessie Macleod,' he said, 'I am going to take back something that I have said about you. Seth can tell you what it is. You are worthy of your happiness, though you have won the heart of the most honorable young man I know.'

'Now you shall be our witness,' said Jessonda, and, taking the pen from Maclure's desk, she wrote, in her fine bold hand, –

I gratefully concur in these sentiments.
Jessonda Lucrezia Maria Giovanni Battista Macleod.

And handed it over for him to sign.

---

[1]Note by Columbine Way: Fictional daughter of Seth Way and narrator of the account.
You can see these marriage lines in the files of the *New Harmony Gazette* in our Public Library.

215

15
MILDRED CARVER, U.S.A.
(1919)

*

Martha S. Bensley Bruère
(1879-1953)

Educated at Vassar College, the University of Chicago, and the Art Institute of Chicago, Martha S. Bensley painted portraits in Chicago from 1895 to 1903. In 1907 she married Robert W. Bruère, an author and specialist in industrial relations. They collaborated on her first book Increasing Home Efficiency *(1912), a work recommending domestic training for both sexes. The Bruères believed that both men and women should know how to manage a household and that women should not be solely responsible for domestic duties. Her eutopian bildungsroman* Mildred Carver *(1919) revises Edward Bellamy's industrial army of* Looking Backward *(1888): women and men enlist for one year in a Universal Service of public works where job assignments depend upon individual preference rather than upon sex. In 1927 Martha wrote a series of articles on Prohibition. She collaborated with Mary Ritter Beard (1876-1958) on an anthology of women's humor called* Laughing Their Way *(1934). To this volume Martha contributed several cartoons. Apparently Martha and Mary were friends of long standing. From 1934 to 1936 Martha served as an administrative assistant in the U.S. Forest Service. This experience led to her writing* Your Forests *(1945). She was also a contributing editor of* Survey. *In addition she was a clubwoman. In 1953 she died of a heart attack. Robert survived her.*

Serialized in The Ladies' Home Journal *from June 1918 to February 1919, before appearing as a book,* Mildred Carver *depicts an upper-class young woman developing a social conscience from her year of Service. Her resolution of her dual need for work and love constitutes the novel's plot. Of this particular issue activist Crystal Eastman (1881-1928) wrote at about this time, 'How to reconcile these two desires in real life,*

216

that is the question.' (Quoted, Sochen, p. 51). Excerpts stressing the complexities of marital choice and commitment to meaningful work follow. The immediately following paragraphs show the relationship between marriage and the Universal Service obligation as well as the democratizing effect of participation in the Service.

REFERENCES
Ann J. Lane, personal communication, 16 February 1983; The New York Times, 11 August 1953, p. 27:4; for background, see June Sochen, *Movers and Shakers: American Women Thinkers and Activists, 1900-1970* (New York: Quadrangle, 1973).

SELECTION
Includes pp. 15, 18, 24, 25, 253-6, 273-6, 286-9.

MILDRED CARVER, U.S.A

---
*

'It looks to me as though you've forgotten that you've got to go
into the Service whether you want to or not. They don't ask
you whether you're going to be married, or vaccinated or
graduated or anything else – they ask you if you're eighteen
years old and if you are you have to go. In your normal frame
of mind you know this as well as I do. Mildred has got to go
into the Service too. And you ought to know, if you don't, that
the law doesn't recognize any marriage between people who
haven't served their year.' . . .

'Universal Service isn't a thing you can dodge, my son. Every
excuse that can possibly be thought of has been tried already
and unless you are physically disabled or mentally deficient –
and I'm proud to say you're neither – you've the choice of
going into the Service or going into jail, and incidentally losing
your citizenship, and so has Mildred. Don't be a fool, Nick.'

'But, dad – Mildred – I asked her to marry me this evening!'

. . . Wicks came back around the table, stopped for an
appreciable moment behind her chair, and then with a hand
that was not as steady as the hand of the perfect footman
should be, put beside her a large square envelope, redirected
from New York, and marked in the upper left-hand corner:

Department of Universal Service
Washington, D.C.

Mildred took the envelope uncomprehendingly and opened
it. A stiff printed announcement, – large, formidable, –
summoning her, Mildred Carver, by the authority of the
President and Congress of the United States, as she was
eighteen years old to enter the National Service on the first day

of October and to remain in it for twelve months thereafter. She was to indicate on the inclosed blanks the division of the Service she preferred, and be ready for departure when she was notified. It was signed by the Secretary of Universal Service. . . .

'. . . say, Wicks,' [Nick] called, 'come and tell us about the Forestry Service.'

The footman was much embarrassed. It is one thing to talk to a young gentleman, man to man, when you are going to a fire with him in the middle of the night, and quite another to stand in your distinguishing but not honorable uniform and tell a lovely young girl whom you serve, and her quite obviously accepted lover about the greatest year in your life – and that so small a thing compared with what they may expect for themselves! But after a moment Wicks forgot himself in telling what it meant for him to be living with boys who had come from every other part of the country – to have been given the sort of academic training he could have got in no other way – training in the structure of trees, in the cell theory of growth, in the lives of insects and their habits.

'Why, I just got to see how it was the world was goin' on – trees and insecs and the way the rocks happened, too. You can't never feel the same about anything again.'

And the thing that the footman didn't say in words, but which was implied in every syllable – and he became very much less of a footman as he did it – was the great difference it made for him not to be working for any one individual but for everybody together. . . .

Two days later as John Barton came down the Carvers' stone steps whose costly whiteness he was blind to, a young man stepped up to him.

'Is this Mr. Barton?' he asked; 'I'm Nicholas Van Arsdale. If you are going to your hotel, may I walk with you?'

John Barton had never heard of Nicholas Van Arsdale, but he expected surprises in New York and the lad did not look formidable.

Nick had to call on every bit of that Dutch determination which had held him building roads in the desert because he thought it was his duty to his country, in order to get started on his talk with John Barton. Out of the corner of his eye the boy studied the man of whom he had heard so much; whom he hated with a fierce, young jealousy; whom he wanted to persuade. Nick appreciated the tall, thin figure, the strong, clean features, and most particularly the charm which his age and experience might have for Mildred, as he plunged desperately into his talk. As they swung up Fifth Avenue through the alternate patches of bright light and deep shadow, the city was tidying up for the night and putting itself to bed. The last rumbling buses went by with their young Service conductors whistling on the back step; Universal Service postmen were making their last collections from the boxes; burly night policemen had begun their rounds. New York was settling slowly upon its pillows.

'Do you want to marry her yourself?' John Barton asked bluntly when Nick had blurted out the case between them as he saw it – the case which determined Mildred's career by her marriage and hung her happiness on the man she accepted as a husband.

Nick was silent while their heels beat out the time for half a block.

'No,' he said slowly, 'I don't! If it were a question of marrying Mildred – just that all by itself, it's – well, you know how I feel about that I guess. But I couldn't take her out to wherever I might be making roads; she'd be miserable! And I couldn't come back to New York and just live the way her people do.'

'They seem pretty comfortable to me.'

'They are – they're deadly comfortable – I couldn't *stand* it.'

'Couldn't stand being comfortable!'

'Not that way – not giving up the work I know I ought to do – not stopping helping making roads that the government needs to move the crops and the ore and the lumber on! I can't go back on my duty to my country because I want to marry Mildred! I'm not such a poor sort as that!'

'But you'll be moving about and perhaps you'll get into something better than road making. If you waited a few years don't you think you'd be able to support her comfortably?'

'It isn't that,' said Nick, 'it isn't being able to support her, it is being able to make her happy! That's why I am talking to you, Mr. Barton. What I want is to make you see the reasons why Mildred ought not to marry me, are just exactly the reasons why she ought not to marry you. If you care anything like as much as I do, you have no right to marry her at all.'

John Barton stopped abruptly and turned on Nick. He was

obviously angry with the slow white anger of New England that turns men speechless. His hands clenched themselves in his pockets, his teeth set hard. How dared this young whippersnapper try to dictate what he should or should not do!

Nick faced him bravely. Like two primitive warriors they stood opposite each other fixing the destiny of the woman they both desired. To them she was a lovely and desirable appendage – the flower of some man's life – only they differed widely from their prehistoric ancestors in that it mattered desperately to both of them that she should be happy. Was not the life they took for granted for her the natural life of the fortunate woman? Wasn't the choice they conceded to her the choice between possible husbands? Weren't they torn now with the intention of saving her from the contingency of a foolish choice? If she was not literally the prize of some man's bow and spear, she was at least the prize of his powers of persuasion. That she might be expected to have plans for herself not bounded by marriage had not occurred to either of them. At last John Barton turned and walked on up the avenue.

'You don't seem to remember that she has promised to be my wife,' he said finally.

'Yes, I'm considering that and also the fact that she once promised to be mine.'

'What!' cried the man, turning on him.

'Oh it was when we were both kids – before we went into the Service. Nobody would let us be engaged then and when our Service year was over I couldn't stop working for the U.S. just because I didn't have to any more. So I didn't come back.'

'I see. You thought you couldn't give up your work and she wouldn't be happy the way you had to live. Well, it's different in Minneapolis. I can give her a good home there. I guess we'd be able to hire help if she needed to. I can get a brick house through one of those building and loan associations and furnish it up right. I'm saving money every year. They tell me the schools are first class when we get around to need them. The city is pretty and the climate good. I'm not going to say how much I care for her, because that is a question between her and me, but I will make it quite plain to you, young man, that I care enough.'

'You don't care enough if you marry her – you wouldn't marry her if you did. You don't care as much as I do, if you don't just let her alone!'

The older man kept himself in hand.

'I look at it this way; the girl is grown up and she has the right to choose what man she'll marry. If she wants you, all right. You are young and good looking, and I suppose you're well educated. Road making isn't the job I would pick out for myself, because you can't settle down and have a home of your own – and a woman likes a home of her own, and ought to have it; but you look smart and I guess you could get into something else easily enough. You knew her pretty well before she went into the Service, and I have known her pretty well since, and I don't see any reason why she wouldn't be happy enough if she married me. It all comes back to what she wants to do.'

'No,' Nick broke in, 'she might want to do something that would make her miserable. I want to save her from the chance of making mistakes.'

'And still you don't intend to ask her yourself?'

'No, I don't. Because I think she oughtn't to marry either of us – the kind of a girl she is, and the life she's had!'

'She was a good little worker in the mill', said John Barton.

'I know,' said Nick desperately, 'it isn't that! Mildred would work or do anything else she had to do. It's the things outside of your work or mine that would make the difference. It's the whole life that matters – she ought to be quite a different kind of a girl.'

'Well,' said John Barton slowly, 'you haven't convinced me and you haven't persuaded me. I care for her and I am going to marry her. You have got the right to cut me out, if you can – but she's engaged to me now and I'll keep her if I can. There is just one thing I think that we ought to agree about. That is, not to tell her that we talked it over. I should think it would make a girl mad to be talked over like this.'

'Yes,' said Nick, 'I think it would, and if you told her that I have been trying to persuade you not to marry her, I know just what she would think of me.'

The older man held out his hand and Nick with his lips trembling and his brown eyes filling, put his slowly into it.

'I don't think,' said John Barton slowly, 'she would make a mistake in taking either of us.'

'And I think,' said Nick unhappily, 'that it would be just like death for her to marry either you or me.'

To neither of them did it occur that Mildred Carver might be anything but the natural 'second' in the game of some man's career. She had spent her required term in the government service, but what of that? Wasn't she the same feminine complement she had been before?

Nick knew that having had a year of work, it was his patriotic duty to go on with it. John Barton's work was his personal, inseparable religion. But both of them took it for granted that the duties of Mildred's citizenship had all been paid.

Nick flung round and started south again and John Barton stood watching him.

'Poor kid – he's in love with her all right, but I don't see what I can do about it. Besides he probably wouldn't be able to support her for a good while.'

John Barton walked on to his hotel, thinking contentedly of the little home in Minneapolis – out in one of those new suburbs where he could buy through a building and loan association. He'd get her an upright piano – perhaps a Victrola, if Mildred would rather have it – and they'd keep a girl. His mind pictured transiently a golden oak dining table with a highly varnished top and machine carved chairs and a sideboard to match. He seemed to get a flash of bright color from the rug and see lace curtains hanging primly at the windows. All these dreams of the future were plain to John Barton, but the realities of the present were heavily obscured. He could see the straight road from the mill where he earned his modest salary to the little red brick cottage where he meant to spend it, but he never even suspected the devious network that led from mines and mills and factories, from railroads and public utilities, from government bonds and steamship securities, from foreign investments and domestic holdings, to the house on Washington Square. The signs of great wealth were not visible to him because they manifested themselves in forms he did not know. Had Mrs. Carver been bedecked with diamonds instead of wearing around her neck a modest string of what looked to him like white beads, – had she rustled in silk – had Mildred's arms clinked bracelets and her clothes dripped lace he might have understood. But what was a simple red brick house facing an imperfectly groomed park that it should enlighten him? He intended to have a red brick house himself shortly and there were plenty of parks in Minneapolis. Of the cash equivalents of pictures and draperies, rugs and china he knew nothing. He had never bought a chair or a table or a dish in his life. There did seem to be a good deal of 'help' about, but that was probably a New York custom – and they did have a motor. Well, didn't he hope to buy a Ford when they got the house paid for? The Carvers were well off – he could see that – but he was not conscious of any overwhelming financial disparity between him and Mildred. And then his mind settled on something very small and soft and warm, being rocked by the fireside, and something very fat and blond learning to walk, and something very active and vigorous, and perhaps a little unruly swinging his books by a strap on his way to school. And John Barton's eyes crinkled up at the corners and his teeth gleamed between his lips and he entered the lobby of his modest hotel.

The next day Nick entering the Carver house just as luncheon was over, saw John Barton catch at Mildred's hand as they left the dining room.

'Nick,' cried Mildred when she saw him. 'Oh, Nick!' and then recovering herself, she held out her hand quite formally. Mrs. Carver greeted him with a little anxious catch of the breath and Ruthie and Junior fell upon him in glee.

Mildred turned to introduce the two men but John Barton said gravely:

'I met Mr. Van Arsdale last night.'

There was something of the condemnatory preacher in his tone.

Mildred looked from one to the other in surprise.

'We took a walk together – and had a talk.'

'Yes,' said Nick with a quaver in his voice, 'we had a talk and I want to have another now – and Mildred with us.'

'I don't think that would be necessary – and I don't see that we have anything to talk over anyway. – I thought we settled it last night.'

Mildred, the last vestige of color gone from her face, turned into the library.

'Come in here, please,' she said in a high little voice.

Her mother hesitated on the threshold and then let the three go in without her. She realized that her work on that situation was done. She had written for Nick and he was here. The immemorial triangle of two men wanting the same woman had been created and they must solve it between them. – As she went up the long curving stairs she was trembling – so much hung in the balance of the next half hour!

Out by the great fireplace Mildred faced the two men, though her cheeks were white and her lips trembling.

'Well?' she questioned in a clear, light voice, as sober as a bell and as insistent.

They were dumb before her – she seemed to them both quite suddenly, to be another person from the young girl whose happiness they were so concerned in safeguarding – an individual, an independent human being quite able to determine her own life and with plenty of characteristics in addition to charm and lovableness. They had both thought of her as looking at life through eyes only half opened to the things they saw in it. What could the obligation to serve the state mean to her now that her Service year was done. But she stood as a new thing, – a judge set over them.

'Well?' she questioned insistently.

John Barton turned to Nick as if to offer him the first chance to speak and Nick regarded him resentfully.

'Mildred, I heard that you were going to marry Mr. Barton and I came back to ask you not to!'

John Barton interrupted him:

'He waited for me when I left you last night and tried to persuade me not to marry you – I thought we agreed not to mention the matter to you – but Mr. Van Arsdale seems not to have understood it that way.'

'I know that was what we said, but I've been thinking of it ever since and I know we were wrong and that I hadn't any right to keep my agreement about it. It's so awful anyway that just breaking my word doesn't seem to matter. I care so much more about not having you miserable than looking like a cad,' Nick plunged ahead.

'I did ask him, – Mr. Barton, not to marry you. I told him he's no right to ask you to live in such a different way and among such different people. And the things girls like to do just aren't in Minneapolis to be done. You'd hate it! You wouldn't be happy and I couldn't stand it not to have you happy – Mildred!'

Nick, growing incoherent, put the weakest side of his case foremost. As Mildred looked at him her color came back and her eyes began to flash with a light that was not at all gentle.

'I don't see, Nick, how it can matter to you.'

The boy crimsoned.

'I know Mildred – I should think you'd feel just that way – only – you know, don't you – that's the reason I stayed away? I knew you'd hate the kind of life out there in the desert or anywhere else where there weren't any roads and had to be some built. It wouldn't be right to take you way out there – even if – you –'

'Even if I wanted to go?'

Nick looked at her unhappily.

'What do you think I want to do, Nick?'

'Why, what every other girl does, I suppose, – have a good time and get married.'

'Well, I don't – or at least that's only part of it. I want to work! I'm a citizen just as much as anybody else and I've got to give my share of partriotic service just like any man or any ten men. I've got to do something that needs to be done!'

A light began to grow in Nick's eyes and he stepped hastily towards her; this was a new Mildred he had never dreamed of – but she drew near to John Barton's side and slipped her hand in his –

'And so I'm going to marry the most splendid and noble man there could be, Nick. It doesn't matter whether I live in Kamchatka or the middle of the Sahara Desert – it's all the same. I'm going to help him to see that the flour's made right and packed right, and shipped on time; and I couldn't help being happy doing that, could I? I can get along without the concerts and the dances and the dinners and the shows – we didn't have any of these things in the Service and I didn't miss them half as much as I miss the Service now. And as for the *people* – Why, Nick, I met every kind of people there are while I was out there, and now I just meet all the same kind. It's so *dull*. I can't *stand* it, being so uninterested all the time! And so I'm going to be married, Nick, and work and do a lot for the country just as though I were in the Service all my life. You needn't bother about my being happy – I couldn't be anything else!'

Nick stood looking at her, his mouth a little open – he tried to interrupt her several times and failed. He was younger than John Barton and the implications of what she said struck him more quickly – the real Mildred of the new day was more visible to him. He felt that he must define his own changing attitude, but John Barton drew Mildred's hand through his arm and stood beside her.

'You said, last night, Mr. Van Arsdale, that if I cared for Mildred, I wouldn't marry her because the life she'd lead would make her unhappy. I guess you can see that that wouldn't be so. Of course she won't have to work the way she's thinking of. I earn enough to take care of her.'

'Not work? Why, of *course* I'll work. It isn't a question of *having* to! It's what I want to do!'

It was evident that John Barton didn't take her seriously. He had got just so far in democracy as the idea that it was the patriotic duty of all men to serve their country all the time, but he hadn't extended his idea to include all women, – certainly not to include his prospective wife.

Nick felt he must try to make her see.

'But just marrying and going to live in Minneapolis isn't all there is to it, Mildred; – and just working in Minneapolis doesn't make the people or the place any different. If you don't mind the way it is away from New York – why, you know, it isn't much worse in Arizona or Kansas or anywhere else where they're making *roads*. – And they're as important – roads are – as anything! Why, you can't even get the wheat up to the flour mill without them! So, if you'd go to Minneapolis to live – why wouldn't you –'

Nick was stopped because he couldn't understand why Mildred was looking at him from some remote glacial epoch. He had no idea what he had done, but he stopped abruptly in his certainty that he had done something.

'Nick,' said Mildred at last, very slowly and with a dangerous iced intensity, 'Nick, suppose you don't go on with that. You don't seem to understand that I *love* John Barton.'

. . . John Barton had waited his whole life for this splendid young mate. His heart sang and the blood sped to his cheeks as he tramped up the beach beside her. It was love of her little hands and trim feet – of her blue eyes and her gold hair – her swift gleaming smile and the quick up-scale laugh that followed it – the soft red that flooded to her low, well set little ears when he kissed her suddenly. In between these moments of joy he tried to make love to her in words.

But here he met with difficulty. Mildred wanted him, when it came to talking, not to tell her how beautiful she was, or how he thought of her night and day, or how happy they were going to be in Minneapolis, but of the wonderful work of feeding the people and how she was going to help him do it. She wanted him to paint her future as an assistant priest at the altar. It was a sort of religious exaltation she craved from him, a thing that neither the church nor any social effort had ever been able to give her – nothing but John Barton himself speaking as the Priest of the Service. She wanted from him the same things that earlier generations had got from the perfume of ascending incense, from the Perpetual Adoration and the chanting and the rolling organ; what, earlier still had come through the witch dances and the dervishes; and way, way back in the dim, almost prehuman stage, from the shaking of the war gourds, the sight of the war feathers and the swift rush of the tribe on the common foe, – this, and a chance to put her developing creative instinct into work, – a chance to serve her country. With John Barton it was the mating instinct, strong, clean and direct. With Mildred it was something quite different, more complex, and far more difficult to satisfy. She got much more joy out of the sound of his voice telling how the farmers of the north-west organized the Nonpartisan League, than out of the touch of his lips on hers. She didn't analyze her own sensations, was quite unconscious what they meant; but again and again she turned the love talk into talk of the things he was doing and that she would do with him; and again and again he turned it back. At last he seemed to understand and fell silent. They were climbing up Tode Hill Road when they came to a little leafless wood with a carpet of fallen oak leaves and the blue bay spread out before them. Mildred stopped to catch her breath. Her cheeks were flushed with the crisp air, her eyes were shining, her lips were smiling with happiness. Never had she looked more beautiful.

'Will you be too cold if we sit here on this little wall for a moment?' he asked very gravely.

He took her left hand out of her muff – pulled off the glove finger by finger, and put it gravely to his lips.

'Mildred, I love you with all the love there is in me – but I'm afraid that you don't love me.'

The girl protested in frightened haste.

'I know you think you love me, dear – it isn't that. It's that you don't know.'

It was a very sober hour for both of them when John Barton put the case against himself. Honestly and deliberately he did it, as an upright man who would not take what was not his merely because he could get it. The case was two-fold, – the first and lesser part, that the things she must give up as his wife would make life a hardship for her. The second and great part, that she didn't care for him as she thought she did. John Barton said in everything but words that the rôle of prophet wasn't the one he cared to fill. He was a lover and he wanted to be loved, not as a leader, but as a man.

There was one moment when Mildred turned to him, holding out her hands.

'But I can't give it up – I can't! Don't leave me with nothing in the world to *do*! Why, it's like being dead!'

Then he caught her to him again, but only for a moment. He sprang to his feet and tramped resolutely up the road and resolutely back. Out of his pocket he took a little case and out of it a ring, perfectly conventional and set with a little diamond. Catching up her bare left hand, he slipped it on the third finger.

'Mildred, this is a sign that I'm not going to marry the woman I love more than my own soul – will you wear it for me?'

When they got back to the house in Washington Square she was white and drawn as she had never been before.

'I must see your father and mother before I go.'

John Barton stood bravely before them, his arm around Mildred.

'I want to tell you that we are not going to be married. I have found that I love your daughter too much to take her, even with her own consent, unless I am sure that she loves me more than she loves the work I am doing. She has told me that she hasn't anything to do – any real work – that she cares about. I wish that you would let her go on working. She made a good record in the mill, and in the field, too. I don't suppose you knew that what she was really going to marry me for, was a job – and that's almost as bad as marrying for a home. I'd just like to say, now that I'm at it, that I appreciate the way you've acted toward me – you've been white. I know how you must have felt about Mildred's marrying me – brought up as she's been and living the way you do. You didn't think I cared about the money, I know, because I guess it must have been pretty plain I didn't know about it. You knew I wasn't a fortune hunter, anyway. It's a bad thing when anything has got to come between a man and a woman except not loving each other – when we get the world fixed right, there won't. Well, good-bye.'

... They stood apart from each other – these two young citizens of the democracy in embarrassed silence, frightened at their own emotion. This was not what they had intended. It had done itself.

Mildred looking at Nick thought that he had never seemed so definitely an aristocrat, so far removed from any possible understanding of the new kind of things she had grown to care for – of work, and what it ought to mean to everybody to be a citizen. And yet never had he seemed so attractive, so personally dear and desirable. But she knew she was going to stand by her resolve!

'Mildred,' said Nick, and there was a new tone of assurance in his voice, 'Mildred, I've come back to ask you to marry me. I've tried to make myself believe that I could get on without you and I find I can't. I'm not going to wait while you try and decide whether you love me more than anybody else or even if you love me at all. I'm just going to make you marry me because I love you so much.'

The girl colored with resentment.

'I know I acted like a fool when I was here before, – when I talked to Mr. Barton. I guess I didn't know how sore I was till afterward, and I know I hadn't an idea how much I loved you. But you've just got to forgive me because I know better now – you've got to.'

Mildred looked down at her fluttering fingers – they were a little stained with ink with which she signed the firm letters – Henriette couldn't get it all off. When he paused for breath she began.

'Nick!' her voice was very low, 'Nick, I've got to tell you something right away. It's – it's very important. I – I don't think you'd like to marry me now – even if you think you would – I'm quite different from what you think I am – from what I used to be – I'm not the kind of a girl you'd like any more at all.'

'Not the kind of a girl? Oh, Mildred, there couldn't be anybody else in the world I'd care for. I know you're trying to let me down easy. And I can't bear to think of it – but – but.'

'Nick!'

'But I've got to make you understand.'

Mildred's face was changing, – the boy plunged on.

'You see, Mildred, I just can't go on with the kind of thing you're used to – not after my Service year, I can't. Why, when I think of Torexo and seats under every tree and the cut grass; and then of the way it looks in Arizona when you're up on a rock at sunrise and the valley below gets blue and purple and pink – and then you plan out where a road ought to go and *help to put it there* – Oh, Lord! I got to thinking of that house in Fifty-sixth Street father's keeping for me to live in – just the same sort of a house I've always seen – and even when I thought of your being there, I couldn't seem to stand it at all. It's beastly to say this to you only it would be worse for me not to.'

Nick caught his breath but he didn't look up and forced himself to go on.

'And so, Mildred, that was why I stayed away. I didn't think I had any right to ask you to go away from everybody you knew and everything you cared for. And I knew I hadn't any right to give up my work. I couldn't be a slacker, Mildred, even if there wasn't any war. I never thought you'd feel the same way about it till you said how you were going to work with John Barton – and even then I thought you didn't understand it yourself. And I was too jealous of him to try and think it out anyway. But I met him in North Dakota and he told me that you weren't going to be married after all, and how you were working on super-steel that I'd never heard of before. And after that I thought I'd *never* get leave to come here, and then that the train would *never* get in!'

Nick stopped literally for lack of breath. Mildred still stood fluttering her ink stained fingers.

'I – I was going to tell you too, Nick, that you'd be disappointed in the way I felt about things – you see I couldn't tell myself last year what I know now! But it's so dull here! I like to ride and dance and everything – only there's nothing else at all! And when I was driving a tractor in Minnesota and sometimes not seeing anything but a rabbit for half a day – why I was part of everything myself! I was part of the government and I was almost as important as the crops themselves. Why, it mattered to everybody in the country how I did my work! But it doesn't matter to anybody how I dance or dress and that's all I had to do here. I couldn't stand it so I'm working every day in father's steel mill. They're making super-steel for reaper blades because I broke so many in Dakota. And I'm finding other things that ought to be made of steel that won't break, and trying to get people to make them of it and then to use the things after they're made. Oh, Nick, it's *wonderful*! And that's what I wanted to tell you about – I've got to do my work as a citizen too. I can't give it up!'

Mildred tried to look at him dispassionately in the light of her weakening resolution. She repeated to herself that in spite of what he said about his work he hadn't cared enough about her to come back all winter – and was surprised to find that this had become a matter of no importance! She called up the intention to devote her life to the great work of feeding the world, – and found that it didn't stand in her way! How was it that the Chinese lilies in the corner smelled so much like the late tuberoses at Torexo? What was this sea of riotous disquieting perfume that invaded the staid drawing room in Washington Square? Mildred trying to lift her chin above it, looked straight into the eyes of Nick Van Arsdale. Was he coming toward her or was it her own footsteps that were bringing them together? She tried to pull herself together and decide what she was to do. Then in answer to her own question she heard her voice say:

'Nick, if you think we could do it together –'

ANNOTATED BIBLIOGRAPHY UNITED STATES WOMEN'S UTOPIAN FICTION, 1836-1983

---*---

Any bibliography requires explanation concerning criteria for selection and, if annotated, definition of categories used to classify the works. A note on format may also clarify the annotations.

The following list of 137 works stresses book-length *eutopias*, that is depictions of imaginary good societies as opposed to bad societies or *dystopias*. *Utopia* includes both good and bad. Short stories and juvenile fiction publishd before 1930 appear, but time prevented similar investigation after 1930. Similarly because of the recent large number of eutopias published after the 1960s, no dystopias appear unless incorporating a eutopia. With borderline cases, I have chosen to include rather than exclude. An asterisk (*) before an annotation marks a selection appearing within this anthology.

Many of the categories of classification are self-explanatory – alternative future, communitarian romance. Categories for the last two decades reveal the strong influence of science fiction upon recent Utopias – extraterrestrial or interplanetary adventure, sword and sorcery (the latter including sword fights and supernatural magic).

Terms referring to gender depiction may be less clear. By *feminist* I will mean 'favoring women's rights and valuing that which is female,' a narrow definition. *Anti-feminist* thus means 'anti-female.' *Sexist*, by analogy to racist, means 'sex-biased or accepting gender-role stereotyping.' People of either sex can be sexist toward their own or the other sex.

The bibliography is arranged chronologically by year and alphabetically within the year. Subtitles appear unless they are very long. Works are listed by year of first publication, so far as I know, with additional editions, reprint, or microfilm collection so noted. Three microfilm sources occur. I provide the full citation for each here and abbreviations henceforth:

1 *American Periodicals, 1741-1900*, Ann Arbor, Michigan: University Microfilms, 1963. Citations appear as coll. American Periodicals, Series II. 675.

2 *History of Woman: A comprehensive microfilm publication*, New Haven: Research Publications, 1976. Citations appear as coll. History of Women 4896.1.

3 Wright, Lyle H., ed., *American Fiction 1774-1900*, vols I, II, III, New Haven: Research Publications, 1968, 1971, 1971, the volumes based upon Wright's bibliography of the same title. Citations appear as coll. Wright I.1073.

A Brief list of Selected Critical References follows as well as a bar graph showing the distribution over time of the 137 works annotated. An alphabetical list of authors appears at the end to facilitate use, and finally recent additions.

REFERENCES (bibliography, definition, tradition)
Arthur O. Lewis, Jr, 'The Utopian Dream,' in Stanley Weintraub and Philip Young, eds, *Directions in Literary Criticism: Contemporary Approaches to Literature* (University Park: Pennsylvania State University Press, 1973), pp. 192-200; Frank E. Manuel and Fritzie P. Manuel, *Utopian Thought in the Western World* (Cambridge, Mass.: Harvard University Press, 1979); Glenn Negley and J. Max Patrick, eds, *The Quest for Utopia: An Anthology of Imaginary Societies* (New York: Henry Schuman, 1952); P. Nicolls, ed., *Science Fiction Encyclopedia* (New York: Doubleday, 1979); Lyman Tower Sargent, *British and American Utopian Literature 1516-1975: An Annotated Bibliography* (Boston: G.K. Hall, 1979).

I SELECTED CRITICAL REFERENCES

The following includes additional useful items on women and Utopia not appearing elsewhere in the volume.

Alternative Futures: The Journal of Utopian Studies 4, nos 2-3 (Spring/Summer 1981): 'Women and the Future.'
Barr, Marleen and Nicholas Smith, eds, *Women and Utopia: Critical Interpretations*, Lanham, Maryland: University Press of America, 1983.

Baruch, Elaine Hoffman, ' "A Natural and Necessary Monster": Women in Utopia,' *Alternative Futures* 2, no. 1 (1979):29-48.

Frontiers: A Journal of Women Studies, II, no. 3 (Fall 1977): 'Fantasy and Futures.'

Heresies: A Feminist Publication on Art and Politics, 3, no. 3 (1981): no. 11, 'Making Room: Women and Architecture.'

Heresies: A Feminist Publication on Art and Politics, 4, no. 1 (1981): no. 13, 'Feminism and Ecology: earthkeeping/ earthshaking.'

Kaplan, Barbara M., 'Women and Sexuality in Utopian Fiction,' Diss. New York University, 1977.

Khanna, Lee Cullen, 'Frontiers of the Imagination: Women's Worlds,' *Women's Studies International Forum*, forthcoming.

Lane, Ann J., Introduction, *Herland* by Charlotte Perkins Gilman, New York: Pantheon, 1979, pp. v-xxiv.

LeGuin, Ursula, 'Is Gender Necessary?' In *Aurora: Beyond Equality*, Vonda N. McIntyre and Susan Janice Anderson, eds, New York: Fawcett, 1976, pp. 130-9.

Quest: A Feminist Quarterly, II, no. 1 (Summer 1975): special issue on women and the future.

Rohrlich, Ruby and Elaine Hoffman Baruch, eds, *Women in Search of Utopia*, New York: Schocken, forthcoming 1984.

Rothschild, Joan, ed., *Machina Ex Dea: Feminist Perspectives on Technology*, Elmsford, New York: Pergamon: 1983.

Staicar, Tom, ed., *The Feminine Eye: Science Fiction and the Women Who Write It*, New York: Ungar, 1982.

Women's Studies International Quarterly, 4, no. 1 (1981): 'Women in Futures Research.'

II DISTRIBUTION OF UTOPIAS BY UNITED STATES WOMEN

1830-1980 (n 137)

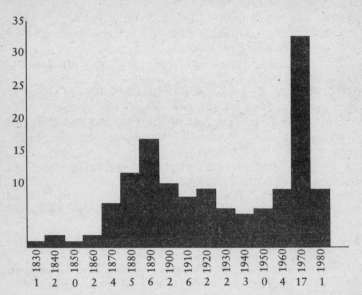

(The number beneath the decade identification indicates the number of feminist Utopias.)

III ANNOTATIONS

1836
*Griffith, Mary (-1877), 'Three Hundred Years Hence' in *Camperdown; or News from our Neighborhood*, Philadelphia: Carey, Lea and Blanchard; rpt Philadelphia: Prime Press, 1950; *American Utopias: Selected Short Fiction*, Arthur O. Lewis (ed.), New York: Arno, 1971; coll. Wright I.1073.
In a dream vision of the United States placed three hundred years into the future, the central place and accomplishments of women amaze the male narrator. Dream novelette.

1841
[Chamberlain, Betsey (-   )], Tabitha (pseud.), 'A New

236

Society,' *The Lowell Offering* I:191-192; rpt *The Lowell Offering: Writings by New England Women (1840-1945)*, Benita Eisler (ed.), New York: Harper & Row, 1977; coll. American Periodicals, Series II.675.

A Lowell mill worker's dream vision of the resolutions to reform her world stresses family responsibility, fair labor practices, mental and physical work for all, and education specific to each sex. Sketch.

1848

*[Appleton, Jane Sophia (-1884)], 'Sequel to "The Vision of Bangor in the Twentieth Century" ' in *Voices form the Kenduskeag*, Bangor: D. Bugbee; rpt *American Utopias: Selected Short Fiction*, Arthur O. Lewis (ed.), New York: Arno, 1971; coll. Wright I.39.

An unenlightened United States man receives guidance from a twentieth-century gentleman, who corrects the former's mistaken underestimation of women in all areas of life. Sex differences are recognized and accepted. Dream dialogue; novelette.

1853

Hale, Sarah Josepha [Buell] (1788-1879), *Liberia; or Mr. Peyton's Experiments*, New York: Harper & Brothers, Publishers; rpt New Jersey: Gregg, 1968; coll. Wright II.1064.

Virginia planter Mr Charles Peyton experiments with ameliorating Black lives – first a collective Virginia farm, second a Canadian community, and finally the Liberia Colonization Society. This final Utopia is less patronizing of Blacks than typical of the era and demonstrates the energy and ability of a people freed. Communitarian polemic.

1866

Davis, Rebecca Harding (1831-1910), 'The Harmonists,' *The Atlantic Monthly* 17:529-38.

A man recalls having visited Economy, Pennsylvania, with a physician and his son. The father decides not to join the Rappites because their narrow patriarchal viewpoint has twisted their lives: the hoped-for eutopia does not exist, but instead an ironic caricature of soured ideals. Short story.

1869

*Corbett, Elisabeth T. (-   ), 'My Visit to Utopia,' *Harper's New Monthly Magazine* 38:200-4.

In post-Civil War United States, eutopia for women is marriage made to her order. Short story of present alternative.

1870

*Cridge, Annie Denton (-   ), *Man's Rights; or, How Would You Like It?* Boston: William Denton; coll. Wright II.658.

A woman dreams of satiric role reversals that make ludicrous the 'cult of true womanhood' when it is practised by men. Five such dream visions.

1873

Alcott, Louisa May (1832-1888), 'Transcendental Wild Oats: A Chapter from an Unwritten Romance,' *The Independent* 25:1569-71; rpt *The Woman's Journal* 5 (21 February 1874); *Silver Pitchers*, Boston: Roberts Brothers, 1876; Harvard, Mass.: Harvard Common Press, 1981.

A short autobiographical romance set in 184– New England depicts 'Fruitlands' as a communitarian experiment where women's labor made men's rumination possible. The community might better have been called 'Apple Slump,' Mrs Abel Lamb suggests in conclusion. Narrative essay.

1874

*Howland, Marie [Stevens Case] (1836-1921), *Papa's Own Girl; A Novel*, New York; Jewett, coll. Wright II. 1290; *The Familistere; A Novel*, Boston: Christopher, 1918, rpt Philadelphia: Porcupine Press, 1975.

Engagingly readable, the novel makes equitable relations between women and men basic to the improved conduct of socity in L—, Massachusetts, where a European count finances a Social Palace. Feminist. Communitarian romance.

*Phelps [Ward], Elizabeth Stuart (1844-1911), 'A Dream within a Dream,' *The Independent* 26:1.

A dream vision reveals marriage to be a potential earthly utopia.

1879

Douglas, Amanda M[innie] (1837-1916), *Hope Mills; or, Between Friend and Sweetheart*, Boston: Lee & Shepard, coll. Wright III.1611.
Though the romance concludes typically with marriages, they are inter-class. The mill-class hero implements his vision of industrial community, modeled after English and French Utopias; mill women establish a cooking school. The experiments prosper. Idealistic; not feminist. Communitarian romance.

1881

*[Lane, Mary E. Bradley (-   )] *Mizora: A Prophecy*, *The Cincinnati Commercial*, November 1880-February 1881; rpt New York: G.W. Dillingham, 1889; coll. Wright III.3203; New York: Gregg, 1975.
Reached through an entrance at the North Pole, Mizora is an all-female society where education is the highest concern. Society though non-violent is hierarchical and white-racist. Amazonian society.

1882

[Wood, Mrs. J. (-   )], *Pantaletta: A Romance of Sheheland*, New York: American News Company; coll. Wright III.6064.
General Gullible voyages by balloon to Sheheland, where Capt. Pantaletta in the Republic of Petticotia demonstrates the negative outcome of gender role-reversal in a satire on female power and governance. Conservative politically; anti-feminist. Space travel.

1883

*Phelps [Ward], Elizabeth Stuart (1844-1911), *Beyond the Gates*, Boston: Houghton, Mifflin; coll. Wright III.5755.
The domestication of heavenly 'mansions' shows a father housekeeping while awaiting the arrival of the rest of his family, and a daughter at last finding her destined heart-mate. Alternative vision.

1885

Shelhamer, M[ary] T[heresa] (-   ), *Life and Labor in the Spirit World, Being a Description of the Localities,*

Employments, Surroundings, and Conditions of the Spheres, Boston: Colby & Rich.

The spirit of a woman deceased in 1877 permits us glimpses of a future afterworld more conducive to the development of human potential – whether belonging in an earlier life to someone common or uncommon; female or male; black, Indian, or serf. Instructional methods and co-operative societies provide strategies for improving the lives of all. Spiritual fantasy.

1887

Dodd, Anna Bowman [Blake] (1885-1929), *The Republic of the Future; or Socialism a Reality*, New York: Cassell; coll. Wright III.1557.

A Swedish nobleman writes in dismay to his friend Christiania about the New York Socialistic City he finds in December 2050. Though women now perform only two hours of domestic work, still foreign courts so dislike contact with female arbitrators that the latter concede rather than negotiate! The narrator bemoans a loss of individuality. Alternative future.

Phelps [Ward], Elizabeth Stuart (1844-1911), *The Gates Between*, Boston: Houghton, Mifflin; coll. Wright III.5762.

Heaven provides the society within which a male physician learns to be a sensitive parent and spouse. Alternative vision.

1889

*Ford, Mary H. (-   ), 'A Feminine Iconoclast,' *The Nationalist* (November):252-7.

A streetcar eavesdropper reports a conversation in which one woman reveals to another the patronizing and paternalistic view of woman inherent in Edward Bellamy's Nationalism. Short story.

*Mason, Eveleen Laura [Knaggs] (1838-1914), *Hiero-Salem: The Vision of Peace*, Boston: J.G. Cupples; coll. Wright III.3633.

Set in northern Wisconsin in the near-past, the Eloiheem Commonwealth established by one founding couple seeks to remove religious, racial, class, and sex inequities. Spiritual community.

Mead, Lucia True Ames (1856-1936), *Memoirs of a Millionaire*, Boston: Houghton, Mifflin; coll. Wright III. 3675.

Set in then-contemporary United States, the novel presents a scheme for ameliorating lives of the earth's helpless and degraded peoples – especially the women – through a Christian Missionary Fund, established by benefactress Mildred Brewster when she inherits millions from a former lover. Economic utopia.

[Woods, Katharine Pearson (1853-1932)], *Metzerott, Shoemaker*, New York: Crowell; coll. Wright III.6058.

In a troubled world realistically presented, Metzerott participates in an urban commune whose members espouse a eutopian socialism. They encounter upper-class resistance, but though membership changes, a group continues. One of its activities is a boarding facility. Communitarian romance.

1890

Pittock, Mrs M.A. Weeks (-   ), *The God of Civilization: A Romance*, Chicago: Eureka.

A Pacific shipwreck leaves a California woman and friends stranded upon a tropical island suggestive of Hawaii. The bronze-skinned natives with their relaxed appreciation of natural and human sensuality win her allegiance: she marries, refusing to leave when chance permits. Romantic fantasy.

Stone, Mrs. C.H. (-   ), *One of 'Berrian's' Novels*, New York: Welch, Fracker; rpt Wright III. 5264.

Couched as fiction by Bellamy's future novelist Berrian from *Looking Backward* (1888), his work accepts Bellamy's traditional gender roles though women as well as men head institutions in St Louis of 1997. Not feminist. Futuristic romance.

1891

[Bartlett, Alice Elinor Bowen (1848-1920)], Birch Arnold (pseud.), *A New Aristocracy*, New York: Bartlett; coll. Wright III.359.

In the suburbs of a Western United States metropolis, a Christian community Idlewild demonstrates a 'new aristocracy of head and heart' where capital and labor exist harmoniously to mutual benefit and where strong women may marry on their own terms. Communitarian romance.

Brodhead, Eva Wilder McGlasson (1870-1915), *Diana's Livery*, New York: Harper; coll. Wright III.677.

Kentucky Shaker community appears less than eutopian as individual members resort to alcohol or suicide. Instead marriage promises greater possibility for satisfied living as a young woman Naamah chooses to leave the community to live with the man she loves, an artist and landowner. Communitarian romance.

Yourell, Agnes Bond (-   ), *A Manless World*, New York: Dillingham; coll. Wright III.6170.

An old man tells his newly affianced nephew of a dystopian prophecy – a theory of a manless world where noxious gases make procreation impossible, where anarchy increases after Gentiles annihilate Jews, and the last woman takes her own life. The nephew discounts the theory by assuming his uncle suffered early loss of love. Alternative future.

1892

[Moore, M. Louise (-   )], *Al-Modad; or Life Scenes beyond the Polar Circumflex. A Religio-Scientific Solution of the Problems of Present and Future Life*, Shell Bank, Cameron Parish, Louisiana: Moore & Beauchamp; coll. Wright III.3817.

An 1879 diary of travels to the Arctic records visitor Al-Modad's observations of a co-operative industrialized society where women and men are equals, their sexuality freely expressed and kinship with all people practiced. Interesting. Communitarian utopia.

Tincker, Mary Agnes (1831-1907), *San Salvador*, Boston: Houghton, Mifflin; coll. Wright III.5500.

Set in a remote and mountainous area, the Christian community of San Salvador exists to protect the needy and defenseless. Gender roles are conservative. The birth of a son concludes the novel. Communitarian romance.

*[Jones, Alice Ilgenfritz (-1906) and Ella Merchant (-   )], Two Women of the West (pseud.), *Unveiling a Parallel: A Romance*, Boston: Arena; coll. Wright III.5627; New York: Gregg, 1975.

A male traveler to Mars visits two societies where ideal women are the equals of ideal men, though one society values the material and the other the spiritual. The parallel unveiled is the common human nature of women and men. Space travel spiced by satiric repartee.

1894

Knapp, Adeline (1860-1909)], 'One Thousand Dollars a Day: A Financial Experiment' in *One Thousand Dollars a Day: Studies in Economics*, Boston: Arena; coll. Wright III.3178.
    Distributing income from the Golconda mines daily to those 18 years and over – 'every man and every woman' – solves wealth inequity. But for the strategy to succeed, a San Francisco man innovates a labor exchange to provide needed services. Economic fantasy.

*Waisbrooker, Lois [Nichols] (1826-1909), *A Sex Revolution* ..., Topeka, Kansas: Independent; coll. History of Women, 4896.1.
    Pacifist as well as feminist, the 'sex revolution' occurs when women refuse to follow men's lead to war: Mother Love is the force empowering social amelioration. All occurs in one woman's dream vision.

1895

[Sherwood, Margaret Pollack (1864-1955)], Elizabeth Hastings (pseud.), *An Experiment in Altruism*, New York: Macmillan; coll. Wright III.4914.
    A woman narrates an abstract tale of a group pursuing altruistic goals with slow progress yet perseverance. Spiritual alternative.

Von Swartwout, Janet (-), *Heads or the City of Gods: A Narrative of Olumbia in the Wilderness*, New York: Olumbia Publishing Company.
    A group travels through the Adirondacks to enjoy the wilderness and to search for truth in their discussions of a 'new order of builders' for the general good. Eutopia more discussed than established, though the group of four men and four women observe their own principles so far as eight people constitute a society. Communitarian alternative.

1897

*Graul, Rosa (-), 'Hilda's Home,' *Lucifer, The Light Bearer*, nos 641-86 (Series 3: vols 1-7, 1897-1903), rpt Westport, Connecticut: Greenwood, n.d.
    In the United States of the 1890s, a woman's ideal and a man's fortune permit a group committed to 'free love' to establish a co-operative home in the 'west.' The venture then expands to include the establishment of a co-operative

business emporium in which all are partners, and the construction of a home for emporium partners. Communitarian romance.

Orpen, [Adela Elizabeth Rogers] (1855-   ), *Perfection City*, New York: Appleton.

Eastern settlers arrive in the commune of Perfection City, Kansas, a mere village founded by Mme Morozof-Smith, viewed by its residents as an 'earthly paradise.' The city disbands as villagers realize that not the ways of the world, but 'the human heart needed reforming first of all.' Communitarian romance.

1898

[Clarke, Frances H. (-   )], Zebina Forbush (pseud.), *The Co-opolitan; A Story of the Co-operative Commonwealth of Idaho*, Chicago: Kerr.

Between 1897 and 1917, a group solidly establishes Co-opolis in Idaho, an economic and political co-operative for women as well as men. An important figure is novelist Caroline Woodberry Braden, also wife and mother, whose success receives ample recognition. Communitarian romance.

Mason, Eveleen Laura [Knaggs] (1838-1914), *An Episode in the Doings of the Dualized*, Brookline, Massachusetts: E.L. Mason; coll. Wright III.3632.

This brief work peopled by many *Hiero-Salem* characters demonstrates the human potential of dualized (androgynous) beings. Spiritual community.

1899

[Adolph, Mrs. Anna (-   )], *Arqtiq: A Study of Marvels at the North Pole*, Hanford, California: Author; coll. Wright III. 30.

Narrator Anna, in a dream, travels to the North Pole where she experiences a society without birth, marriage, or death, where women rule equally with men, and education continues for life. Dream vision of exotic journey.

Morgan, Harriet (-   ), *The Island Impossible*, Boston: Little, Brown.

In a children's dream world, closer to a Robinsoniade than to eutopia proper, one remains a child, can travel great distance in little time, escape all evil, enjoy equality of the sexes – even superiority if one is female. Coming adulthood requires departure from the island. Juvenile fantasy.

1900

Mason, Caroline A[twater] (1853-1939), *A Woman of Yesterday*, New York: Doubleday; coll. Wright III.3631.
To escape a loveless marriage, heroine Anna Benigna Mallison joins a North Carolina egalitarian community Fraternia where she resumes training interrupted by marriage and regains direction of her own life. Finally she departs for India as a teacher. Communitarian romance.

Richberg, Eloise O. Randall (-), *Reinstern*, Cincinnati: Editor Publishing.
A woman's dream vision of train travel to an unknown planet reveals a society of loving, broadly educated individuals where both sexes train for and participate in parenting and adult working responsibilities occur in conjunction with those for child rearing. Extra-terrestrial vision.

1901

Henley, Carra Dupuy (-), *A Man from Mars*, Los Angeles: B.R. Baumgardt.
Asylum resident Professor Darlington, interviewed by a stenographer, relates his visit to Mars, after a head injury. Martians are cerebrally highly developed and enjoy apparent sex equality. Alternative vision.

1902

*Cooley, Winnifred Harper (c. 1875-after 1955), 'A Dream of the Twenty-first Century,' *Arena*, 28:511-16.
By New Year's Day 2000, women will have obtained a just place in United States society, according to a woman's dream on New Year's Day 1900. Short story.

1903

Kinkaid, Mary Holland [McNeish] (1861-1948), *Walda; A Novel*, New York: Harper.
Prophetess Walda, beloved of the school master in Zanah – a religious colony located in a secluded United States valley, defies colony rules repressing sensuous and sensual expression by leaving for the love of a visiting stranger. Communitarian romance.

1905

Evans, Anna D. (-   ), *It Beats the Shakers, or a New Tune*, New York: Anglo American.
The novelette stresses the relation between the sexes as crucial to social improvement: marriages require shared rights and responsibilities between partners to realize the human possibility of 'pure Eden on Earth.' Lacks specifics. Dream vision.

Fry, Lena Jane (-   ), *Other Worlds: A Story Concerning the Wealth Earned by American Citizens and Showing How It Can Be Secured to Them Instead of to the Trusts*, Chicago: Author.
On the planet Herschel, the family Vivian provides a model for controlling the trusts so that industrious people may enjoy their own wealth. Both women and men participate in economic management. Families are central social units, but women enjoy greater independence than was true for 1905. Economic romance.

Rogers, Bessie Story (-   ), *As It May Be: A Story of the Future*, Boston: Gorham.
Mary Tillman, deceased in 1905, regains consciousness in 2905, a future society resembling the 'perfect harmony' believed in 1905 to exist in heaven. The brief eutopia sketches a society where violence no longer occurs and social supports permit women to live without excess housekeeping or home-caring burdens. Alternative vision.

1908

Martin, Nettie Parrish (-   ), *A Pilgrim's Progress in Other Worlds; Recounting the Wonderful Adventures of Ulysum Storries and His Discovery of the Lost Star 'Eden,'* Boston: Mayhew.
Balloonist/sky cyclist Ulysum Storries progresses from one perfect planetary world to another, each exhibiting a different arrangement between the sexes, blends of innovation and conservatism. As Ulysum never admits to having a wife on Earth, he attracts women as guides, each querying him about Earth so as to reveal their own more equitable condition for women. Space travel.

1909

Wiggin, Kate Douglas [Smith] (1856-1923), *Susanna and Sue*,

Boston: Houghton, Mifflin.
A mother Susanna, with her daughter Sue, escapes a drunken philandering husband by entering the Shaker community of Albion, Maine, where she finds temporary relief as she defines her personal needs. A change in her husband convinces Susanna to leave and reunite her family. Stresses people's requiring differing living alternatives. Juvenile communitarian romance.

1911

Gilman, Charlotte Perkins [Stetson] (1860-1935), *Moving the Mountain*, *The Forerunner* 2; rpt New York: Charlton, 1911; rpt Westport, Connecticut: Greenwood Press, 1968; excerpt *Charlotte Perkins Gilman Reader*, Ann J. Lane (ed.), New York: Pantheon, 1980.
A male narrator lost for thirty years returns to United States of 1940 to find women filling positions formerly allotted only to men. Futuristic romance.

1915

Gilman, Charlotte Perkins [Stetson] (1860-1935], *Herland*, *The Forerunner* 6; rpt New York: Pantheon, 1979, excerpt *Charlotte Perkins Gilman Reader*, Lane, (ed.), New York: Pantheon, 1980.
Discovered by three adventurous United States men, remote Herland, an all-female society, makes Motherhood its highest office. Many invidious – as well as humorous – comparisons emerge as the adventurers receive education about Herland. Amazonian society.

1916

Fisher, Mary Ann (1839-   ), *Among the Immortals: In the Land of Desire*, New York: Shakespeare Press.
A gossipy, ethnocentric, spirit afterworld set about 1916. Women less inferior, but class hierarchy remains. Marriage differently defined. Ambivalent view of women. Spiritual fantasy.

Gilman, Charlotte Perkins [Stetson] (1860-1935), 'With Her in Ourland,' *The Foreruner* 7; rpt Westport, Connecticut: Greenwood Press, 1968; excerpt *Charlotte Perkins Gilman Reader*, A.J. Lane (ed.), New York: Pantheon, 1980.
A Herlander woman tours our world just after World War I

erupts. The contrasts between our ways and hers astonish her into satiric commentary. Blend of satiric dialogue-travelogue from viewpoint of visitor from eutopia.

Jones, Lillian B. (-   ), *Five Generations Hence*, Fort Worth, Texas: Dotson Jones.

Grace Noble, 'high brow' daughter of an ex-slave, teaches and writes while her close friend Violet Gray becomes an African missionary. Grace later marries a physician and raises children. Each achieves her 'dream of life' and the improvement of her race. Alternative future.

1917

*[Snedeker, Caroline Dale Parke (1871-1956)], Caroline Dale Owen (pseud.), *Seth Way: A Romance of the New Harmony Community*, Boston: Houghton, Mifflin.

An historical romance of Robert Owen's New Harmony, the novel shows the community faltering but the relations between man and woman established by an egalitarian contract. Historical romance.

1918

[Bennett, Gertrude Barrows (1884-?1939)], Francis Stevens (pseud.), 'Friend Island,' *All-Story Weekly*, September 7; rpt *Under the Moons of Mars*, Sam Moskowitz (ed.), New York: Holt Reinhart Winston, 1970.

Retired sea-captain, questioned by young man, recounts her shipwreck on Friend Island, a sentient, hospitable Pacific Island with a heart and a name, Anita. Feminist sex-role reversal. Short story.

1919

*Bruère, Martha [S.] Bensley (1879-1953), *Mildred Carver, U.S.A.*, *The Ladies' Home Journal*, 35-36, June 1918-February 1919; rpt New York: Macmillan.

In post-World War I United States, a Universal Service in public-works projects enlists women and men for one year with regard not to gender but to interest and aptitude. Work becomes as crucial for a woman as marriage for a man: each needs both. Alternative future.

1920

Johnston, Mary Ann (1870-1936), *Sweet Rocket*, New York: Harper.

The Sweet Rocket Road leads school teacher Anna Darcy into Virginia woods hundreds of thousands of miles away: the mind becomes the vehicle for space/time travel. Her visit with former student Marget Land refreshes by showing new selves being born as consciousness widens in an encouraging environment. Alternative vision.

1922

Kayser, Martha Cabanné (-   ), *The Aerial Flight to the Realm of Peace*, St Louis: Lincoln Press.
An unidentified narrator records a balloon flight to a dream world where all are healthy, happy, and loving. Education is central. Abstract, not feminist. Dream vision.

Scrymsour, Ella M. (1888-   ), *The Perfect World; A Romance of Strange People and Strange Places*, New York: Stokes.
A strange, underground, Earth-dystopia: an earthquake destroys the dystopia just after characters launch a trip to Jupiter, a Utopia where only men work and women must wait to be asked in marriage. Sexist. Post-catastrophe romance.

1923

[Thompson, Harriet Alfarata Chapman (-1922)], *Idealia; A Utopia Dream; or Resthaven*, Albany, New York: Lyon.
A woman visits a community – for the elderly, the orphaned, the invalid – modelled after a resort. Its male director explains special features – wheeltables, parlorettes, and social activities. Communitarian alternative present.

1924

Cleghorn, Sarah N[orcliffe] (1876-1959), 'Utopia Interpreted,' *Atlantic Monthly* 134:56-67, 216-24.
Four varied interpretations explain the evolutionary causes for the existence by 1995 of a eutopian Family Order of society and the Discipline of Happiness: control of natural energy; social ills shared by concerned women; unequal ownership abolished; nomadry as 'open pasture for human spirit.' Brief alternative future.

Pettersen, Rena Oldfield (-   ), *Venus*, Philadelphia: Dorrance.
Two women from Utopian Venus land near Chicago to

educate a young woman in phases of past existences. Love is the universal Utopian condition and mating between women and men, its highest expression, is initiated by women. Spiritual romance.

1925

Dell, Berenice V. (-   ), *The Silent Voice*, Boston: Four Seas.
After an unnatural post-catastrophe interim of women's rule, women return to their natural place at home and fulfill their duty to bear Aryan children. Women have greater control in marital relationships, but state represses the individual. Paradise is ideal sexual union. The 'silent voice' in each is an understanding of real liberty, the true America. Futuristic romance.

1928

Cazella, Edith Virginia (-   ), *The Blessing of Azar, A Tale of Dreams and Truth*, Boston: Christopher.
Azar, a commercial magnate, establishes and finances a community called The Friends, founded upon equitable commerce. Azar sees the sexes as two halves of a perfect whole, in which each sex enjoys liberty comparable to the other: a male, or head of state, oversees legislative functions; a female, or the body, guides the masses. Communitarian romance.

1929

Snedeker, Caroline Dale Parke (1871-1956), *The Beckoning Road*, New York: Junior Literary Guild.
An historical romance of the Harmonists and the failure of their community, this juvenile work stresses Pestalozzi pedagogy and the triumph of young love. Juvenile utopia.

1930

Vassos, Ruth (-   ), *Ultimo: An Imaginative Narration of Life Under the Earth*, New York: Dutton.
Brief, abstract utopia, reported by male narrator as he is about to depart the stiflingly perfect society existing inside the earth after temperatures on the surface fell too low to sustain life. Little on women (the word never occurs) save indication of 'birth-permission cards' but otherwise free cohabitation. Space travel.

1935

Spotswood, Claire Myers (-   ), *The Unpredictable Adventure: A Comedy of Woman's Independence*, New York: Doubleday.
Set in the land of Err, a satire about woman's independence includes a eutopia of the New Chimera, where love rules freely. Women's independence is satirized, yet demonstrated in this comic adventure. Picaresque satire.

1937

Sterne, Emma Gelders (1894-   ), *Some Plant Olive Trees*, New York: Dodd, Mead.
An historical romance of Napoleonic refugees' Vine and Olive colony in Demopolis, Alabama, the novel depicts failed ideals. The focus upon the relation between a colony founder and his wife includes her critique of his treatment of her and hence attention to women's position in Utopia.

1938

DeForest, Eleanor (-   ), *Armageddon; A Tale of the Antichrist*, Grand Rapids, Michigan: Eerdmans.
In an anti-Semitic and anti-feminist dystopia set in California and Palestine, twin sisters compete for love and survival during the years of intrigue preceding the arrival of a Christian millennium after a bloody 'armageddon.' Future fantasy.

Morris, Martha Marlowe (1867-   ) and Laura B. Speer (-   ), *No Borderland*, Dallas, Texas: Mathis, Van Nort.
The borders exist between lives, times, and states in this exotic adventure where past prefigures future as two male archeologists explore. Spiritual alternative.

Rand, Ayn (1905-1982), *Anthem*, London: Cassell; rev. ed., Los Angeles: Pamphleteers, 1946.
A male narrator envisions an extreme individualism as a positive alternative to a state-controlled community. Anti-feminist. Anti-socialist eutopia.

1943

Dardenelle, Louise (-   ), *World Without Raiment, A Fantasy*, New York: Valiant.
After all man-made goods have disintegrated from a

251

climactic increase in temperature, a nudist colony spreads from California throughout the United States. People appreciate a natural world without the products of technology and become healthy, loving individuals. Both sexes enjoy freely given, non-exclusive love. Futuristic romance.

1945

McElhiney, Gaile Churchill (-   ), *Into the Dawn*, Los Angeles: Del Vorse.
Jeanne Wallace, aviator, is downed on Pacific Island of Heaven. She acquires 'astral' powers enabling her to communicate with parents and the man she loves. A goal of loving contribution to world's welfare, re-united with her lover, will guide Jeanne's future. Spiritual fantasy.

1949

McCarthy, Mary [Therese] (1912-   ), *The Oasis*, New York: Random House.
A vacation colony as ideal community disintegrates. Satiric treatment explodes utopian hopes and particularly bares marital discord. Communitarian satire.

Short, Gertrude (-   ), *A Visitor from Venus*, New York: William Frederick Press.
Accustomed to all-female Venusian society, a visitor reports her dismay at Earth's sex-unfair arrangements. Satiric. Extra-terrestrial Amazonian alternative.

Sutton, Paralee Sweeten (-   ), *White City: A Novel*, Palo Alto, California: Palopress.
Aviators lost over Antarctica find a eutopian White City where the white light of understanding has raised all to greater levels of teamwork, equality, and achievement. Gender roles unclear, though male visitor predominates; father and daughter reunited. Futuristic romance.

1950

Barber, Elsie Marion Oakes (1914-   ), *Hunt for Heaven*, New York: Macmillan.
Pastor John Bliss begins his 'hunt for heaven' after the 1886 Haymarket riot and trains his daughter Rebecca to carry on the principles establishing his Christian Colony. It fails because the kingdom of heaven can be founded only within a given individual. Rebecca abandoned such principle for passion. Historical romance.

1952

Barnhouse, Perl T. (-   ), *My Journeys with Astargo; a tale of past, present, and future*, Denver: Bell Publications.

An ambivalent consideration of technology with its power to
Young men from Colorado in spaceship Astargo travel among planets and discover a utopia on Perfecto (described in three of 57 chapters), where conditions improve through each passing year. Vague; not feminist. Space travel.

1955

Brackett, Leigh [Douglass] (1915-1978), *The Long Tomorrow*, Garden City, New York: Doubleday.

An ambivalent consideration of technology with its power to destroy or ameliorate. A technological social remnant exists within a twenty-first century agrarian society akin to New Mennonites of the 'past.' Two adolescent youths find the other technological past. Futuristic romance.

1957

Maddux, Rachel (1912-   ), *The Green Kingdom*, New York: Simon & Schuster.

The Green Kingdom is a condition of realizing potentiality, whether creative or affective. Men fare better than women. But the dream contains its antithesis as well — isolation, violence, death. Spiritual romance.

Norris, Kathleen [Thompson] (1880-1966), *Through a Glass Darkly*, Garden City, New York: Doubleday.

Characters move from one world to another, from eutopian afterworld back to present dystopian world to alleviate ills. Heroine works to help children; concludes with her marriage. Spiritual romance.

Rand, Ayn (1905-1982), *Atlas Shrugged*, New York: Random House.

Against a panorama of United States business and industrial corruption, a small group of the best minds — predominantly male — gathers to await a future moment when they can return from their Colorado mountain hideout to establish morality, intelligence, and individuality. A female hero Dagny Taggart figures prominently as an executive responsible for transcontinental railroad operation. Her three successive lovers parallel stages in her changing understanding of her own motivations and goals. Economic, anti-socialist eutopia.

St Clair, Margaret (1911-   ), *The Green Queen*, New York: Ace.
With eutopia lurking at its edges, dystopian planet Viridis oozes intrigue. Sexist. Extra-terrestrial adventure.

1961

Henderson, Zenna [Chlarson] (1917-   ), *Pilgrimage: The Book of the People*, New York: Doubleday; rpt New York: Avon, 1961; sequel, *The People: No Different Flesh*, New York: Doubleday, 1967.
Episodic, each narrative increases a reader's comprehension of the People of the Group who emigrated from the planet Home. People can levitate, mind-read, and mind-heal. Having a strong oral tradition, an Assembling of People for recalling the past is the occasion for each episode as one Group member shares a personal experience significant for Group self-identity. Spiritual travel.

1962

Leslee, Jo (-   ), *It Shall Be Conquered*, Boston: Christopher.
Present-day interplanetary voyage to unknown planet Maresdon in space ship captained by woman. Seven earthlings visit its eutopian society, only vaguely specified, which stresses mental development and exhibits sex equality. Extra-terrestrial alternative.

Smith, Evelyn E. (1927-   ), *The Perfect Planet*, New York: Avalon.
On Artemis, an all-female society is devoted to physical culture in a satire on concerns about health and beauty. Not feminist, sex-biased, humorous. Extra-terrestrial satire.

1964

Lawrence, Josephine (1890?-1978), *Not a Cloud in the Sky*, New York: Harcourt.
A dystopian Tranquil Acres populated by 'our aged' instead of producing satisfied elderly leads to the formation of a eutopian 'rambunctious retired' who win their campaign for irregularity. Not feminist; satiric. Alternative future.

1968

Mannes, Marya (1904-   ), *They*, Garden City, New York: Doubleday.

A near-future eutopia in which those born before 1925 are segregated from the rest of society – effectively eradicating memory of past individuality. 'They' – youthful barbarians, in the view of the exiled five main characters – have violently communized society. Individualistic eutopia of 'us.'

1969

Carroll, Gladys Hasty (1904-   ), *Man on the Mountain*, Boston: Little, Brown.
   In twenty-first century Great Country, inhabitants are divided among four States according to their ages. Through separation all have become lonely for and suspicious of each other. Explorations of the youngest evoking concern from the eldest will permit reconciliation. Not feminist. Alternative future.

LeGuin, Ursula [Kroeber] (1929-   ), *The Left Hand of Darkness*, New York: Walker; rpt New York: Ace, 1969.
   On the planet Gethen in the distant future, visitor from Ekumen, Genly Ai arrives to accomplish a trade alliance. The unusual feature of Gethens is their ambisexuality, the novel being an early science fiction attempt at imagining alternative gender roles. Extra-terrestrial futuristic fantasy.

Lightner [Hopf], Alice M. (1904-   ), *The Day of the Drones*, New York: Norton.
   In the future country of Afria, a young black woman Am Lara prepares to become its future head. Blacks discover white survivors of nuclear disaster. Future peace requires new civilization integrating whites with blacks. Post-catastrophe alternative future.

1970

Piercy, Marge (1936-   ), *Dance the Eagle to Sleep*, Garden City, New York: Doubleday; rpt New York: Fawcett, 1971.
   Franklin High School students led by Amer-Indian Corey revolt. Objecting to an insensitive administration, they band together and eventually set up an alternative rural community. Though not feminist, young women begin to recognize gender-role confinement. Communitarian Utopia.

Russ, Joanna (1937-   ), *And Chaos Died*, New York: Ace; rpt Boston: Gregg/G.K. Hall, 1978.
   Several centuries into the future on another planet, a male visitor guided by a female mentor learns that a select group

of Earth people have developed ESP. Bisexuality is also common in Edenic landscape. A dystopian future Earth provides background contrast. Extra-terrestrial futuristic fantasy.

1971

Alexander, Thea [Plym] (-   ), *2150 A.D.*, Tempe, Arizona: Macro Books.

A Macro Society set in 2150 A.D. and based upon expanded awareness of self and others helps individuals develop capacities only imagined in 1976 – for example, telepathy, psychokinesis, levitation. The novel's chapters alternate between the journal of Jon Lake – left to his friend Karl Johnson, in which Jon records his dream projections into 2150 – and the discussions between Jon and Karl about those 'dreams.' Futuristic romance.

Bryant, Dorothy [M. Calvetti Ungaretti] (1930-   ), *The Comforter*, San Fransisco: D.M. Bryant; rpt *The Kin of Ata are Waiting for You*, Berkeley: Moon/Random, 1976.

Ata is an alternative world available to whoever chooses to dream of it. It is a world of the spirit, where visions of the moment reveal one's being. Its ideal member is a comforter, who nurtures or heals. Ata symbolizes human possibility through a fantasy world at once communal, pastoral, and feminist. Alternative vision.

Elgin, Suzette Haden (1936-   ), *The Communipaths*, New York: Ace; *Furthest*, New York: Ace, 1972; *At the Seventh Level*, New York: Daw, 1972; rpt *Communipath Worlds: Three Complete Novels*, New York: Pocket, 1980.

A eutopian novella, plus two sequels, follows the missions of intelligence agent Coyote Jones on three planets with differing societies: heroines in each case demonstrate unusual abilities. One communal eutopia and two dystopias reveal both a feminist social critique of war and sexism, and a feminist vision of human growth and potential. Space travel.

Wetherell, June Pat (-   ), *Blueprint for Yesterday*, New York: Walker.

From 2032 AD, a heroine searches for her grandfather's secrets with the help of a legacy from her grandmother. Successful, she escapes the United States with her male friend to underground activist Red Rebels headquarters in Delos. Alternative future.

256

1972

Farca, Marie C. (1935-   ), *Earth*, Garden City, New York: Doubleday; dystopian sequel *Complex Man*, Doubleday, 1973.

On a future EARTH – ours or another – a pastoral society lives in self-sufficient ecological balance. A visitor from Earth (possibly our own, as a future dystopian technocracy) arrives to explore and takes away three clones, also leaves three clones behind. (A sequel permits all six clones to meet on EARTH.) Extra-terrestrial futuristic fantasy.

LeGuin, Ursula [Kroeber] (1929-   ), *The Word for World Is Forest* in *Again, Dangerous Visions*, ed. Harlan Ellison, Garden City: Doubleday; rpt new York: Putnam; New York: Berkeley, 1976.

On Altshe called a 'paradise planet' where a matriarchy still manages a pastoral, ecologically balanced existence, an invasion of Men destroys and forever changes the society by the introduction of killing; particularly the female Altsheans are Men's targets. Extra-terrestrial invasion.

1973

[Arnold, June] (1926-1983), *The Cook & The Carpenter; a novel by the carpenter*, Plainfield, Vermont: Daughters, Inc., 1973.

Thirteen women and their children live as an intentional community in Texas, with the aim of establishing a school/center to provide alternative health services. Members join and leave the group; differences develop and dissolve; all develop capacity to change. Alternative present; feminist.

1974

LeGuin, Ursula [Kroeber] (1929-   ), *The Dispossessed*, New York: Harper & Row; rpt New York: Avon, 1975.

The people of the planet Anarres, the ambiguous Utopia, practice an anarchistic communitarianism. At the novel's center is an atypical male Shevek, a theoretical physicist, the structure of whose story demonstrates the possibility of reconciling contradictory concepts of time – as both linear and circular: the novel completes a circle by ending where it began with the convergence of two linear plot lines. Extra-terrestrial alternative.

1975

[Neeper, Carolyn A. (1937-   )], 'Cary Neeper' (pseud.), *A Place Beyond Man*, New York: Scribner's.

Two planets of the near-future contain non-human, intelligent and sentient beings, ellls and varoks. Tandra, a scientist from Earth, creates a new family with her daughter, and an elll and a varok, each male. Love permits social construction and universal benefit when expressed across planets and species. Extra-terrestrial future fantasy.

Russ, Joanna (1937-   ), *The Female Man*, New York: Bantam; rpt Boston: Gregg/G.K. Hall, 1977.

Whileaway, an all-female eutopia, exists ten centuries into the future. The main character is split among four women, each having an identical genotype, but each living in a different time or place. A visitor from Whileaway arrives on present Earth, meets two Earth women from different times and all three encounter a fourth from a time between our present and Whileaway's future. Extra-terrestrial Amazonian society.

Staton, Mary (?1945-   ), *From the Legend of Biel*, New York: Ace.

On planet MC6, an Earth visitor Howard Scott dreams of finding the 'perfection' he willingly dies to protect from Earth's discovery, but instead births into MC6 society, a sharer of Biel's gene pattern. Her 'legend' of possible human development carefully fostered by a mentor constitutes the bulk of the novel. Extra-terrestrial alternative vision.

1976

Bradley, Marion Zimmer (1930-   ), *The Shattered Chain*, New York: Daw.

The Free Amazons enact a eutopian existence for women by providing personal autonomy, home residence, sororal companionship through a system of urban guilds located throughout the planet Darkover. Three diverse and strong women carry the plot – a châtelaine, an intelligence agent, and a Free Amazon. Feminist sword and sorcery.

Holland, Cecelia [Anastasia] (1943-   ), *Floating Worlds*, New York: Knopf.

Two thousand years into the future, Paula Mendoza – a black, anarchist, interplanetary diplomat – leaves a eutopian commune on Earth to negotiate the best truce possible among dystopian societies on several planets. Space adventure and suspense.

McCaffrey, Anne [Inez] (1926-   ), *Dragon Song*, New York: Atheneum; rpt New York: Bantam, 1977.

On the planet Pern where Terran colonists settled some five generations before, Benden Weyr is a eutopian community where women are effective healers and beneficent rulers. A young singer recovers and her rare gift for music at last receives encouragement. Sword and sorcery.

Piercy, Marge (1936-   ), *Woman on the Edge of Time*, New York: Knopf; rpt New York: Fawcett, 1976.

A future eutopian Mattapoisett, Massachusetts, contrasts with present New York City mental institutions. Connie Ramos, a Chicana incarcerated for violence (provoked by the deprivation she has continuously experienced), finds herself periodically in a society, at once communitarian, environmentally aware, bias free, and human potential enhancing – a future compensatory of all the wrongs she has ever known. Alternative vision.

Wilhelm, Kate (1928-   ), *Where Late the Sweet Birds Sang*, New York: Harper & Row; rpt New York: Pocket, 1977.

Environmental pollution and radiation wastes land and cities; all die save one extended family gathered in a mountain valley where they develop cloning to compensate for sterility. Population decreases to one fertile male and group of breeder females. Conclusion is stereotypic; a heterosexual couple expecting a child in a world where individuality again predominates. Extra-terrestrial futuristic romance.

1978

Balizct, Carol (-   ), *The Last Seven Years*, Lincoln, Virginia: Chosen Books.

Set in Tampa, Florida, 1988-1995, the author sees a future utopia as a Christian heaven on Earth, the last seven years of a polluted, corrupt, and disintegrating world verifying Biblical prophecy. Major actors are male. Sexist. Futuristic religious romance.

Broner, E[sther] M[asserman] (1930-   ), *A Weave of Women*, New York: Holt, Rinehart Winston; rpt New York: Bantam, 1982.

A community of women living in contemporary Jerusalem

create rituals affirming women's experience, refuse self-defeat, move from birth through death to life and love. Novel centers first upon one then upon another community woman and her experience. An irreverent – often funny – celebration of womanhood. Alternative present.

Charnas, Suzy McKee (1939-   ), *Motherlines*, New York: Berkley; a sequel to dystopian *Walk to the End of the World*, New York: Ballantine, 1974; rpt Berkley, 1978.
After surviving the Wasting brought about by Holdfast men in *Walk to the End of the World* (1974), the Riding Women tribes and the free fems seek a peaceful co-existence. Protagonist Alldera bears a daughter – who seems likely to start a new motherline – and promises to lead a return to vanquish Holdfast. Amazonian post-catastrophe future.

LeGuin, Ursula [Kroeber] (1929-   ), *The Eye of the Heron* in *Millennial Women*, Virginia Kidd (ed.), New York: Delacorte; rpt New York: Harper & Row, 1983.
On Victoria planet, two settlements of outcasts from Earth exist in uneasy balance – hierarchical Victoria City and consensual, nonviolent Shantih. The latter permits leadership to women and men – though the former suffer less severe casualties. Inspired by a woman who chose to leave Victoria City, a group from Shantih set out to build a new world in the wilderness. Extra-terrestrial alternative.

McIntyre, Vonda [Neel] (1948-   ), *Dreamsnake*, Boston: Houghton, Mifflin; rpt New York: Dell, 1979.
On post-catastrophe Earth, varied communities exist, one woman-headed tribal group being particularly concerned with human welfare. Future fantasy.

Randall, Marta (-   ), *Journey*, New York: Pocket.
After twelve years on their planet Aerie, the Kennerin family continue to journey toward creating a world of human interdependence and achievement with the arrival of 200 refugees whom they rescue from social dissolution on planet New Home. The novel stresses group-defined goals suitable to female and male, nonhuman and human beings. Extra-terrestrial future fantasy.

1979

Carr, Jayge (-   ), *Leviathan's Deep*, Garden City, New York: Doubleday.
On the planet Delyafam, a future society of humanoids

exhibits a gender-role reversal with the Noble Lady maintaining a household in which boys serve her. The Delyen non-competitive, co-operative society struggles to survive against the off world Terrene, whose technological superiority enables them to subdue inhabitants of planets they visit, but the possibility of equality between Delyen-Terrene individuals exists. Matriarchal future alternative.

[Cherry, Carolyn Janice (1942-   )], 'C.J. Cherryh' (pseud.), *The Fires of Azeroth*, New York: Daw.

Mirrind and Carrhend, two eutopian villages run by elder women and their men, are destroyed in the process of trying to free the world from limitless power and freedom of the Gates, through which one can travel through space and time. The destruction results from the woman Morgaine, who in closing the Gates must sacrifice the villages. Sword and sorcery.

Clayton, Jo (1939-   ), *Maeve: A Novel of the Diadem*, New York: Daw.

On a future planet Maeve, Starwitch Aleytys arrives en route to finding her son. While there, she uses many unusual talents in the process of saving from control by the Company, two nonhuman populations, the forest cludair and urban ardd. Although once found she had planned to take her son with her, she realizes he will be happier without her. Disappointed she leaves, but quickly feels excitement about the new worlds she'll visit. Future fantasy, partial eutopia.

Cox, Joan (1942-   ), *Mind Song*, New York: Avon.

The Terran society of Delpha is eutopian, particularly respecting political and sexual expression. DonEel from Scarsen travels through time and space to discover the nature of the threat to Delpha. He reveals his own and other's capacity for telepathy through space and time, a 'mind song of desire' for Eden. Extra-terrestrial, inter-planetary sword and sorcery.

Gearhart, Sally Miller (1931-   ), *The Wanderground*, Watertown, Mass.: Persephone Press.

The Hill Women roam their Wanderground, located beyond the Dangerland separating them from the City. A pastoral, spiritual, all-female eutopia where new language and new ritual flourish. The Hill Women live in a communal life in tune with flora and fauna around them. Episodes feature the experiences of first one then another member of the group. Amazonian community.

Lynn, Elizabeth A. (1946-   ), *Watchtower*, New York: Berkley.

In the midst of a sword and sorcery fantasy is eutopian Vanima, a land of summer isolated in mountains, its approach known only to those who have been there. A pacific, pastoral people.

Marinelli, Jean (-   ), *From Blight to Height*, New York: Vantage.

A brief, amateurish eutopia, present and near-future United States, depicting the development of a multi-ethnic society of equals ruled by a male elite and subdivided into self-sufficient Regions of 60,000 apiece. Alternative future.

White, Mary Alice (1920-   ), *The Land of the Possible: A Report of the First Visit to Prire*, New York: Warner.

Charles Aldworth, Ph.D., makes his first visit of one week to seven varying communities in the land of Prire. The Utopia focuses upon governmental, labor, industrial, environmental, economic, and educational arrangements. The society appears strikingly equitable and cooperative. Alternative present.

Young, Donna J. (-   ), *Retreat: As it Was!* Weatherby Lake, Missouri: Naiad Press.

A pastoral all-female eutopia on the planet Retreat experiences disruption when visitors from planet Home are attacked and irradiated en route. Emphasis upon closeness to nature, healing skills, storytelling as instruction. Partheno-genetic reproduction; genetic variation through Ordeal of Sharing. Extra-terrestrial Amazonian alternative.

1980

Randall, Marta (-   ), *Dangerous Games*, New York: Pocket.

On Aerie-Kennerin planet, from New Time 1242-46, the Kennerin family led by matriarch Mish struggles against internal and external dangers to maintain their autonomy as a family as well as their community with extra-human beings, the Kasirene, a nonviolent agricultural society. Extra-terrestrial future fantasy.

Sargent, Pamela (-   ), *Watchstar*, New York: Pocket.

Heroine Daiya learns during her ordeal of passage on far-future Earth that her agrarian society enforces a group illusion. A visitor to Earth takes her to another world having an infinity of possible ways of being. Daiya chooses to remain on Earth with the hope of teaching the larger mindcraft she now understands. Extra-terrestrial futuristic fantasy.

Singer, Rochelle (1939-   ), *The Demeter Flower*, New York: St Martin's.

Set in California's Sierra foothills about 2020 AD, the village of Demeter is a pastoral communitarian society of women established during the social breakdown of the 1980s. The arrival of a runaway heterosexual couple rouses the village toward establishing a second village and forces the women to face male treachery. Tea from the seeds of Demeter flowers causes pregnancy. Amazonian communitarian future.

Slonczewski, Joan (1956-   ), *Still Forms on Foxfield*, New York: Ballantine.

In 2133 AD, representatives from UN Interplanetary arrive on Foxfield, a planet where 92 years ago a group of Philadelphia Friends established a First Settlement at Georgeville. The conflict concerns the rights of small groups versus those of a universe. Major characters are women, who have greater endurance and perform better under stress than men. Extra-terrestrial futuristic fantasy.

Vinge, Joan [Dennison] (1948-   ), *The Snow Queen*, New York: Dial; rpt New York: Dell, 1981.

A dystopian Winter planet Tiamat ruled by Snow Queen Arienrhod is about to undergo, after 150 years, the Change to eutopian Summer. To prevent such evolution, the Queen has cloned herself. A complex plot and large cast of characters – human and nonhuman – demonstrates the uncertainty of achieving ideals. Extra-terrestrial fantasy.

1981

Holland, Cecelia [Anastasia] (1943-   ), *Home Ground*, New York: Knopf.

A present collective in northern California supports itself on the sale of marijuana. The utopia appears in the ambivalent and painful process of becoming. The heroine remains in the group though the man and young woman who love her leave; shares pot from her field after bust. Communitarian romance.

1982

Paxson, Diana L. (-   ), *Lady of Light*, New York: Pocket/Timescape.

In Westria some two centuries after Cataclysm, a near-feudal but ecologically sensitive society has developed. A king goes in search of a queen, who will be 'mistress of his heart' and mistress of four Jewels of Power, as well as bear an heir. Partially eutopian, non-feminist, post-disaster future.

Petesch, Natalie L.M. (1924-   ), *Duncan's Colony*, Athens, Ohio: Swallow/Ohio University Press.

Duncan, a former seminarian, gathers a colony of eight people – four men and four women – to prepare for the coming nuclear holocaust. Colonists break all the rules he has set as they choose individual responses to the fact of their own mortality. A near-past communitarian gathering and disbanding, this novel shows the utopian impulse meaningfully expressed not in a colony but in social activism.

1983

Cherryh C.J. (1942-   ), *The Dreamstone*, New York: Daw.

The dreamstone permits its wearer to enter Ealdwood, where death and destruction are scarce, where a protectress nurtures growth and uses magical powers. Also the remote mountainous Steading, a refuge for the lost or the chased, is a eutopia existing as an escape (chs 2, 3). More fantasy than Utopia, the book is set in an undetermined past.

IV ALPHABETICAL LIST OF AUTHORS (with cross listings for dual authors, married names, and pseudonyms; and asterisk marking authors collected)

Adolph, 1899

Alcott, 1873

Alexander, 1971

*Appleton, 1848

Arnold, A., see Bartlett, 1891

Arnold, J., 1973

Balizet, 1978

Barber, 1950

Barnhouse, 1952

Bartlett, 1891

Bennett, 1918

Brackett, 1955

Bradley, 1976

Brodhead, 1891

Broner, 1978

*Bruère, 1919

Bryant, 1971

Carr, 1979
Carroll, 1969
Chamberlain, 1841
Charnas, 1978
Cherry/Cherryh, 1979, 1983
Clarke, 1898
Clayton, 1979
Cleghorn, 1924
*Cooley, 1902
*Corbett, 1869
Cox, 1979
*Cridge, 1870

Dardenelle, 1943
Davis, 1866
De Forest, 1938
Dell, 1925
Dieudonné, 1887
Dodd, 1887
Douglas, 1879

Elgin, 1971
Evans, 1905

Farca, 1972
Fisher, 1916
Forbush, see Clarke, 1898
*Ford, 1889
Fry, 1905

Gazella, 1928
Gearhart, 1979
Gilman, 1911, 1915, 1916
*Graul, 1897
*Griffith, 1836

Hale, 1853
Hastings, see Sherwood, 1894
Henderson, 1961
Henley, 1901
Holland, 1976, 1981
[Hopf], see Lightner, 1969

*Howland, 1874

Johnson, 1920
*Jones, A.I., 1893
Jones, L.B., 1916

Kayser, 1922
Kinkaid, 1903
Knapp, 1894

*Lane, 1881
Lawrence, 1964
Leslee, 1962
LeGuin, 1969, 1972, 1974, 1978
Lightner, 1969
Lynn, 1979

McCaffrey, 1976
McCarthy, 1949
McElhiney, 1945
McIntyre, 1978
Maddux, 1957
Mannes, 1968
Marinelli, 1979
Martin, 1908
Mason, C., 1900
*Mason, E.L., 1889, 1898
Mead, 1889
*Merchant, 1893
Moore, 1892
Morgan, 1899
Morris, 1938

Neeper, 1975
Norris, 1957

Orpen, 1897
*Owen, see Snedeker, 1917

Paxson, 1982
Petesche, 1982

265

Pettersen, 1924
*Phelps, 1874, 1883, 1887
Piercy, 1970, 1976
Pittock, 1890

Rand, 1938, 1957
Randall, 1978, 1980
Richberg, 1900
Rogers, 1905
Russ, 1970, 1975

St Clair, 1957
Sargent, 1980
Scrymsour, 1922
Shelhamer, 1885
Sherwood, 1895
Short, 1949
Singer, 1980
Slonczewski, 1980
Smith, 1962
*Snedeker, 1917, 1929
Speer, 1938
Spotswood, 1935

Staton, 1975
Sterne, 1937
Stevens, see Bennett, 1918
Stone, 1890
Sutton, 1949

Vassos, 1930
Vinge, 1980
Von Swartwout, 1894

*Waisbrooker, 1894
*[Ward], see Phelps, 1874,
    1883, 1887
Wetherill, 1971
White, 1979
Wiggin, 1909
Wilhelm, 1976
Wood, 1882
Woods, 1889

Young, 1979
Yourell, 1891

V RECENT ADDITIONS

1979
Elgin, Suzette Elgin. *Star-Anchored, Star-Angered*, Garden City,
    NY; Doubleday.

1982
Sargent, Pamela. *The Golden Space*, New York; Simon &
    Schuster/Timescape.

1983
Bradley, Marion Zimmer. *Thendora House* (sequel to *The
    Shattered Chain*, 1976), New York: DAW.

1984
Forrest, Katherine V. *Daughters of a Coral Dawn*, Tallahassee,
    FL; Naiad Press.

P A N D O R A   P R E S S

an imprint of Routledge and Kegan Paul

For further information about Pandora Press books, please write to the Mailing List Dept at Pandora Press, 39 Store Street, London WC1E 7DD; or in the USA at 9, Park Street, Boston, Mass. 02108; or in Australia at 464 St. Kilda Road, Melbourne, Victoria 3004, Australia.

ELIZABETH GASKELL : FOUR SHORT STORIES

The Three Eras of Libbie Marsh · Lizzie Leigh · The Well of
Pen-Morfa · The Manchester Marriage

In her unaffected, direct description of the lives of working class
women as lived out between the mean streets and the cotton mills
of nineteenth century England, Elizabeth Gaskell chose to break
with the literary conventions of Victorian ladies' fiction (which
demanded genteel romances) and give her readers, instead, the
harsh realities, the defiance and courage those lives entailed. Far
from being delicate drawing room flowers, the characters in these
four stories (collected here for the first time) are women who live
unsupported by men, who labour and love and scheme and
survive in strangely modern tales shot through with Gaskell's
integrity of observation and deep compassion. The stories are
prefaced by a long appreciation of Gaskell's life and work by Anna
Walters.

'Mrs Gaskell draws the distinction between male and female
values quietly, but forcefully' *School Librarian*

0-86358-001-7 Fiction/Criticism 122pp 198 × 129 mm introduced by
Anna Walters paperback.

ALL THE BRAVE PROMISES

Memories of Aircraftwomen 2nd Class 2146391

Mary Lee Settle

Mary Lee Settle was a young American woman living a comfortable life in Washington D.C. when the Second World War broke out. In 1942 she boarded a train, carrying 'a last bottle of champagne and an armful of roses', and left for England to join the WAAF. She witnessed the horror of war – the bombing raids, the planes lost in fog, the children evacuated, a blacked-out Britain of austerity and strain. She also witnessed the women, her fellow recruits, as they struggled to adapt to their new identities and new lives at the bottom of the uniformed pile. Dedicated 'to the wartime other ranks of the Women's Auxiliary Air Force – below the rank of Sergeant', this rare book captures women's wartime experience; a remarkable and important story by one of America's prizewinning novelists.

'One of the most moving accounts of war experience ever encountered' *Library Journal*

0-86358-033-5 General/Autobiography 160pp 198 × 129 mm paperback

not for sale in the U.S.A. or Canada

MY COUNTRY IS THE WHOLE WORLD

an anthology of women's work on peace and war

Cambridge Women's Peace Collective (eds)

Women's struggle for peace is no recent phenomenon. In this book, the work of women for peace from 600 BC to the present is documented in a unique collection of extracts from songs, poems, diaries, letters, petitions, pictures, photographs and pamphlets through the ages. A book to give as a gift, to read aloud from, to research from, to teach from, *My Country is the Whole World* is both a resource and an inspiration for all who work for peace today.

'an historic document . . . readers will be amazed at the extent of the collection' *Labour Herald*

'a beautifully presented and illustrated book which makes for accessible and enlightening reading' *Morning Star*

0-86358-004-1 Social Questions/History 306pp A5 illustrated throughout paperback

DISCOVERING WOMEN'S HISTORY

a practical manual

Deirdre Beddoe

Rainy Sunday afternoons, long winter evenings: why not set yourself a research project, either on your own or in a group or classroom? This is the message from Deirdre Beddoe, an historian who tears away the mystique of her own profession in this step-by-step guide to researching the lives of ordinary women in Britain from 1800 to 1945. *Discovering Women's History* tells you how to get started on the detective trail of history and how to stalk your quarry through attics and art galleries, museums and old newspapers, church archives and the Public Records Office – and how to publish your findings once you have completed your project.

'an invaluable and fascinating guide to the raw material for anyone approaching this unexplored territory' *The Sunday Times*

'Thrilling and rewarding and jolly good fun' *South Wales Argus*

0-86358-008-4 Hobbies/Social History 232pp 198 × 129 mm illustrated